FIETLEBAUM'S ESCAPE

FIETLEBAUM'S ESCAPE

Scott D. Mendelson

iUniverse LLC
Bloomington

FIETLEBAUM'S ESCAPE

iUniverse books may be ordered through booksellers or by contacting:

iUniverse LLC
1663 Liberty Drive
Bloomington, IN 47403
www.iuniverse.com
1-800-Authors (1-800-288-4677)

ISBN: 978-1-4759-9767-5 (sc)
ISBN: 978-1-4759-9768-2 (ebk)

Library of Congress Control Number: 2013912159

Printed in the United States of America

iUniverse rev. date: 07/13/2013

CHAPTER 1

Fietlebaum hummed an old Yiddish tune as he clocked Burb Plorbus's rotational velocity. "*Vey iz mir*[1]," he remarked. "He's hit three-hundred RPM." A repeat of the measurement confirmed his results. *This* boychik[2] *is sick*, he decided.

The Drusidi cadet's gyrations had been disrupting classes at the Transgalactic Merchant Marine Academy. On the previous day he had twirled headlong into the control panel of the academy's new hyperdrive simulator. It had been the pride of the alumni association and now was damaged beyond repair. The board of directors demanded action, which brought Plorbus before the student health clinic's psychiatrist, Dr. Isaac Fietlebaum. It was Fietlebaum's job to determine what was causing the odd behavior and how to stop it.

Fietlebaum struggled to discern the nature and etiology of the malady as he watched Plorbus spiral across the floor of his office. He listened intently. Each burble and snort emitted by the peripatetic cadet triggered a cascade of diagnostic pictures, diagrams, and digitext projections in Fietlebaum's memory. The memories coalesced and the name of the illness sprang fully formed into his

---

1 "Woe is me." An expression of surprise and/or dismay. A glossary of all of the Yiddish words and phrases used in *Fietlebaum's Escape* is provided at the end of the book.

2 an affectionate term for boy

consciousness. "Pseudotrigortism," Fietlebaum said to himself.

A flap of one of Plorbus's tentacles generated a sudden, resounding crack that further jarred Fietlebaum's memory. He was in medical school. He saw the languid turning of the old ceiling fans in the lecture hall. He smelled the fetid cologne of Burgan Plotzi, the Janpooran student who sat behind him in Professor Norsint's exopyschiatry course. Norsint discussed the etiology of pseudotrigortism and variations in its presentation. A Drusidi whirled his way across the digitext screen as Norsint described the phenomenon, pointing out the fine details with his laser penlight.

Fietlebaum was reconstructing the final moments of Norsint's lecture when Norja Borket broke his reverie. She was one of the academy's guidance counselors and had accompanied Plorbus to the clinic. She found it all disturbing. "Something has to be done," she insisted.

Fietlebaum lifted his head. "What?" he asked with palpable irritation.

Norja Borket blew through her teeth and generated the high-pitched wheezing sound that was the Ergastian expression of annoyance and befuddlement. Plorbus kept spinning. "Why does he keep *doing* that?" she implored.

"I don't know," Fietlebaum replied with a shrug. "That's what I intend to find out."

Plorbus spun faster. Centrifugal force lifted his tentacles up and outward, with one finally clipping the corner of a picture of Fietlebaum's father, Morris, that hung on the wall. It fell to the floor with a crash of splintering glass.

"*Oy gevalt*[3]!" Fietlebaum exclaimed.

"It's not normal, is it?" Norja Borket asked plaintively. "All this spinning, I mean. I don't see how he can get his school work done." She wheezed through her teeth again,

---

3 "Oh, God forbid!" An expression of surprised dismay

and her rising consternation activated chromatophores beneath her translucent skin. Fractal patterns of red and yellow spiraled across her face. "You are going to do something about it, aren't you?" she demanded to know.

She's going to drive me meshugeh[4], Fietlebaum thought to himself. He took a deep breath, and slowly exhaled. "Norja—if I may call you that—let me explain something about pseudotrigortism."

"Pseudo what?" she inquired with another loud wheeze through her teeth.

"Tri-gor-tis-mmm" he replied, taking time to enunciate each syllable, less for clarification than as a means to rein in his growing irritation. He paused to construct an explanation within her grasp. "This spinning isn't always abnormal for Drusidi," he began. "Back home on Drusid, they spin like this every three years when their moon, Trigort, makes its closest pass by the planet. It's part of their sex lives."

The red and yellow on Norja's face flashed bright purple. Rings of deep green pulsed and spun around her frontotemporal horns. "How interesting," she murmured. She leaned in closer for more of Fietlebaum's explanation.

"The sexual behavior of Drusidi is tied to the arrival of Trigort. It's rooted in their biology. When Trigort gets close, the gravitational pull of Drusid heats the interior of the moon and causes vapors to boil off its surface. Those vapors drift down and blanket the planet in a thick fog."

"I don't see why that would make them want to spin," Norja noted incredulously. "A gloomy fog makes me want to stay in bed."

"Yes," Fietlebaum replied with a dour expression, "I'm sure it does. But this is *special* fog."

Norja rolled her eyes. "What could be so *special* about it?" she remarked in challenge.

---

4 crazy

At that moment, Fietlebaum realized Plorbus's trajectory would send him whirling into the bookstand upon which sat his ancient, first edition copy of Freud's *Civilization and its Discontents.* It had been a graduation gift from his father. He leapt up to grab the revered book and, after stowing it safely under his desk, he returned to his chair and impromptu lecture.

"Gasses in this fog from Trigort stimulate the growth of the plants the Drusidi use for food," he went on to say. "When Trigort arrives, the plants grow lush and food is abundant." He paused for effect. "But the plants don't just grow—they change! The fog makes them produce chemicals that mimic the Drusidi's natural sex hormones. The Drusidi eat the plants and get, uh—" He struggled for the word Norja might best appreciate, only to disappoint himself by surrendering to, "very, very sexy."

Norja's eyes opened wide. Her olfactory tentacles throbbed. "It's all so *fas*cinating!" she cooed.

"And the fog doesn't change only the plants," Fietlebaum persevered. "It changes the Drusidi, too!"

Norja's mouth fell open. She stared at Fietlebaum with rapt attention. "Really?" she asked. "What does it do to them?"

Fietlebaum again excused himself, got up, and moved the umbrella stand that stood in Plorbus's path. He returned to his chair. "The fog affects their brains," he continued. "First it stimulates the appetite centers of their brains and makes them want to eat even more of the hormone-rich plants."

"Plorbus gained twenty pounds last week," Norja noted. "When he's not spinning, all he does is eat."

"There you go!" Fietlebaum responded. "I'm not surprised." He stopped to shift his feet to be less of an obstacle as Plorbus spun by. "As the fog gets denser, it starts to activate nerve centers deep in their brains. The outflow of neural pulses from those motor systems generates the spinning motion in the males, as we see with young Plorbus. At first, it is subtle, an occasional slow and graceful pirouette in an otherwise ordinary walk across a room. But as the fog thickens, the graceful turns become more vigorous and frequent. Before long, the males are whirling like dervishes through the streets."

"My God!" Norja cried. "How exciting!"

"That's not the half of it," Fietlebaum advised her. "It also activates sexual excitation in the males and release of sexual pheromones."

"How intriguing," Norja interjected. After an awkward pause, she queried, "What are pheromones?"

"They are sort of like cologne," Fietlebaum explained, "but more potent. They're from glands beneath their two front tentacles. When the males spin, the tentacles move up and down and the axillary bristles beneath them vibrate and waft the pheromones into the air. It makes a funny, high pitched whirring sound." He took a stab at mimicking the sound, but found no success in it, and abruptly returned to his explanation. "The pheromones from the males stimulate the brains of the females," he added. "It makes the spinning and sexual advances of the males impossible to resist."

"Hmmm," Norja sighed dreamily. Her communicator buzzed. She glanced at the message that flashed across the screen, and a pained look of disappointment fell across her face. She punched in a reply and stood up. "I have to go," she said apologetically. "One of our new cadets from Korpia has barricaded herself in the dorm showers and is refusing to come out." As she slithered toward the door, she slowly turned and tentatively proposed to Fietlebaum, "Perhaps, we could meet later and you could finish your stimulating explanation."

"Perhaps not," Fietlebaum quickly replied. Norja wheezed through her teeth, turned back around, and slithered out of the clinic. Fietlebaum heard the door slam shut. "*Got tsu danken*[5]," he said out loud. "Now I can get back to work."

He leaned back and watched Plorbus continue to spin with a detached and discerning eye. He spun ever faster. His tentacles moved up and down. The axillary bristles rubbed against one another and vibrated with an abrasive atonal screech. As Fietlebaum had anticipated, pheromones were released. An overpowering stench of asparagus-laden urine filled the room. "*Feh*[6]," Fietelbaum muttered under his breath.

A particularly vigorous spin sent Plorbus reeling towards the windows. His tentacles tangled in the cords of the venetian blinds, and his rotational momentum ripped the blinds from the wall. The blinds and the cadet crashed to the floor in a billowing cloud of disintegrated plaster. "*Genug es genug*[7]," Fietlebaum murmured under his breath. He requested the orderlies to sedate Plorbus and place him in the low stimulation room. He needed peace and quiet to consider the problem.

On Drusid, he reflected, *this kind of behavior is perfectly normal. But we're a full ten light-years from Drusid. And right now, Trigort isn't even close to the planet*. He sighed in mild consternation. He saw no obvious reason for Plorbus to gorge himself, spin, and exude pheromones as he was.

Fietlebaum gave a *kvetch*[8] as he lifted himself up from the chair. He shuffled across his office, poured a cup of now cold coffee out of a grimy carafe, and returned to his chair behind the desk. He set his elbow on the desk and propped his chin in the web of his thumb and index finger. He fell deep into thought. *What's at the bottom of this?* he wondered.

---

5 "Thank God"

6 An expression of disgust

7 "enough is enough"

8 A groan of complaint

Pseudotrigortism could arise out of an overabundance of the Drusidi neurotransmitter, progmolatine. This would stimulate the motor nuclei that drove the abnormal behaviors. But a trial of the progmolatine antagonist, progmutimab, had failed to give Plorbus any relief. "It's no simple neurochemical imbalance," Fietlebaum murmured under his breath. "Is it psychological?" he asked himself. Homesickness could cause unstable young Drusidis to develop pseudotrigortism. But, there was little to suggest this possibility in Plorbus. He had heard of nothing in his early development that might result in weakness or predisposition to neurosis.

There was a knock on the door. Oy[9]! he thought, *It's that* meshugeneh[10] *Norja Borket!* "*Gai avec*[11]!" he barked. There was another knock. He leapt from his chair and stomped to the door. "Leave me alone!" he bellowed as he flung the door open. In the doorway stood Porzint Blop, commander of the Transgalactic Merchant Marine Academy.

Fietlebaum recovered himself. "Commander Blop!" he gushed. "Please, come in."

Blop himself was Drusidi. He had a special interest in Plorbus's case. He emitted a belching sound, and Fietlebaum's cybertranslater conveyed that he had come to see how the young Drusidi cadet was progressing.

"Of course, Commander," Fietlebaum replied, as he led him to a chair. "It's lucky you came by at this moment. You might be able to help me."

"I'll do what I can," Blop burped.

"Plorbus seems a strong and intelligent young fellow," Fietlebaum asserted. "I see no reason for him to exhibit pseudotrigortism. Have you had any concerns?"

---

9 Oh!

10 Crazy woman

11 "Go away!"

Blop shook his head. "I've had no concerns at all," he gurgled in reply. "He's done well at the academy. His grades have been good. He has friends, and he's well regarded by the faculty. He has everything to look forward to."

Fietlebaum ran through a list of possibilities with Blop, but none panned out. He didn't use drugs. He didn't owe money. At home, he had the expected pair of hermaphroditic fiancés, and the wedding was planned for the day after he graduated. He was a rising star, a straight shooter. "Thank you," he told Blop. "I'll let you know as soon as I've discovered the cause of the problem." Blop burbled his appreciation and scuttled out the door.

Fietlebaum fell back into thought. "Is it structural?" he finally asked himself. "A small hemorrhage? A tumor?" He ordered a quantum microvibrational imaging study of Plorbus's brain. "To hell with the expense," he said to no one in particular. With Plorbus still heavily sedated, it was a perfect opportunity to perform the imaging study without the additional motion artifacts from the pseudotrigortism. The sleeping Drusidi was wheeled to radiology for the study.

An hour later, the radiologist called Fietlebaum. "There's a shadow," she said. "It's small, about four by six millimeters, in the medial aspect of the radial outlay of the dorsal motor nuclei. It's in the neuropil just upstream of the neural processing unit."

Fietlebaum called Commander Blop. "I'll be right over," Blop bleated.

"It's a small tumor," Fietlebaum told him. "But it's easily treated." The cybertranslator conveyed his conclusion to Blop, and a look of relief fell across his face. "It's interfering with normal function of his brain and causing the pseudotrigortism. He will require a brief course of tri-focal radiation to destroy the lesion," Fietlebaum explained. "There will be some swelling in the neural tissue, and inflammation. For a few days the symptoms might even get worse. But he should be fine within a week or two."

Blop shook like a wet dog, a Drusidi expression of joy, and generated a series of ebullient burbles and snorts. After a second series of fervent wet dog shakes, he slid a long ventral tentacle into the pouch that hung around his abdominal segment and grasped a plug of aluminum that he quickly placed and folded into Fietlebaum's hand. Although worthless in most areas of the galaxy, the aluminum was of inestimable value on Drusid. "You shouldn't have," Fietlebaum said, with an inflection of voice that betrayed his impression that Blop truly should not have given him the valueless lump. But his lack of enthusiasm in receiving the gift was lost in cybertranslation. The happy and grateful Commander abruptly turned and scuttled back out of his office, ostensibly to go inform all of Plorbus's parents about the good news.

Fietlebaum called out to him before he reached the front door of the clinic. "Please, Commander Blop, give Norja Borket the good news. She will be relieved." He sat back down in his chair. "And she'll leave me alone," he added with no one to hear it.

Fietlebaum relaxed for a few moments before reviewing notes on the final patient of the day. But, the patient was a no-show. The young Cypian cadet, who had been emergently scheduled for that time slot, had been having increasing difficulty adjusting to the academy's rigorous scholastic demands. He was failing in his courses. He had been causing concern among his advisors from crying out at night in his dorm room. His health was deteriorating, and wherever he crawled he left a trail of iridescent green scales. It was a sign of profound distress in his species. Apparently, the cadet had even been contemplating suicide. But on the afternoon of his appointment, he had broken into the transporter pool garage, stolen a personal transport vehicle, and set a trajectory for the Cypian star system. Though

Fietlebaum mildly resented the cadet's failure to appear, he had to admire his initiative. "I didn't think the little *pisher*[12] had it in him," he said with a laugh. "*Nu*[13]? You never know."

The vacant hour weighed upon him. He drummed his fingers on his desk. "Well," he murmured, in reflection upon the progress he had made in the Plorbus case, "at least the day wasn't for nothing." The room's empathic sensors recognized the fatigue in his voice. "Perhaps you should go home, get some supper, and relax Dr. Fietlebaum," the room suggested in motherly tones. "Yes," Fietlebaum replied. "I think you're right." As he rose from his chair, he felt a pain in his arthritic left hip and gave a *kvetch*. "*Oy*," he groaned. "I'm not young anymore."

He grabbed his old jacket off the rack beside his desk and walked toward his office door. The room took it upon itself to open it. As he stepped through the door, the room gently shut itself behind him and turned off its lights to spare him the trouble. "Thank you," Fietlebaum mumbled absently.

He shuffled out the front door toward the parking lot. His Silesian nurse called out, "Good night, Dr. Fietlebaum." He answered, "Umm hmm," without lifting his head, and continued on to where his transport capsule was parked. As he reached for the door, he caught the sobering sight of his reflection in the polycarbonate window. He rarely looked at himself anymore. *When did Isaac Fietlebaum get so old and tired?* he wondered. No answer was forthcoming. He opened the door, tossed in his jacket, initiated the propulsion system, and headed home.

---

12 pisser

13 "So?"

CHAPTER 2

Fietlebaum sped through the acrid, yellow cloud layers of Polmod. His transport capsule was buffeted by the turbulence of thermal currents rising off the star-baked, barren land. "What a planet," he murmured as he gazed down upon the endless stretches of gray land scarred by centuries of germanium strip-mining. "*Feh*[14]!"

It was a planet of ravished landscapes, squalid huts, and wind eroded farms in the middle of nowhere. But it was precisely in the middle of nowhere that Fietlebaum had wanted to be. Other than the Transgalactic Merchant Marine Academy, there was little to speak of on the planet. Prior to the training of merchant transport officers and starship crews, the primary industry on Polmod had been the mining of germanium ore that for years had been the essential metal in the construction of the metatemporal ion drives that powered the great transport ships across the galaxy. The academy had been built there to provide gainful employment for inhabitants of the planet who would otherwise have had no future other than a low paying job in the mines. Ironically, it was the lighter and more durable copper titanium alloy developed by engineers at the Transgalactic Academy that replaced germanium in the ion drive engines and spelled doom for the mining industry on the planet.

The building of the academy had been a political move by galactic bigwigs that scraped up just enough votes

---

[14] An expression of disgust

among the poor to keep their party in power for another six years. When they were subsequently swept out of office, less sympathetic governors from another planet in the star system became the stewards of Polmod. The planet gradually fell back into a state of general neglect, perhaps even worse off than it had been before.

Fietlebaum's capsule swooped in and slid across the ground, sending up billows of Polmodi dust. It came to a stop in front of a squat, four room bungalow beside a poorly maintained travelers rest stop on a ragged edge of Industry City, the once thriving but now dying urban nerve center of the mining industry on Polmod. Fietlebaum pressed the door release button. The retaining ring that held the button in place broke, and the spring underneath it that restored it to position after being depressed launched both itself and the red plastic button across the personal transport vehicle just out of sight and reach behind the adjoining seat. Fietlebaum sighed another weary "*Oy,*" and decided to postpone retrieval of the button assembly. Perhaps he would have the Polmodi live-in attendant at the rest stop repair it in the morning. No traveler had visited the rest stop for at least two months, so he should have no trouble working the task into his schedule. Thankfully, the door of the vehicle opened. Fietlebaum climbed out and walked to the front door that immediately recognized him and welcomed him home.

"Good evening Dr. Fietlebaum," the door said. "We hope you have had a nice day."

"Yes," he answered in a tone utterly devoid of enthusiasm. "It's been terrific."

The door opened for him, and Dr. Fietlebaum shuffled through. The door closed itself securely behind him. The day was over. He walked to his leather lounge chair, and eased down in it. "*Oy,*" he sighed as he felt the sturdy old chair accept his full weight. He reached for the cold, half-cup of coffee he had left on the side table earlier that morning before he left for work and sipped from it. A brief attempt at reflecting on the day's events met resistance, and he abandoned it in favor of simply reminiscing.

Ten years before, he would never have imagined himself on this *farkakteh*[15] little planet. He had held positions at the Galaxy's most prestigious universities. He had been celebrated at galas and toasted at dinners of the Galaxy's most respected professional organizations. He had stayed at the finest hotels and eaten in the finest restaurants. He had been *ongeshtopt mit gelt*[16].

Now, at 68 years of age, he was content to live alone in his run down little bungalow and sustain himself on meals generated by a beaten up, old food synthesizer. The synthesizer had long ago burned out its field insulators, and static electricity from passing communal transports would sometimes scramble the synthesizer's processing codes. Beef steak might then taste like burnt cabbage. Chicken might have perfect flavor but the consistency of highly congealed tapioca pudding. He ate it anyway. "*Nu*? What difference does it make?" he would ask rhetorically. "I know what it's supposed to taste like. *Iz nisht geferlech*[17]."

It was astonishing how quickly it had all unraveled. When his wife, Sophie, died unexpectedly, he felt as if his reason for living had been taken away. Though he had counseled tens of thousands of patients in exactly the same circumstance, his wisdom and experience did not spare him the overwhelming sense of emptiness and disillusionment. "*Der shuster gaien borves*[18]," he would say.

His hair had thinned and gone white. His face was thin, and had lost its youthful color. He studied his hands. "*Oy*," he lamented. "I'm turning yellow." He glanced around his

---

15 shitty

16 stuffed with money

17 It's not so terrible

18 The cobbler is barefoot.

bungalow. The furnishings were spare. The carpet, once white, had gone mousey gray from the Polmodi dust that relentlessly worked its way in beneath the door and through imperceptible cracks in the window frames. A picture of Sophie hung by itself on the far wall. The expanse of pale, empty wall around it made her portrait appear shrunken and detached. The adjacent wall was entirely bare. *I should hang something up*, he often thought. He had *tchotchkes*[19] for the walls and tables but had forgotten where they were. He had lived there for eight years after moving from Silesia, and still had unpacked boxes in his closet.

It had been one calamity after another. Not long after he lost Sophie, his accountant was found to have embezzled his clients' funds, including Fietlebaum's entire lifesavings. The *gonif*[20] high-tailed it to a poorly charted star system near the galaxy's black hole. With the appearance of lacking perspicacity in having his money stolen by a mere hireling, Fietlebaum was asked to step down from his prestigious position of chairman of the board of the Silesian pharmaceutical conglomerate, Frodrisht and Plork. Then the sharks smelled blood in the water.

Several years before his fall, a new medication had been marketed to improve the behavior of school children on the planet Jorgon. Not long after it was released, the drug, gestiron, was discovered to have caused irreversible neurodegenerative disease in many of the children that received it. There was a furor. The Galactic Senate Subcommittee on Health and Welfare began an investigation.

Unbeknownst to Fietlebaum, several of the senators on the investigative committee had invested heavily in Silesian Dynamics, the company that had produced and sold the drug. They were anxious to dilute the company's

---

19 Decorative doodads and trinkets

20 thief

responsibility for the tragedy. With all the problems Fietlebaum had been having, and no longer having a cadre of high-priced corporate lawyers to defend him, it seemed a reasonable strategy to pin some of the blame on him. He had become an easy target. "*Nu?*" he grumbled. "*Az der oks falt, sharfen alleh di messer*[21]."

"Those dirty *momzers*[22]," Fietlebaum whispered aloud as he recalled the events. "And *that alta kocker*[23], Lornst!" The chairman of the Senate hearing on the matter had been an elderly, Silesian senator named Dorshint Lornst. He kept mispronouncing Fietlebaum's name.

"Dr. Fertlebond," he recalled the senator saying, "witnesses have informed us that they had voiced serious concerns to you about this medication, gestiron, but you did nothing to stop the sale of the drug."

"It's Fietlebaum, senator," he replied, "and I had absolutely nothing to do with the sale of that medication."

"So you say," Lornst went on. "Yet, we have heard testimony that you, Dr. Fiessenbloom, did everything you could to silence controversy over the drug."

"It's Fietlebaum," he insisted, "and the allegations you make are absurd. I was involved in some of the first studies of the drug. However, I saw early indications the drug might be dangerous, and I abandoned my research. After I had those suspicions, I not only warned the research community, but personally advised Dr. Horshint Bestish, the CEO of Silesian Dynamics, against marketing the product."

"Of course you did," Senator Lornst replied in a patronizing tone. "But isn't it the case, Dr. Feiggenblott, that you were positioned to make a great deal of money off the sale of gestiron?"

---

21 When the ox falls, everyone sharpens his knife.

22 bastards

23 old fart

"It's Fietlebaum, damn it!" he shouted. "And you need to get it through your head that I had nothing to do with either the manufacture or sale of that *farkakteh* drug, and I had absolutely nothing to gain from its financial success!" But before he could regain his composure and further defend his position, a buzzer buzzed and the senators glibly announced the meeting would be adjourned to allow them to vote on an important pork barrel bill that had just been placed before the senate. The gavel fell, and that was that.

Even years later, in his bungalow on Polmod, it infuriated him to think about it. He shook his head in disgust. "I would never have engaged in such despicable behavior," he said out loud.

After the senate hearing, more accusations were made and more investigations were mounted. Prosecutions and harsh penalties were promised. The scandal became the subject of news hour "special reports" and media exposés. It was several years before the senate subcommittee conceded that Fietlebaum probably wasn't involved in the tragic series of events. But it was too late. His reputation was irreparably damaged. His soul was torn. By the time his innocence was clearly established, the story was out of the news cycle and supplanted by more salacious stories. No one apologized. None of his lofty friends in government or the pharmaceutical industry ever came to his aid. "*A freint bleibt a freint biz di kesheneh*[24]," he lamented.

Fietlebaum had had enough of high finance and corporate intrigue. One fortuitous day, while he was about to throw out a stack of old medical journals from his office in Silesia, he looked down and noted an ad that had been placed by the Transgalactic Merchant Marine Academy. They were looking for a psychiatrist for their new mental health clinic on out-of-the-way Polmod. *Where the hell is that, anyway?* he wondered at the time. A map search

---

[24] A friend stays a friend up to his pocket.

showed the planet to be in thinly populated space far out on the galaxy's spiral arm. The prospect was immediately appealing. But the deal was cinched when he contacted the academy and they didn't know who he was. He relished the thought of being anonymous on a desolate planet in the middle of nowhere. No one else had applied for it, so the job was his.

He sighed and waved away the now bitter cup of coffee as if it, too, had perpetrated a betrayal. He got up to grab something more substantial for the end of a trying day. *Schnapps*[25], was the thought that came to mind. He poured two fingers of ancient scotch from an antique crystal bottle. "Please play William Byrd's third fantasia," Fietlebaum requested of his living room. The dark drones of ancient Earth viols filled the room and echoed off the bare walls. He sipped his *schnapps*. The music, *schnapps*, and the day's last heartfelt "*Oy*" relieved him of enough angst to relax, sigh, and eventually dismiss it all. "*Ich hob es in drerd*[26]!" he groaned in a long, leisurely exhalation. He nestled down into his newly recovered serenity.

It was not his time, and certainly not his culture, but the droning viols of the dark consort music of William Byrd had a haunting, primal quality to it that reached out to him across the centuries and light-years. At times he felt a stronger closeness and affinity for the long dead composer than to those with whom he shared time and space.

He eased back into his chair. He looked across the room at the picture of Sophie. He missed her. He missed his colleagues with whom he had researched and published scientific papers. He missed his students. He did not miss the life of the corporate executive that had accumulated around him. That life had evolved slowly and insidiously, like the delicate but weighty encrustations of ice that

---

25 whiskey

26 "To hell with it!"

envelope the countryside in a Earth storm of freezing rain. It was beautiful, but incarcerating and destructive. He was better off without it.

The music and *schnapps* worked their magic. The bonds of time and incarnate existence loosened. He neither reflected nor reminisced. The melodies carried him to other worlds, across landscapes of tenor and pitch interweaving in filigreed polyphony. Unlike the course of events in his life, the melody, no matter how melancholy or complex, always resolved in a simple, but comforting, major chord. It offered the promise that his turmoil and conflicts too might resolve.

The music ended. The silence was replaced by the sound of a Polmodi windstorm whipping across the injured plains. The wind-blown sand peppered the walls of his bungalow in waves of white noise as hypnotic as Byrd's viols. Lulled into trance by music, alcohol, and the rhythmic Polmodi sandstorm, Dr. Isaac Fietlebaum drifted off to sleep.

CHAPTER 3

"He's in the end room, Dr. Fietlebaum," the nurse whispered as she led him to his patient. "The police brought him in last night." The ward was dimly lit. The ordinary sounds of the sick—the moans, sneezes, belches, and coughs—were here joined by the cackles, cries, screams, and rants of the galaxy's mentally ill. Isaac Fietlebaum's resolute and regular footfalls lent a sense of order and cadence to the cacophony that echoed down the hallways.

One day a week, Fietlebaum rounded on patients held in the psychiatric unit of the Industrial City General Hospital. He did it as part of an agreement between the academy that paid him and the hospital that desperately needed his services. Fietlebaum made out that it was an enormous imposition and insisted on extra compensation for it. In fact, he thoroughly enjoyed it. He could gain only so much satisfaction from treating love-sick cadets and the neglected, bitter spouses of overworked professors. He needed the stimulation of treating the truly ill.

The long-limbed Silesian nurse led him to the patient's bedside and hurriedly retreated. The room was small. It was being kept hot and humid. "Like a *schvitz*[27] bath," Fietlebaum thought out loud. The institutional, cardboard brown paint on the walls exaggerated the claustrophobic atmosphere. In the middle of the room was a bed stripped of sheets. He lay naked on the bed, writhing in four-point restraints.

---

27 A sweat bath

He was an Astaran whose name was Lors Argsglar. His species was amphibian. When out of water, fatal dehydration was prevented by a thick slime exuded by glands distributed across the surface of their body. Exposure to the air polymerized the slime into a rubbery outer skin, as black and shiny as patent leather. His head was enormous, and contributed a third of his body's mass. His mouth made up most of the size of his head. Rows of small but extraordinarily sharp and strong teeth lined the gaping mouth. They acted like rasps to grind algae-like growth off the rocks at the bottoms of lakes and rivers of Astara. The webbed feet and hands were rimmed by claws, as strong as steel, to cling to the rocks off which they fed.

Despite their fearsome appearance, Astarans were ordinarily phlegmatic and sedentary. Yet, Lors Argsglar was in restraints to prevent him from grabbing whoever might be walking by and shredding the flesh from their limbs with his rasping teeth. He had killed three Polmodi in this fashion the night before, after which the police brought him in chains to the emergency department.

Argsglar now called himself, "*ghomgijdahm,*" which the cybertranslater understood to be Astaran for "God already dead." He repeated the name over and over in a deep, booming honk such as might be made by a profoundly tormented tuba. At times he bellowed with such force he rattled the walls.

He had come to believe he was God of the Universe and that he was dead. With he, that is, God, being dead, time had stopped, and with time having stopped, existence was without direction and meaningless. Nothing was any longer of consequence, and the only salient feature of his existence was agony. His was an agony without beginning or end, unbounded in space with no possibility of change. The impossibility of his experience seemed so great that on the previous night he had felt compelled to prove it. To determine if his impression of meaninglessness was true, he felt it necessary to perform the most vile of acts. True to his suspicion, he had no feelings of either gratification or remorse from gnawing the flesh off the ones he had just killed. The agony of his nihilism only intensified.

Lors Argsglar was beyond engagement. He gave no meaningful information. Fietlebaum remained at his bedside another few moments. After he had gleaned what he could from watching and listening to the suffering creature, he walked back to the nurse's station to review the medical chart.

The nurse's face was ashen. Her saucer-eyes were wide, with the cat-like pupils dilated. Her mouth trembled. "Dr. Fietlebaum," she whimpered, "I can't bear to hear him bellow any longer. What made him go mad?"

Fietlebaum gave a wry look. "It could have been any of a hundred reasons," he replied. "It may have been a chemical imbalance, maybe a drug or a poison. An infection, a tumor, or a stroke might have altered his behavior." He paused. "*Nu*," he said with a palpable air of disappointment in having to consider something more mundane. "Maybe the poor fellow had struggled too long. There's no shortage of *tsuris*[28] in this world."

The nurse scurried off, and Fietlebaum sat down to pour through the Astaran's chart. The hospital's internists had already determined there to be no structural lesions in the Astaran's brain. Electromagnetic field analyses revealed no aberrations in its electrochemical activity beyond what would be expected in states of extreme excitement and fear. His circulatory, respiratory, digestive, and endocrine systems were intact. Samples of the Astaran's deep purple blood had been obtained, and revealed normal levels of blood gases, hormones, and ribose, the Astarans' primary

---

28 troubles

metabolic carbohydrate. Culture and sensitivity tests revealed no indications of invasive organisms. The standard toxicological screen was also negative, thus eliminating the most common set of intoxicants Astarans used to alter their mood and perceptions. With the most obvious medical contributions ruled out, Fietlebaum was left with his usual puzzle to resolve. Was this psychological, neurochemical, or both?

Who is this fellow? he wondered. He called the Astaran's Polmodi landlord, and learned that for thirteen years Lors Argsglar had been a perfect tenant. The local police chief told him he had no police record. His boss at work informed Fietlebaum that the Astaran had never missed a day of work. He was conscientious to a fault. One day he left the office with a government pen in his pocket and made the forty-five minute return trip from his home to return it that same evening.

Argsglar worked in the accounting department of the city's mass transportation office. His interests were narrow. His obsession was tracking expenditures for the lubricants that kept the doors of the communal transporters opening and closing smoothly. In his spare time, he collected antique subway tickets from around the galaxy. *Not my idea of a good time*, Fietlebaum reflected. He had no family or social life on Polmod. But that was common. Many out-worlders lived in similar circumstances.

Something is missing, Fietlebaum decided. He requested that another blood sample be drawn from the Astaran, and every molecule in it identified by the hospital's mass spectrometer. The results would be compared against existing catalogues of all of the molecules that had been identified in the blood of normal populations of Astarans. Meanwhile, Fietlebaum asked police to search the Astaran's home and see if any unusual items, letters with troubling news, a suicide note, or any other documentation of a mind in disintegration were lying about.

A half an hour later, the lab technician trotted back into the room. "Dr. Fietlebaum," he said excitedly, "the results of the analysis are back." He laid the printout in front of Fietlebaum and pointed to the surprising column of figures. "Lors Argsglar's blood contained trace amounts of a substance not seen in the blood samples of twenty-three thousand normal Astarans."

"It might be at the bottom of the fellow's misbehavior," Fietlebaum told him. "Let's find out what it is."

Fietlebaum had the lab tech concentrate the sample and run it back through the mass spectrometer at high gain. In another fifteen minutes, the results printed out. "I'll be damned," Fietlebaum whispered.

The substance was an alkaloid. It was from a rare plant, *prastaad*, that grew on a moon of Silesia. On Silesia, the leaves of *prastaad* were chewed to produce an altered state of consciousness much prized by certain subcultures on the planet. *Prastaad* had been elevated to the status of a sacrament, and some religious cults on Silesia made use of it in their worship services. While chewing *prastaad*, the worshipers often reported experiencing closeness with God and a new understanding of their place in life.

When the police returned, they gave Fietlebaum some of the items they had found in Lors Argsglar's home. Among them was a journal he had been keeping. With the assistance of the cybertranslater, Fietlebaum read through it.

Lors Argsglar had been miserable for years. He felt lonely and misunderstood. Astarans were seen as dull, boring and shallow. No one cared or even suspected he might be searching for his soul. Yet his existence was a painful mystery to him. He was grasping for the meaning of being alive in the universe and how something so solid and real could be so temporary for each individual who lived in it. He struggled with the meaninglessness of life that ended in death. He could not find the answers, but neither could he retreat from the pursuit of them.

Lors Argsglar wrote of his need to experience a oneness with the guiding process of the Universe and to feel part of it. It was near the end of his journal that he mentioned his intention to use *prastaad*. He had heard about its use by Silesians in their meditation practices. It was said to "open the soul." He hoped it would expand his consciousness and give him a new understanding of life, consciousness and God. The madness and murderous behavior of the tormented Astaran may have been a spiritual quest gone wrong.

Fietlebaum nodded his head in recognition of what must have occurred. "*Prastaad*!" he exclaimed. He found it fascinating that enough neurochemical processes were shared among species, even those that had evolved on planets light-years apart, that a single substance could be psychoactive in very different nervous systems. It was explained by the basic building blocks of life, amino acids, carbohydrates, deoxyribonucleic acids, phospholipids, having long ago been scattered across neighboring areas of the galaxy by comets, meteorites, and other forms of celestial collision. This was the so-called panspermia theory. The seeds of life had spread widely throughout the galaxy, and probably the entire Universe, by common and well-known processes of chemistry and physics. In some cases, primitive forms of life that had already evolved after billions of years were themselves transported to other star systems and planets by such processes. Thus, while evolution was unique on each planet, and the divergent nature of evolution generated radically different solutions to the challenges of life in differing environments, many of the same processes of biochemistry and physiology were common throughout the galaxy.

Unfortunately, the *prastaad* may have had an effect on Lors Argsglar that was dramatically different from the calming and spiritually illuminating effect experienced by Silesians. The effects of *prastaad* in Argsglar may have been mediated in a part of the brain that processed a very different aspect of reality than was the case in Silesians. Rather than a sacrament to open his mind, Lors Argsglar may have placed pure hell in his Astaran mouth.

The old research into what was sometimes referred to as psychedelic drugs had noted that the nature and tone of the "trip" always depended upon the individual's mind set and the environment in which they pursued their psychedelic experience. The unfortunate Lors Argsglar had a head full of loneliness and fear. Alone in his dreary room, the *prastaad* multiplied his loneliness and isolation a thousand fold. While pursuing God, Lors Argsglar became *ghomgijdahm*, God already dead.

As Fietlebaum was entering his report into the hospital's digital records, he heard a shout from the Polmodi nurse in Lors Argsglar's room. There was a call on the intercom for the Code Blue team to come. The Astaran's vital signs had suddenly accelerated, as if he wrestled with some enormous new strain. Just as suddenly, he fell still. His bellowing ended, and his limbs gave up their fight against the restraints. His one, large compound eye was open, but he vacantly stared at the ceiling. His vital signs plummeted. The Code Blue team arrived, but their efforts were useless. Lors Argsglar was pronounced dead.

Because the exact cause of his death remained unknown, the case was discussed at the hospital's weekly morbidity and mortality meeting. Some of the physicians maintained the most likely cause of death was cardiac failure due to the Astaran's persistence in struggling against his restraints despite having already propelled himself into an extreme state of exhaustion. His compound hearts had likely given out. It was argued that more should have been done to sedate him and to support his cardiovascular system. Fietlebaum was not convinced. It was his impression that the Astaran had simply willed himself into death, and nothing more could have been done to save him. The truth he had discovered was too terrible for him to live with, and he accepted the one remaining kindness the otherwise empty universe had to offer.

CHAPTER 4

Fietlebaum's first patient in the academy's clinic that morning was a native Polmodi. She was one of the relatively few left on the planet. Most of the Polmodi had either been killed off by the more powerful and advanced life forms that had colonized Polmod centuries before, or had fled their home planet for refuge in even more remote areas of the galaxy.

Minforp Graj was short, with the radially structured body of all Polmodi life. Radial, rather than bilaterally symmetrical, was the anatomical structure typical of most life forms in this sector of the galaxy. Unlike the primitive Earth creatures with radial bodies, such as starfish and jellyfish, the Polmodis were upright and compartmentalized into anatomical structures analogous to the abdominal, thoracic and cephalic compartments of the more highly evolved Earth animals.

With a radial design to their bodies, the Polmodi had no front or back. They presented with three sides that were virtually identical in appearance. In a bird's eye view, or the view Fietlebaum enjoyed from high up in his commutes to and from the clinic, the Polmodi looked like spiny equilateral triangles. While the three sides did not differ in gross structure or function, like humans, who favored a right or left side, the Polmodi tended to favor the use of one of the three facets. The dominant side of a Polmodi was immediately obvious to all others of their race, but to the unpracticed eye, such as Isaac Fietlebaum's, it was utterly indistinguishable from the other two. Fietlebaum would begin speaking to a Polmodi without realizing the face he was addressing lacked the desire or capacity to interact with him in any meaningful fashion. He found it disconcerting.

Minforp presented with an increasingly common problem on economically blighted Polmod. "Doctor," she told Fietlebaum, "I don't care anymore. I don't do my house work, and I haven't taken a bath for over a week." This was something Fietlebaum had suspected, as she had a pungent body odor. *Like dead fish and burnt cinnamon*, Fietlebaum decided. "I'm tired all the time," she added. "I hardly sleep anymore."

Fietlebaum noticed her skin hung limply on her frame, like dry, wrinkled red curtains. This prompted him to ask, "How is your appetite?" She shook her head to convey that she had none. Fietlebaum nodded in recognition.

The forks of her tongues darted in and out of her mouths. They writhed and turned deep blue and purple, the colors that mirrored her despondency. Her gurgling Polmodi speech, reminiscent of the ululation of excited Middle Eastern women, increased in pitch and volume. Purple saliva dripped down her chests. "I've never been like this!" she cried.

Fietlebaum offered her a wad of tissues to mop herself dry. "When did it start?" he asked her.

"When my husband lost his job!" she was quick to exclaim, as if she had long been desperate to reveal that fact. "After that, he was angry all of the time," she complained. "He criticized everything I did. When the money ran out, he wanted to fight about the bills. When our baby, little Plorpet, got sick, it was all my fault." She snorted and shook her head. "Only a few months ago," she lamented, "everything was fine. Now all we do is fight."

She paused. "Sometimes," she began. She hesitated.

"What happens sometimes, Minforp?" Fietlebaum asked.

The skin on her faces sagged further. Her drooling grew more profuse, and the forks of her tongues turned black and writhed more vigorously. "Sometimes," she reluctantly confessed, "I don't want to go on living." After uttering those words, she made a loud bleating sound, like a frightened goat.

The sound carried Fietlebaum to the side of a young Polmodi making the same anguished cry. She was a teaching case, a rare patient for the Medical School of Forgion University. She cried out and, before anyone could stop her, she pulled a small, but razor sharp, Polmodi knife from her tunic and slashed her anterior cervical artery. He again smelled the pungent odor of dark Polmodi blood. He felt emergency staff push past him to try, unsuccessfully, to staunch the bleeding. He saw her collapse to the floor. Minforp's cry was the same sound and suffering.

Regardless of the planet or species, sentient beings were everywhere the same in one regard. None could suffer defeat after defeat without eventually feeling something deep in their soul break. At some point the suffering creature found itself unable to carry on. This sense of no longer being able to continue to battle the stresses of life was described in many different languages, but a common semantic thread ran through every description he heard. Some said they were beaten down. Others were weighed down, slowed down, or pushed down and unable rise. The complaint was always a variation of a word cybertranslated into the English word, "depressed."

Minforp Graj was beyond the point of being soothed by mere words. A medication would be necessary to restore her capacity to deal with stress, and lift her to a state in which she could begin deal with the very real problems that had beset her and her family. The galaxy's big pharmaceutical companies had little to gain from developing psychiatric medications for the poverty stricken Polmodi. There was no ready-made miracle on the shelf to prescribe to Minforp. Thankfully, Fietlebaum had been down this road before.

Almost all species had developed medications from herbs and roots that grew on their home planets. The Polmodi had developed a sophisticated folk medicine of extracts of plants and lower forms of animal life. After he arrived on the planet, Fietlebaum had used the academy's mass spectrometer to analyze the more efficacious herbal concoctions in the folk pharmacopeia. The proteomics program he had developed determined which neurotransmitter receptors in the brain were likely to be affected by the active components of the folk medicine. The program also suggested how the addition of a chlorine atom here, or a methyl group there on the native molecule might produce a more potent and effective medication. By this method, Fietlebaum had tailor made a variety of psychotherapeutic medications for his Polmodi patients.

Fietlebaum peered into his desk drawer, grabbed a small bottle of pills, and handed it to Minforp. "Take one of these every morning, dear," he told her, "and in a few weeks you should begin to feel better."

Her tongues relaxed and grew lighter in hue. "Thank you doctor," she said.

"I have one more question before you leave," Fietlebaum said. "Will you be safe at home?"

"Yes," she responded without hesitation. "Now that I have somewhere to turn, I know I will be safe."

"Good!" he replied. "I'll see you in a week. Please make an appointment on your way out."

Ten minutes later a young human, James Dennison, was led into Fietlebaum's office. Dennison had been reluctant to come, as he had seen no need. His family had arranged the appointment. He had stopped going to classes. Dirty dishes and rotting food piled up in every room of his apartment. He had not washed or changed clothes for nearly two months. When he walked down the street, people stopped and stared. Parents pulled their children away.

Fietlebaum introduced himself and said, "Please have a seat."

Dennison tilted his head back and gazed down his nose at Fietlebaum in a look of grave suspicion. Without breaking his gaze, he backed up cautiously and sat down.

"I'm a clone," Dennison said nonchalantly.

"Is that so?" Fietlebaum replied.

"It happened years ago," Dennison continued, "but I found out only last month."

"Tell me more," Fietlebaum requested.

"James Dennison is my gene donor," he explained. "Agents removed pieces of tissue from him during Transgalactic Lifespan Synchronization Time. They sent the genetic material to a lab and cloned us."

"So you're *not* James Dennison," Fietlebaum recapitulated. "You are merely a James Dennison clone."

"I was number twenty-three," he replied matter-of-factly. "I was cloned from Dennison's big toe—his left one."

"This boy is *meshugeh*," Fietlebaum whispered to himself.

Fietlebaum had seen several such cases in the past. Cloning evolved out of the science of genetic engineering. The process opened vistas in the treatment of cancer, degenerative neurological diseases, and resolved otherwise intractable problems in organ and limb transplantation. No one considered it might have psychiatric sequelae. Yet, throughout history, delusions have always reflected the technology of the times. Prior to the industrial revolution on Earth, delusional humans were possessed by demons. After Marconi's work, they were controlled by radio waves. Television soon replaced radio as the favored medium for messages from God and the Devil, and, not long afterward, people thought themselves commanded by telecommunication satellites. After the development of genetic technologies, it wasn't long before being a clone came into vogue among the delusional.

"Being a mere clone of Mr. Dennison," Fietlebaum posed to his patient, "you feel no need to go to his classes, clean his house, or wash your genetically engineered facsimile of his body?"

Dennison shrugged and replied in the age-old, rhetorical question, "Why bother?"

Though tempting from a common sense point of view, Fietlebaum had learned, from years of experience, that it was useless to argue with patients such as Dennison. No manner of logic and proof could dissuade him. Despite all their suffering, the tenacity with which these patients held on to their beliefs made it seem they preferred their delusions to reality.

The treatment for delusional disorders in humans had not changed for thousands of years. Delusions were aberrations of thought similar to the aberrations of perception that manifested as hallucinations. It was over-activity of the neurotransmitter dopamine in the brain that fueled both forms of neuropsychiatric derangement. Accordingly, Fietlebaum hoped a dopamine antagonist might dampen the intensity of Dennison's delusions. However, the more important component of treatment would be convincing Dennison that being a clone did not free him from the basic duties and responsibilities of existence. Nor did it prevent him from partaking in, and possibly even enjoying, what the universe had to offer. The task would not be to convince him his delusion was wrong, but irrelevant.

Fietlebaum reached into his pharmaceuticals drawer and grabbed a bottle of tablets. "This is a month's supply of plestidol," he told Dennison. "I want you to take one tablet every morning."

'I'm a clone!" Dennison pointed out with a dismissive laugh. "Your pills can't change that."

Fietlebaum peered over the rims of his glasses. He pulled his brow ridges down into deep, disapproving furrows. "Indulge me," he retorted.

Dennison tipped his head back and again gazed at Fietlebaum with his piercing stare of suspicion. Fietlebaum steadfastly met his gaze, and Dennison eventually abandoned his opposition. "Okay," Dennison said with indifference, "if you say so."

"I say so," Fietlebaum insisted, "and I want you to return next week for psychotherapy." He opened the office door for the delusional young human, and directed him to the front desk to make a new appointment.

The last patient of the day was a Drajan, who sat silently in the waiting room. The appointment had been made at the last minute. The only rationale for the visit was a sentence hurriedly scrawled on a slip of paper explaining that the patient was depressed after the untimely death of his mother.

The Drajan was small, but wiry. His scales were deep purple, thinly edged in brilliant, iridescent green. His bulging eyes were the same green, with narrow, black slits for pupils, like those of a snake. Sharp, serrated green teeth extended out beneath the margins of his thin, purple lips.

Fietlebaum beckoned him into his office. The Drajan sidled past and sat. Fietlebaum closed the door and asked him what kind of help he was seeking. The Drajan said nothing. The air whistled through his narrow nostrils as he slowly breathed in and out. Aside from the occasional twitch of his long, green tail, there were no obvious indications of psychic burdens.

It was not Fietlebaum's habit to pressure a patient after asking a question. He had long ago learned that there was always a reason for silence. If allowed to, that reason would often reveal itself. After he had decided there was nothing more to gain from waiting, he asked more insistently, "How can I help you, sir?" The Drajan then pulled from his coat pocket a badge that identified him as agent Erd Glesh of the Galactic Intelligence Agency. The cybertranslater reported the Drajan as saying, "Dr. Fietlebaum, we expect your assistance in resolving an important matter of Galactic security."

Fietlebaum wondered if the revelation was true or if the Drajan had a problem more serious than the one the note had suggested. *Maybe he's delusional*, he thought. He called him out. "So, agent Glesh," he inquired, "what kind of work do you do for the Galactic Intelligence Agency?"

Glesh discerned Fietlebaum's incredulity. He responded by lifting the thin metallic cover of his identification badge to expose a holographic platform upon which a miniature version of the director of the Galactic Intelligence Agency strode out and announced, in no uncertain terms, that the bearer of this badge, agent Erd Glesh, was indeed an employee of the GIA and on official business of urgent nature. Fietlebaum came to the conclusion that such a device was not likely to be counterfeited and that agent Glesh was almost certainly genuine. At the same moment he realized it would have been better for everyone had Mr. Glesh simply been *meshugeh*.

CHAPTER 5

Fietlebaum agreed to meet Glesh after work at a well known, but past its prime, Gorsidian restaurant in the center of Industrial City. As he flew to the center of town to meet Glesh, he considered the situation. He hadn't a clue as to what it was all about, but he suspected it wouldn't be pleasant. "I need this like a *loch in kop*[29]!" he groaned.

His capsule dipped down from the clouds, and the grimy towers and litter strewn streets of central Industry City soon came into view. The capsule guided itself down to street level, and veered into a parking lot beside a dilapidated old restaurant with flashing lights and a sign in Gorsidian script that read, "Gorsidian Gardens." A capsule with galactic identification numbers was already parked, and he assumed it belonged to Glesh.

Fietlebaum stepped out of his capsule. The Polmodi wind howled. Dust, desiccated fragments of vegetation, and weathered scraps of discarded paper blew across the parking lot and swirled around him. He turned up his collar and ambled toward the door. He pushed it open and stepped in.

Despite its decline, it was still a popular eatery. Gorsidian food appealed to a variety of tastes throughout the galaxy, and species from many different planets were drawn to the restaurant's spicy dishes and cheap prices—particularly the cheap prices. The place was poorly lit. He could barely make out individuals at back tables and in grimy booths. Light reflected faintly off a vague

---

29 a hole in the head

constellation of eyes—single eyes, compound eyes, eyes on stalks that waved about when Fietlebaum glanced in their direction. The restaurant's old sound system spit Gorsidian music into the room. The music was dark and bubbly, like the wounded, mammalian cry of uilleann bagpipes. It was punctuated intermittently by the crackle and static of fatigued wires. The air was heavy with the smoky, sweet aromas of Gorsidian food. It smelled good. The manager spotted Fietlebaum, slithered across the floor and, without so much as a cybertranslated word, stretched a tentacle up to his shoulder and guided him, a little too insistently for his taste, to the back room where Glesh was waiting.

"Thank you for coming, Dr. Fietlebaum," Glesh said.

"A *shtik naches*," Fietlebaum replied in deadpan as he took a seat at Glesh's table. The cybertranslator conveyed Fietlebaum's message as, "a great pleasure," ignoring his use of the Yiddish idiom in a tone of voice to mean exactly the opposite.

"May I order you something to eat?" Glesh inquired.

Though he was famished, Fietlebaum refused to be beholden to Glesh even for the mere price of a dinner. "No, thank you," he replied. "I'm not hungry at the moment. Besides, I have a lovely dinner waiting for me at home. My food synthesizer works miracles."

"If you don't mind," Glesh said, "I will order something for myself. I'm starving."

"I wouldn't dream of stopping you," Fietlebaum replied without conviction.

After giving his order to the waiter, Glesh turned back toward Fietlebaum. "Let me tell you why we need your assistance," he said

"I'm all ears," Fietlebaum told him.

"The Galactic government uses large quantities of rare elements in its military computing and navigation devices," Glesh explained. "Without a reliable source of those materials, we cannot maintain our weapons systems, and thus cannot maintain a battle ready posture."

"Of course," Fietlebaum half-heartedly agreed, "a battle ready posture."

"The Galaxy's primary sources of neodymium and thallium are the mines on the planet, Janpoor," Glesh went on to say.

"Sure," Fietlebaum noted, "Janpoor."

"The mines have, up until recently, been providing a steady supply of those elements. However, recent labor unrest on the planet has led to some compromises in that supply."

"Okay," Fietlebaum acknowledged with an impatient nod, "thallium, Janpoor, compromises. But what does this have to do with me?"

"You must let me continue," Glesh said curtly.

"By all means," Fietlebaum allowed. "Continue."

"Janpoor is ruled by a government with strong ties to the Galactic Central Committee, and they have always been able to direct their affairs in our best interest. However, a Janpooran rabble rouser, by the name of Teysoot Motzo, has recently gained a following among miners on the planet. He has been organizing them, demanding a lot of safety regulations and benefits, and threatening to go on strike if the demands aren't met. A strike would stop the flow of materials critical for our military. We can't allow that to happen."

"Of course, we can't," Fietlebaum was barely willing to admit.

"There are also large populations of Janpooran workers on other planets in the star system, and Teysoot Motzo holds sway over many of them as well. A variety of military projects and plans critical to the Galactic government are being jeopardized. This needs to be stopped, now."

"But I *still* don't know why I'm here!" Fietlebaum complained.

Glesh sighed with annoyance. His tail twitched. "The Janpoorans," he told him, "are ignorant, primitive, and superstitious creatures. They don't tolerate weakness and they don't tolerate craziness. That's why you're here."

Fietlebaum was exasperated. "I don't see where you're going with this," he protested. "If Teysoot Motzo is mentally ill, I'll be happy to treat him. I don't need this *meshugeh* cloak and dagger business. Why can't you just tell me what you want from me?"

Glesh stared intently at Fietlebaum. His tail thumped on the floor, and the scales on his chest began to quiver. He contained himself. "Teysoot Motzo may not be mentally ill now," he replied with a smirk, "but with your help, Dr. Fietlebaum, he soon will be."

Oy! Fietlebaum thought. Suddenly, it was clear. *Why assassinate an enemy of the state and make him a martyr when you can coerce a psychiatrist into turning him into a disreputable lunatic?* He was angry at Glesh for dragging him into this, and angry at himself for being so naive. "So," Fietlebaum responded in measured tones, "what you are asking me to do is use my medical knowledge to drive Teysoot Motzo insane and make sure it happens in a very public fashion."

"Precisely," Glesh replied.

Fietlebaum was incensed. "Agent Glesh," he said as he leaned back and tried to maintain his composure, "it was only a few years ago the government decided I was an easy target for its tricks. God had taken my wife. My accountant had taken my money. My company had taken my livelihood. So, your government did me a kindness and took my reputation!" Fietlebaum felt his temper rise. "Now you are asking me, a victim of your galactic character assassination squad, to help you destroy another innocent being?" He leaned in toward Glesh and shook his head in disgust. "Glesh!" he growled. "*Shtup es in tuches*[30]!"

---

30 Shove it up your ass!

He rose from the table and stomped out of the room. The manager slithered out of a corner and extended a long tentacle in an attempt to stop him, but Fietlebaum simply pushed it aside. The Gorsid looked back to Glesh for direction. Glesh shook his head and waved a dismissing hand at Fietlebaum. "Let the old fool go," he said.

"*Vey iz mir*," Fietlebaum mumbled as he strode out the door to his capsule. "A perfect ending to a perfect day." He climbed into his capsule and nestled into the seat. "A real *macher*[31], that Glesh. Who does he think he is?"

He asked the capsule to fly him home. It was a relief to have escaped Glesh's presence, but he continued to seethe. "That *momzer*," he kept grumbling, "—the nerve of that dirty *momzer*." He ruminated on it half the way home, until enough was enough. "Ach!" he growled, "What's the sense in it? If I can't keep him from making me crazy, how can I expect to help my patients?" "*Ich hob es in drerd*[32]," he sighed, and let it go.

His transportation capsule dropped from the sky and parked itself in front of his bungalow. He was hungry. He had not eaten all day, and not even the aggravation of meeting with Glesh could rob him of his appetite. As he walked through the front door he realized his circumstances called for comfort food. He strolled into his kitchen and uploaded a recipe for *lokshen kugle*[33] into his food synthesizer. It came out in three minutes and looked delicious. He dished himself out a plate and sat at the table. With high expectations, he lifted a forkful of *kugle* to his mouth and ate. It tasted like anchovy. He heaved a cataclysmic, "*Oy*!" and spit it out. He wiped his mouth and shook his head. "Of course!" he grumbled. "The way things have gone today, I should have seen this coming!" He threw

31 Big shot

32 To hell with it!

33 A noodle pudding

out the *kugle*, and poured himself two fingers of *schnapps*. He listened to music for a few minutes, but this night not even his beloved Byrd could relieve his consternation. He abandoned the music and went to bed early.

That night he tossed and turned. He suffered nightmares. The Senate had re-opened their investigation into the gestiron scandal. It seemed the deleterious effects of the drug had been greatly underestimated. Jorgon children were changing. They were growing tentacles. Senator Lornst appeared and showed Fietlebaum the evidentiary holograms. Some of the children had completely transformed into spitting images of the manager of the Gorsidian Gardens. Parents were furious. "Go tell it to Fietlebaum!" Lornst cackled. Tentacles of angry children reached in under his doors. Tentacles were swinging from the light fixtures. They crawled out from under his bed and insinuated their way into his sheets. Suddenly, Glesh stood at the foot of his bed. "Did you think you could escape?" he asked accusingly.

He woke with a start. "*Gevalt*!" he cried out. He switched on the light and looked around. There was nothing there. "*Vey iz mir*. I thought this *meshugas*[34] was over." He took a deep breath and rubbed his forehead. "The government still sees me as a patsy." He sat up a few more minutes until he was certain he could dismiss it all as a dream, then lay back down and crawled in under the covers. "Well, he murmured, "maybe it's over, and maybe it's not. But one thing is certain, *azes vert nit besser, vert memaileh erger*[35]."

---

34 craziness

35 If it doesn't get better, it will probably get worse.

CHAPTER 6

Fietlebaum arrived at his office and prepared for his day of seeing patients. It had been several months since the meeting with Glesh at Gorsidian Gardens. Although he was able to push his personal affairs to the back of his mind and concentrate on his work, he couldn't help but think about Glesh and wonder when the other shoe would drop. Certainly, Glesh wouldn't simply let it go. But it made no sense to worry about things he couldn't control. He had been telling his patients that for years. Surely he could benefit from the same advice. If Glesh had further plans for him, he would just have to cross that bridge when he came to it.

The morning started with Hisht Jorvond, an adolescent Horgentian suffering what was politely called, "an emotional disturbance." What Fietlebaum disliked most about his practice at the academy was his obligation to see the children of employees who were having problems growing up. Try as he might, he just didn't like the little *pishers.*

The young Horgentian shambled into the room and poured himself into the chair in front of Fietlebaum's desk. He resembled a large sea cucumber. He had no clearly defined head, but on top of his ovoid body were two enormous eyes and, just below, a large, lipless mouth. He had no limbs—none permanent, anyway. Rather, across the surface of his body were colonies of amoeboid cells that could almost instantly assemble themselves into a variety of pseudopodia. Their structural complexity ranged from mere stumps, to fingered hands with dexterity sufficient for virtuoso piano performances. As he slouched in the chair, pseudopodia sprang up and down across his body in rapid, random fashion. *Fidgeting*, Fietlebaum decided.

Fietlebaum smiled faintly. "I'm Dr. Fietlebaum," he said. "How can I help you?"

Hisht generated a series of sounds in response to Fietlebaum's inquiry, but the cybertranslater could not compute. It was an enormous source of annoyance. No matter the species, the cybertranslaters had to be re-educated every few weeks to maintain their ability to understand the slang teenagers were tossing about. *The mumbling doesn't help either*, Fietlebaum thought.

"Hisht," Fietlebaum said, "I'm not one of your young friends. I can't understand what you're saying." Hisht rolled his eyes as if an unbearable imposition had just been placed upon him.

"I'm old," Fietlebaum admitted with theatrically apologetic tone. "Pretend that I'm your grandfather." He hoped that might help him say something the cybertranslater could understand.

When the cybertranslater conveyed that message, the Horgentian emitted a loud warbling sound, which Fietlebaum correctly assumed was the little *pisher* laughing at him. "If it pleases you grandpa," Hisht said in slow and measured cadence, "I communicate to you my belief that you resemble grandma's excretory organ." He emitted another long burst of warbling, and, along with the warble, a peculiar odor emanated from him and spread across the office. That was another thing Fietlebaum disliked about teenagers.

Genug es genug, Fietlebaum thought, *the little* gruber yung[36] *needs the truth.* "Listen," he snapped. "I don't want to talk to you anymore than you want to talk to me." Hisht stopped warbling and looked in Fietlebaum's direction. "I

---

36 Rude boy

think you're a snot-nosed, little *pisher*, and you think I'm a senile *alta kocker*," Fietlebaum continued. "But the two of us are expected to talk. My boss says we have to, your parents say we have to, and that means we have to. So, the sooner we get this over with the better."

That did the trick. The boy let loose. He revealed far more than Fietlebaum had hoped for. He talked about his problems at school, his awkward attempts at dating, his parents' never ending accusations that he was experimenting with hallucinogenic booja leaves, his confession that he actually *was* experimenting with hallucinogenic booja leaves, and his fears that he was masturbating too much.

There is nothing wrong with this little putz[37] *that isn't wrong with every other little* putz *in the universe*, Fietlebaum thought as he listened to the endless tales of adolescent woe. He glanced at the clock on the wall. The allotted hour was nearing an end. "That's it," he told Hisht. "Now, let me give you some advice. Your parents are a pain in the *tuches*[38], but they're the best friends you'll ever have. Take their advice and try not to hurt them too much. You have to get up off your lazy butt and do something! Go out for sports, get a hobby, make some music. Masturbate more, not less. It never hurt anybody, and it will give you something to look forward to every day. And remember, girls don't bite." He stopped for a moment trying to recollect if Horgentian females did in fact bite or not, but he couldn't quite recall. "Anyway," he concluded with mild consternation, "you can be sure they are as clueless as you are."

"Okay," Hisht said meekly. "Thank you."

"And for God's sake," Fietlebaum added, "take a bath once in a while!" He got up, strolled to the door, and opened it for the young Horgentian. "On your way out, tell my clerk

---

37 prick

38 ass

I want to see you in two weeks." He was relieved the hour was over.

After a few minutes to collect his thoughts, he asked his nurse to walk Minforp Graj back to his office for her follow up visit. "I'm feeling better, doctor," she told him. He noted she moved in more spritely fashion than when he first saw her. She had gained back some of the weight she had lost and no longer looked gaunt. She was sleeping better. "These are good signs," he told her. Perhaps most importantly, the medication he had started was not causing her any new problems. The ancient edict, *primum non nocere*[39], was still his guiding principle. Fietlebaum remained hopeful the choice of medication was a good one, and that she would continue to feel better over the next weeks and months.

With the first hints of improvement evident, it was time she began to talk more about the events that precipitated her fall into depression and consider what changes she could make to improve her life and marriage. Psychotherapy was a sophisticated skill, but Fietlebaum believed that simply talking was important. He had long ago concluded that most of people's problems came from feeling unable to say something to someone else. Fietlebaum enjoyed the neurochemistry and psychopharmacology that made each patient a unique and challenging puzzle. But talking with the patients and watching them recover their lives was what made his job worthwhile. When the session ended, Minforp shimmied her way to the door, turned, and said, "thank you, doctor." Though he had been in practice for nearly forty years, those words sounded as sweet as they did the first time.

Fietlebaum had time for a quick cup of coffee before he returned to his office for his next patient. His nurse led Fejdut Lops, a young Korpian female, to the chair in front of his desk. At least, he thought she was female. Korpians

---

[39] first do no harm, in Latin

were among several advanced species in the Galaxy that underwent sex transformation when numbers of their own sex became too high. The identification of gender was extraordinarily important in Korpian society, to the extent that gender transformation of words, such as in human Romance languages, was exaggerated and generated entirely different forms of address in conversation. When the cybertranslater failed to address her gender properly, she became irate.

"I refuse to speak to that machine!" she asserted. "Unless you want me to leave, you're going to have to get a different one in here."

Fietlebaum restrained the impulse to tell her to go ahead and leave, and decided he would indulge her. A new cybertranslater was brought in, and he asked her what problem led her to come to the clinic.

"I don't know," she snapped as if being greatly imposed upon. "I thought *you* would know. *You're* the doctor!"

"Miss Lops," Fietlebaum replied, in as calm and accommodating a voice as he could muster, "It would help us both if I knew what you hoped to gain from seeing me."

"Now you sound like you're angry at me!" she huffed.

"*Oy gevalt*," he murmured under his breath. He had seen such patients many times before. They were the ones who demanded you, "go away a little closer." There would be no pleasing her. This frustrating, unreasonable behavior was an epiphenomenon that arose from some as of yet unidentified interactions of early life deprivation, unrequited desire, and disappointment. No matter what species or planet, there were always individuals who could see no shades of gray in their relationships with others. They either loved you or hated you, and this could change in the blink of an eye. If they hated you, they really hated you, and they kept on hating you until you told them there was simply no use in being around someone who so fervently hated you, at which time they would tearfully beg you to stay and threatened to kill themselves if you didn't. Unfortunately, relenting made them hate you all the more.

The literature abounded in theoretical explanations for the behavior, but none were entirely satisfactory. At such times, Fietlebaum's mind leapt to most the obvious and straightforward explanation for such childish and infuriating behavior—"she's *meshugeh*[40]!" He had noted to colleagues that, despite the lack of technical sophistication in the term, there was often no better characterization of the problem.

After noting his strong countertransference toward the Korpian, and warning himself to avoid falling prey to it, he reminded himself that her borderline personality disorder was something he would have to deal with in a more productive and therapeutic manner. He decided the best approach was to simply eliminate himself from the conversation and use her experience as the sole basis for their interaction.

"I hear you telling me that I seem angry," he finally replied.

"I just came for help, and you act like I am doing something terrible!" she shouted back.

"How does that make you feel to be seen as doing something terrible?"

"I try my best and nobody understands me. It makes me angry and it makes me want to cry." The cybertranslater had difficulty finding an adequate translation for the Korpian word that it eventually decided to refer to as "cry." The actual behavior of the Korpians was a loud gargling sound accompanied by vigorous shaking of the cephalic structures.

"It makes you angry and it makes you want to cry, doesn't it? Immediately the room filled with an astonishingly loud and heartfelt gargling. Her head shook

---

[40] Crazy!

with such force and velocity that he feared the row of olfactory tentacles atop her midsagital crest might fly off. "Ah," Fietlebaum thought to himself, "this is what she needed to do." He made no effort to stop her.

After a very long ten minutes or so, the gargling and shaking stopped. "I feel better now," the Korpian whimpered.

"Yes, you feel better now," Fietlebaum echoed.

"Thank you, doctor," she sighed. "Can I see you next week?"

"Yes, of course," he answered. "Please make an appointment on your way out." The second those words left his mouth he was struck by the horrible realization that his suggestion she do something on her way out might be interpreted as him ordering her out of his office, and the "go away a little closer" behavior would start up all over again. Thankfully, she was feeling unburdened enough by her emotional catharsis that she understood his suggestion as it was intended.

"Yes, I will," she said. "Thank you."

It had been a good morning. Minforp Graj was doing well, and even the hours with the little *pisher* and the *meshugeneh*[41] had worked out better than he had expected. Just before his next appointment, the nurse informed Fietlebaum that a small package had been delivered while he was in with his last patient. "It's on the counter," she said, adding parenthetically that it was not the usual service that delivered it.

He was not expecting anything, and he puzzled over what it could be. But when he saw the package itself, he knew Glesh had something to do with it. It was wrapped in government packing. The pinstripes on the brown paper were formed of continuous lines of the finely scripted letters, GIA. The package was too small to

---

41 Crazy person

contain documents. It was about an inch high and wide, by four inches long. *What the hell is it?* he wondered. He entertained possibilities consistent with the size of the box, and his suspicions frightened him.

His heart pounded and beads of blue perspiration erupted on his skin. His hands trembled as he fought to tear the tenacious wrapping from the box. He worked a claw underneath a stubborn strand of tape and tore off the last layer of paper. He prayed the box held a holographic projector or an electronic messaging device of some sort, but his worst fears were confirmed when he pried the box open and saw a severed finger lying inside. The finger was covered with shiny orange scales, and had two parallel rows of blue hair running across the dorsal side. A note lay underneath the finger. It read: "Dr. Fietlebaum, we have your grandson, Aaron. His finger is the proof you need. We expect you to cooperate with us. Please call at your earliest opportunity. Agent Erd Glesh, GIA."

CHAPTER 7

Isaac Fietlebaum was born on Hijdor, an Earth-sized planet on the outer side of the far spiral arm of the Milky Way Galaxy. Most of what Fietlebaum knew about the history of Hijdor, he learned from the Blahjdiri elders. Civilization had flourished on Hijdor for more than twenty thousand years, until wars, pestilence, rape of the planet's resources, and catastrophic climate change returned the planet to a stage of existence Humans might refer to as the Stone Age. The extraordinary intelligence of the Hijdori did not keep them from destroying their planet, and the decline was more precipitous than any of them could have imagined.

Hijdor had been rich with plant and animal life. It's oceans had been filled with creatures that swam and crawled on the ocean floor. Its forests had echoed with the calls of a myriad animals. Winged creatures of countless shapes and colors had glided through it's skies. Over a period of a few hundred years, the lush and vibrant surface of the planet was reduced to a wasteland.

After the fall, life on Hijdor was reduced to a daily struggle to wrestle a mouthful of food and a drop of water from the planet's uncharitable surface. More than seven billion had lived on the planet, but the desolate hunk of rock it became could sustain no more than a few thousand. With the protective elements torn from its atmosphere, the surface of Hijdor was too arid and exposed to stellar radiation to be safe for more than brief excursions into its open plains. Most of life was lived in the night and in the caves that riddled the planet's hills and mountains.

The water that dripped in the deep recesses of the caves provided just enough moisture to keep the Hijdori alive. Their staple food was the nutrient poor lichen that grew in the cracks and crevices of rocks that gave shielding from the lethal rays of the planet's star. On lucky days, the insect-like creatures that lived among the lichen became extra protein in their meager diet. With protein at a premium, even the flesh of the dead was eaten. Dead friends were eaten in solemn ceremony, dead foes in raucous celebration. Rabbi Goldman had once remarked, when that delicate subject was broached, "Your cousins probably aren't *kosher*, but you did what you did to survive. That's an exception to the rules God always allows."

To survive during the "dark years," as the Hijdori called them, one had either to be strong and willing to take whatever was needed without hesitation or remorse, or clever enough to keep what one had while sneaking away with what others had managed to scrape up. Shades of gray across the spectrum of intelligent to intimidating were useless. Thus, two clans rose to supremacy over the Hijdoris who survived. The Grojdiri were brutes who killed and scavenged. The Blahjdiri were shrewd and cunning creatures who lived by their wits while manipulating, as best they could, the half-witted Grojdiri.

In one to one combat, the larger and stronger Grojdiri had the advantage. But the weapons fashioned by the more artful Blahjdiri, their razor-sharp knives and well balanced spears and atlatls, equaled the odds. When captured in battle, those weapons became prized possessions of the technologically backward Grojdiri. Otherwise, the weapons of the Grojdiri were the stones they threw and stalactite fragments they wielded as bludgeons.

The Blahjdiri's best weapon was guile. Their favorite trick was to mimic the sound of dripping water to lure the Grojdiri into ambushes in dead-end arms of the caves. They practiced ventriloquism and threw their voices. By manipulating light and shadow, they made themselves appear as many rather than few. They cast fear and doubt. They practiced illusion, distraction, and the arts of misperception. "They were as good as any Las Vegas magician," his father, Morris Fietlebaum, once noted with admiration. By those means they balanced their power with the Grojdiri. But it was merely balance. In battles where lives were lost, Blahjdiri lives were always among them.

By the time the planet was discovered by the Galactic Planetary Resource Survey, Hijdor had been in its state of devastation for over three-thousand years. Telemetry systems had informed the galactic surveyors that the planet had life, perhaps even multicellular life, but the surface was so inhospitable that complex or intelligent life seemed unlikely. None were anxious to explore the planet, let alone attempt to establish contact with anything that might be crawling across its surface. But, one group decided that Hijdor was exactly what they had been seeking.

After leaving Earth, and the war torn Middle East that had finally combusted in an apocalyptic war of mutual annihilation, the surviving progeny of the Israelis had set out on the starship *Magen Dovid*[42]. They travelled through the star systems searching for a planet on which to establish New Jerusalem. Their ancestors had long ago made the Negev and Sinai deserts bloom. "If anyone could coax the dry and barren soil of Hijdor to life," Morris had proudly proclaimed, "it was the men and women of the *Magen Dovid*." They set course for Hijdor. "We were going," Morris Fietlebaum later told his son, "and nothing was going to stop us."

Seven years later, the *Magen Dovid* arrived. Though they celebrated the landing, none could deny that gazing across the barren landscape of the planet was a sobering experience. The glare of the red sun that burned above Hijdor revealed little more than lifeless plains and rocky

42 Star of David

hillsides as far as the eye could see. Morris shook his head when recounting the story of the first days. "There was nothing out there," he said. "Absolutely nothing." By all indications, the only witnesses to their landing were the silent moons that crossed the gray Hijdori sky. It would not be easy to transform the wasteland into a garden. Still, they dedicated themselves to the task and pledged they would succeed or die.

Some of the settlers constructed shelters, while others surveyed the planet to determine what resources it had to offer and what dangers might be lurking about. The initial surveys did little to alter the initial impressions of the forbidding surface of the planet. There was water vapor in the atmosphere, but no evidence of any liquid water on the ground. The only indications of flowing water were few and far between erosions in the hillsides that told the more trained eyes among them that rivulets of water had once run there.

The heat and violent windstorms on Hijdor were constant threats, not merely to progress, but to life and limb. Morris Fietlebaum recalled how, several months after the landing, two settlers were killed when a powerful gust of wind brought down a stone wall they were constructing. "*Vey iz mir*!" he marveled, "—like a hurricane, that wind!" The windstorms that raked the sand across the desert plains soon also revealed that intelligent life had once flourished on Hijdor. Now and then, the winds would uncover what looked like ancient structures. The discovery was fascinating but disquieting. It suggested an advanced civilization, perhaps one with technologies more sophisticated than their own, had been defeated by insurmountable forces of nature. Yet, they were spurred on by the assumption that the planet had life-sustaining resources. "We knew that Hijdor was hiding something," Morris explained, "so we kept looking."

It was finally assumed that if there were water, it was underground. Survey teams fanned out through the hills to find caves and map their resources. In that surveying they learned that intelligent life on Hijdor had not died out. While mapping one of the larger caves in the area, something was spotted in the beam of a helmet light. It was a knife, fashioned from native volcanic glass. A blue residue on the blade was still moist, making it almost certain it had only recently been used. "*Gevalt*!" Morris exclaimed. "When I heard about the knife, you could have knocked me over with a feather!"

The settlers were elated when they found the first spring deep within one of the caves. It was a small spring, only half a liter per hour in flow, but it was a start. It gave hope that the planet, like Israel of old, might someday be terraformed into a land of milk and honey. They installed a pump and laid pipe to carry the water down to the cluster of settlements. The water would be used to drink and for drip irrigation systems, like those that allowed cultivation of the Israeli deserts.

That night there were toasts and celebrations. But, the following morning the flow of water had stopped. A team was sent into the cave to investigate, and they found that the pipe from the spring had been smashed and the pump destroyed. It was obvious the as of yet unseen Hijdori were not only intelligent and resourceful, but had no intentions of sharing their water. "*Nu*?" Morris asked in retrospect, "Who could blame them?"

Over the next few months, more springs were found. More pumps and pipes were placed, but most were later found broken and ruined. The surveying teams also found increasing evidence of violence within the caves. With more water being discovered and pumped out to the irrigation projects, it was likely becoming a scarcer and more valuable commodity among the Hijdori. It was more worth fighting and dying for. More stone knives and bludgeons, often spotted with what was assumed to be blue blood, were found in the caves. Pools of blood lay in the dust on cave floors. Where the dust was thick enough, foot prints and ragged furrows remained as signs of violence and struggle.

All were curious about the Hijdori, and many had hoped to see the body of a native creature killed in battle. "We weren't morbid," his father explained apologetically, "we were curious. *Mein Got*! Who wouldn't be?" It was puzzling that no bodies were found at the scenes of what appeared to be ferocious battles. "It was only later," Morris noted, "we learned the bodies were being carried away to be butchered and eaten." He shrugged and projected his lower lip in quizzical fashion. "Who knew?" he asked rhetorically.

Guards were stationed by the pumps and pipelines, and the vandalism stopped. Apparently, the Hijdori were intelligent enough to see the futility in fighting the well-armed settlers. Thereafter, the water flowed and progress in the irrigation projects accelerated. Greenhouses were built to protect the crops from the harsh elements of Hijdor and to provide optimal atmospheric conditions for plant growth.

When the first fruits of their labor, a handful of radishes, were brought to the table of the communal hall there were tears, prayers, and celebration. "What a proud night that was!" Morris later told Isaac. Indeed, some had died in the quest to build New Jerusalem and bring life to the arid land. Others had died on the long journey to the planet. That night gave them reason to believe their sacrifices had not been in vain, and that their hopes and dreams would be fulfilled. "Still," Morris admitted to Issac, "what Rabbi Goldman said that night reflected what everyone felt—*Alts, dos hartz hot mir gezogt*[43]!"

Efforts were redoubled. The settlement grew. More cave springs were tapped and water production was increased. A

---

43 I always knew in my heart it would happen!

clinic, a power station, a communications center, a school, and other structures of civilized existence were built on the surrounding land. It wasn't long before the quantity of produce grown in the drip-irrigated greenhouses went beyond what was needed by the settlement itself. They began to export the surplus to neighboring planets and space outposts. Contracts were signed to supply mining companies and Galactic Armed forces units with fresh produce. The settlement was not merely a success in planetary survival. It was becoming an economic success as well. "We started to make a *shekel*[44]or two," Morris observed with pleasure.

With demand for their goods increasing, they were able to attract out-world workers to the planet. New areas of Hijdor were explored and developed. The exploration for water in the caves of the hills and mountains of Hijdor expanded. The beleaguered Hijdori continued to struggle with one another. On occasion, the clashes and cries of battle were even heard echoing through the caves on the edges of the expanding settlement. Footprints, blood trails and broken weapons continued to be found, but no traces of the Hijdori themselves were seen. "*Nu*?" his father recalled. "We knew you were there."

---

44 An ancient Heberew coin

CHAPTER 8

"I'm the one who found you," Morris was fond of saying. He had told the tale many times over the years. He was one of the starship's physicians and part of a surveying team. "We were in a cave looking for water," his story would begin, "when we came upon another one of your battle scenes. I was looking around when I saw something move on a ledge. I almost *pish*-ed my pants! I shined my light and saw orange scales. I stepped up on a rock underneath the ledge and eased myself up for a better look. There you were!"

Around this time, time young Isaac would roll his eyes and try to slip away. "Stay *boychik*," Morris would plead. "Stay, and listen." Usually, Isaac would relent.

"You didn't try to get away," Morris would say, "and at first I thought you were wounded. But, when you gurgled and wriggled your little legs I knew you were only a baby! I suspected your momma had hidden you on the ledge to keep you safe when the fighting broke out. I lifted you off the ledge and held you. You nestled your head under my chin and purred like a cat. Everyone told me I had the biggest smile they had seen on my face in thirty-five years!"

"*Oy*!" Morris would say. "You were a cute little *pisher*!" The *pisher* statement was, more often than not, accompanied by Morris wrapping his arm around Isaac's neck in an affectionate headlock.

"My God, Dad," Isaac would respond, with only partially feigned annoyance. "You've told that story a million times!"

"*Nu*?" Morris would innocently reply. "Then one more time couldn't hurt."

"For a moment," Morris would say wistfully, "I thought about putting you back for your momma to return for you. But I suspected something terrible had happened in that cave. All of the blood on the floor of the cave made me worry there might not be anyone to come back for you." He would nod thoughtfully. "Later we found out your momma was killed in that battle. It's a good thing I kept you."

At first, as Morris himself would admit, he treated "the little *pisher*" like a pet. But he soon realized the Hijdori infant was a being of high intelligence. A milestone was reached the day Morris returned home from work and heard words come out of his mouth. Like any human infant does, he had for months been making sounds that resembled the first attempts at speech. But on that day he cried out, "*Oy vey!*" as clear as a bell. "*Got in himmel*[45]*!*" Morris shouted. "He speaks Yiddish!" From that day on, it was no more "little *pisher*." "Someone who speaks Yiddish deserves a real name," Morris proudly asserted. He called him Isaac, for he would be the child of his old age.

It soon became clear that Isaac's first words of Yiddish were no fluke. Within a few years he was speaking excellent Yiddish, as well as perfect Hebrew, English, Russian, and Silesian. The following years gave further evidence of Isaac's astonishing capacity to absorb and assimilate knowledge. He breezed through arithmetic, algebra and calculus. In his spare time he delighted in deriving new mathematical transformations of classical proofs in geometry and physics. Along with mathematics and science, he delved into the works of the great philosophers. "That Plato was very clever," he announced one morning at age five, much to Morris' delight. He was particularly fond of Spinoza and the great Gorsidian philosopher, Slorjdeg, who, though thousands of years away in time and light-years away in

---

45 God in heaven!

distance, had developed nearly identical understandings of the nature of being, space and time.

Morris introduced Isaac to fine literature. "You'll like this," he would tell young Isaac. "Have a look." He read Shakespeare and Dostoyevsky. With Morris's coaxing, he developed a liking for the classics of the ancient New York Jewish literati, Isaac Bashevis Singer, Saul Bellow, and Phillip Roth. Isaac always wished he could have spent a day with Holden Caulfield.

It was Rabbi Moishe Goldman's opinion that Isaac's abilities to interpret and abstract were most dramatically demonstrated in his introduction to Talmud. According to the rabbi, there was no better instrument than the Talmud to gauge the depth of one's ability to appreciate the subtleties of the interactions of the minds and hearts of sentient beings. It didn't matter if those beings were human, Silesian, Polmodi, or Hijdori. "What difference does it make?" Goldman would ask.

In the study of Talmud, Isaac Fietlebaum went off the scale. He relished the arguments and counter-arguments concerning the fine points of the nature of obligations one has to God and fellow beings. He memorized long tracts of Talmud and discussed classical interpretations, even developing new twists and turns of understanding that left Rabbi Goldman in awe. His reinterpretations of the ancient texts for fresh guidance in the moral questions regarding interactions among sentient species from different star systems who had followed entirely different paths of evolution were, in Goldman's words, "breathtaking." By many accounts, he possessed all the intellectual capacity and brilliance of the *wunderkind*[46] *rabbis of the Renaissance in Eastern Europe two thousand years before. "A klug yingl*[47]*"* Goldman would say admiringly.

---

[46] Wonder child

[47] A smart boy!

Isaac's ability to cut the Talmudic Gordian knot became almost legendary. For centuries, rabbis of the Galactic era had argued over how—in a time of interstellar travel and life on strange planets that circled their stars in periods very different from Earth's—one could determine with certainty when a Jewish boy or girl had actually reached the *b'nai mitzvah*[48] age of thirteen. This was not to mention the complications introduced by Transgalactic Lifespan Synchronization Time. Moreover, since Judaism had spread to include some members of other Galactic races, among them beings with hugely variable lifespans and ages of maturity, there were also questions as to how to determine the appropriate *b'nai mitzvah* ages of the alien converts. It was noted that Brastants, whose world sped around a neutron star, lived high velocity lives of just twelve earth years, while the Poyers of the Maltzeit cluster did not become mature until well into their second century. Significant numbers of those species had converted to Judaism, resulting in Jewish Brastants dying before the age of *b'nai mitzvah* and Jewish Poyers of age thirteen being too immature to perform the religious duties required of them. When posed the seemingly intractable age question during Talmud study, Isaac simply shrugged and responded, "*Alt genug iz alt genug*[49]." "*Nu?*" Rabbi Goldman replied. "I think you're right!"

Yet, as Morris was always quick to point out, Isaac was not only smart, but good company, too. Morris's wife, Sharon, had not survived the trip to Hijdor. As sometimes happened in interstellar travel, she had failed to awaken out of suspended animation. It was missing Sharon that gave Morris an early glimpse into the depth and quality of Isaac's intelligence. One night, while reminiscing over holographic pictures, Morris began to weep as he again watched his

48 The ceremony of religious maturity.

49 Old enough is old enough

beloved Sharon moving with all the grace and charm she had possessed. Isaac came to his side to console him. He placed his hand on Morris's shoulder and let it rest until his tears were done. He gave him a gentle squeeze and returned to his play. "Even at his age," Morris said to himself, "he's a *mensch*[50]."

Isaac was popular among the other settlers of Hijdor. His young human friends were constantly knocking on the door. "Is Isaac home?" they would ask. "Can Isaac come out to play?" Along with calculus and philosophy, he liked sports. He could throw a wicked curve ball and kick a soccer ball with the best of them. He was in every respect an all-around boy. But he wasn't an average boy, and he was soon to discover his roots.

Isaac remembered well one summer when the weather on Hijdor was particularly harsh. There was a desiccating heat spell. The settlers had found Hijdori bodies in the caves that appeared to have died from fluid loss and heat stroke. On one of those broiling afternoons, several dozen Hijdori slowly walked into the settlement. They were silent with hands outstretched in the traditional Hijdori gesture of peace and surrender. They were welcomed with water and the respite of air conditioned shelter. They were given expert medical care. The Blahjdiri emissaries sent word back that the settlers were peaceful and kind. The Blahjdiri boy who had been taken in to live with them appeared to be happy, healthy, and well treated. Over the following weeks, more came in out of the hills and were welcomed.

After several days of analyzing Hijdori speech, the cybertranslators deciphered the intricacies of the grammar and syntax, and acquired enough vocabulary for meaningful conversation between the settlers and the Hijdori natives. As the oral history of the Blahjdiri was revealed by its elders, the settler's admiration and affinity

---

50 A good man, a real person

for these beings grew enormously. They had struggled for centuries with the Grojdiri. They were greatly outnumbered, and the more powerful Grojdiri had claimed the best water sources and weapons quarries. The Blahjdiri were like the Jews of Medieval Europe, who, deprived of land, power and resources, still managed to survive among peoples intent on destroying them through the development of a culture of shrewdness and intellect. This similarity did not escape Morris Fietlebaum, who would jokingly refer to the Blahjdir as the lost tribe of Israel. This, he would explain with tongue in cheek, is where Isaac got his *Yiddishe kop*[51].

Isaac had been told there were others like him on the planet. But, seeing the creatures who looked like his own reflection in the mirror was, to say the least, startling. They were the same height as humans, with orange scales, and short blue hair on their heads. Unlike Isaac, who wore a T-shirt and a of pair blue jeans, his cousins were naked. Thus, he could see that their hair extended in a thin row down the middle of their backs. Rows of the same short tufts of blue hair began on their shoulders and extended down their arms, fanned out at the wrists, and split again to form parallel rows on the sides of each finger. Each finger and opposable thumb ended in a sharp blue claw. Patterns of hair growth similar to the ones on their upper extremities extended from their hips to their toes. Their orange eyes were relatively larger for their faces than those of humans, and their noses smaller. The lip-like structures around their mouths were free of scales and revealed the underlying blue color of the skin. Their tongues were blue and their small sharp teeth were orange like their scales.

The entry of the Blahjdiri into the settlement at that stage of Isaac's life was fortuitous. Around that time Hijdori biology was staging a coup in his brain. After he had gotten over the astonishing discovery of the existence

---

[51] Jewish head

of his own species, he was struck by how attractive the young females were. Their looks, their scent, the lilt in their speech, and the way they moved were intoxicating. With that incentive, Isaac quickly became fluent in Hijdori and devoted considerable time to catching up on Hijdori dating customs. One particular young female caught his eye. Her name was Sofikala, and he called her Sophie for short. Talmud, physics, and calculus lost their charm. He thought about her all the time, and spent every spare moment with her.

The day came when Morris asked Isaac to stay to do some chores around the house as he was leaving to be with Sophie for the day. Isaac snarled and bared his sharp orange teeth. "*Vey iz mir*," Morris said to himself. "A lovesick teenager I've got—with teeth yet!" It wasn't easy, but they got through it. Morris decided to welcome Sophie into their lives and, like Isaac, he grew fond of her. He called her, "my little *shikseh*[52]."

The love between Isaac and Sophie grew, and it wasn't long before they were married under a *chuppa*[53] of olive wood sprouted on Hijdor from fruit that had grown in the land of Israel. At the end of the ceremony, when Isaac stomped on the wine glass, Morris Fietlebaum felt an enormous sense of pride. He was the only father Isaac had ever known, and he felt his job was done. Isaac continued to excel in his studies, and soon after the marriage, he and Sophie moved to the planet, Silesia, where he had been accepted into the prestigious Forgion Transgalactic School of Medicine. There he spent four years in medical school, with another four in residency. He never took notes in class. He listened, and whatever he heard he remembered in detail. Later, in the treatment of patients, the sound of their heart, or a particular wheeze in their chest, would evoke thousands

---

52 A non-Jewish girl, though most often blond and blue-eyed.

53 Wedding canopy

of pristine memories of sounds, symptoms, diagnoses, and treatments. It amazed his professors and humbled his fellow medical students. "His memory isn't *photo*graphic," his father used to say, "it's *phono*graphic." His father always got a big kick out of saying that, which Isaac never understood.

Isaac wasn't able to visit Hijdor during his years in medical school and residency. The two years it would have taken to make the trip by starship would have interfered with his studies. However, after he graduated, he and Sophie returned to Hijdor. By that time, their son, Dovid, and daughter, Rebecca, had been born. Morris was grateful to have lived long enough to see his "grandchildren." He never dreamt he would. He bounced them on his knee, and sang old Yiddish songs to them. It was a joy for him. "*A shtik naches*[54]," he would say.

Even fresh out of residency, Isaac had begun to make a name for himself in medicine and psychiatry. He was invited to return to Silesia to teach and perform research at the medical school. He was also offered a well compensated consulting position with the pharmaceutical giant, Frodrisht and Plork. He regretted having to leave his father, as he was old and probably without many more years left. But Morris insisted he go. "This is an opportunity you cannot ignore," he told Isaac. "*A leben ahf dir*[55]! Don't worry about me."

Isaac took his father's advice, and the young family moved back to Silesia. Several years later, when he got word Morris was ill, he returned to Hijdor. One of the agonies of life on the far-flung planets of the galaxy was that distances were so great that it was often impossible to get from one planet to another for family emergencies. Thankfully, Morris rallied and survived long enough for Isaac to arrive on Hijdor. Not unexpectedly, the rally was short-lived. But

---

54 A great joy, particularly from one's child or grandchild.

55 Live and be well!

Isaac was grateful to have arrived in time to be at Morris's bedside when he died. Through his last hours he suffered delirium, and Isaac feared there was nothing left of Morris Fietlebaum. But in the last minutes of his life, in a final moment of lucidity some of the dying are inexplicably granted, Morris reached out for Isaac's hand and squeezed it. "*Mein boychik*," Morris whispered, "*ich hob dir lieb*[56]."

After Morris's death, Isaac returned to Sophie and his children on Silesia. He taught and practiced psychiatry at the Forgion Transgalactic School of Medicine, and later worked his way up through the ranks of Flodrisht and Plork. When Rebecca and Dovid came of age, they returned on their own to Hijdor. There was nowhere else for them to find a Hijdori mate and start their own families. Isaac and Sophie missed them terribly, but they were glad their children were in the land of their human grandfather and their Hijdori ancestors. They found mates, settled down on Hijdor, and had their own children—his grandchildren. Rebecca married a Hijdori engineer named Rorsht, and had two children, Nijrid and Beth. Dovid settled down with a Hijdori pharmacist, Deborah, and they had a son. They named him Aaron.

---

56 My dear boy, I love you.

CHAPTER 9

It infuriated Fietlebaum to think of the fear and pain Aaron must have felt as Glesh cut his finger off. That it would eventually grow back was no comfort. "The boy never hurt a soul," he cried. "How could that *momzer*[57] have done such a thing? And for what?" Yet, his rage was tempered by his awareness that Glesh's cruelty, and the power of his agency, had no bounds. This would be no merely embarrassing senate investigation. This was something new and dangerous. For whatever reason the government chose him, it was clear they meant business. He suppressed his anger and revulsion, and he resigned himself to cooperate with Glesh for the safety of his family. He called Glesh and agreed to do his bidding.

"I'm glad you've decided to be reasonable," Glesh told him.

"Gai tren zich[58]!" Fietlebaum quickly responded.

"Yes, of course," Glesh glibly replied after consulting his cybertranslater. "If only I could find the time. In any case, you will soon receive instructions." Without another word, Glesh terminated the conversation.

Later that night, Fietlebaum sat pensively in his living room listening to William Byrd and nursing two fingers of *schnapps*. As he thought of Aaron, he felt a wave of guilt sweep over him. Aaron had been at the Young Maccabees vacation camp on the jungle planet of Gashag. Fietlebaum had helped to arrange it. The planet was in the beta sector

---

57 bastard

58 Go fuck yourself!

of the same spiral arm of the galaxy as Polmod. He heaved a sigh. "They thought he would be safer close to his *zaideh*[59]," he lamented. "A lot of good I did."

He took a sip of *schnapps*. "*Oy*!" he exclaimed. "When Dovid and Deborah find out they will be frantic!" Then he realized it would be months before they would get the news on Hijdor. He threw up his hands and let them fall to his lap. There was nothing he could do about that. The transgalactic quantum entanglement communicator was the only way to send immediate word across such a distance, but it was restricted to official government use. They sometimes made special allowance for humanitarian reasons. With the government itself behind the kidnapping, that wasn't likely to happen.

He heard a transport capsule slide up to his front door. Something dropped into his mail box, and a moment later the craft took off again. He shuffled across the floor to the mail box and retrieved an envelope. Inside was a one way ticket to the Pinshett Starport on Janpoor and a note. *Catch the first starship to Janpoor tomorrow morning. Then take an air taxi to the Andromeda Hotel. You will be contacted there. Tell no one where you are going. Do not contact family or friends. Your grandson is safe for now, but departures from the plan will have dire consequences.*

The next morning, he packed a bag with clothes, his music library, and a bottle of good scotch, then called for an aircab to the Polmod Starport. When he arrived at the starport, it was nearly deserted. The few in the ticket lines were off-worlders connected with the academy or the moribund mining industry. A handful of students of various species who had just arrived for admission into the academy were lounging in the gating areas. They were playing computer games, and their shouts and raucous laughter echoed down the small starport's single concourse.

---

59 grandfather

It occurred to Fietlebaum that the only Polmodi in sight were either pushing brooms or carting luggage for paying customers. The injustice pained him.

Fietlebaum checked his ticket and headed for the departure gate. He had to wait only a few minutes before the crew informed the passengers that it was time to board. They filed onto the ship and were led into the observation gallery. There the flight attendants gave a brief talk on the safety devices in the ship and what to do in the case of an emergency. Fietlebaum allowed his mind to drift. He had heard the talk a thousand times and had long known it by heart.

Afterwards, they were led to the suspension dormitories. He was shown to his assigned suspension chamber, and he stowed his things in the adjacent cabinet. As he slipped into his suspension chamber, he glanced down the row of fellow travelers climbing into their own chambers. At the end of the line, a Drajan passenger stared back at him. "This is no coincidence," he murmured. "He belongs to Glesh. My life is no longer my own."

He laid back. *What kind of fellow is this Teysoot Motzo?* he wondered. *Is he as dangerous as Glesh?* As his chamber filled with cold suspension gas, he felt himself begin to go under. New questions, random and unmoored from logic, floated through his mind. *Are Janpoorans ticklish? Why are circles round? Do you see half the world with one eye*? As the last steadfast neurons flickered on and off, a grim reality occurred to him. *Does Aaron have his retainer?* "It cost a fortune to straighten that boy's teeth!" he protested as he slipped into unconsciousness. Then there was darkness.

It was a long trip. The passengers had been awakened as the ship was approaching Janpoor. Fietlebaum sat in the observation gallery recovering from the suspended animation.

"This doesn't get easier," he groaned. He worked a stiff shoulder that had lain ill-positioned during the nine months of lying frozen and motionless in his suspension chamber. As the starship slid into the atmosphere of Janpoor, and down through the purple cloud cover, the surface of the planet gradually came into view. Fietlebaum stared out the porthole and watched the features grow in definition as they descended.

Janpoor retained more natural beauty than Polmod, but only because its resources were discovered later and had been exploited over a shorter period of time. Unlike Polmod, some of Janpoor remained forested. It still possessed an ocean, although much of its life had been killed off by the mining waste and toxic metals that leached out into the rivers and fed back into the bays and estuaries. Moreover, whereas Polmod had an atmosphere of decline and decay, Janpoor retained a boom town feel. There was a great deal of money to be made in mining rare elements, and while most of the inhabitants of Janpoor were poor miners and laborers, there were areas of the planet and its cities where the rich lived well.

The ship neared the Pinshett Starport, and the roar of the low velocity propulsion systems kicked in, replacing the whine of the interstellar engines. The ship stopped in midair and hovered in place until a disembarkation ramp was secured below. The starship dropped slowly onto the tarmac, and the roar of engines abruptly stopped. Fietlebaum gathered his belongings. He lined up in the aisle with the other passengers and waited to file off the ship.

The starport was bustling with activity. It was vacation season, and the wealthy of Janpoor were heading to more trendy destinations to enjoy their traditional month of leisure. A young Janpooran playing a game of chase with an older sibling ran headlong into Fietlebaum's knees, nearly tripping him. The collision left a streak of yellow mucus on his jeans. "A lovely welcome," Fietlebaum mumbled to himself.

Janpoorans, like Polmodi, had radially structured bodies. However, unlike Polmodi, only one side of the Janpooran body developed fully. During fetal development, one of their five sides became dominant, while the other four sides atrophied. The four undeveloped sides shrank together leaving the hairless skin decorated with vestigial remains of limbs, genital structures, and sensory organs that resembled mere warts and wattles.

Janpooran skin was green from the vanadium-rich blood in their veins. Their faces had multiple, lidless black eyes, like spiders. They were land animals. However, it was suspected that early in their evolution, they had been aquatic. An early, evolutionary separation of oral and respiratory systems had allowed them to feed on aquatic plants and animals while still being able to breathe the thin Janpooran air. The respiratory slit, the *ahzha*, was on top of the head. It was surrounded by olfactory tentacles reminiscent of a star-nosed mole. The digestive slit, the *poto*, sat low on the face. It was filled with small but very sharp teeth set in flexible cartilaginous jaws. Chewing was accomplished through the rapid undulation of one toothed jaw upon the other. The separate respiratory and alimentary openings allowed the Janpoorans the remarkable ability to gorge themselves with food and carry on a spirited conversation at the same time. This was something Fietlebaum, and others of species that ate and breathed through the same opening, never got used to observing.

Fietlebaum pushed through the starport crowd, and made his way to the aircab stand. There he took his place in yet another line, and eventually worked his way to the front. An aircab pulled up and the pilot leapt out to open the door and assist him with his bags.

"Where you go, pops?" the cybertranslater generated from the Janpooran street slang.

"The Andromeda Hotel, please," Fietlebaum replied.

"You on you way," the pilot replied as he slammed the stick forward and jetted out into the air lanes.

The Janpoorans loved flying. It was sport. They sped up, slowed down, honked, yelled, slid in and out of the air lanes, and jockeyed for position to slip into the most promising lane and accelerate to the head of the line of traffic. Fietlebaum's pilot pushed his way into the heavy afternoon traffic, rammed the capsule in front, and forced the capsule in the adjacent lane to swerve out into oncoming traffic. That pilot overcorrected, honked, and whacked Fietlebaum's aircab in his return to his lane. Each pilot gave the other a lewd gesture, then abruptly abandoned their conflict to redirect their attention to other contests. "Hmmm," Fietlebaum said to himself, "constitutionally hypomanic." After a few more air lane scrimmages, wild gestures, and words the cybertranslater refused to define, the pilot threw the cab into a steep dive and slid up to the entrance of the Andromeda Hotel. He hopped out, bounded to Fietlebaum's door and flung it open. "Here ya go, pops," he sang. "Andromeda."

The Andromeda wasn't a flop house, but, as his father, Morris, would have said, "it ain't the Ritz." The lobby was filled with businessmen, likely on business trips trying to squeeze out what they could from their companies' minor accounts with Janpooran mining conglomerates. Fietlebaum stepped into the line of cheap suits, worn out luggage, and peculiar body odors smothered by oppressive colognes. He had progressed a few places in line before he heard his name called. He turned to see the concierge, a portly Janpooran in a white caftan, standing beside him.

"Am I correct in assuming that you are Dr. Fietlebaum?" the concierge asked in perfectly articulated English.

Taken aback, Fietlebaum stammered, "Why—uh—yes. I'm Isaac Fietlebaum."

"Please follow me, Dr. Fietlebaum," the concierge replied. "Everything is taken care of."

The concierge led him to an elevator, and they rose to the fourteenth floor. He followed the concierge off the elevator and down the hall until they stopped at the door of Fietlebaum's room. The concierge gave him the key and told him he hoped he would enjoy his stay. He smiled, turned and left. Fietlebaum unlocked the door and pushed it open. In the hallway stood Erd Glesh.

Fietlebaum was unable to speak. He stood there, starring at the *momzer*. Glesh noticed the paralysis in which Fietlebaum was trapped, and believing that he was the cause made his hard expression slowly melt into the Drajan analogue of a Mona Lisa smile. "Good afternoon, Dr. Fietlebaum," Glesh finally said. "I hope your trip was pleasant."

Fietlebaum collected himself. "It was fine, you *putz*[60]," he replied. "Where is my grandson?"

"I'm pleased to hear you had a good trip," Glesh answered, "and you needn't worry about your grandson. I need him to keep you in line, and as long as you cooperate, you and your grandson will both be fine."

"If he doesn't get home to his parents, safe and sound, I will hunt you down and kill you!" Fietlebaum retorted. He was surprised by the tone of his own voice and the strength of his words. Most of all, he was surprised that he meant every word he said.

"Well, Glesh said demurely, "as they say in English, we will have to cross that bridge when we come to it." He paused for effect. "Now, there are things I need to tell you," he continued, "and you need to listen."

"I am listening," Fietlebaum said with resignation. "Say what you need to say."

They sat. Glesh outlined the plan to Fietlebaum and explained where his unique expertise would come into play.

---

60 prick

"Teysoot Motzo has plans to address the Janpooran miner's union in two weeks," Glesh told him. "It is their annual convention, and there will be a lot of union members and representatives from the media there. The word is that he will announce his strategy for the union to demand new concessions from the mining company. He will threaten a strike if those requests are denied." Glesh sneered with disdain. "The executives have no intentions of meeting these demands of Teysoot Motzo and his union thugs," he declared, "and the company has the full support of the Defense Department and Galactic administration in denying them. We will not allow him to jeopardize the defense position of the Galaxy."

Glesh lifted his eyes and stared intently at Fietlebaum. "It will be your job," he stated firmly, "to make certain Teysoot Motzo's speech reveals him as the lunatic he is. How you do it is up to you. I will give you all the materials and intelligence information you need. Your contact will be my agent, Mar Beshted. Do whatever you need to do to succeed. The only thing I forbid is contact with Teysoot Motzo before the night of his speech. There is too much risk of compromise."

Glesh glanced at his watch. His tail writhed and the scales on his chest flared out. "Where is that idiot?" he snarled. At that moment the door burst open. A young Drajan trotted breathlessly into the room and assumed a rigid position of attention. He was smaller in stature than Glesh. His uniform was ill-fitting. *The boy can't ask for a proper uniform?* Fietlebaum mused.

Glesh eased out of his chair and strolled up to Beshted. He stared into his face, then lunged forward and bit him on the side of his face. Fietlebaum winced at the sound of the Drajan's flesh tearing. Glesh pulled back and spit out a piece of Beshted's cheek. Bright green blood bubbled out of the wound, running in tiny rivulets down his face and onto the floor. "Don't be late again," Glesh said as he turned and left the room.

When they were alone, Fietlebaum asked Beshted if he was alright. "I'm fine," Beshted answered stoically. "It's an honor to have my behavior corrected by an agent of Glesh's stature."

Fietlebaum was taken aback. "An honor?" he asked with anger and bewilderment. "It's no honor. It's *meshugeh*[61]*!*" He grew more incensed. "What the hell is the matter with you?" he demanded to know. "You don't deserve treatment like that. Nobody does! Why do you put up with it?" He looked intently at Beshted and noticed that among the dark purple and green scales on his face were patches that had grown in gray and misshapen. He suspected they were previous wounds from Glesh. He heaved a remorseful sigh as he realized that Beshted was as helpless against Glesh as he and grandson were. "I'm sorry," he said. "I don't mean to add insult to your injury. I just hate to see you suffer at the hands of that *paskudnyak*[62]."

Beshted remained at attention as Fietlebaum drew closer to examine his wound. "*Vey iz mir*," he said under his breath as he looked at the torn tissue on his face. "That must hurt." He leaned back to better focus his eyes on the wound. "It's no use trying to stitch it up. The edges are too ragged and far apart." He shook his head slowly and whistled. "He really took a bite out of you. It will have to heal from the inside out."

Fietlebaum turned and strode toward the door. "You stay here," he ordered as he opened the door. "I'm going to the lobby to find some antiseptic for the wound. Bites cause infection." As he walked out the door, he mumbled under his breath, "And God only knows the last time that *momzer* brushed his teeth."

Fietlebaum returned ten minutes later with antiseptic cream from the hotel's convenience store. But, Beshted was

---

61 Crazy!

62 scoundrel

gone. He felt guilty for criticizing him. "Poor *boychik*," he said to himself. "It must be hell working for that *schleger*[63]."

He was tired. "What a day," he reflected. He got undressed, put on his pajamas, and slipped into bed. He tried to consider the task before him, but he was exhausted and his thoughts muddled. "*Genug es genug*," he grumbled with resignation. "A person can do only so much in one day." He plumped his pillow and turned out the light.

He was weary, but could not sleep. "*Oy*," he murmured as he sat upright again. "What I wouldn't do for a little snifter of something."

"Please play the *Credo* from the *Mass for Four Voices*," he asked his communicator. The room filled with Byrd's majestic sweetness.

What did he hear when he listened to music? he wondered. From his studies of comparative neurophysiology, he knew that his ears were similar to those of Byrd's. The range of frequencies he could hear were the same. He could sing the human melodies he had previously heard, and assumed his sense of tenor, pitch, and rhythm were similar as well.

He suspected the greatest differences were in the brains that processed the musical signals. In humans, the sense of smell was physiologically linked to emotion and memory in the brain. Aromas, more readily than other forms of sensory stimulation, could evoke emotion-laden remembrances of things past. In Hijdori, it was the auditory systems of the brain that had evolved and expanded in function to process emotion and lay down memory. In Hijdori, melody, emotion, and memory were synergistic and inextricably bound.

When Fietlebaum listened to music, it unleashed in his mind passionate recollections of all of the people, places and events that had ever in any way been connected with

---

[63] bully

that particular melody. Tones and intervals flooded his mind with sadness, joy, and excitement. It was exhilarating, though, at times, exhausting. *Byrd would have envied me for how music resonates in my soul*, he thought to himself. A moment later he reconsidered. Nu? *Maybe not.*

"Achh," he grumbled as he lay back down. "*Ich hob es in drerd*[64]." He yawned. "Now we're getting somewhere," he sighed. "Why do we yawn?" he wondered aloud. "So far as I know, all species in the galaxy do it, but no one knows why."

His fatigue overcame him. Even the endless crashes and bangs of Janpooran taxis wrangling for lane supremacy outside his window could no longer prevent him from drifting away. He was vaguely aware of trying to recall if Janpoorans yawned as he fell into dreamless sleep.

---

[64] To hell with it.

CHAPTER 10

Fietlebaum needed to create a substance to drive Teysoot Motzo insane. Although Glesh did not care one way or the other, it was also his intent to cause no permanent harm. He felt he owed that to his innocent victim. The drug would have to devastate Teysoot Motzo's thinking, perception and emotion, then, after lingering a few days, completely disappear. "Easier said than done," he sighed.

He considered consulting the scientific literature on what types of substances produce hallucinations and delirium in Janpoorans, but decided on a more direct approach to the problem. He would ask Janpoorans what they used to get high. After finding a suitable mind-warping candidate, he would determine the drug's mechanism of action, and molecularly engineer it to be more powerful, long-lasting, and horrifying in its action.

Beshted spoke Janpooran. Although the cybertranslaters would have sufficed, Fietlebaum saw benefits in the personal touch of direct communication, especially if they were going to be discussing illegal substances with strangers. He called Beshted on the house phone and asked him to come over right away. Two minutes later, Beshted burst through the door. He was out of breath, and there was a fresh abrasion on the arm he had used to push his way into Fietlebaum's room.

"*Gevalt!*" Fietlebaum said. "I'm not Glesh. I won't bite you if you're late. Besides, Drajans probably aren't *kosher*." Beshted gave him a puzzled look. "Never mind," Fietlebaum told him. "Today we're going to hunt for good dope." Beshted gave him another puzzled look. Fietlebaum let it go.

"If I was young," Fietlebaum asked him, "dropped out of college, liked to get high, listen to music, and chase young girls, where would I live in Pinshett?"

"Get high?" Beshted asked. Do you mean use drugs?"

"Yes," Fietlebaum answered. "—get high, loaded, wasted, whacked, stoned, buzzed, fucked up, shit-faced."

"Park Street," Beshted replied.

Then we'll head for Park Street!" Fietlebaum affirmed. "But, Beshted," he added in more subdued tone, "before we go, I have something for you."

"For me?" Beshted inquired. "What is it?"

Fietlebaum lifted a box off the desk and handed it to him.

Beshted tentatively unwrapped the box, opened its lid and lifted out a brand new uniform. His mouth fell open. "What's this?" he asked in bewilderment.

"*Nu*?" Fietlebaum replied. "What does it look like?"

"It—it's—a uniform," Beshted stammered. "But—why?"

"An up-and-coming young agent needs to look sharp," Fietlebaum answered. *Not like a* shlump[65], was his unspoken thought. "I asked one of the housekeepers what size she thought you wore, and I had her order it from a tailor in town. Go try it on."

Beshted took the new uniform into the other room and returned a few minutes later with it on. He was beaming.

"Wow!" Fietlebaum exclaimed. "You look terrific!" *Trog gezunterhait*[66]*!*"

Beshted stepped toward the door. "But don't wear it today, *boychik*," Fietlebaum was quick to add. "Today we need to be discreet."

---

65 A nerdy slob

66 Wear it in good health.

"Of course," Beshted croaked. "I'll go change into something less conspicuous."

He returned to his room and came back in casual clothes. Fietlebaum nodded his head in approval.

"Let's go," Beshted said.

"I'm with you," Fietlebaum agreed.

They took the elevator to the lobby, and the concierge called them an aircab. It pulled up in a cloud of dust, and Fietlebaum and Beshted climbed in.

"Where you go?" the cabbie asked.

"Park Street," Beshted answered.

"Where on Park Street?" the cabbie demanded with thinly veiled annoyance.

"The stretch of Park Street where no one with money ever asks you to take them," Fietlebaum replied.

The cabbie turned, scrutinized the two of them, then rubbed his thumb and forefingers together in front of their faces.

"Relax," Fietlebaum told him as he fanned out a handful of bills.

The cabbie shrugged what passed for shoulders on Janpoor and shot back, "We almost there!"

The aircab rocketed off into the air lanes. Two *thunks*, a whack, and one near-miss head-on collision later, the cab dropped down out of the smog into an old and seedy section of Pinshett City. The cab abruptly shuddered to a halt. "Park Street," the cabbie announced.

Fietlebaum paid the cabbie, and he and Beshted hit the sidewalk. The buildings were two or three-storied storefronts. About every third storefront was vacant, but lights in a few of the upper rooms gave evidence of occupation. *Squatters*, Fietlebaum suspected. Bright colored curtains hung windblown in windows raised for ventilation. Odors of spice, musk, smoke, and perfumed candle flame wafted through the air. Jarring melodies, loud, rhythmic and pulsating, echoed through the alleyways. The sidewalks were crowded. Janpoorans, and the occasional Korpian or Gorsid, were sitting out on stoops talking, laughing, and making the raspy whistling sound of Janpooran singing. On some stoops, three or four huddled together, passing back and forth something that looked like a miniature megaphone filled with orange-colored leaves. There was no smoke or flames involved, just vigorous inhalation through the device the cybertranslator referred to as a *moozore.*

Fietlebaum told Beshted, "I think we're getting somewhere. When I see someone promising, I want you to ask them if they want to earn a little cash." Beshted, who was shy even by Drajan standards, wasn't thrilled about the plan, but he acquiesced. As they walked further down the sidewalk, Fietlebaum spied a possibility and pointed him out to Beshted. He was a Janpooran wearing a bright red caftan with swirls of multicolored dye scattered across it. He held a *moozore* stuffed with the orange leaves. He took a deep inhalation, then stared off into space. Beshted walked up to him and asked him if wanted to make a little cash. After a long pause, the Janpooran looked at him and said something, after which, Beshted motioned to Fietlebaum to move on.

"What did he say?" Fietlebaum inquired.

"Go run home fuck you dog," Beshted dutifully reported.

"Well," Fietlebaum said philosophically, "at least he didn't ignore you."

The next group inhaling the drug was more agreeable. One let out a bubbly Janpooran laugh and handed Beshted the *moozore*. Beshted shook his head, "No." Fietlebaum took it instead. *It's the way to get a foot in the door*, he decided. He held it to his mouth and took in a deep draught of vapor with an odor reminiscent of moth balls. The orange substance they called, "*burzet*" was like catnip. Just smelling it gave the user a "buzz," with the effect greatly amplified by deeply inhaling it.

The Janpoorans, the Korpian and Gorsid in the circle were sent reeling by the drug. However, Fietlebaum's neurophysiology was such that it did absolutely nothing to him. He took one more deep breath, held it in as long as he could, and in exhalation reported, "*bupkis*[67]!" The Janpoorans were, as Beshted translated it, "blown away" by his tolerance.

Fietlebaum's impression was that the *burzet* was more a social lubricant than a mind warping potion. There were likely to be more powerful and sinister substances in the drug subcultures of Janpoor. Certain individuals, regardless of their species, were drawn to such things. Perhaps it was a manifestation of some pathological need to be punished, or a form of extreme nihilism. Yet each species and culture had a seriously ugly chemical to abuse. Humans had PCP, and Gorsids had *basha*. The Janpoorans would surely have some similar stuff that could take your soul away, when *where* it went no longer mattered.

"What have you got that's stronger?" Fietlebaum asked. The Janpoorans laughed. "Come," one of them said. "We go talk business." Fietlebaum and Beshted followed the Janpooran down the sidewalk and into an alleyway. They entered the back door of one of the storefront buildings. The room was lit by candles, and a chokingly thick, musky odor was in the air. The Janpooran, Plosoy Foseff, led the way. As they started up some back stairs, they noticed a Janpooran standing on the landing engaged in peculiar behavior. He stood like a statue. He raised his head, then slowly his arm as if to snatch something out of the air in a slow motion, hallucinatory ballet. He stood still again, transfixed, and made a low grumbling sound until he ran out of breath. Two Gorsids slithered down the stairs and a tentacle of one of them brushed the Janpooran on their way past. The contact sent him into a screaming fit of rage.

---

67 Goat turds, nothing

Hmmmm, thought Fietlebaum, *we're on to something.* He had Beshted ask Plosoy Foseff what the fellow on the stair landing was using. Plosoy Foseff laughed, then shook his head slowly for dramatic effect. "Wicked bad stuff," he said. "That shodom. You grind seed for powder and smoke. Stay fucked up just little while, but *ba-a-ad* fucked up!" He laughed his bubbly Janpooran laugh and added, "*Wick*ed bad fucked up!"

Several minutes later, as Plosoy Foseff had predicted, the Janpooran on the landing was restored to more reasonable behavior. Fietlebaum asked if he could talk to him, but Plosoy Foseff told him it wasn't a good idea. "He nasty fellow," he said. "You not like him. You want shodom, we go upstairs talk Bostoff Metzee. "He nasty, too," Plosoy Foseff said with a laugh, "but he like you money."

Plosoy Foseff led Fietlebaum and Beshted up another flight of stairs and down a dark hallway. Music blared, and through some of the open doors, they saw other Janpoorans in catatonic trances. One suddenly sprang into frantic arm flapping. Fietlebaum noted it with approval. As they approached the last doorway, Plosoy Foseff stopped them and told them to wait. He returned a few minutes later. "Bostoff Metzee say come in, bring you money bag."

Fietlebaum and Beshted stepped through the doorway into Bostoff Metzee's room, and were taken aback. Bostoff Metzee was huge, a head taller than most Janpoorans. He was also twice as wide. He had a scar that ran diagonally from his *ahzha* to his jaw. It was the result of a disagreement he had had years ago with a Gorsidian *burzet* dealer. Word was that the Gorsid's scar was much longer.

Bostoff Metzee sat in an overstuffed chair, and was filling his *poto* with Janpooran noodles dripping with spicy-smelling green sauce. That did not prevent him from chitchatting with the bevy of beauties that was his harem. He pinched one and she shrieked with feigned offense. Then he whispered in the ear of another who bubbled into rails of Janpooran laughter. *A real* macher[68], Fietlebaum thought.

Bostoff Metzee wore a flaming pink caftan with florescent orange embroidery. There must also have been electronics in the thread, as the embroidery occasionally flashed with running stripes of color across the front of the caftan.

Fietlebaum had often pondered the question of how different species experienced color. Species that had co-evolved on the same planet and had developed their visual transduction and processing systems from similar neurophysiologies might be expected to share a similar sense of color. But when species evolved on different planets, all bets were off.

There was nothing inherently "pink" about the wave lengths of electromagnetic radiation that led humans to report they were looking at something pink in color. Bostoff Metzee's caftan was "pink" in Fietlebaum's mind only because his human father had referred to it by that name when they were simultaneously experiencing the phenomenon of "pink" in their own unique human and Hijdori fashions. There was no basis to assume that he and his father were experiencing the color in ways that were at all similar. Still, perhaps by coincidence, both Fietlebaum and his human father would have agreed that the color combination Bostoff Metzee wore was nauseating. Fietlebaum next wondered if Bostoff Metzee's neural processing circuits perceived the jarring pink and orange combination in a vastly different way, or if he simply had horrible taste in fashion. It also occurred to Fietlebaum that the two possibilities were not mutually exclusive.

When Fietlebaum strode up to Bostoff Metzee, the Janpooran stopped eating and talking, and leaned forward to give him a good look. "I never see nobody like you," he

---

68 Big shot

said. He paused for a moment and added, "You bring you money bag?" All the while maintaining his business face, Bostoff Metzee surreptitiously reached an arm around and goosed one of his girls. She shrieked with surprise, leapt off his lap, and ran giggling out of the room, nearly trampling Beshted in the process.

"So," Bostoff Metzee said, "they say *burzet* no good for you and you look for shodom."

"Yes," Fietlebaum replied to Beshted's translation.

"Wicked bad," Bostoff Metzee retorted with a rueful laugh. "Okay, I hear you good boy. I give you shodom."

After the requisite haggling over quality and price, Fietlebaum walked off with his sample of shodom. Back on the sidewalk, Beshted called for an aircab. It whisked them back to the Andromeda Hotel.

CHAPTER 11

Glesh was furious. He heard about the adventure on Park street and had Beshted hauled to his office. His tail thrashed, and the scales on his chest flared out and rattled like the display of a love-starved peacock. He strode across the room to Beshted. He kicked him twice and bit him hard. "What are you doing running around Pinshett making a spectacle of Fietlebaum in some shitty part of town?" he screamed. "You idiot! You brainless fool!"

There was no good answer, and Beshted was naive in thinking he could find one. "Dr. Fietlebaum needed to find drugs that affected Janpooran brains, sir," he tried to explain, "and he asked me to go along with him."

Glesh slapped him and gave him another vicious bite to the face. "If you do something stupid like that again," he snarled, "I will have you replaced, and then I will have you killed! Do you understand?"

"Yes, sir," Beshted replied while fighting the pain.

"Tell Fietlebaum that he is restricted to the hotel. Before you drag him off into public again you need my permission. Now get out!"

Beshted left and arrived a few minutes later at Fietlebaum's room at the Andromeda Hotel. When Fietlebaum opened the door for him, he immediately saw the new damage that Glesh had done.

"My God!" Fietlebaum exclaimed, "Come in, come in. Are you all right?"

Beshted gave a terse nod and quickly changed the subject. "Glesh says no more trips outside the hotel without his permission."

"Am I under house arrest?" Fietlebaum fumed.

Beshted nodded positively again.

"Under whose authority can he do this?" Fietlebaum implored.

"He doesn't need authority," Beshted answered. "He does as he pleases." He paused and added a cautionary note. "I wouldn't argue with him if I were you."

Fietlebaum was irate, but in no position to be defiant. He sighed. "Like a *loch in kop* I need this," he murmured under his breath.

Fietlebaum had started deciphering the mysteries of shodom, and he shared the little he had learned with Beshted. "From my review of the scientific literature," he explained, "shodom is a plant that grows on Bini, the third moon of Janpoor. It's scientific name is *Morphospermi janpoorensis*. But beyond that, information is scarce." He picked up a recent issue of the *Journal of Transgalactic Ethnopharmacology* and read from it. "The drug is currently finding use among the Janpooran underclass as a recreational drug for a short but intense hallucinatory high. The active principle and its mechanism of action remain unknown." He paused. "The only other information in the literature is what you and I have already learned on the street," he added. "We know that it's wicked bad." He reached over and dropped the journal into the trash.

With no existing information on the identity of the psychoactive component of shodom or its mechanism of action, Fietlebaum would have to ferret it out himself. It was a challenge, but he relished the prospect. "I can't wait to get started," he admitted with a grin. Glesh had already ordered his equipment moved from his office on Polmod to his room at the Andromeda, so he had everything he needed. "I'll let you know how it goes," he told Beshted as he escorted him to the door.

Beshted resisted. "Please sir," he allowed himself to say, "I would like to stay."

"*Nu*," Fietlebaum replied. "An extra pair of hands might come in handy. Come on, *boychik*. Let's get started."

Fietlebaum had Beshted grind the shodom seed and roast it to mimic the Janpooran habit of smoking the drug. When he finished, Fietlebaum placed the prepared shodom in a flask of solvent to extract the active molecules. After swirling it and letting it soak, he poured the mixture through filter paper into a second flask. He held the flask of dark brown liquid up for Beshted to see. "There is a mixture of chemicals in this extract," he explained. "One of them is the substance that gets Janpoorans stoned. We have to isolate it and identify it."

He sucked up the liquid in a syringe and injected it into a port in an instrument that consisted of a long spiraled tube, with pumps, gauges, and a moving line of vials that passed underneath the outlet of the tube. "This is a gas chromatograph," he told Beshted. "Molecules of different sizes and configurations pass through the tube at different speeds."

Beshted reflected for a moment, then took it upon himself to complete Fietlebaum's explanation. "So," he said hesitantly, "as the line of vials progresses beneath the outlet, the types of molecules that drip out into them are different." Fietlebaum smiled and nodded with approval. "It's a way to separate them," Beshted concluded.

"Excellent!" Fietlebaum exclaimed. "You're a natural-born scientist!" He patted Beshted on the back. He was pleased to see Beshted flutter his eyes, in Drajans an involuntary expression of joy, like a smile. *Glesh,* Fietlebaum thought, *you're a* shmuck. *You encourage the boy, you don't bite him.*

When the chromatography was done, they ran the fractioned samples through the mass spectrometer to identify and characterize the molecules. "By tonight," Fietlebaum explained, "we'll know what molecules are in shodom. Tomorrow, we'll analyze the proteins encoded in the Janpooran genome to see what types of receptors they have in their brains. My proteomic analysis program will tell us which of the molecules bind to those receptors. One of those molecules will be the active component of shodom."

After two days of work, they had identified three pairs of molecules and receptors that could mediate the effects of shodom. "The answer," Fietlebaum told Beshted, "will come when we determine which of these three receptors is in a part of the Janpooran brain where disruption would cause an altered state of consciousness."

In consulting the literature, Fietlebaum determined that two of those receptor proteins were known and their distributions mapped in the Janpooran brain. One was in an area that processed odors. He all but ruled that one out. "Funny smells aren't likely to drive anyone *meshugeh*," Fietlebaum surmised, though from recollection of horrifyingly odiferous teenage patients, he allowed it as a remote possibility.

Another of the receptors was in a part of the brain that controlled heart and respiratory rate. "This one's out, too," Beshted quickly volunteered, with a glance toward Fietlebaum to gauge his response. "I agree completely," Fietlebaum responded.

The last candidate was an unknown receptor whose distribution in the Janpooran brain had yet to be mapped. "This one's it," Fietlebaum said with a smile. It was exhilarating to find such a receptor, particularly one that mediated dramatic, mind-altering effects. "Under different circumstances," he told Beshted, "this could be a wonderful discovery." Nu, he thought. *Someday this might help someone.*

Fietlebaum needed one thing more before he could synthesize designer shodom that would blow Teysoot Motzo's mind. Like all beneficiaries of panspermia in the galaxy, Janpoorans carried a variant of DNA. In knowing Teysoot Motzo's genetic code, he could determine if this receptor in his brain had any unique qualities that might make him more or less susceptible to alterations in the active molecule of shodom.

Janpoorans secreted a yellow mucous-like waste product from their respiratory systems. Children let it drip, but adults disposed of the secretions by wiping it away with a special cloth, a *fasha*. Fietlebaum asked Beshted to retrieve a used *fasha* from Teysoot Motzo's house. It would be loaded with DNA.

That night, Beshted snuck through an open window into Teysoot Motzo's house and rifled the laundry basket for a soiled fasha. The following morning he brought Fietlebaum a *fasha* with Teysoot Motzo's monogram in Janpooran script in the corners. It was still slimy with mucous. Fietlebaum invited Beshted to stay for the analyses, but Glesh had demanded he return immediately. *Glesh doesn't like us alone together*, Fietlebaum suspected.

Fietlebaum proceeded in the usual way. He extracted the DNA from the sloughed off cells in Teysoot Motzo's mucous. He sequenced the DNA, and then derived the amino acids and proteins encoded in the sequence. With his proteomics program, which predicted the most likely patterns of protein folding in typical Janpooran physiological conditions, he digitally constructed the shodom receptor in his brain. Guided by his receptor/ligand interactions program, he replaced two methyl groups on the aromatic ring of the active molecule of shodom with methoxy groups to increase the binding affinity. He added a double bond to lock the molecule into a configuration with the highest affinity for the binding site. The finishing touch was replacing a hydrogen atom with fluorine to resist enzymatic degradation.

Fietlebaum calculated that the synthetic shodom would be 17,251 times more potent than the native molecule. He further determined that effects of the fluorine-altered shodom would last about ten days, well beyond the usual fifteen minute high. "Wicked bad," Fietlebaum said to himself. After a moment to savor his success, he called for Beshted to return.

Beshted arrived minutes later. Fietlebaum informed him of what he had accomplished, and enthusiastically described the astonishing potency and staying power of the shodom he had molecularly engineered. "Now we need a means to administer it," he concluded.

They considered the problem. Beshted spoke up first. "When I broke into Teysoot Motzo's house last night," he noted, "I saw a bag of *burzet* and a silver *moozore* on his bedside table. He probably settles down with it every evening."

Fietlebaum gave a nod of understanding. "What are you suggesting?" he asked.

"I can return to his room and spike his *burzet*," Beshted replied.

Fietlebaum was taken with the idea, but saw a problem. "*Burzet* is enjoyed by inhaling its vapors," he explained. "The shodom likely isn't volatile enough to be carried along in sufficient concentration in the air sucked in through the *moozore*."

"Then we can spike the *moozore*!" Beshted quickly countered. "I can paint the end of his *moozore* with the new shodom so that touching it to his *ahzha* will deliver the dose."

"Brilliant!" Fietlebaum replied.

After giving Beshted a few congratulatory pats on the back, Fietlebaum shared a final concern. "From what I've heard about Teysoot Motzo, he seems a sturdy, roll-with-the-punches sort of fellow. A sudden, uncharacteristic display of insanity might raise suspicions of foul play among his followers. We need to induce a prodrome."

"What do you mean, a prodrome?" Beshted felt free to inquire.

"Severe psychiatric illnesses rarely sprang into being all of a sudden," Fietlebaum explained. "They usually begin as a buildup of lesser symptoms, a prodrome, that gradually evolves into the signs and symptoms of the more severe illness. A discernible prodrome would make it appear more as if a genuine psychiatric illness has driven him into insanity. Do you understand?"

"Yes," Beshted replied.

"This needn't be dramatic," he went on to say. "It could be as simple as a drop in motivation, an increase in fatigue, or complaints of feeling weak and out of sorts." He paused to allow Beshted to digest the information. "Of course," he was quick to add, "a little crying and screaming wouldn't hurt."

The plan that came to Fietlebaum was to expose Teysoot Motzo to a viral infection that caused fatigue and general malaise. A trip to Pinshett General Hospital's medical floor would provide them with what they needed. Beshted immediately called Glesh and asked permission for he and Fietlebaum to go on a mission to the hospital. After a long hesitation on Glesh's part, permission was begrudgingly granted. They called an aircab.

When they arrived at the hospital, they donned white clinic coats and nonchalantly walked into the nurse's station. They scoured the ward charts until they found the records of an elderly Janpooran patient who had been hospitalized for a respiratory infection. It was a flu-like illness, viral in etiology, that had caused the old fellow to stop eating, become dehydrated, weak, and finally unable to get out of bed. It seemed the elderly and frail of all species were susceptible to viral infections. "Pneumonia is the old Janpooran's friend," Fietlebaum whispered to Beshted.

Beshted went to the bedside and swabbed away some of the yellow secretion from the old Janpooran's *ahzha*. Fietlebaum stood in the hallway and nodded approvingly. Beshted left the room with the virus-laden secretion. A nurse passed by. He did not recognize either Beshted or Fietlebaum. "May I help you?" he inquired, in a tone that meant he had no intention to do so.

"Do I look like one of your nursing students?" Fietlebaum demanded in response. "Do you commonly interrogate consulting physicians who are called to the floor?"

The nurse shook his head, "No."

"Do we need to speak with your charge nurse?" Fietlebaum continued.

"No, sir," he answered apologetically. "That isn't necessary. Is there truly anything I can help you with?"

Fietlebaum asked him to fetch a bottle of viral growth medium to culture the secretion Beshted had obtained. The medium contained cloned respiratory membrane cells, and would provide a means for the virus to proliferate. When the nurse returned with it, Beshted complemented his professionalism. "I wish we had nurses as fine as you in our hospital!" he exclaimed. Fietlebaum nodded his head in agreement. "Your care, concern, and performance have been impeccable," Beshted continued. "I would like to—" He was stopped by a wry look from Fietlebaum, who announced they needed to get the sample to the lab, "*stat*!" Beshted sheepishly nodded his head in agreement. They expeditiously left the hospital and aircabbed back to the hotel.

After returning to the hotel, Beshted reluctantly returned to his room and Fietlebaum set to work. The virus they obtained from the hospital affected Janpooran respiratory membranes. The only change that Fietlebaum wanted to make was to optimize the likelihood of the virus causing emotional disturbance. Some viruses adept in affecting the nervous system could produce all of the symptoms of a full blown psychiatric illness. Fietlebaum synthesized segments of neuron-selective Janpooran DNA and inserted them into the virus to provide it affinity for brain tissue. With a fresh sample of brain tissue he had Beshted obtain from the city morgue, Fietlebaum confirmed the altered virus enjoyed the company of Janpooran neurons. The virus could be counted on to wreak a bit of havoc not only in Teysoot Motzo's lungs, but in his brain as well.

Fietlebaum prepared a simple aerosol apparatus to expose Teysoot Motzo to the virus. The union talk was in two weeks, the infection, including the so-called post-viral syndrome, usually lasted about ten days, and the incubation period for infection was about two days. They needed to expose him soon. Fietlebaum hatched a plan, and called Beshted to give him the details.

The next day, Beshted staked out Teysoot Motzo on the street outside his downtown office. When he spied his prey coming out the door, Beshted followed him down the sidewalk. Teysoot Motzo stopped to purchase a Pinshett city news digitext, and when he re-entered the foot traffic, Beshted bumped him hard from the side, knocking the digitext and change from his hands. He apologized profusely to Teysoot Motzo, brushed him off, and insisted on taking him to the emergency room of the hospital. "You crazy!" Teysoot Motzo bellowed. "This little bump, it nothing!" As the big, angry Janpooran bent down to collect his effects off the sidewalk, Beshted stealthily sprayed a mist of genetically engineered virus into the air around his *ahzha*.

CHAPTER 12

Teysoot Motzo was big. He liked to throw his weight around. He didn't take orders, he gave them. He was similar to Bostoff Metzee, the shodom dealer, in temperament and stature. The most noticeable differences were that he had no scar on his face and ever-so-slightly better taste in clothes. Moreover, unlike Bostoff Metzee, he had established himself, albeit somewhat tenuously, in polite society. It was he that presided at the union's charitable events, and he that passed out the *galarka* roasts to the rank and file on *Pozonto*, the annual Janpooran holiday of ancestor worship. Teysoot Motzo's success as labor leader had even led some to suggest that he run for government office. He had to admit the possibility held appeal. But sacrifices would be involved. Kickbacks, under the table payoffs, and weekends of debauchery on Boojo Island would be harder to hide from public scrutiny as a public official. Besides, Teysoot Motzo had only begun to exploit the rewards of his office. In the upcoming meeting of the union, he was hoping to receive a mandate from the rank and file to expand union authority and oversight to mining operations on Janpoor's moons as well as to neighboring planets. He was also trying to leverage control of the industries that shipped and contained the various ores after they were mined. That would mean more money and power. The upcoming meeting and speech were important to him.

But Teysoot Motzo had acted strangely the last week or so. Everyone had noticed. He was tired, and did not know why. He had always been moody, but he had been even more moody than usual. He threw his improperly prepared breakfast against the wall, and "cried" when his soup was cold. The outward expression of sadness and disappointment in Janpoorans, their behavior most analogous to crying in human beings, was to inhale deeply, and tighten the lips of the *ahzha* while forcing air back through them. While engaged in the behavior, Janpoorans sounded very much like a child's balloon being deflated through the tautly stretched open end. No non-Janpooran could bear to be around the behavior. Janpoorans didn't much care for it either. Later that day, while walking from his car to his office building, his legs hurt and he cried again. This was not the behavior of an adult Janpooran male, particularly an important and powerful one. Others began to talk. His friends suggested that he was getting sick. He did have a respiratory discharge consistent with an infection. But, he refused to hear of it. "I never had sick day in my life," he yelled back at them.

Two days before the union address, he was even more exhausted and irritable. The press came to interview him, and he screamed at them to go away. He threw a full glass of glosett juice, his favorite drink, at his secretary when she voiced her concern about his acting that way around the media. Teysoot Motzo was clearly in a tailspin. Fortunately for Fietlebaum, he continued to use his *burzet*. He had told his assistant that it was all that was getting him through the last week. Yet he was starting to worry about his planned talk at the union meeting. Though it was important to him, he himself wonder if he should cancel it.

On the morning of the day of the union talk, Teysoot Motzo was feeling better. He could not explain why. Perhaps, unbeknownst to him, the effects of the virus were beginning to wane. In any case, he didn't cry that morning, and for the first time in more than a week he was looking forward to the meeting.

Beshted kept surveillance on Teysoot Motzo's house. When he saw him leave for his office that morning, he picked the lock, entered his house, and quickly found the *burzet* and *moozore.* He took the small vial of molecularly engineered shodom and painted a hefty dose of it on the end of the *moozore.* He replaced the *moozore* to where it had lain, then snuck back out and returned to the hotel. There was nothing more to do than wait for Teysoot Motzo to come home and enjoy his *burzet* that evening. Glesh was informed of the plan and the high likelihood that Teysoot Motzo would be in a drug-induced delirium that evening at the union meeting. He had made certain that an emergency medical team would be there to attend to Teysoot Motzo and take him to Pinshett General Hospital for treatment when the need arose.

Teysoot Motzo spent the day at his office, rehearsing his speech and strategizing with his political cronies. It was an ideal time for him to consolidate control of the union and for the union to flex its muscles. He was back in control. He was feeling strong again. He brushed aside any suggestions that the talk be postponed. When his advisor mentioned that he had had several crying spells in the previous few days, Teysoot Motzo punched him in the face. He hit him with such force that he fell backward over a chair. "Hah!" Teysoot Motzo laughed, "maybe *you* go cry now!"

A few minutes before leaving for the meeting, Teysoot Motzo excused himself and retired to his study to partake in a bowl of *burzet.* His secretary told him that he needed to hurry, as in only a few more minutes they would have to leave. "Let them wait!" Teysoot Motzo bellowed. He filled his *moozore* with *burzet*, and sniffed the aroma of the drug that lingered on his fingers before refolding the bag of *burzet* and replacing it in his drawer. He held the *moozore* lovingly in his hand before lifting it to inhale. As the *moozore* touched his *ahzha*, he felt a peculiar sting that he had never felt before. He reflexively brought the *moozore* back down to inspect it, but, at the same time, his secretary reminded him again that it was getting late. "Hah!" he shot back. "They love me, even if they wait." Feeling pressured for time, he ignored the peculiar stinging sensation and placed the *moozore* back in his *ahzha*. He inhaled, long and deeply.

As Teysoot Motzo climbed into the transport capsule, he felt strange. He felt as if he was being pulled away. As he climbed into his transport capsule, he had the enigmatic sense of simultaneously climbing into his Uncle Teysoot Pasho's old transport capsule that he had last ridden in eighty years before. He was stretched across time and space. A policeman flew by in hot pursuit of a transgressor with his lights flashing and siren blaring. The blue flashing of the lights was suddenly the pulsing of his own arterial blood extending out into space. The light that fell on him felt "heavy," despite his understanding that the sensation made no sense. The sound of the siren reverberated in his head, with waves of sound spinning off synesthetic eddies of whirling color inside him. A weariness such as he had been feeling the previous week again crept over him. He closed his heavy eyelids. Colors and sparks spun with frantic velocity across what had before been a curtain of comforting darkness. "Maybe they right about sick," he cautiously told himself. "Maybe I *bad* sick!" But he was on his way to an important meeting. With the sheer strength of his will, he banished the visions, sensations, and uncertainties from his mind. They remained banished for about a minute and a half.

On route to the auditorium, the crowds on the sidewalks were looking at him. He was certain they knew that something was wrong. Their facial expressions were uniformly sinister and accusing. He arrived at the auditorium to tremendous applause from the crowd of union members, but the sound was terrifying. It was thunderous and mechanical, like the screech of metal scraping against metal, like starships colliding. With a halting and hesitant gait, he fought his way to the podium. As he gazed out across the crowd of miners, he saw them shatter into a myriad of colors. They became a swirling sea of crystalline forms, melting, moving, and flowing into one another. He, too, began to melt. Then he froze. The cheering of the crowd faded to startled silence, from which rose a growing chorus of boos and catcalls. After what seemed an eternity, Teysoot Motzo's movement was restored. But the disconcerting feeling of paralysis was replaced by an overwhelming sensation of heat and vibration rising up from his abdomen. He could not resist the upwelling of energy. His face flushed bright green. He shook his head, flapped his arms, and exploded into a violent, high-pitched cry. The speech was not going well.

Things got worse. His assistant ran to the podium to lead him away, but Teysoot Motzo did not recognize him. He saw him as transformed into a creature with fiery skin and rings of malevolent energy radiating from him. Teysoot Motzo shrieked and beat him with the microphone. His secretary ran to the podium to help, but he attacked her as well. He screamed that she had poisoned him and was trying to kill him. In the midst of squeezing her *ahzha* shut to suffocate her, he froze. When his spasmed muscles relaxed, he sat and cried again. The irritating sound of his Janpooran crying was compounded by his continuing to hold the microphone, with the raspy, balloon-deflation sound generating an even louder screech of similarly high-pitch feedback through the auditorium's public address system. It was a disgraceful display by Janpooran standards. The boos and hoots from the crowd grew louder and more angry.

The police that Glesh had arranged to be on site sprang into action. They rushed the stage and grabbed Teysoot Motzo. He fought back and they pinned him to the floor. Teysoot Motzo was terrified, and the terror made him freeze again. Time dilated, and the policeman became part of a dark, hallucinatory tableau. They moved in slow motion in stroboscopic spasms. Their skins grew dark with swirls of phosphorescent colors spinning in and out of existence across their faces. Their voices slowed and fell in pitch until they growled like loud, lazy thunder. With an explosive return of motor function, Teysoot Motzo sprang to his feet and screamed with fear. He punched one police officer, picked up another, and threw him off the stage. The officers took out their clubs and pummeled him into submission. They cuffed him and dragged him off the stage in chains.

Teysoot Motzo was led through the auditorium. His head was down. He wailed and cried. Yellow mucous dripped from his *ahzha* and down his face. Every few moments, the catatonic paralysis set in again. He froze solid, and the police had to shove him forward to maintain their progress to the transport capsule that waited outside. The rank and file of hardened miners were not impressed. The auditorium echoed with their derisive cries, boos, and curses. Bottles, half eaten sandwiches, and wadded balls of paper flew through the air toward Teysoot Motzo. For a moment there was concern that the crowd might push their way through and assault him. But the Pinshett police made sure they didn't. "He's through," Glesh thought with great satisfaction from his surveillance position on a catwalk far above the crowd. "Fietlebaum," he whispered out loud, "perhaps you are as clever as they say you are."

The police dragged, pushed, and, at one point, carried Teysoot Motzo to the transport capsule. They threw him in the back, slammed the doors, and shot off into the air lanes toward the emergency department of Pinshett General Hospital. By Glesh's arrangement, an emergency medical services technician was on board the capsule. He slammed a hypodermic needle into Teysoot Motzo's right abductor muscle, and pumped in a massive dose of the powerful

Janpooran sedative, prosteridine. Within five seconds, he was in a deep, drug-induced coma.

The capsule continued on to the hospital, where they were met by the emergency medicine physicians and several of Glesh's handpicked security specialists. Teysoot Motzo was tossed onto a gurney and wheeled into the emergency room. A perfunctory effort was made to ensure that he was medically stable, but the assumption was that he was simply crazy, stoned, or, more likely, both.

The most immediate plan was to strap him down and make sure that he didn't hurt himself or anyone else when he woke up. Meanwhile, the legal gears turned. The emergency physicians appealed to the district court for an emergency psychiatric hold to keep him in the hospital, against his will if need be. With Glesh's help, the paperwork was expedited, and the hold papers, signed, and officially sealed, were back in the physician's hands within half an hour.

One of Glesh's agents informed the emergency physician that, by lucky coincidence, one of the most experienced and highly regarded psychiatrists in the galaxy happened to be visiting Janpoor at the time. The agent noted that Teysoot Motzo was a very important citizen of Janpoor, and no effort should be spared to give him the best psychiatric care. He suggested to the emergency staff that they immediately contact this illustrious visitor, Dr. Isaac Fietlebaum, at the Andromeda Hotel. Fietlebaum arrived at the hospital an hour later.

CHAPTER 13

Teysoot Motzo was in four point restraints when Fietlebaum arrived at his bedside in Pinshett General Hospital. By this time, he had been moved from the emergency department to the third floor acute Psychiatric ward. It was a locked unit. Distraught creatures of various species wandered the hallways, writhed in their beds, or sat stone-faced in the socialization room. The air was heavy with the spicy, musky odors of the esters, ethers, and amines generated by alien metabolisms. The aromas mingled with the more pungent, rancid body odors of those who could not be coaxed to shower on a daily basis. Moans, grumbles, and whimpers rose and fell across the ward, but, with liberal use of psychotropic medications, the screams and cries were held to a minimum.

Some of the patients were there by choice, but most were there against their will. They had either been committed by the court, or, like Teysoot Motzo, were on a court sanctioned physician hold awaiting commitment. In either case, they were not free to leave. The criteria for commitment were being an imminent risk to one's self, a risk to others, or being so crazy that one was unable to care for him- or herself. Most of those who had been committed had been crazy in one way or another, but were behaving in safe, if not entirely reasonable, fashion on the ward because of the medications they received. Only a few continued to present as serious risks to safety. Those individuals were under close observation, in seclusion rooms or, as was the case with Teysoot Motzo, in a seclusion room as well as in restraints.

They were not the worried well. Some on the ward suffered severe emotional disturbance and were suicidal. One such patient, a Polmodi laborer, had lost his job in the Janpooran mines and had no money for passage for the return trip home. He became suicidally depressed over the likelihood of never seeing his home planet again. In an age of transgalactic travel, severe homesickness was a common condition in psychiatric units across the galaxy. It was no longer a problem of children being a few miles from home for the first time. It was a serious and, at times, fatal condition, when being away from home meant living on an alien planet, hundreds of millions of miles away, with alien minds and faces, strange plants and animals, and unfriendly climate. The vastness of space was humbling under any circumstances. But when one longed for a pinpoint of light in the night sky, with no possibility of return to it, the sense of distance and isolation could become unbearable.

Many on the ward were not merely depressed, but psychotic. Some were both depressed *and* psychotic. They were disorganized, delusional, or suffered hallucinations. The most common forms of hallucinations in the galaxy were visual, auditory, and olfactory. However, some species had developed special forms of sensory perception that were also subject to distortions from chemical imbalances.

Rodrantians, like salmon, migrated back to their place of birth to reproduce and die. Their journey was guided by Rodrantia's powerful magnetic field. On occasion, psychiatrically ill Rodrantians experienced hallucinatory magnetic sensations that compelled them to follow illusory homing signals. The imaginary magnetic signal would sometimes be followed until the sufferer fell exhausted or died from an unfortunate encounter with a cliff or large body of water that fell between them and their magnetic destination. The condition was particularly heart-wrenching to observe when the homing signal was perceived as coming from directly above. "*Oy!*" Fietlebaum once said in describing the extraordinary phenomenon to a colleague. "All the *hopken mit shpringen*[69] up and down—it's enough to give you a headache!"

Fietlebaum observed with fascination a Rodrantian on the ward with such magnetic hallucinations. He was a massive creature. Fietlebaum watched his muscles ripple and sinews grow taught beneath his scaly skin as he moved his appendages. *Legs like tree trunks,* Fietlebaum idly noted. The Rodrantian's feet had worn spots in the hallway floor by slip-sliding beneath him as, hour after hour, he strained to propel himself forward while his upper body remained stationary against the unmovable concrete wall. Nurses and orderlies informed him repeatedly that his ancestral home was on a planet situated in the completely opposite direction from the one he was struggling to go. But it did no good. All through the day and night, he pushed against the wall and cried out in anguish that he had to get home, ever mindful that he was going nowhere.

On the psychiatric ward, Fietlebaum was back in his element. He was pleased when Dr. Doftor Feydoss, the Drusidi psychiatric attending on the ward, slithered up and introduced himself. It was flattering to hear from the young doctor that his earlier writing had led him into the field of psychiatry. But, the moment was bittersweet. He was burdened by his sense of guilt from compromising the freedom and integrity of an innocent sentient being. He felt only partial absolution in having been forced to do it.

Dr. Doftor Feydoss asked Fietlebaum if he would be willing to attend to Teysoot Motzo during his hospitalization. When Fietlebaum agreed, Doftor Feydoss thanked him and asked if he could then give him the medical report. "Certainly," Fietlebaum replied. It pained

---

[69] Hopping and jumping

him to withhold from Doftor Feydoss that he already knew much of Teysoot Motzo's history and was actually responsible for some of it. However, it was necessary to act as if he was hearing of this patient for the first time. His grandson's life and, for all he knew, his own and Teysoot Motzo's lives, depended on it.

They walked into the seclusion room, where Teysoot Motzo remained in the drug-induced coma. He was in a hospital gown, strapped to the bed. He was unresponsive to commands and had no reaction to painful stimuli, such as pinching or pressing knuckles into sensitive places. Fietlebaum noticed that there was a motion sensor attached to the bed rails designed to sound a loud alarm to alert the staff if he tore his restraints and tried to get out of bed. It occurred to him that the alarm was redundant, as Teysoot Motzo's screams would be far louder than the alarm if he awakened to find himself in restraints.

Dr. Doftor Feydoss delivered the standard medical report to Fietlebaum. "This is a ninety year old male Janpooran with no known psychiatric history. He was brought by police from the Pinshett City Conference Center where he had been giving a speech to the Janpooran Miners Union. Only recently, he had been enjoying his usual state of good health. However, by all accounts, he had over the last two weeks begun to exhibit unusual behavior. He was complaining of fatigue, poor concentration, lack of appetite, sleep disturbance, and emotional lability. This emotional lability was marked primarily by irritability, but he had also exhibited several bouts of extreme sadness and crying that were described by those who know him well as uncharacteristic."

This doctor did his homework, Fietlebaum thought. *That's exactly what happened.*

"The patient's condition worsened dramatically on the evening of an important talk that he was to give at the miners' union meeting," Dr. Doftor Feydoss continued.

"At that time, he was described as emotionally labile. He exhibited a wide range of emotions including anxiety, fear, anger, and sadness. He also appeared to be experiencing psychotic features. He was responding to internal stimuli and likely suffering paranoid delusions. He not only attacked the assistant that had worked for him for over eleven years, but also assaulted his personal secretary, whom he accused of trying to poison him."

The poor shmuck[70], Fietlebaum thought, *it was me that poisoned him*. But, he nodded appreciatively and asked Dr. Doftor Feydoss to continue.

"The standard toxicology screen determined that he had significant levels of *burzet* in his blood. However, he is known to be a habitual user of the substance. Moreover, it is unlikely that the relatively mild effects of *burzet* could have contributed to the psychotic break exhibited by the patient."

Fietlebaum anxiously waited to hear if *shodom* had been found in Teysoot Motzo's blood, but it had not. Apparently, the modifications he had made in the molecule to enhance its effects had also changed its antigenic properties enough to prevent it from being detected by the toxicological immunoassay. He had completely overlooked the possibility of being discovered by the "tox screen." "Dumb luck," Fietlebaum told himself with mild recrimination.

"As for his medical history," Doftor Feydoss asserted, "aside from a recent development of mild hypertension, and a remote surgical removal of an infected left tordask gland, the history is unremarkable. He has no chronic illnesses. He takes no prescribed medication."

Burzet, a harem of females, eats like a chazer[71], *and healthy as a horse. He must have a constitution like iron,* Fietlebaum thought. Got tzu danken[72]. *He'll need it.*

---

70 Prick, in the pitiful sense. A fool

71 pig

72 Thank God

"As for his psychosocial history, he was born and raised in the slums of Pinshett, and dropped out of school at an early age to work in the mines and support his family. He was married once. His wife died of circumstances unknown to us. He has no children, at least none that are legitimate. Twenty-five years ago, he spent three months in prison for assault. He subsequently spent time in jail for breaking and entering, and living off the avails of prostitution. Several years ago, he was tried but acquitted on racketeering charges. Although his legal history is compelling, he has had no significant interactions with the police for at least twelve years."

No angel, this fellow, Fietlebaum surmised.

"His more recent psychosocial history," Dr. Doftor Feydoss continued, "is remarkable for his being a successful and important union leader after working for thirty years himself as a hard rock miner in the Janpooran mining industry. He has become a very powerful figure, both in Janpooran and interplanetary union affairs as well. It is reasonable to suspect that his primary sources of psychosocial stress are the enormous demands placed upon him by his responsibilities as a union leader."

You don't know the half of it, Fietlebaum wanted to tell him, but, instead, he said "thank you, doctor," when Dr. Doftor Feydoss finished his presentation. "What is your differential diagnosis for this patient?" he inquired.

Dr. Doftor Feydoss hesitated for a moment, then noted, "Dr. Fietlebaum, you yourself have written some of the literature's most important and insightful papers on species bound psychiatric syndromes in the galaxy. Your study of Janpooran mental illness is still read by psychiatric residents here on Janpoor. Thus, with your indulgence, my differential diagnosis includes a toxic psychosis, and until we image the brain, we cannot fully rule out a lesion or central nervous system infection. Because this is the patient's first psychotic break, it will also be important to rule out any form of partial complex seizure. However, in my opinion, the most likely diagnosis is Major Depression, with psychotic features." Fietlebaum nodded in appreciation.

Bolstered by Fietlebaum's recognition, Doftor Feydoss elaborated. "Of course, both the patient and his fellow Janpoorans would likely interpret the history of present illness as being consistent with "*leshte po noc*," or screaming ghost disease. This cultural understanding of the illness does not alter the underlying neurophysiological basis of the condition, but it will certainly affect how the patient sees and understands his condition as well as how well he will be able to reintegrate himself back into his life as he recovers." He paused, then soberly added, "As you are certainly aware, Dr. Fietlebaum, the stigma of *leshte po noc* will be hard for a fellow such as Teysoot Motzo to overcome."

Nu? Fietlebaum thought. *You're right. But there is nothing I can do about it now.*

Fietlebaum officially accepted the transfer of patient Teysoot Motzo to his care. He felt an awkward satisfaction in hearing that his sequential introduction of the genetically engineered virus and modified shodom had almost perfectly mimicked the natural history of a common psychiatric illness of the Janpoorans. *From* mensch *to* schlemiel *in seconds flat,* he thought, *all through the miracles of modern science*. He sighed in resignation, and considered his next step in his interaction with the unfortunate Teysoot Motzo. The most likely series of events would be keeping Teysoot Motzo safe and sound on the psychiatric ward until a commitment hearing could be held. After that, he would be transferred to another facility, almost certainly one of Glesh's choice, for more prolonged treatment. By then, word of his suffering *leshte po noc* would have leaked out. He would be disgraced and no longer a threat to the military resources Glesh held so dear.

He was certain that the effects of the chemically modified *shodom* would still be strong at this time, and that it would be a relief for Teysoot Motzo to be "knocked out" until some of its terrifying effects had worn off. Nonetheless, sooner or later he would have to stop the injections of the powerful sedative, prosteridine, and allow Teysoot Motzo to regain consciousness. He felt it both medically and morally imperative to make certain that, *Got zol ophiten*[73], no permanent damage had been caused. Moreover, the court would demand to know if Teysoot Motzo's behavior and general condition had improved between the onset of his dangerous psychiatric condition and the day of his commitment hearing. This would not be possible to ascertain while he was unconscious. Thus, with some misgivings, Fietlebaum ordered the nurses to withhold the next injection of prosteridine. Then he waited.

Fietlebaum had sat at Teysoot Motzo's bedside for several hours, watching and waiting. "*Nu?*[74]" he murmured quizzically. Then, Teysoot Motzo moved his arm. A moment later, he groaned and opened his eyes, all six of them. He screamed and fought against the restraints. He cried in loud, squeaky, Janpooran fashion. "*Vey iz mir!*" Fietlebaum blurted out. He then asked Teysoot Motzo through cybertranslation if he was okay and if he knew where he was. But Teysoot Motzo only shrieked and struggled more loudly. The few words he screamed made no sense, at least not in the opinion of the cybertranslater. Meanwhile, the nurses came running, prosteridine needle in hand.

"Please, nurse," Fietlebaum ordered, "go ahead and inject the medication. We can try to withhold it again tomorrow."

---

73 God forbid

74 So?

Teysoot Motzo's eyes rolled back and his head fell to the pillow. "*Gai shloffen*[75]," Fietlebaum whispered to him. "I'm sorry," he added as he lingered at his bedside. "I will try my best to make it up to you."

Though he had not been observant for more than thirty years, the *Kol nidre* prayer, the Jewish prayer for release from ill promises made under duress, suddenly came to Fietlebaum's mind. He absently recited a few lines before shaking his head and letting the rest go. He was left with a sad sense of brotherhood for all those beings in the Universe who over the millennia had been forced to do evil in order to avoid something still worse. "It's not easy," he told himself.

---

[75] Go to sleep.

CHAPTER 14

Fietlebaum was bored to death. He had nothing to do all day but sit at Teysoot Motzo's bedside and watch him breathe. Dr. Doftor Feydoss, the attending psychiatrist on the acute psychiatric ward, dropped by and asked him if he would be willing to mentor a psychiatric resident who was working in the outpatient clinic. "Teysoot Motzo will be fine," Doftor Feydoss insisted. "The nurses and I will be there to keep an eye on him." Beshted said that as long as Doftor Feydoss was there to cover for him, and he didn't leave the hospital, there wouldn't be a problem. It seemed a welcome respite, and Fietlebaum said he would be happy to do it.

Dr. Doftor Feydoss led him downstairs to the outpatient psychiatric clinic where the resident was waiting. He was Dr. Jorshgo Klarj, a young Gorsid who had graduated from medical school only a few months before. He had four years of psychiatric residency to complete, and he had chosen to work on Janpoor, where his father, an electrical engineer, was employed in the mining industry. He would be spending the next four years at Pinshett General Hospital treating psychiatric patients on the acute inpatient ward and in the outpatient clinic.

Like all students of psychiatry, Klarj had read several of Fietlebaum's most famous papers. He tried his best to appear professional and nonchalant, but his twitching tentacles belied his anxiety in meeting the renowned psychiatrist. Fietlebaum extended his hand and said, "I'm Isaac Fietlebaum, and I am very pleased to meet you."

The resident extended his dominant, left anterolateral tentacle and shook Fietlebaum's hand. "I—I—I'm Jorshgo Klarj," the resident stammered, "and I am very honored to meet you, sir."

Fietlebaum noticed Klarj's anxiety. "No need to be intimidated by an *alta kocker*[76] like me," he told him. "A few years ago, I might have eaten you alive, but not now." The resident seemed to relax, even smile in Gorsidian fashion, after the cybertranslator delivered Fietlebaum's words. "Come, Dr. Klarj," Fietlebaum told him. "Let's see what they've arranged for us." Dr. Doftor Feydoss led them to an office where they would meet their patient. Then he returned to monitor Teysoot Motzo.

The patient that entered the room was an adolescent Blossian male who was accompanied by his mother. A younger sister tagged along with them. "Good morning," Dr. Klarj said. The young male nodded back in response. The mother also nodded in salutation, but then quickly brushed past him to peer left and right through the window. She drew the drapes closed, then re-opened them before she backed up and sat down in a chair next to her son. "My son, Klorpo," she began, "has no energy. He can't—" She stopped in mid-sentence, wriggled in her a seat few times, stood up, walked over to inspect a picture on the wall, strolled to the desk, picked up and inspected a blown glass paper weight, set it down, made sure it was returned to the correct position, then sat back down in her chair and stared with wide-eyed countenance at Dr. Klarj.

The disconcerted Dr. Klarj asked if she could again explain what problems she believed her son was having, and what help she hoped to receive for him. But before he could finish his question, the daughter ran over to Fietlebaum, snatched a writing pen out of his pocket, and ran out the door with it. The mother ran after her and a moment later

---

[76] An old shitter, old fart

returned with her in hand. Still somewhat out of breath, she immediately launched into a critique of the office décor. Then the daughter grabbed a letter opener off the desk and ran out the door again with her mother in hot pursuit. All the while, Klorpo, the patient, calmly sat in his chair.

"Don't you see?" the distraught mother implored on her return. "He is always this way! He scares the hell out of us! His father is worried sick!" She stopped and walked over to more closely inspect the drapes, pulled several loose threads off of them, and asked if the weather had been unusually warm or if she simply had not yet grown used to the Janpooran climate. When the daughter ran out a third time, the mother yelped and gave chase. This gave the resident a little time to review the medical records the mother had brought.

The records showed that Klorpo had been seen by a number of specialists on his home planet of Bloss prior to their having moved to Janpoor. The diagnosis that Klorpo had received from the last Blossian outpatient psychiatrist was APHD, which was short for "Attention-Prolongation Hypoactivity Disorder." He was said to have a severe case, exhibiting all four of the major diagnostic criteria of the disorder, that is, having the tendency to fixate on single sensory experiences, remaining sedentary for minutes at a time, engaging in linear thought processing, and possessing emotional reserve. The Blossian psychiatrist had recommended a potent stimulant, but the family moved to Janpoor before a trial of the medication could be started.

The Blossians evolved over millions of years on their planet in open savannah country in the midst of a variety of ferocious predators that at any given moment were prone to chase them down and rip them to shreds. Their means of survival was to evolve a constant shifting of attention, to look here and there, to touch this, sniff that, listen, and run away to another set of stimuli to look at, touch, and sniff.

Blossian anatomy and neurophysiology reflected the species relatively low place in the planet's food chain. They had the wide set eyes of animals who are prey. This allowed them a wide field of vision to spot predators who might be creeping up from the side or behind to catch them. Their eyes moved independently, like those of chameleons, and were constantly in motion. Their ears grew large, like those of rabbits. They extended a foot or more in the air on each side of their head, and could pivot to maximize the collection of sound from different directions. The mother's and daughter's ears, though not Klorpo's, twitched and shifted position every few seconds. Their olfactory transducers grew out bilaterally, on stalks, much in the fashion of hammerhead sharks. They sucked in air over receptor-laden turbinates that provided exquisitely sensitive olfactory sense, including an astonishing ability to locate the source from which an odor emanated. The accuracy of the system was such that even with eyes closed they could determine the source of an odor within a few feet at a range of a hundred yards.

Blossian brains were trip-wired. Small movements stimulated them. Small changes excited them. Loud sounds sent them through the roof. They were restless, edgy, easily shocked and excited. They were a talkative, mercurial species. For non-Blossians, they were hell to be around. Over the course of their evolution the Blossians who did not engage in the typical, erratic Blossian behavior tended to get eaten. At the present stage of their civilization, Blossians who failed to exhibit the expected forms of behavior were not eaten. They were diagnosed as being mentally ill. This had been the case with Klorpo.

The Gorsidian resident was at a loss. Fietlebaum sensed the resident's distress and suggested he speak with Klorpo without interference from his mother and sister. Following Fietlebaum's lead, the resident asked the mother if she might sit in the waiting room while he spoke with Klorpo alone. "Yes, of course," the mother said, quickly adding, "There's a sale on hats at Hofdozz Department store this afternoon." After stopping briefly to inspect the contents of the office trash can, she grabbed her daughter and left the room, leaving the resident and Fietlebaum free to speak privately with Klorpo.

Klorpo had sat calmly the entire time he was in the office. He remained so after his mother and sister left the room. After the door closed behind them, Dr. Klarj asked him, "How are you doing?"

"I'm fine," Klorpo replied.

"Do you think you need the help of a psychiatrist?" the resident inquired.

"No," Klorpo answered, "unless you could help me with my algebra homework." From previous experience with Blossians, Fietlebaum was able to inform the resident that the reply was made with a wry smile.

"W—well," Klarj stammered, "why do you think your mother is so upset?"

"She worries about me," Klorpo replied.

"Are you worried about yourself?" the struggling resident inquired.

"No," Klorpo calmly told him.

"Is your father worried about you?"

"Yah. He's like my mother. They keep telling me, 'Get with it!' But I feel fine."

With further inquiry, Fietlebaum and the resident learned that Klorpo was cheerful and pleasant most of the time. He had friends. He was intelligent and articulate. Notwithstanding his quip about algebra homework, he was doing well in school. He didn't do drugs. He had not been in any trouble with the police. He had plans for his future.

"Is there anything we can do for you?" Klarj asked in closing.

Klorpo thought for a moment. "No," he replied. "I'm fine."

Fietlebaum saw that the tips of the resident's tentacles were beginning to curl. It was a sign of consternation among Gorsids, and an indication of impending emotional breakdown if not explosion. It was time to rescue him.

"Klorpo," Fietlebaum said, "why don't you go sit with your mother and sister in the waiting room for a few minutes while I discuss your situation with Dr. Klarj. When we're done, we will have you and your mother come back in to talk things over."

"Sure," Klorpo replied in agreement. Then he walked out to join his mother and sister.

"What do I do?" the mildly frantic Dr. Klarj begged Fietlebaum. "The mother insists that Klorpo is sick. But Klorpo says he is fine. And he seems fine. But in comparison to other young Blossian males, he is probably crazy!" The resident shook his head in bewilderment. "If you want to know the truth," he added, "I think it's his mother who's crazy. But, by Blossian standards she is probably normal."

Fietlebaum noticed that the tips of Klarj's curled tentacles had also begun to quiver. *Oy*! he thought. "Dr. Klarj," he said calmly but firmly. "Let me explain something to you. It is not unusual for a family to believe that one of its members is crazy. Sometimes they're right. That individual may be suffering. They can't work or love. In some cases, they are a danger to themselves and need treatment whether they want it or not. But in some cases, it is the family that is crazy, and the individual is merely what we refer to as the designated patient. Sometimes, the designated patient is the only sane member of the family."

Klarj's tentacles stopped quivering. "The best way to maintain your therapeutic perspective," Fietlebaum continued, "is to keep in mind that your obligation is to your patient—not his family, his society, or his species. The others can *kvetch* as much as they want. But, if the patient says he doesn't want or need your help, and if he isn't acting in a manner at odds with his own safety and expressed desires, then there is nothing you need to do for him, regardless of what anyone else wants."

"Dr. Fietlebaum," Dr. Klarj asked plaintively, "are you saying that Klorpo is fine and does not need treatment?"

"Fine, *shmine*," Fietlebaum replied with a shrug. "Fine is a meaningless concept. Because he is so different from other Blossians, he will almost certainly have some trouble in his future. But, everyone has a little *tsuris*[77]. The important fact is that he doesn't want treatment, and he meets no criteria for you to force it upon him. His mother will be unhappy, but she is not our patient. Klorpo is."

Dr. Klarj asked Klorpo, his mother, and his sister to come back into the office. "Your son doesn't want treatment," he told Klorpo's mother, "and we have no basis to force medication over his objections."

"What?" she shrieked. "Are you telling me that there is nothing wrong with my son?" She picked a piece of lint off of the resident's suit collar, straightened his tie, and yelled, "This is outrageous!"

The ends of Klarj's tentacles curled again. "We do think," he squeaked, "that your family should seek counseling to deal with the differences in opinions you have about your son's behavior. Perhaps you can come to accept him for who he is."

She was livid. "Are you suggesting this is our fault?" she demanded to know. She noted that the janitors did a terrific job maintaining the floors at the hospital, then demanded to see the director of the hospital. "This is unacceptable!" she screamed. She warned Fietlebaum, "Your shoe lace is untied," then stomped out of the office with Klorpo and his sister in tow.

"*Vey iz mir*," Fietlebaum said. He turned to young Jorshgo Klarj and added, "There are many lessons to be

---

[77] troubles

learned from this case. It illustrates the differences that can exist among species, how family conflicts affect patients, and how clinical solutions arise from understanding the nature of the obligations you have to your patient. But the most important lesson to learn from this case is that whether you're a psychiatrist or a plumber, you can't please everybody."

CHAPTER 15

Glesh was not happy that Teysoot Motzo had been allowed to awaken from his coma. He was equally displeased that Fietlebaum had left Teysoot Motzo to go and mentor a resident. Thus, Fietlebaum was not surprised the next morning to discover a new Drajan GIA agent, Kan Kesset, stationed with him in Teysoot Motzo's seclusion room. He was there to tighten the reins.

Kesset was not only a seasoned and loyal intelligence agent, but had also served as a corpsman in the Drajan Planetary Army. He had some rudimentary medical knowledge, though Fietlebaum quickly found his reach to be beyond his grasp. Kesset made it clear that it was Glesh's intention that Teysoot Motzo not wake up any time soon. He also conveyed Glesh's insistence that the prosteridine injections be converted to a hanging IV drip to minimize any chances of lapses in sedation. From the smirk on the Drajan's face, Fietlebaum suspected that this particular idea had originated with Kesset, himself.

Meanwhile, Glesh was leaving no stone unturned. The hospital staff was informed that Teysoot Motzo was of "special interest" to the Galactic government, and that any medical orders, even Fietlebaum's, needed to be okayed by agent Kesset. The commitment hearing had been postponed, so that Glesh could arrange to have his own, hand-picked judges on the panel. To destroy any reputation Teysoot Motzo may have managed to hold onto, Glesh had also leaked to the press rumors that Teysoot Motzo had been seen crying in bars and other night spots weeks before his breakdown at the union meeting. The possibility of *leshte po noc* was mentioned. To prevent any further reckless behavior on Fietlebaum's part, Glesh had Kesset remind him on a daily basis that his grandson's life hung in the balance until the Janpooran was legally out of sight and mind.

Unlike Beshted, Kesset had no warmth or empathy. He was manipulative and cruel. Fietlebaum discovered this first hand when he informed Kesset that Teysoot Motzo would likely become tolerant to the prosteridine, and that the dose would need to be increased with time.

If we don't increase the dose," Fietlebaum tried to explain, "Teysoot Motzo may suddenly awaken all on his own. This would likely be terrifying for him and, at best, inconvenient for us."

Kesset summarily dismissed the possibility. "I wouldn't worry about it," he replied with disdain. To prove his point, he placed a knuckle on the boney ridge below Teysoot Motzo's left lateral eye and pressed hard. This area was exquisitely sensitive in Janpoorans, and any failure of the prosteridine to maintain deep sedation would have resulted in some form of response from Teysoot Motzo. Fietlebaum watched as Kesset ground his knuckle into Teysoot Motzo's flesh. The pressure he exerted was sufficient to part the flesh from the underlying bone. He seemed to relish the damage he was doing. Teysoot Motzo remained still. Kesset turned to Fietlebaum, stared into his eyes for a moment without saying a word, then turned away. "Things will stay as they are," he said.

Fietlebaum had been right. Over the next few days, despite the constant IV drip of the once effective dose of prosteridine, Teysoot Motzo stirred. He groaned and mumbled incoherently. At times, he seemed to be trying to convey something, but quickly fell back into meaningless garble. Kesset had been out meeting with Glesh, and when he returned to see Teysoot Motzo on the edge of consciousness he screamed at the nurse to immediately increase the administration rate of the IV pump loaded with prosteridine. He said nothing to Fietlebaum. *But if looks could kill*, Fietlebaum thought.

Fietlebaum later explained to Kesset that while Teysoot Motzo needed to remain sedated, the court would eventually have to see what Teysoot Motzo was like while conscious and without psychotropic medication. Without that information, they would be unable to gauge the need for further treatment. The last attempt at withdrawing the prosteridine showed the Janpooran to still be psychotic and agitated, but that had been nearly a week ago. There was no compelling reason to assume that he would continue to be so severely ill. "We need to see what he is like awake and without psychotropic medication," Fietlebaum told him. Kesset did not like to be challenged or told what to do. "I will speak to Glesh," he curtly replied, then turned back to his business.

Beshted came by that afternoon. As he walked into Teysoot Motzo's seclusion room, he was taken aback by Kesset's presence. Kesset cocked his head to look at him as he entered, but said nothing. Fietlebaum noted Beshted's discomfort, and asked Kesset if he could speak with Beshted in private. Kesset gave no indication that he had heard the question. But after a moment he stood up and left. "Ten minutes," he said as he strode out the door.

Beshted remained uneasy. "What's wrong?" Fietlebaum asked.

"Glesh took me off the case," Beshted replied.

"Yes, I know," Fietlebaum said. "It doesn't astonish me." Beshted's discomfort convinced him something else was going on. "But that's not what's troubling you, is it?" he gently inquired. "Sit. Tell me about it." He was surprised at how little coaxing Beshted needed.

"My father died, yesterday," he said without obvious signs of emotion.

"Oooh," Fietlebaum groaned, "I'm sorry. That's a painful loss for you."

Beshted noticeably stiffened and retorted, "No, it isn't. He was a bastard."

"When your father dies," Fietlebaum replied, "you not only lose the father you had, but also the father you wanted."

Beshted fell silent. Fietlebaum had hit a nerve. It was an utterly new and foreign experience for Beshted to reveal to another how he felt. But, a look of sadness came over him, and for a moment Fietlebaum thought he might begin to tremble and moan in the Drajan manner of expressing grief. He glanced up at Fietlebaum for the briefest moment with pain in his eyes, but fought to shake it off. "It was Glesh that gave me the news," he said. He paused, and added, "I think he did it."

"It sounds like more than coincidence, doesn't it," Fietlebaum observed. "That *paskudnyak*."

"He may think I'm a fool," Beshted admitted, "and maybe I am. But, I'm still an agent with Galactic Intelligence. He can't have me killed without some kind of investigation being held. I suspect this was his best way of telling me I had better leave and be quiet."

"You need to be careful," Fietlebaum advised him.

Kesset pushed through the door. "*Er iz shoyn du, der nudnik*[78]!" Fietlebaum noted. The cybertranslater complained that it did not know how to translate those words. "Just as well, my silicone friend," Fietlebaum whispered kindly.

Kesset sauntered into the room without acknowledging Fietlebaum or Beshted. He sat and, without turning his head in their direction, said, "Ten minutes is up. Get out."

---

[78] So, the nuisance is here already!

Beshted rose and started out the door, but then turned to convey his appreciation to Fietlebaum. "Thank you," he said.

Fietlebaum looked into Beshted's eyes and let his gaze linger for a moment before simply nodding his head in acceptance. Beshted walked out.

Kesset said nothing. After a long silence, he said with disgust, "He's weak."

"Well," Fietlebaum observed, "not everyone can be a *gantseh macher*[79] like you." After the cybertranslater included the insult inherent in the statement, at Fietlebaum's request, Kesset became angry. "You may live to regret your smart remarks!" he snarled.

"*Nu*?" Fietlebaum replied. "Who doesn't have regrets?"

After another long and sullen silence, Kesset informed Fietlebaum that Glesh had granted permission to wean Teysoot Motzo off the prosteridine. "I convinced him it was necessary," he rushed to add.

"*Mazel tov*[80]," Fietlebaum replied without enthusiasm, then he quickly stepped to the intravenous pump and dialed it back.

Over the next few hours, as the blood levels of prosteridine fell, Teysoot Motzo slowly rose back into consciousness. But, as Kesset had hoped and Fietlebaum feared, he remained under the powerful effects of shodom. When he opened his eyes he cried. Kesset called his name, and Teysoot Motzo turned in response. He stared at Kesset's face. Fietlebaum thought that Teysoot Motzo called out a name that sounded like "Gorsh," "Glarsh," or even "Glesh," but he admitted that he could have been mumbling almost anything. To the best of his knowledge, Teysoot Motzo had

---

79 A big shot

80 Congratulation, but sometimes spoken in a sense of derisive sarcasm

no idea that Glesh existed. *The murmurings of delirium*, Fietlebaum concluded.

As Teysoot Motzo climbed further out of his sedation, deeper fears took hold of him. He screamed and cried louder. He struggled against his restraints. "Put him under," Fietlebaum ordered. Kesset turned slowly toward Fietlebaum, stared a moment in passive defiance, then turned back toward Teysoot Motzo. He hovered above him, enjoying the Janpooran's torment. Teysoot Motzo shrieked in horror, and fought against the restraint until they cut into his flesh. "You passive aggressive *kuppe drek*[81], turn up the prosteridine!" Fietlebaum shouted. But Kesset did nothing. *"Gai tren zich*!" Fietlebaum shouted, as he pushed past Kesset to increase the IV dose of prosteridine. The cybertranslator seemed pleased to convey to Kesset Fietlebaum's suggestion in Yiddish that he go fuck himself. In a few moments, Teysoot Motzo stopped his crying, closed his eyes and returned to his drug-induced sleep.

Fietlebaum was incensed. "I know that you and Glesh are in control. You're holding all the cards. But when I tell you to do something in regard to the care of this patient, Goddamn it, you do it!"

Kesset smirked in the sly Drajan fashion, but said nothing. He sat and looked out the window. After Fietlebaum appeared to have cooled down, Kesset turned and blithely informed him that the commitment hearing would be held in the morning. "Be ready," he told him.

"How long have you known this?" Fietlebaum demanded.

"Since yesterday morning," Kesset replied.

"Didn't you think I needed to know this sooner?" Fietlebaum asked.

"I decide what you need to know, and when you need to know it," Kesset retorted.

---

[81] Piece of shit

"Kesset," Fietlebaum replied with feigned affection, "do me a favor," adding, after a pregnant pause, "*un gai in drerd*[82]!"

It had been a perfectly lousy day. Ever since Teysoot Motzo's admission to the psychiatric ward, he had been stuck in the hospital. He desperately needed some respite. "Kesset," he said, "I have to get out of here. I need to go back to my hotel for a night."

"No!" Kesset barked derisively. "Do you take me for some kind of idiot?"

"Yes," Fietlebaum retorted, "the worst kind!"

"I could handcuff you to your crazy friend's bed for the night if you like!" Kesset bellowed in reply.

Fietlebaum saw that his antagonism of Kesset was only making matters worse. "Look," he began in more congenial fashion, "I apologize. But you and Glesh need my help, and I can't give it to you if I'm exhausted. Please, call Glesh and ask if I could have a night to myself."

Kesset turned away without replying and stomped out into the hallway to the room he had set up as his temporary office on the ward.

Well, Fietelbaum thought to himself, *that's that.*

Several minutes later, Kesset returned. "Glesh agreed to let you go tonight," Kesset answered dryly, "but I'll be watching you every second."

Hmmm, Fietlebaum thought. *Like God's own* malach ha mavis[83] *he'll be watching.* Still, he forced himself to say "thank you."

Kesset leaned closer, placed a tracking device in Fietlebaum's pocket, and whispered, "Kiss my ass."

Fietlebaum ambled toward the locked double doors that opened out to the foyer and the bank of elevators down to the lobby. The patients had received their evening

---

82 Do me a favor, and drop dead!

83 Angel of Death

medications and the ward was calm, at least relatively so. Through one doorway he passed, he heard the muffled weeping of the suicidally depressed Polmodi who longed for the planet he would never see again. He side-stepped the Rodrantian who continued to grind himself against the wall in his fruitless march towards his magnetic hallucination of home. A Gordisian who suffered paranoid delusions suddenly sidled up to Fietlebaum, but was intercepted by a portly Polmodi orderly and unceremoniously led away to a quiet corner. When Fietlebaum reached the locked doors, the same orderly spotted him and lumbered over as quickly as he could with the key. "Goodnight, Dr. Fietlebaum," the Polmodi said as he worked the tumblers of the lock.

"Good night, and thank you," Fietlebaum replied. A good boy, he thought to himself, a sturdy, dependable fellow.

He rode to the lobby and caught an aircab outside the hospital. The traffic was sparse, and the cabbie enjoyed few opportunities to joust with other cabs. He seemed disappointed in the lack of sport that night and offered Fietlebaum none of the usual banter during the flight. *Even the cabbies are* ongeblozzen[84] *tonight,* he observed. The cab dropped him off in front of the Andromeda Hotel, he shuffled into the lobby and caught an elevator up to his floor.

When got in his room, he unbuttoned his collar, loosened his belt, and poured himself two fingers of *schnapps.* As he sunk into the chair, he caught sight of a flashing light in his peripheral vision. He looked up and saw that a small surveillance camera had been installed in the corner of his room. "Nothing gets past that *paskudnyak,*" he noted.

He put on some music, an old English mass by William Byrd. The *schnapps* and the music worked their magic.

---

84 moody

For the first time in a week, he was able to relax. "*Vey iz mir*," Fietlebaum sighed. He took another sip of *schnapps* and considered his situation. "What have I been dragged into?" he lamented. "That *momzer*, Glesh!" he growled. "If it wasn't for Glesh, my grandson would be safe. If it wasn't for Glesh, I wouldn't be tormenting poor Teysoot Motzo. If it wasn't for that *putz*, I would be back in my little flat on Polmodi, looking forward to another day in my clinic." He gave another long sigh. "If, if, if," he muttered as he shook his head in resignation. "*Az di bubbe volt gehat beytsim, volt zi gevain mayn zaideh*[85]."

[85] If my grandmother had balls, she would be my grandfather.

CHAPTER 16

Fietlebaum had graduated at the top of his class at Forgion Transgalactic School of Medicine. "The most promising student in the last ten years," the dean had said of him. After residency at Silesian General Hospital, he was awarded a coveted psychopharmacology fellowship at the Yang Chi Institute of Transgalactic Neuropsychiatric Studies. There he developed techniques for the rapid identification of active molecules in native botanical medicines. He discovered new classes of psychoactive drugs and cured illnesses previously thought to be intractable. Isaac Fietlebaum became a big name in transgalactic psychiatry.

Though primarily a psychopharmacologist, Fietlebaum was well-versed in psychoanalytic theory. The expansion of psychotherapeutic treatment to non-humans had strained psychoanalytic notions of how psychodynamic conflicts drove individuals to illness. The profound differences in childhood experiences among the various extra-terrestrial beings had left classical psychoanalysts nowhere to hang their hats. Some of Fietlebaum's earliest scholarly papers addressed gaps in theory by describing commonalities in psychodynamic conflicts among various sentient beings of the galaxy. The papers were considered groundbreaking.

Fundamental to Freud's psychoanalytic theory was the Oedipal conflict, which arose in every little boy out of feeling sexual attraction to his mother while fearing reprisal from his father. He subconsciously wanted to kill his father, but feared his father would cut his penis off in revenge. For Freud, this conflict explained what drove the behaviors of individuals and societies. He theorized that the manner in which the boy resolved the Oedipal conflict determined if he became a contented, law abiding member of society, or a twisted, social wreck. But questions and controversies persisted. What about girls and the Oedipal conflict? What did women want?

The importance of the Oedipal conflict was seriously called into question with the discoveries of sentient species that had neither penises nor mothers and fathers. The Morvodians, for example, were all females and reproduced by parthenogenesis. The Zostonds were the products of the sexual congress of four hermaphroditic parents. The Korpians, who spontaneously changed from one sex to another one or more times in their lives, also fell through the cracks of psychoanalytic theory.

At a conference Fietlebaum attended on psychodynamic processes of various sentient species in the galaxy, an argument broke out. Some maintained that only members of species with a mother, a father, and a sex organ to lose could suffer the angst that drove neurosis. Fietlebaum vehemently objected. "Any being in the Universe that is born, lives, loves, and knows he will die can go *meshugeh*," he declared, "and for damn good reason!" His position garnered wide support, and his statement later came to be known as "Fietlebaum's Law." It solidified his position among the psychiatric elite.

The panel assembled to decide Teysoot Motzo's fate was diverse. It consisted of three psychiatrists, a Human, a Gorsid, and a Janpooran; as well as three judges, two of whom were Janpoorans, and the other a Silesian on loan from the Galactic Regional Court of Appeals. With the illustrious Fietlebaum under his thumb, Glesh had little concern about the psychiatrists. He was confident that they would follow Fietlebaum's lead. As for the judges, the Silesian was a wild card. But, the two Janpoorans, whom

Glesh had known to be burdened with considerable gambling debts, were already bought and paid for.

The commitment hearing was held under the auspices of the Pinshett District Court of the Janpoor Planetary Judicial Council. The courtroom was garish. It was bright red and illuminated by strings of colored lights, such as might celebrate the grand opening of a toy store. The walls were slung with banners upon which were written words of Janpooran judicial wisdom—"You going get what you deserve," "If you behave you self, you not be here," and "You going wish you not do that." The floor was littered with food wrappers, and the crumpled notes and documents from previous hearings. Though Fietlebaum was not in the room to appreciate it, the air was heavily laden with the aroma of *burzet*.

The judges and consulting psychiatrists crowded behind a long wooden counter. Each judge wore a shiny, green robe that tied in the front and carried scarlet Janpooran script on the back giving his name and district of jurisdiction. To Fietlebaum, they were reminiscent of the robes Earth's ancient professional wrestlers wore into the ring. The psychiatrists wore what were in Fietlebaum's estimation, more sensible, gray business caftans.

Teysoot Motzo appeared in court through a holographic feed from his room in the Forensic Psychiatry Unit of the hospital. His image manifested in a space in front of the judges. He remained in bed in four-point restraints. The panel watched him writhe and strain against the polymer straps. The shouts and mad ramblings of the other patients echoed in the background, and served as a constant, grim reminder of exactly where Teysoot Motzo was. Glesh had made certain that the gag in Teysoot Motzo's *ahzha* had been removed for his own screams and cries to be better appreciated by the panel.

Fietlebaum testified holographically from an office in the psychiatric unit. His likeness appeared in the courtroom next to Teysoot Motzo's. Holographic platforms carried the panel's and Teysoot Motzo's likenesses back to Fietlebaum. What the commitment panel did not know was that a third platform in Fietlebaum's office carried another live image. In that image, Glesh sat behind Fietlebaum's grandson and held a razor-sharp knife against his throat.

The lead judge, one of the Janpoorans, grabbed an enormous gavel and pounded it on the counter to bring the court into session. He made the standard pronouncements concerning the nature of the proceedings and their basis in law. "Decision we need for make," he went on to say, "be whether or not Teysoot Motzo suffer psychiatric condition that make him unable care for self, or make him danger for self or others." He pounded his gavel one more time, then addressed his first question to Teysoot Motzo.

"Teysoot Motzo," the judge asked, "you have attorney present?" In fact, Teysoot Motzo had been assigned an attorney by the district court, but the young, Borgostian lawyer had been so terrified of his client that at the last minute he bolted. It wasn't clear if it was in response to the question about his attorney or purely out of coincidence, but Teysoot Motzo emitted a long, pathetic moan, like a heavy door slowly closing on a rusty hinge. The judge thought for a moment, then shrugged. "Teysoot Motzo probably not benefit much from attorney anyway," he said. "We go on."

"Teysoot Motzo," the judge went on to inquire, "you understand question before court?" Teysoot Motzo mumbled incoherently. The cybertranslater noted an inability to translate what he was saying. "The words make no sense," the machine plaintively reported. *Word salad,* Fietlebaum thought. *The shodom must still be affecting his brain.* The human psychiatrist on the panel expressed concern about Teysoot Motzo not clearly understanding the proceedings, but the judge was not impressed. "We not going stop now!" he barked.

The judge then turned to Fietlebaum. "Dr. Fietlebaum," he began, "you here for help us decide if Teysoot Motzo have psychiatric disease and need more treatment. We need for know if you real expert." The Janpooran psychiatrist immediately suggested to the court that they forego that exercise, as there was simply no question about the doctor's knowledge and integrity. The other two psychiatrists readily agreed. Fietlebaum winced and silently apologized for betraying their trust. "Okay for me," the judge replied as the rest of the panel nodded in agreement. He slammed his gavel down. "You credential accepted!" he declared. "Now we get down for business."

"Dr. Fietlebaum," the judge continued, "you think Teysoot Motzo suffer psychiatric illness?" Fietlebaum hesitated a moment. Out of the corner of his eye he saw Glesh shift the knife in his hand as he held it against his grandson's neck. It was shameful using his knowledge and reputation to destroy Teysoot Motzo. But, he could not allow his grandson to suffer harm at the hands of Glesh.

"Your honor," Fietlebaum reluctantly began, "it is my opinion that Mr. Teysoot Motzo does indeed suffer a psychiatric illness." The holographic Glesh stared intently as Fietlebaum explained. "I would formally diagnose his condition as Major Depression, with psychotic features. However, I am compelled to add that the signs and symptoms of Teysoot Motzo's illness are identical to the condition referred to by Janpoorans themselves as *leshte po noc*, or screaming ghost disease." The holographic image of Glesh nodded with approval, and beckoned with his hand for elaboration.

"The syndrome," Fietlebaum continued, "is unique to Janpoorans. They believe the ghosts of those who die unfulfilled search the world for strong, productive people and suck the energy from them, leaving them fatigued and listless. If the victim resists, a battle ensues. If the ghost wins, it takes control and seeks vengeance for the disrespect it has been showed. The symptoms of such a lost battle, and ones suggestive of *leshte po noc*, were those exhibited by Teysoot Motzo."

The junior Janpooran judge sprang up. "You not need tell us about *leshte po noc*!" he protested. "Everybody know *leshte po noc* when they see!"

"Shut up!" the lead judge demanded. He slammed the big gavel down.

The junior Janpooran sullenly flopped back into his seat. The lead judge turned back to Fietlebaum. "Dr. Fietlebaum," he continued, "you think *leshte po noc* make Teysoot Motzo dangerous?"

Glesh's holographic image again nodded his head in the affirmative. "I do, your honor," Fietlebaum felt compelled to reply. "Teysoot Motzo has a history of violence. Some years ago he spent time in jail for assault. Violence is part of his nature." Teysoot Motzo bellowed, as if in protest. He screamed and struggled against his restraints. Glesh was delighted. "Your *haken a tsheinik*[86] isn't doing you any favors," Fietlebaum mumbled under his breath.

"Gag him!" the judge angrily demanded. A nurse at his bedside deftly placed a cloth around his *ahzha*. "You continue, Dr. Fietlebaum," he ordered.

Fietlebaum described to the court the peculiar changes in Teysoot Motzo's behavior in the weeks prior to the night at the union meeting, as well as how he acted at the meeting itself. The judges and psychiatrists on the panel took notes and grunted intermittently to affirm their understanding of what had transpired.

After a lengthy account of the catastrophic events at the union hall, Fietlebaum described what happened subsequent to his arrival at the hospital. "In the emergency department, Teysoot Motzo continued to be agitated and violent. He screamed and struck out at the doctors and

---

86 Literally, "beating a tea kettle," making a lot of loud noise

nurses. He presented such a threat to the hospital staff that he had to be sedated and placed in restraints. He was wheeled to the psychiatric unit, and placed in a quiet room to allow him the rest he needed. But it was to no avail. We have tried on several occasions over the last few days to stop the intravenous sedation, but, as you yourselves saw only a few minutes ago, he becomes agitated and aggressive. His dire psychiatric condition has persisted."

The junior Janpooran judge again leapt to his feet. "Hah!" he bellowed. "This boy got *leshte po noc*. He crazy. Case closed!"

The Janpooran psychiatrist seated next to him quickly rose in protest. "You big jackass[87]!" he cried. "That what we psychiatrists here for decide."

The young Janpooran judge leaned in close to the psychiatrist's face. "Case closed, I say!" he barked in response. "We send him for crazy house!"

The psychiatrist snarled and poked the judge in the abdomen, which prompted the judge to snatch the gavel from in front of the lead judge and swing it at the psychiatrist's head. The psychiatrist grabbed the head of the gavel, and the two wrestled for possession of it. The Gorsid psychiatrist resented the judicial over-reach, and darted a tentacle up and around the judge's *ahzha* to clamp it shut. The Silesian judge then overcame his usual self-containment, cried, "Contempt of court!" and poked the Gorsid in the eye. Angry voices boomed. Arms flailed. Tentacles flew. Green judicial robes billowed. All the while, the holographic representation of Teysoot Motzo continued to writhe and fight against his restraints.

Oy, Fietlebaum thought, *they can all share a room at the asylum.*

---

87 "Jackass" was the cybertranslation. The actual statement was "Bogog" a similarly maligned stubborn, stupid Janpooran creature.

The lead judge intervened. "Order!" he boomed. "Order! I decide when we reach verdict!" He thrust out his hands around the *ahzhas* of the Janpooran judge and psychiatrist, squeezed them shut and forced the pair to relinquish control of the gavel. He retrieved the gavel and repeatedly slammed it down upon the counter, sending court papers flying and fluttering to the floor. "Shut up for Fietlebaum continue!" he demanded.

Fietlebaum heaved a sigh. "I have no more to tell the court, your honor," he said with resignation.

"Oh," the judge croaked anticlimactically. He quickly recovered his fervor and bellowed, "Then it time for bring Teysoot Motzo witness."

At this point in the hearing, Teysoot Motzo would have had the right to call witnesses on his behalf. They might have vouched for his character. They might have helped explain why commitment was unnecessary, or offered an alternative course of action. But no such witnesses appeared. Glesh had seen to that. The decision to commit or not commit Teysoot Motzo would be drawn entirely from Fietlebaum's testimony. Yet, Teysoot Motzo's behavior had been so abnormal, even a medical student could have convinced the panel that Teysoot Motzo met criteria for commitment. *Besides*, Fietlebaum realized, *Glesh has half the panel in his pocket. The decision is already made.*

The judge glanced around the courtroom and, with no witnesses for the defense forthcoming, he slammed his gavel down. "Does panel have question for ask?" he inquired.

Each member of the panel asked a few obligatory closing questions, but none asked the critical ones. None asked if Teysoot Motzo had enemies. None asked if Fietlebaum had a conflict of interest. None asked about the GIA. When there were no more questions from the judges or psychiatrists, the lead judge issued the standard closing set of inquiries. "For conclusion, Dr. Fietlebaum, you believe

Teysoot Motzo mentally ill and still likely for hurt self or others?"

"Yes I do, your honor," he answered.

"You think he maybe have *leshte po noc*?"

With an insistent stare from Glesh, Fietlebaum reluctantly replied, "Yes, in all likelihood, he suffers *leshte po noc*."

"You believe Teysoot Motzo need more treatment?"

"I do."

"You think he able for make good decision about his own treatment?"

"No, your honor," Fietlebaum answered. "I do not."

"Dr. Fietlebaum," the judge asked in somber tone, "you think court must commit Teysoot Motzo for such treatment?"

The holographic image of Glesh pushed the knife more firmly against his grandson's neck. "Yes, your honor," Fietlebaum answered. "I do."

The judge pounded the gavel three times. "We issue commitment order for Teysoot Motzo!" he proclaimed. "He crazy from *leshte po noc*." Then he turned slowly, but intently, toward his fellow Janpooran judge. "Now, you jackass," he said with a smirk, "case closed!"

Upon conclusion of the hearing, Fietlebaum had expected Glesh to loosen his grip on his grandson. He did, but not until after he had drawn the knife ever so slightly through the top layer of scales and skin, allowing a barely perceptible streak of blue blood to slowly rise into the painful, but otherwise harmless wound. Two of his henchmen led Aaron away as Glesh reminded Fietlebaum, "Your cooperation is still expected."

Glesh made certain the transcripts of the hearing, the commitment order, and the diagnosis of *leshte po noc* were widely circulated by Janpooran media. Teysoot Motzo was done. Among the strong-willed, and superstitious laborers of Janpoor, the mere suspicion of *leshte po noc* was a death knell for political power. Their union would not allow itself to be led by one inhabited by a screaming ghost. With commitment, Teysoot Motzo could legally be transported to an off-world, long term facility against his will. Most important to Glesh was that now no one would care.

CHAPTER 17

The plan had been to transfer Teysoot Motzo to a psychiatric hospital on Gajdon, a small, sparsely populated planet in Janpoor's star system. Except for Polmodi, there was no more desolate a place. After his name had faded from public memory, he would be released to Gajdon to live out the rest of his life in obscurity. At least, this is what Fietlebaum had been made to understand. But word came that the deadly and extraordinarily contagious Visuvian Fever had broken out in a mining camp on Gajdon. The Janpooran health authorities placed a quarantine on travel to or from the planet. Until other arrangements were made, Teysoot Motzo would have to stay in Pinshett General Hospital. His intravenous drip of prosteridine was continued, and Fietlebaum was ordered to stay with him and make certain that he remained in his chemically induced coma.

Fietlebaum knew the effects of prosteridine on Teysoot Motzo were diminishing with time. He also suspected the effects of the modified shodom preparation would be wearing off. The following morning, while Kesset was out making new arrangements for transfer, Teysoot Motzo rose a little further out of his state of unconsciousness. Being curious about his condition, Fietlebaum let it happen.

Teysoot Motzo twitched and moaned. He mumbled incoherently. Among the random pieces of "word salad" one particular phrase was uttered repeatedly. But, his speech was so slurred by sedation that the cybertranslater could not make it out. Fietlebaum asked for a statistical analysis of the phonemic structures and the most likely possibilities of what he was saying. The cybertranslater reported that the most likely phrase in the Janpooran language, with confidence limits of 77.3%, was, *zhorvdhoz*, which translated into "dirt bombs." "Why the hell would he say that?" Fietlebaum asked himself. "It makes no sense."

With Teysoot Motzo continuing to repeat the word, "*zhorvdhoz*," Fietlebaum suspected it had to mean something. "Dirt bombs, dirt bombs." All he could make of it was the possibility that Teysoot Motzo was involved in something more sinister than leading his labor union in a rebellion against the government. Perhaps explosives had been buried underground as part of a terrorist plot. But it seemed farfetched. "I can't put stock in the mutterings of a delirious patient," Fietlebaum sighed.

Kesset returned a few hours later. The new plan was to transfer Teysoot Motzo to a Forensic Psychiatric Unit in a far flung outpost on Monton in the Vartan star system. He would leave in three days. Teysoot Motzo remained in the state of delirium, now and then mumbling and repeating the mysterious phrase. It angered Kesset that the state of coma had not been maintained. He cast a dirty look at Fietlebaum and accused him of deliberately failing to adjust Teysoot Motzo's proteridine dose. Kesset inched up the prosteridine level in the intravenous pump to a dangerously high level, and Teysoot Motzo fell silent.

For the rest of the day, Teysoot Motzo's words preyed on Fietlebaum's mind. Perhaps the ominous words were more than the product of chemically induced confusion. Maybe Glesh had been correct to fear the intentions of this Janpooran firebrand. Perhaps he knew of something that Teysoot Motzo had been planning.

The possibility of innocents being killed while there was information to save them was more than Fietlebaum's conscience could bear. He could not allow Teysoot Motzo to remain sedated with lives at risk. *But, what can I do?*

he wondered. Both he and Teysoot Motzo were watched constantly, if not by Kesset, then by a nurse instructed to keep a close eye on them and report back to him with anything she thought suspicious. There was no way he could stop the prosteridine drip for long without being caught and punished. As he considered the problem, something occurred to him.

Fietlebaum sprang up and cried out while clutching his abdomen. He crumpled to his knees and, by every indication, collapsed from intense pain. Kesset was horrified. He tried to rouse Fietlebaum, but he was unresponsive. He frantically ran into the hallway to find medical assistance. Fietlebaum leapt up, and rifled the storage drawers for a new bag of saline. After finding one, he detached Teysoot Motzo's IV line from the bag that contained the prosteridine solution, and replaced it with a new one that contained only saline. He grabbed the bag of prosteridine he had removed, and ran into the restroom that adjoined the room. He slammed the door and disposed of the bag by stuffing it under a layer of paper toweling in the trash can.

Kesset rushed back with a young doctor he had grabbed and was startled to find that Fietlebaum was gone. He looked under furniture and screamed out his name. When Fietlebaum nonchalantly strolled back into the room from the toilet, Kesset was livid. "I thought you were dying!" he shouted at Fietlebaum. "What the hell was wrong with you?" Fietlebaum hiked his shoulders in a shrug of innocence while he patted his belly with both hands. "*Mein kishkes*[88]," he replied.

"You're no psychiatrist," Kesset screamed, "you're a lunatic!"

"*Nu*," Fietlebaum said innocently. "When you gotta go, you gotta go."

---

[88] My guts

"Damn you, Fietlebaum!" Kesset snarled. "Watch him," he ordered the nurse. "He's up to something!" He escaped down the hallway to his office, pushed his way in, and slammed the door shut.

"Something must have upset him," Fietlebaum said to the nurse with feigned surprise and concern. "He's been under a lot of strain lately." She nodded in half-hearted agreement. "This erratic behavior of his is no trivial matter," he added in somber tone. "Galactic Security can't be interested in Teysoot Motzo for nothing." The mention of Galactic Security brought a look of alarm to her face.

Fietlebaum paused for a moment in a portrayal of deep reflection. "Maybe we should tell agent Glesh about these outbursts of his," he said. "What do you think?" he asked her.

"I, I don't know," she said hesitantly. "Maybe we should."

"You're absolutely right!" he exclaimed. "You have me convinced! Kesset has confiscated my communicator. Lend me yours and I'll give Glesh a quick call before he comes back."

He stuck out his hand for the communicator, and before she could think too much about it, she reached into her pocket, grabbed it, and handed it to him.

"No need to drag you into this business," he told her in a voice drenched with fatherly concern. As he said it, he tossed his head in the direction of the door as a suggestion for her to step out into the hallway for moment.

The second she left the room, Fietlebaum called Beshted. He hoped that Beshted's growing fear and loathing of Glesh would lead him to participate in a minor betrayal.

After what seemed an eternity, Beshted answered. "I don't have much time," Fietlebaum told him. "I need an important favor."

"What kind of favor?" Beshted asked cautiously.

"I have to speak with Teysoot Motzo, alone, tonight. I need you to call Kesset away. Perhaps you could use GIA channels to give him an official looking message that he needs to meet Glesh in town."

There was a long silence. Fietlebaum feared he may have overestimated Beshted's willingness to be disloyal. He might call Glesh and tell him of the intrigue he was hatching. Oy! he thought, *I'm dead.* He heard Kesset walking back down the hallway toward Teysoot Motzo's room. His heart pounded. "Alright," Beshted said, then hung up.

As Kesset pushed through the doorway, his communicator buzzed. A text message appeared on his screen. "Damn it!" he exclaimed with stifled anger.

"What's the matter?" Fietlebaum asked.

"None of your goddamn business!" Kesset growled. He turned and stomped back down the hallway toward the elevator. "I'll be back." He got on the elevator, and as the doors were closing he called out, "When I get back, there had better not be anything funny going on."

Fietlebaum found the nurse down the hallway and gave her back her communicator. "Glesh was very pleased to be kept informed," he told her. "It's a good thing you suggested I call him."

"Uhhh, thank you," she replied with bewilderment. "—I think."

Fietlebaum strolled back to Teysoot Motzo's room, sat down, and waited. With no more prosteridine dripping into his veins, Teysoot Motzo began to wake up. His vision was blurry, and his tongue was thick. "*Nu*?" Fietlebaum said while staring intently into Teysoot Motzo's face. "Why do you keep saying *zhorvdhoz*?"

Teysoot Motzo stared up at Fietlebaum and struggled to bring his face into focus. "What you name?" he asked with considerable annoyance. "What you talk about?"

"You said it over and over again while you were delirious from the sedative," Fietlebaum replied. "You kept saying, *zhorvdhoz, zhorvdhoz*!"

"You idiot!" Teysoot Motzo said with a classic Janpooran sneer, "Why in hell I say that? Dirt bomb? Dirt bomb? You crazy! It make no sense!"

"I thought that, too!" Fietlebaum protested. "But you kept on saying it all the same."

"What you name?" Teysoot Motzo again demanded.

"I'm Isaac Fietlebaum. I'm a doctor, and you're in a hospital. We don't have much time. So, tell me. Why did you keep saying *zhorvdhoz*?"

Teysoot Motzo shook the dullness out of his head, then took another moment to clear his thoughts. He slowly realized the nature of the confusion. "I not say *zhorvdhoz*," he growled, "I say jorftoss." Then he paused for effect before repeating the word louder and with exaggerated enunciation, "jorrff-tosss!" The cybertranslator confirmed the word "jorftoss," and added that it was not a Janpooran word. It was Kladagi. The word sounded familiar to Fietlebaum, and he searched his mind for the connection . . . Kladagi . . . jorftoss. Then it occurred to him. "*Oy gevalt!*" he blurted out. Jorftoss was a drug. It was worth a fortune and highly illegal throughout the galaxy. Mere possession of jorftoss was punishable by death. Fietlebaum shook his head in dismay. "*Vey iz mir*," he croaked. "What have I gotten myself into?"

A second later, Kesset stepped off the elevator. Half way to the rendezvous point with Glesh, he had received a second message cancelling the meeting. He was in an ugly mood. Fietlebaum heard his footsteps stomping up the hallway toward Teysoot Motzo's room. *Nu*? he muttered. "Moishe Pupik[89] is back.

"Quick," he told Teysoot Motzo, "scream."

"You crazy?" Teysoot Motzo replied.

"Scream, damn it, trust me!" Fietlebaum insisted.

---

89 Moishe Bellybutton, best thought of as Mr. Nobody.

Teysoot Motzo screamed a series of loud, blood curdling screams. Kesset broke into a sprint down the hallway. He rounded the corner into the room and found Fietlebaum bending over Teysoot Motzo. "Quick!" Fietlebaum ordered him, "go get the nurse, he needs a shot of prosteridine! *Stat*!"

Teysoot Motzo lifted his head and cried, "no more that stuff!" Fietlebaum pinched him, hard, and he screamed again, this time quite involuntarily. Kesset ran and got a nurse, who followed him back with a syringe full of prosteridine. Just before they raced in, Fietlebaum used his sharp Hijdori teeth to bite a little hole in the saline bag that fed the intravenous pump, and the remaining fluid in the bag drained out.

The nurse hurriedly injected Teysoot Motzo, and he quickly fell back into sedation. Kesset noticed the deflated bag. "The bag ran dry!" he screamed with annoyance. "Don't you watch for these things?" he angrily inquired of the nurse. Fietlebaum stood behind Kesset and, beyond his field of vision, slowly shook his head and waved his palms to advise the nurse to simply be quiet and let Kesset vent. He gave the impression that he was looking out for her. She apologized and hung another bag of prosteridine solution. The solution flowed, and Teysoot Motzo remained quiet for the rest of the night.

Fietlebaum was exhausted by it all. "What a day," he told himself as he prepared to go to sleep on a cot next to Teysoot Motzo. As he lay there he thought of all that had happened. The transfer had been postponed and now the destination of the transfer was changed. He had risked his neck getting Teysoot Motzo out of his drug-induced coma, if only a little while. His suspicion that Teysoot Motzo might be involved in terrorism had all been the workings of his imagination. But, he had learned something just as ominous—that he was in some way tied up in the jorftoss trade.

Fietlebaum's thoughts drifted toward what degree Glesh might also be involved in jorftoss trafficking. He recalled thinking that Teysoot Motzo had spoken his name, perhaps after seeing Kesset and mistaking him for Glesh. He had then suspected that it was only his imagination. Now, he wasn't so sure. All the while he had been concerned about Glesh's ruthless behavior as an agent of the Galactic government. But if he was acting outside of his role as a government agent, if he was acting as a criminal, then what wouldn't he do to get his way? *This is dangerous business,* he realized. At least Beshted had sided with him against Glesh. That was one comfort to embrace.

As he was about to drop off to sleep, the nurse who was complicit in his earlier scheme crept into the room. She appeared nervous, glanced around the room to make sure no one was watching, then handed Fietlebaum a small, folded piece of paper. "I was told this was very important," she whispered. Then she quickly scooted back out into the hallway. It was a message from Beshted. It read, "When Teysoot Motzo arrives on Monton, Glesh is going to have him killed."

"*Oy*," Fietelbaum sighed. "Of *course* he's going to have him killed. I should have seen this coming." He got up off the cot and paced the floor. "I won't be a party to something like this," he said to himself. "I won't be involved in the cold-blooded murder of another sentient being, no matter how unsavory he might be. *Shoyn genug*[90]." He looked upon Teysoot Motzo, who again lay sedated and helpless in his bed, and the ancient words of the Hippocratic Oath came to his mind—*I will prescribe regimens for the good of my patients according to my ability and my judgment, and never do harm to anyone.*

What have I done? he thought. He stepped over to the big Janpooran and whispered in his ear, "I'm getting you out of here."

---

[90] Enough already

CHAPTER 18

Fietlebaum needed a way out, and there wasn't much time. Arrangements had been made to transport him and Teysoot Motzo to Monton the following morning. He had just over twenty-four hours. After a night of thinking, and a lot of tossing and turning, he hatched a plan.

Fietlebaum got up and looked for the nurse who had the previous day lent him her communicator. "Good news!" he whispered to her when he found her in the medication room. "Agent Glesh was so grateful to hear about Kesset's odd behavior that he wants to reward everyone involved in passing on that information. I told him I would get back to him with your name. That is, if you agree."

"I don't see why not," she said, trying but failing to hide her excitement over attention from the galactic government.

Fietlebaum stuck out his hand, and after a moment to realize what it was he wanted, she handed him her communicator. He snatched it out of her hand, strolled to the toilet, closed the door, and called Beshted.

"There is another, bigger favor I need from you, my friend," he told Beshted. "There is an instrument maker in town. His name is Thabah Gossoff. At one time, he worked in the Physics Department at The Silesian Planetary University constructing equipment for their experiments. I never met him, but I heard he does excellent work. He retired from the University and returned to Janpoor. He opened a shop in Pinshett to keep busy. I want you to visit him."

He heard footsteps in the hallway that stopped beside the door. "*Oy*!" he loudly moaned. "*Mein kiskehs*! Never eat hospital food! *Drek* they serve here, pure *drek*!" The footsteps quickly led the interloper away down the hall.

"Now, listen very carefully," Fietelbaum continued. "Ask him to make a minibot. It must move, about ten feet per second, in random directions, and it must be resilient enough to bounce off walls without damage. Most importantly, it must carry a powerful magnetic field generator, at least 500,000 gauss, and have enough battery strength to run for fifteen minutes. Insist that it be finished tonight. Tell Thabah Gossoff that I will pay him double what he would ordinarily ask for if he can get it done by then. Tell him my life depends on it. When you get it, send the news back to me somehow, and I will send word to you what to do with it."

"I understand," Beshted replied before clicking off his communicator.

Fietlebaum secreted the communicator back to its owner, then set to work. By this time, Kesset was keeping tight rein on him. He was no longer allowed to leave the hospital. Thus, he asked permission to use the hospital's lab and synthetic equipment under the pretense that he had to come up with some way to lessen the adverse effects the prolonged prosteridine treatment was having on Teysoot Motzo. His suggestion that Teysoot Motzo might die before being transported off Janpoor scared the hell out of Kesset. He granted him the request. He sent an orderly along to prevent any "funny business."

Fietlebaum needed antidotes, but not for Teysoot Motzo. His goal was to reverse the psychotherapeutic effects of medications used to treat a few of the most psychotic patients on the psychiatric ward. In many psychotic illnesses, too much of a natural neurotransmitter in the brain resulted in the over-activation of its matching set of receptors. The medication acted by binding to those receptors, but blocking rather than activating them. This antagonism of neurotransmitter over-activity was keeping many of the patients on the acute psychiatric ward of Pinshett General Hospital calm, pleasant and relatively reasonable. To reverse the therapeutic effects of the medication, he would have to chemically alter the molecule so that, like the natural neurotransmitter, it activated rather than blocked the receptor. The most dramatic effects would be obtained if the medication were altered in such a way as to make it far more effective than the natural neurotransmitter itself.

Fietlebaum reviewed the pharmacology of the medications that maintained the civility of two of the biggest, strongest, and potentially craziest Janpoorans on the ward. He also studied the medication that calmed a Gorsidian patient who, at the time of her admission, was suffering a florid paranoid psychosis. Although the Janpoorans were strong and intimidating, the Gorsid was fast, slippery, and had six tentacles that could be very difficult to restrain if her behavior deteriorated. It would literally be like trying to slap hand cuffs on an octopus. He anticipated chaos.

Fietlebaum's computer analysis of the medications gave indications as to what modifications might be made to each psychotherapeutic molecule to achieve the effect he desired. If modified properly, the altered molecules should make the recipients even crazier than they were before receiving treatment. He entered the planned modifications of the molecules into his computer and ran simulations of their actions at their respective receptors. Theoretically, at least, they worked like a charm. He programmed the pharmacosynthesizer to produce the new molecules. He synthesized enough for a hefty dose of reversing drug for each of the three target patients on the ward. He then dissolved each drug in an aliquot of dimethylsulfoxide, a unique organic solvent that would not only dissolve the drugs, but also carry them into the bodies of the patients if the solution was splashed on their skin.

After a long morning of work, he placed three separate vials of medication antidotes into his pocket. As he was walking out of the hospital lab, with the supervising orderly in tow, he spotted a maintenance worker. He asked him for an instrument derived from older, more primitive technology—a small crow bar. "I've got a sticky drawer upstairs," he explained. The maintenance worker handed him the crow bar. "Bring it back when you're done with it," he called out as Fietlebaum left. "I don't wanna have to pay to replace it!"

Early the next morning, Fietlebaum uncapped the vials of the counteractive medications he had created, and surreptitiously splashed them on the respective recipient's skin. Then he strolled back to Teysoot Motzo's room and shut off the intravenous pump that pulsed prosteridine into his bloodstream. He prayed that Beshted would be able to enter the hospital with the minibot without difficulty. He knew that Beshted would not be able to access the psychiatric ward where he and Teysoot Motzo were, as Kesset would have immediately called hospital security. But, he figured that getting on to the floor above would be less problematic. The only remaining problem would be waiting to see if the device that Thabah Gossoff had built would work.

Fietlebaum breathed a sigh of relief when a sympathetic nurse informed him that Beshted had arrived at the hospital with the "package." He trusted her to return to Beshted a folded piece of paper with instructions. "A matter of life or death," he told her. As Fietlebaum had requested in the note, Beshted placed the minibot on the floor of the hallway directly above the spot where, in the hallway of the floor below, the magnetically hallucinating Rodrantian had permanently launched himself against the wall. He switched on the magnetic field. For the first time in months, the Rodrantian stood erect and stretched his head toward the new source of magnetic attraction. Beshted flipped the switch to activate the minibot's motion, then walked away.

The minibot took off. The Rodrantian on the floor below took off as well, following the path of the magnetic field generator, matching precisely its speed and direction. The minibot collided into the wall and bounced off in the respective angle of reflection. The Rodrantian simultaneously collided with the wall on the floor below and ran off at the identical angle in pursuit of the minibot's magnetic signal. Unfortunately, while the minibot's pathway was clear, the Rodrantian's pathway was blocked by the breakfast cart that was at that moment being wheeled down the hallway. He collided with the cart. Trays, plates, and food went flying. Torrents of juice splashed out across the hallway. The Rodrantian spun and fell on the slippery floor, flailed his arms and legs in a fight for balance, then continued his desperate pursuit of the new magnetic core of his psychic existence. He trampled patients in his way and pushed aside staff that sought to restrain him. Patients, nurses, and orderlies slid across the slick hallway, crashed into doors, walls, and each other. The Rodrantian continued his pursuit, speeding up, turning, stopping, pirouetting, leaping, and anything else he had to do to maintain his proximity to the newer, stronger, magnetic homing signal. Alarms were sounded, "Code 99" was frantically and repeatedly called over the intercom, security teams were marshaled.

Meanwhile, the potions that Fietlebaum had splashed on the patients to reverse the therapeutic effects of the psychotropic drugs were starting to produce their desired effects. Three patients who had for weeks been calm and cooperative, suddenly relapsed into the behaviors that first brought them to the psychiatric unit. The larger Janpooran screamed and waved his arms. When one of the hospital security guards ran by him on his way to subdue the Rodrantian, the Janpooran grabbed him and hurled him back up the hallway, knocking over guards, patients, and hospital staff like so many bowling pins. Apparently the guard, a newly hired Ergastian immigrant to Janpoor, resembled the apparition that had for years been haunting the nightmares of the Janpooran patient. Now the Janpooran wanted to end the torment once and for all. He ran up the hallway in pursuit of the Ergastian, screaming, crying, and expressing every intention to rip the hapless guard's limbs off.

By this time, the Rodrantian had followed the magnetic siren's song to the nurse's station. He slammed into the glass partition, shattered sheets of glass, and sent papers, pills, and patients flying into the air. The second Janpooran that had been splashed with counter-therapeutic solution was one of the patients the Rodrantian sent flying. He wailed, cried, and climbed into a frantic state of dysphoric mania. He scrambled up off the floor where he had landed and took off in pursuit of the Rodrantian, who by that time had followed the minibot's signal back up the hallway where he had first collided with the breakfast cart.

Kesset heard the commotion and peeked out of Teysoot Motzo's seclusion room into the hallway onto the scene of bedlam. "My God!" he exclaimed. "What the hell is going on?" "Stay here!" he barked to Fietlebaum, as he ran out to join the effort to quell the disturbance. He commanded the first orderly he saw to go back and keep an eye on him.

About this time the Gorsidian recipient of Fietlebaum's concoction had begun to twitch and entertain suspicions about the hospital staff. As Kesset ran past the increasingly disgruntled creature, she shot out two tentacles and wrapped them around his legs like an Argentinean bolo. He fell on his face. As he lay moaning on the floor he was trampled by the Rodrantian who had yet again reversed his direction, and soon after trampled again by the screaming Janpooran who was pursuing him up and down the hallway.

The Gorsid made a loud, long gurgling sound, and reeled Kesset in. "Oh shit!" is what the cybertranslater made of Kesset's last words.

Teysoot Motzo had also begun to stir. He sat up and shook off the chemical haze he had been under. Fietlebaum grabbed him, warned him to be quiet, and told the big Janpooran to follow him. With chaos as their cover, they ran to the back door of the ward, where Fietlebaum handed Teysoot Motzo the crow bar. "Pry it open, and let's get the hell out of here!" he said. Teysoot Motzo slid the crow bar between the door and its frame, leaned his full weight against it, and cracked it open in seconds flat. They ran out into the stairwell and started down before Fietlebaum reminded Teysoot Motzo to stop and toss the crow bar back through the door onto the ward. "I promised not to run off with it," he explained.

The two of them ran down the three flights of stairs to the ground floor. "We'll catch a cab," Fietlebaum spat out between gasps for breath. They stumbled outside to the street, flagged down an aircab, and jumped in. Before the cabbie could ask about the destination, Fietlebaum yelled, "Just go!"

The cabbie did a double take, and turned around to better see his passengers. "Teysoot Motzo?" the cabbie asked as he shot off into the air lanes. "I thought you go crazy."

"Hah!" Teysoot Motzo bellowed. He made a fist, shoved it into the cabbie's face and said, "I show you crazy! Now shut up and fly!"

"We fly!" the cabbie replied as he slammed and banged his way into the line of traffic. "Where we go?" he finally thought to ask.

Fietlebaum suspected it would be unwise to show up at the Pinshett starport, and decided the starport in the smaller, nearby city, Kintot, would be the wiser choice. "Kintot Transgalactic Starport!" he called out.

"Pinshett Starport much closer," the cabbie observed. Teysoot Motzo displayed his fist again, and the cabbie sang out, "Kintot Starport, here we come!"

As they took off, Fietlebaum realized that none of his plans extended beyond getting out of the hospital. He had given no thought as to where they would go once they got to the starport. He had to get himself and Teysoot Motzo to safety. Most importantly, he had to get his grandson back. But, he had no idea how he would accomplish these things. He was then struck by the sobering thought that his helping Teysoot Motzo escape would put Aaron at even greater risk. "*Oy*!" he groaned. He felt helpless and confused. His head ached.

On the way, Fietlebaum revealed to Teysoot Motzo all that had taken place. This was partly out of obligation to him, and partly as a means to think out loud. He told how Glesh had taken his grandson, and how he had tortured the boy. He explained how Glesh had coerced him into finding a way to make him look crazy and have him taken to the psychiatric hospital. "You clever boy, Fietlebaum," Teysoot Motzo had to admit. "That shodom wicked bad!"

"It sure was!" Fietlebaum gushed, until a pang of remorse swept the enthusiasm away. He apologized for everything he had done, but insisted he had no choice. He swore to Teysoot Motzo that he had no idea Glesh had planned to kill him.

Teysoot Motzo laughed. "You funny boy," he said. "Kill mean nothing for Glesh. He no care for me, no care for you, no care for you grandson. Jorftoss all he care about."

"So," Fietlebaum exclaimed, "Glesh *is* involved in the jorftoss trade!"

"Hah!" Teysoot Motzo laughed. "Glesh up to his skinny little Drajan ass in jorftoss!"

"*Oy, gevalt,*" Fietlebaum sighed as he shook his head. "What do we do now?"

"Listen, Fietlebaum," Teysoot Motzo said with sudden and uncharacteristic gravity. "If we got jorftoss, we got power. If Glesh got jorftoss, we got dead! Jorftoss only on Sholoso. So, we got go Sholoso."

"*Nu*," Fietlebaum said with a shrug. "I guess we go to Sholoso"

CHAPTER 19

Fietlebaum had learned of jorftoss many years before while he was in medical school. Professor Zort Broslip, a Kladagi endocrinologist and ethnobotanist, had been assigned to lecture the pharmacobotany class. But one day, as he made his way to the podium, it was evident that something was wrong. He looked fatigued and disheveled. When he got to the podium he stood silent for a long moment, as if lost. "If you could save a life," he haltingly began, "you would not hesitate to put your skills to use." He paused, glanced nervously to his side, then shook his head defiantly at someone in the wings before turning his face back to the auditorium. "Why then," he asked plaintively, "would you hesitate to extend that life?"

Fietlebaum and other students heard a commotion from behind the stage. Silesian and Drajan agents, wearing the black uniforms of the Galactic Contraband Interception Squad had gathered. They edged their way onto the stage. Broslip discerned their intentions, and his lecture quickly degenerated into a rant. "Jorftoss is a gift from God!" he cried. "They conspire to steal God's own gift of life from our hands!" As the agents approached, he scuttled toward the front of the stage to escape, but was apprehended. "You've no right!" he bellowed at the agents that surrounded and laid hands on him. He kicked and screamed as they dragged him off. "You're killing my father!" he screamed. "Murder! Murder!" The distraught dean of students rushed to the podium and cancelled the class. "Go study in the library," he called out to the students, before he himself was led off by the agents for questioning.

The confused and troubled young Fietlebaum sought out Dr. Pesht Meshond, his professor and mentor, for an explanation. He knocked on Meshond's door, and the old Silesian professor called him in. "I shouldn't discuss this with you, Isaac," Meshond said after hearing what had happened. "The powers that be have decided that jorftoss is a legal issue, not a medical one. It's not an appropriate subject."

But Fietlebaum was insistent. "I'm sorry, sir," he confessed, "but I don't understand. Professor Broslip was arrested, and he suggested that it was only for trying to save his father's life? How could that be a crime, and what could this plant, jorftoss, have to do with it?"

Meshond sighed deeply. He laid his glasses on his desk, leaned back and folded his hands. "I wanted to avoid a conversation like this," he said wearily, "but I owe a bright young fellow like you an explanation." He paused for prudent reflection, but in a sudden betrayal of his customary pedagogical reserve, he thrust his head toward Fietlebaum and pronounced with a scowl, "To hell with the Galactic Contraband Interception Squad!"

Abandoning any further pretense, he continued more candidly. "Do you know of the Chang Tze procedure?" Meshond asked.

"No, sir," Fietlebaum reluctantly admitted.

"Well, that's good," Meshond said, "because you shouldn't." He shifted in his seat, trying to find a comfortable position for the uncomfortable conversation. "As you know," he continued, "it's genetic factors that determine the length of life of beings in the galaxy. One common mechanism of ageing is the shortening of telomeres on the ends of chromosomes. Telomeres are clipped off each time a strand of DNA is replicated, and when the last telomere is gone, a cell can no longer divide and replace itself. Like sand through an hour glass—when the last telomere is clipped off, your time is up. Another genetic mechanism is apoptosis, or what is often called the program of cellular suicide. Both lead the individual down the pathway to death."

Fietlebaum nodded in recognition. "Yes," he said, "I'm familiar with those processes."

"As well you should be," Meshond noted before he went on. "Other systems, ones that maintain the body and protect it from invaders or internal rebellions of cancer cells, then begin to fail, also according to genetic time tables. Regardless of the species, death is no accident. It's a natural, finely regulated process."

Meshond was treading on dangerous ground. Getting closer to the heart of the matter, he paused, cleared his throat, then continued his explanation. "It was the human molecular geneticist, Chang Tze, who discovered that most of the genetic mechanisms that lead to death could be over-ridden. He developed what came to be known as the Chang Tze procedure. It was a step down the pathway to immortality."

"What did it involve?" Fietlebaum inquired.

Meshond looked intently at Fietlebaum. "The Chang Tze procedure was a grueling one," he asserted. "A virus vector, which varied according to species, was used to transfect the patient and carry new genetic information into his body. One goal of the transfection was to insert variants of telomerase DNA into cells to maintain the capacity for replication of genetic material.

"That would stop the flow of sand through the hour glass," Fietelbaum interjected.

"Yes, very good," Meshond replied with a nod of appreciation. "You're a bright fellow, Fietelbaum." Meshond repositioned himself and continued his explanation. "In the Chang Tze procedure," he went on to say, "the apoptosis genes were also manipulated to prevent cell death while still allowing the weeding out of abnormal cells, such as cancer cells. Genes engineered to stimulate mitochondrial replication were transfected to maintain optimal cellular energy production. To maintain vitality of the body, his process included yearly administration of stem cells into organs that had weakened. That replenished the population of healthy cells in those tissues."

Meshond stopped and nodded thoughtfully. "The procedure was quite effective," he said with obvious admiration. "Chang Tze himself was the first to undergo the process, and he lived to the age of two-hundred and thirty-seven years before he finally succumbed to old age."

But Fietlebaum remained puzzled. "I realize that two-hundred and thirty-seven years is a long life for a human," he protested, "but that certainly isn't immortality. And what does jorftoss have to do with it all?"

"Be patient, young Fietlebaum," Meshond gently admonished, "I will tell you."

"While the Chang Tze procedure prolonged life well beyond the expected range," Meshond went on to say, "it had serious, often fatal drawbacks. The virus used to transfect genetic information into the cells could cause life-threatening infections and allergic reactions. In some species, the fatality rate of the procedure approached twenty-five percent. Moreover, as you correctly pointed out, while the procedure tripled or even quadrupled one's lifespan, it could not extend life indefinitely. Of course, the procedure was also extremely expensive." He paused again for effect. "Jorftoss resolved the first two problems," he said, "but it greatly compounded the third."

"What does the jorftoss do?" Fietelbaum inquired.

"I'll try to explain," Meshond answered. "There are over 100 quadrillion known plant species in the galaxy, and many of them produce complex chemical substances. It was a statistical certainty that somewhere in the galaxy there would be a plant whose cellular machinery synthesized substances that could promote longevity. It happened that one such plant grew in the high mountains of Kladag. It was referred to by the native species as "jorftoss," which in their language meant, "God leaves." For thousands of years, the Kladagi prized the plant. They believed it increased strength and resilience to stress. It improved endurance, enlivened the old and frail, and improved memory and concentration. They used it as a tonic for all their ills. It was fundamental to their folk medicine."

"Many important medications were initially discovered from refinement of herbal folk preparations," Fietlebaum pointed out.

"You are quite correct," Meshond replied in validation, "and the initial scientific evaluations of jorftoss confirmed remarkable benefits from its ingestion. The substances in the plant's leaves were found to bolster the immune system. They protected against oxidation, inflammation, and other enemies of cellular integrity. They stopped cross-linkage of proteins, protein glycation, and other destructive processes of ageing."

Meshond's communicator buzzed. It was his secretary. "Dr. Meshond," she said anxiously, "the Galactic Contraband Interception Squad is interviewing the faculty and demanding to speak to you."

"Tell them they'll have to wait," Meshond replied, "I'm with a student."

He looked at Fietlebaum, nodded in a gesture of self-affirmation, and continued. "What was remarkable about jorftoss," he further explained, "was that the large, multi-ringed molecules it contained were extraordinarily pleomorphic. That is, they possessed the ability to twist and turn through various confirmations, each of which was pharmacologically active in different ways."

"Like having ten medications in one," Fietlebaum volunteered.

"Exactly," Meshond responded. "Good observation!" he added with a wink. "The chemical, genetic, and enzymatic mechanisms that mediated the genetic determinants of longevity varied considerably from species to species. However, there was something about the collection of pleomorphic molecules in jorftoss that gave it the ability to benefit individuals of most species across the galaxy." He paused, then noted, "Pure chance, I suspect."

Then Meshond leaned forward to deliver the thrust of the explanation. "Jorftoss saved most patients from the life-threatening infections and allergic reactions from the viral transfections of the Chang Tze procedure. But most remarkably," he asserted, "studies showed that in those that underwent the procedure, intravenous administration of extracts of jorftoss tremendously increased its effectiveness. For reasons that no one completely understood, it appeared to give virtual immortality. In the four-hundred years since the development of that technology, individuals of a number of relatively short-lived species have been reported to have lived through twenty-five life expectancies without natural death or significant decline in vital capacity. To the best of our knowledge, they remain alive."

"Then jorftoss works!" Fietlebaum exclaimed.

"Yes," Meshond admitted with a sigh. "The evidence suggests that it does."

"But why," Fietlebaum asked, "would such a miraculous treatment be outlawed?"

"I understand your confusion," Meshond replied. "Eternal life would seem a magnificent gift. But in reality, the promise of immortality brings catastrophic problems."

"Why?" Fietlebaum asked incredulously.

Meshond sighed again. "You are young," he said, "but at some time in our lives life, most of us ordinary individuals with ordinary lifespans, come to terms with the fact of our impermanence. While sad and disillusioning, the humbling recognition of the transient nature of life is a prerequisite for love, sacrifice, and courage. It is the dues we pay to become full members of the family of living, sentient beings." He paused again to find the best words to explain the phenomenon. "On the other hand," he continued, "experience has taught us that the mere possibility of eternal life breeds utter ruthlessness. Those that purchased the promise of immortality allowed nothing to jeopardize it. Since only the extremely wealthy could afford the treatments, those same individuals had tremendous resources at their disposal to zealously guard against any compromises of the physical existence that was imperiled no longer by time, but only by accident or malice aforethought. Mere suspicions of threat became paranoid delusions, and delusions led to acts of murderous rampage. The "immortals" spared no effort or cruelty to insure their supply of jorftoss. Lying, stealing, and killing, were of no consequence to them when eternal life was at stake. As the numbers of those receiving the Change Tze procedure and jorftoss supplementation increased, the numbers of incidents of murder, blackmail and corruption soared."

His communicator buzzed again. It was his secretary. "They demand to see you now, sir, and they won't take 'no' for an answer."

"I understand," Meshond replied with a scowl. "Tell them I shall be there shortly"

"It was for those reasons," he went on to say, "that the Chang Tze procedure and jorftoss were banned throughout the galaxy. All of the jorftoss growing in the tropical jungles of Kladag was rooted out and destroyed. Those that cultivated the plant had their lands confiscated, and those that trafficked in jorftoss were sentenced to death. That is the way it remains."

Meshond stopped and simply stared at his desk for a moment. "But all sentient beings are greedy," he added in reflection. "You will discover that as you grow older, Isaac. They are greedy for life and greedy for money. Thus, trade in jorftoss simply went deep underground. Cultivation of the plant spread to neighboring planets and moons where geography and climate were similar enough to those of Kladag for small plots of jorftoss to be planted and carefully nursed to maturity. The illegal trade generated enormous profits for those brave or foolish enough to risk the consequences. Unfortunately, the fight for control of the galaxy's only pathway to never ending life has continued to spread violence and death across the stars."

Meshond stood up. "Speak to no one of this conversation," he sternly warned Fietlebaum, "for both of our sakes. In fact, I suggest you forget all about it."

"Thank you, sir," Fietlebaum replied, "I won't bring it up again." Then the two of them walked out, Fietlebaum to return to his dormitory room, and Meshond to the dean's office to placate the Galactic Contraband Interception Squad.

Soon afterward, Fietlebaum learned that Professor Broslip had been convicted of possession of jorftoss and transferring it to his ill father. He was sentenced to death and executed. His name was stricken from the University's records. The incident was never discussed, and Fietlebaum all but forgot about it. He didn't hear the word, "jorftoss" again until forty years later when he heard it uttered by the half-delirious Teysoot Motzo while strapped to his bed in the psychiatric ward of Pinshett General Hospital.

"*Nu*?" Fietlebaum told himself, as he boarded the starship to Sholoso with Teysoot Motzo. "I could have waited a little longer."

CHAPTER 20

A day away from Sholoso, the starship sprang back to life. Artificial intelligence systems snapped back into being. Cabin lights flashed on. Life support systems switched from life suspension to reanimation mode. Heaters and fluid pumps kicked into operation, and oxygen and water generators hummed. The glass lids of the life suspension chambers popped open.

Fietlebaum hated the transition from suspended animation into consciousness. He had gone through it scores of times, but had never gotten used to it. The sensations he felt were similar to those one might describe in a leg that had "gone to sleep" after resting too long in an awkward position. However, in awakening from this form of sleep, the prickling, tingling, and oxymoronic painful numbness seemed to arise from every fiber in his being. Even his thoughts felt tingly and raw.

Teysoot Motzo was in the life suspension chamber next to his. He groaned as he slowly rose to a sitting position. "Fietlebaum," he said. "Fietlebaum, that you?

"Yes," Fietlebaum said, "it's me."

"Fietlebaum," Teysoot Motzo croaked. "Pity me. I feel like hell!"

"You look like hell, too," Fietlebaum confirmed.

"Hah, you funny boy, Fietlebaum," Teysoot Motzo responded. Then he groaned once more and lowered himself back down onto the chamber bed to rest a moment before attempting to get up again.

Fietlebaum climbed out of his chamber and stepped over to help Teysoot Motzo out of his. Then the two of them crept slowly to the observation gallery to sit and regain some equilibrium. They sat and gazed out upon the vast expanse of space through the gallery's large polycarbonate viewing panels. Sholoso's star, Morvoa, shone brilliantly, and the planet itself had swung into view. It appeared as a bright, white and red speckled ball, the size of a full moon in the Earth sky.

"It's beautiful, isn't it? Fietlebaum said.

"Enjoy now, Fietlebaum," Teysoot Motzo said with a rueful laugh. "You not think that when we there."

The starship fell into orbit around Sholoso. Fietlebaum waited for the deceleration that would mark descent to the surface, but it didn't happen. Instead, the public address system announced that transport craft would be launched to ferry passengers to the planet.

"Why isn't the starship landing?" he asked Teysoot Motzo.

"Sholoso dangerous place," he replied.

"Then why are we going there?"

"No need for worry," Teysoot Motzo told him. "You just follow me."

They climbed onto one of the communal transport capsules and it descended to the surface of Sholoso. As they stepped out onto the surface, Teysoot Motzo warned Fietlebaum, "If you want stay alive on Sholoso, you better watch out. They wicked mean here. They *crazy*, wicked mean since Jorftoss start for die."

"What?" Fietlebaum asked incredulously. "The jorftoss is dying?"

"Yes," Teysoot Motzo replied.

"Why?" Fietlebaum implored.

"Nobody know. Plant get sick. Plant die. All across galaxy, farmers watch jorftoss shrivel up. Now, jorftoss grow only on Sholoso. Big-heads think bug, maybe virus, killing jorftoss, but nothing they can do about it."

"Why didn't you tell me this?" Fietlebaum demanded to know.

Teysoot Motzo shrugged. "You not ask."

Something occurred to Fietlebaum. "If the jorftoss is dying," he said to Teysoot Motzo, "and the supply is disappearing, then the jorftoss you can get a hold of must be worth a fortune." Teysoot Motzo nodded his head affirmatively. Does this have something to do with Glesh trying to have you killed?"

"Hah!" Teysoot Motzo laughed, "You clever boy, Fietlebaum!"

"*Gevalt*!" Fietlebaum cried, "My grandson is kidnapped, and I'm on this *farkakteh* planet on the other side of the galaxy because you and Glesh are in a drug war?" He was disgusted and infuriated. However, realizing that this was not a good time or place to alienate Teysoot Motzo, he struggled to rein in his anger. "Okay," he said with resignation. "Now what do we do?"

"That easy," Teysoot Motzo replied. "Only jorftoss left in universe is what grow on Sholoso. Everywhere else, jorftoss dead. We buy up all jorftoss on Sholoso. Then Glesh in big trouble, 'cause he got keep customers happy. We make deal with Glesh. We all make big money."

"But he has my grandson," Fietlebaum reminded him. "That's the only reason I'm here."

"Glesh only care about jorftoss and money bag. We make big money and make bargain with Glesh. That get you grandson back."

"Do you have any money to buy up the jorftoss?" Fietlebaum thought to inquire.

"Well, no," Teysoot Motzo admitted, "But my credit good. Everybody know Teysoot Motzo!"

"That's what I'm afraid of," Fietlebaum replied.

The sarcasm wasn't wasted on Teysoot Motzo. His face flushed a vivid green. He cast six wary eyes at Fietlebaum, and for a moment he looked as though he might rip his ears off. But he laughed and let it go. They hailed an aircab to take them on into Dasholos, the only city—really nothing more than a little town—on Sholoso, where they could rent a room, rest, and think things through.

An aircab dropped out of the pink Sholoson sky, and Fietlebaum and Teysoot Motzo climbed in. The pilot was an Astaran. "Good morning," the cabbie said. The gravelly, honking sound of his voice carried Fietlebaum's thoughts back to the death bed of Lors Argsglar, the Astaran who had so catastrophically sought God. The tortured cry of "*ghomgijdahm*" boomed in his head. He heard the death rattles in Argsglar's throat. He extricated himself from the memory of the hospital room and refocused his attention to this Astaran on Sholoso. "Good morning," Fietlebaum replied.

There were a many of his amphibian species on the planet. They felt at home in the swamps and steamy climate of Sholoso. Their drab, unassuming personalities allowed them to assimilate without difficulties into the culture that greatly resented intrusion. No Sholoson had aspirations to pilot an aircab, which left the Astaran immigrants free to quickly corner the aircab market. It was a source of pride for them. *Like the pride of being the world's tallest midget,* Fietlebaum surmised.

"To the hotel?" the Astaran asked them.

After learning that there was only one hotel on the planet, Fietlebaum simply answered, "Yes."

The transports had landed at the starport situated several miles outside of Dasholos, thus the flight into town allowed Fietlebaum his first brief glimpse of the Sholoson landscape. As Teysoot Motzo had suggested, Sholoso was far more beautiful from space than it was from the surface of the planet. The striking red and white speckles he had so admired from 400,000 miles away were expanses of iron rich swamp water and miasmic fog, respectively. It was oppressively hot. There was a damp, rottenness in the air.

Aside from jorftoss growing well in its swamp lands, there was little else to distinguish the planet. Hundreds of years before, the planet had been mined for its iron ore by off-world companies funded by Silesian and Drusidi venture capitalists. If it wasn't for the investments and improvements the companies had made during that period of mining, there probably would not have been any development on Sholoso—no Dasholos, no roads, no starport.

The Sholosons themselves rarely travelled, and almost never patronized the starport. Most had no desire to live in Dasholos's manufactured housing, preferring to live in their mud huts in the swamps. The town itself was a hodgepodge of modular buildings in various states of ruin. When a building became too dilapidated to occupy, a new modular building was slapped together nearby. If the occupants of the new building fell down on their luck, a common occurrence in Sholoso's shaky economy, they simply moved back into the old dilapidated one and made do. Nothing was ever torn down in Dasholos.

The aircab glided to a stop in front of one of the larger ramshackle structures that Fietlebaum correctly assumed was the Dasholos Hotel. Out of the corner of his eye, he caught sight of someone coming out the door toward the cab. When he reflexively turned to face the approaching Sholoson security guard, a sudden and spontaneous wave of revulsion swept over him. Sholosons were, charitably speaking, unusual in appearance.

Anatomy, facial structure, aesthetic sense, and taste varied considerably across the galaxy. There was astonishing variety in the appearances of hundreds of species. There was also remarkable tolerance for differences. Still, the general consensus among the various sentient beings in the galaxy was that Sholosons were ugly. Their exteriors were marked by large, irregularly shaped, randomly placed holes lined with pheromone-secreting excretory glands. In many respects, their skin resembled the cut surface of a large round of Swiss cheese. The major distinction between their external surface and that of the cheese was that their skins were bright red in color and in-between the holes sprouted large, sharp spines similar to those of African porcupines. Only a practiced eye could discriminate males from females. Sholosons themselves often made mistakes.

Their legs and feet had evolved to negotiate the swamps and mud flats of Sholoso. Their legs were spindly but strong, and their feet were large and round. In embryological development, isolated sections of flesh between the pedal bones withdrew to create holes through the feet. These holes served to relieve the vacuum created while lifting the large foot up out of mud. From a distance, they appeared to be walking around on snow shoes. Their four spindly arms ended in three-fingered hands. The ipsilateral pairs of arms were often used locked together in tandem, with the resulting coupled hands being extremely strong and versatile in their actions. Sholoson heads were shaped like bullets, with unruly patches of porcupine-like spines at the point. With so many of the aforementioned holes all over their exteriors, it was sometimes difficult to distinguish the holes on their heads that served as eyes, olfactory sensors, and mouth.

As Fietlebaum would soon discover, the temperaments of the Sholosons were as ugly as their bodies, perhaps uglier. They would *kvetch* and complain over the most trivial concerns. They fought at the drop of a hat, and if you offended a Sholoson, you made an enemy for life. Their language sounded very much like the sounds made by cats screeching at romantic rivals. There was no word for loyalty in the language. The only redeeming feature of the Sholosons was their greed for money and the weapons it could buy them. Certainly, greed is rarely considered a redeeming quality, but in the case of Sholosons, it was the one thing that could be depended upon to dissuade them from truly vicious and disgusting behavior. Of course, this quality entailed their willingness to go to any length to punish anyone foolish enough to steal money from them or hedge on a deal.

The hotel's Sholoson security guard strutted up and demanded that the Astaran open the door of the cab. He gave Fietlebaum a perfunctory frisking, then turned to Teysoot Motzo. "Hands up, fatso," he commanded. When he finished frisking Teysoot Motzo, he begrudgingly nodded an acceptance and stepped back out of the way. After Fietlebaum regained his composure, he grabbed his bag and climbed out of the cab. Teysoot Motzo, who had no composure to lose, followed suit. They walked to the door, bags in hand, and waited momentarily in expectation that the Sholoson would open it for them. He didn't. Then they pushed their way through the door and walked into the lobby.

The town of Dasholos was mostly for off-worlders. The hotel was entirely so. The only Sholoson at the hotel was the guard. The front desk was staffed entirely by long-tentacled Gorsids. The custodian squeegeeing swamp water off the threadbare carpet was an Astaran with aspirations to someday pilot an aircab. Several Silesian guests sat in a circle of folding chairs and watched the news flash by on a beat-up old communicator screen set up in the lobby. A married trio of Drusidis got off the elevator and scuttled past on their way to the diner that adjoined the hotel. Joe Henderson, an elderly human who swore to never return to Earth, had rented out a third floor room for the last seven years. A year before, the Sholoson owner had finally agreed to give him a monthly rate. Joe had come down to the lobby in search of a light bulb. Otherwise, he would remain in his room for weeks at a time.

After signing in on Fietlebaum's tab, they walked to the elevator to go up to their third floor, "penthouse" rooms. Fietlebaum was still exhausted from the trip and his continuing recovery from suspended animation. "I'm going to my room and sleep," Fietlebaum said. "I'll see you in the morning."

"You sleep, Fietlebaum, "Teysoot Motzo replied. "I walk down street see if Dasholos still got hot nightlife." When he saw the desired look of astonishment burst upon Fietlebaum's face, he laughed. "Only fooling," he said, "I go for sleep, too." He stepped down the hallway, but turned to add, "Good night, Fietlebaum. Don't let bedbug bite—really, they *big* here."

CHAPTER 21

Early the next morning, Fietlebaum awakened to a knock on his door. It was Teysoot Motzo. He was dressed in a khaki shirt with matching shorts, knee socks, and hiking boots.

"All you're missing is a pith helmet," Fietlebaum blurted out.

"Really?" Teysoot Motzo asked. "Maybe, it not too late for pick one up."

"No, no," Fietlebaum answered in quick recovery. "No one will fault you for the lack of one."

Teysoot Motzo shrugged. "I go see Sholosons," he said. "I make deal, and come back for let you know how much jorftoss they have for us. I be back for dinner time."

"I'm going with you, "Fietlebaum insisted.

"Hah!" Teysoot Motzo laughed. "You bighead not belong in Sholoso swamp. You get eaten by gorbo snake. You stay here until I get back. You not worry. Everybody know Teysoot Motzo. I make good deal. We make big money."

With serious reservations, Fietlebaum let him go. Through the window, he watched Teysoot Motzo hail an aircab, get in, and speed off towards the outskirts of town. "Well," Fietlebaum said in an effort to reassure himself, "I'm sure he knows what he's doing." Almost exactly twenty-five minutes later, Fietlebaum received a text message on his communicator.

"Fietlebaum," the message read, "this Teysoot Motzo. I tied on tree, by creek, at foot Batso Hill. They got demands. They got blasters. Come quick. Bring you money bag."

It took a moment to sink in, then Fietlebaum exploded. "That *shmuck!*" he screamed. "That big, stupid *schlemiel*[91]! He's gone twenty-five minutes and he's been kidnapped for God's sake!"

More often than not, Sholosons killed intruders. However, they decided to spare Teysoot Motzo. Teysoot Motzo had been correct in claiming that everyone on Sholoso knew him. It was only his impression of the regard in which they held him that was flawed. Contrary to his own belief, the Sholosons saw him as a buffoon. Nonetheless, they suspected that he was a well-connected one, with rich and powerful friends. Thus, after a lengthy discussion among themselves, a discussion that spurred two fights and several death threats, the Sholosons decided that he was worth more as a hostage than as fertilizer for the jorftoss. They tied him up and told him to call his travelling companion. They were looking for a sizeable ransom.

Fietlebaum was in a quandary. If no ransom was paid for Teysoot Motzo, they would probably kill him. But if he brought the ransom money to the Sholosons, there was nothing to prevent them from keeping the money and killing them both! "*Vey iz mir*," Fietlebaum grumbled. "Right about now, I could kill him myself." He paced the floor of the cramped little hotel room, back and forth until he came up with a way out.

He got dressed, rode the elevator down to the lobby, walked out the front door and hailed an aircab. "I need to get to Batso Hill," he told the cabbie. "There is a creek at the foot of the hill. My friend is there. Some Sholosons are holding him captive, and he needs my help."

---

91 Silly fool

The Astaran gave him a puzzled look, shrugged his shoulders, and told him, "We're on our way." He repositioned himself in his seat, but before he took off, he turned back around to Fietlebaum and added, "Please, pay in advance."

Fietlebaum paid the money the cabbie requested and they took off. They flew to the outskirts of town, then slowed down at Fietlebaum's request to look for Teysoot Motzo and the band of Sholosons that had kidnapped him. The cabbie located Batso Hill and glided slowly around its base. "There!" Fietlebaum shouted, when he spotted a group of Sholosons on the ground next to the creek that Teysoot Motzo had described.

The cabbie flew toward the big tree to which Teysoot Motzo was likely tied, then thought better of it and dropped down about a hundred yards away. "This is as close as I get, pal," the cabbie insisted. Fietlebaum got out and started walking toward the Sholosons.

"Good luck," the cabbie cried out.

"It may come to that," Fietlebaum admitted.

The aircab flew off. Fietlebaum walked to where the Sholosons stood, and as he got closer he saw that Teysoot Motzo was indeed tied up. When got within about twenty feet, the Sholosons pointed their blasters at him and motioned for him to put his hands in the air. He did as they demanded, and continued to walk with his hands up to where Teysoot Motzo was tied.

"Fietlebaum, "Teysoot Motzo cried, "you bring money?"

"Shut up!" the Sholoson nearest to him yelled, only to then himself demand to know, "Fietlebaum, did you bring any money?"

"No," Fietlebaum said. "No money."

"No, no, Fietlebaum, you not say that!" Teysoot Motzo cried. "You gotta have money! They going blast me for death!"

"Shut up!" the Sholoson demanded before turning back to Fietlebaum. "No money?" he asked with astonishment.

"No money," Fietlebaum repeated. After a pregnant pause he added, "I have something better."

"Nothing better than money!" Teysoot Motzo protested.

"Shut up!" Fietlebaum yelled at Teysoot Motzo. Then he turned and more reservedly said to the Sholoson, "I've got something better than money. Take me to your boss."

"Is this some joke?" another Sholoson asked with contempt.

"No joke," Fietlebaum insisted. "I've got something that your boss will want to know about."

The Sholoson tilted his head in the universal look of incredulity.

"He will be very angry if you pass up something better than money," Fietlebaum insisted.

The Sholoson relented. "Okay," he agreed half-heartedly, "follow me."

"Don't go anywhere," Fietlebaum said to Teysoot Motzo as he walked away with the Sholoson.

"Hah! You funny boy, Fietlebaum," he called back.

"Shut up!" Fietlebaum heard a Sholoson holler from behind as he strode after his guide.

He followed the Sholoson around the base of Batso Hill, then plodded behind him on a soggy trail into the depths of the swamp. As they progressed along the trail, the vegetation became more luxuriant and the canopy above them more dense. The air was warm, humid, and laden with odors of mud and rot. Despite the gloom of shadows, Fietlebaum was startled by the beauty of the plants and flowers that sprang up along the trail. He spotted an enormous flower with petals like flames of red and violet. As he drew near, its scent wafted toward him on a sudden breeze. He nearly vomited.

"*Oy*!" he retched. "An *ipish*[92] like I can't remember!" The aroma of the sewage treatment plant on Hijdor had been vaguely similar.

Vapor from the heart of the swamp drifted as a thick fog across low sections of the trail. It choked him. The heat was oppressive, and blue sweat dripped down his face and stung his eyes. His feet sank in mud. There was a buzzing sound. Insects as big as Fietlebaum's outstretched hands swooped from overhanging trees and swirled around his head. One landed and sunk a needle-like proboscis into the meat of his neck. He screeched more from shock than pain. The Sholoson heard his cry, deftly turned, and swatted one of the stinging insects out of the air with a mighty backhand. He scooped the dead one up out of the mud, ate it, and left the rest to swarm around Fietlebaum's head. Without a word or gesture of comfort for Fietlebaum, he turned back to the trail and slogged on. For the first time he could ever recall, Fietlebaum wished he were back on Polmod.

After another mile of trail, they broke through the jungle and came to a clearing. Fietlebaum did not immediately connect the clearing with habitation. It appeared more the consequence of a natural disaster—a storm or flood that had uprooted trees and piled up scattered mounds of dirt and vegetation. Then Sholosons of all ages and sizes poured out of what Fietlebaum realized were ill-constructed mud huts and lean-to hovels to see who was being brought into their midst. The Sholoson guide turned to Fietlebaum and barked, "Stay here! I will get Hagatt."

Fietlebaum was alone and surrounded by dozens of gibbering Sholosons. They were naked and smelled of fetid mud and swamp water. He suspected they had never seen a Hijdori before. They gazed at him in fear and

---

[92] A stink

wonder, walked around him, sniffed, reached out to touch his orange, scaly skin with their fingertips. Several of the villagers spat on him. One young Sholoson tried to poke him with a stick. "*Vey iz mir,*" Fietlebaum groaned. "These creatures have my life in their hands."

"Get away from him!" a voice boomed. The crowd parted, and Fietlebaum saw Hagatt, the largest Sholoson he had so far seen, stride up surrounded by an entourage of five or six Sholosons of lesser stature. Several had to run to keep up with him.

Hagatt was an intimidating sight for Fietlebaum, even more so when he stood directly in front of him. But proximity also revealed qualities of refinement that set him apart from the rest. Unlike the others, his body was free of caked mud and swamp debris. The porcupine-like quills on his face were trimmed, and the hollows and crevices of his body scraped free of the odiferous exudates that tended to collect there. It was a pleasant surprise when Hagatt rattled through several languages hoping to find one in which to directly converse. It was an enormous relief when Hagatt asked if he spoke Silesian, one of the languages in which Fietlebaum was fluent.

Hagatt had acquired his fluency in Silesian and other galactic languages while working in a lower management position for the last Silesian owned mining company on Sholoso. This was before the market collapsed and the operation became unprofitable. Prior to the fall of the company, they had even sent him for business training at one of the nearby Silesian off-world universities.

"I was told you have something to offer us that is better than money," Hagatt said to Fietlebaum in perfect Silesian. "Why don't you join me in the lodge house and explain this to me."

"Of course," Fietlebaum replied.

"Please walk this way," Hagatt said.

Fietlebaum followed Hagatt to the lodge house, the most substantial structure in the village. The Sholoson pushed aside the grass curtain in the doorway and beckoned him in. It was a large woven hut, with a dirt floor and low wooden tables for serving food during village meetings and ceremonies. Bones from the last feast—stinking from putrid, bits of flesh that still clung to them—lay in scattered piles around the room. *But, very neat piles*, Fietlebaum granted. "Please, sit down," Hagatt said, and immediately called for drinks and tidbits of food to be brought.

"Before you explain what you have for us," Hagatt said, "perhaps you could start by telling me who you are and why you have come to Sholoso. I have never seen anyone of your species before, and I must admit that I am very curious about you."

"I would be happy to tell you everything you want to know," Fietlebaum replied.

A tray of food was brought to the table. Fietlebaum had not eaten and was hungry. However, the small, green bean-like objects moved away from his fingers when he attempted to pick them up, and he decided to restrict himself to the fruit juice on the tray. After taking a sip of acrid juice, Fietlebaum explained that he was a psychiatrist and scientist. He added that he had formerly been a businessman in the pharmaceutical industry before he became disgusted with it and left to practice psychiatry in peace at the Transgalactic Merchant Marine Academy on Polmod. He told Hagatt of Erd Glesh kidnapping his grandson to force him to compromise the integrity of Teysoot Motzo and get him into a psychiatric hospital under false circumstances.

"It turned out that Glesh was intending to assassinate Teysoot Motzo," Fietlebaum told him, "and I wouldn't be a part of his despicable plan."

Hagatt tilted his head in quizzical fashion as if to ask "Why not?" but he didn't pursue the question.

"So," Fietlebaum continued, "we got off Janpoor and came here to figure a way to save my grandson and Teysoot Motzo."

"Hmmm," Hagatt murmured, "I know this Erd Glesh. He is a very dangerous fellow." He fell silent for a moment, seemingly deep in thought. "But why," he finally asked, "did you come to Sholoso in particular?"

"After we escaped the psychiatric ward," Fietlebaum explained, "we realized we had to have some leverage to protect ourselves from Glesh. Teysoot Motzo said that if Glesh was the problem, then jorftoss was the solution." Hagatt's eyes opened wide at the mentioning of the valuable plant. "Teysoot Motzo was under the impression that Sholoso was the only planet where there were still jorftoss plants free of the infection that has been killing it all over the galaxy. So here we are," Fietlebaum concluded.

"I see," Hagatt replied. Then, after another moment of silent contemplation he said, "So tell me what it is you have that is better than money."

"The jorftoss is dying throughout the galaxy," Fietlebaum began. "It is almost certainly an infection, probably a virus, and it appears to be very contagious. I suspect it was spread from planet to planet by jorftoss dealers hiking out to jungle plots to buy up leaves from the small farmers. Now I understand that the virus has reached Sholoso, and it is starting to kill your plants." Hagatt tipped his head in confirmation. Fietlebaum then fixed his gaze at Hagatt. "The virus is extremely virulent," he said. "It is only a matter of time before the infection kills all of the jorftoss on Sholoso as it has on the other planets. No one will be able to replace the money you will lose if the jorftoss dies." Hagatt reluctantly nodded in agreement.

"I have spent my life in medical science, laboratories, and research," Fietlebaum went on to say. "I will find a way to prevent your plants from becoming infected, and thus save the jorftoss trade on Sholoso. That's what's better than money."

Hagatt simply sat and stared silently at Fietlebaum. Then he replied in solemn tone, "It may already be too late. The infection has come to Sholoso, and many plants have already shriveled and died."

"Then we haven't a moment to lose!" Fietlebaum insisted.

Again, Hagatt sat deep in thought. After what seemed an interminable time, he looked up and asked, "What do you need to start?"

CHAPTER 22

Hagatt arranged for Fietlebaum to move into a larger room at the Dasholos Hotel. It was the "Presidential Suite," the main distinction from his previous "Penthouse" being that it had an extra couch and a walk-in closet. The closet would serve as his laboratory. It was a far cry from the state-of-the-art facilities he enjoyed when he worked years before at Forgion Transgalactic, but he would make do.

He had given Hagatt a list of pieces of equipment he needed. A few were already on Sholoso. An incubator and a refrigeration unit had sat unused in the health clinic that had been built, supplied, and then abandoned by the defunct mining company. An old, but serviceable microscope, once used to examine ore samples, was collecting dust in the boarded-up field office of the company. Glassware and tubing were found in the company's old chemical engineering office. Hagatt's crew brought them by.

The starship that had brought them to Sholoso was still in orbit around the planet awaiting its departure date. Fietlebaum saw it as another potential source of equipment and material. He rode the shuttle craft back up to see what he could arrange.

The mechanical engineer on the starship was an intelligent and industrious fellow with experience in building and repairing equipment. His shop on board was well stocked, and blueprints for almost any device were accessible from the starship's computer. Fietlebaum paid him to construct a few other instruments he needed—a centrifuge, a gel electrophoresis unit, and a solid-phase

DNA synthesizer that could also be used for protein synthesis. Fietlebaum soon learned that a few extra Silesian *horki* were also sufficient to turn the engineer's back when he spied a computer, a router, and other electronic items that were too useful to pass up. Piece by piece, he assembled his laboratory.

Several days after their conversation, Fietlebaum made arrangements with Hagatt to journey out to collect samples of jorftoss. There were thousands of plots of illegal jorftoss scattered throughout the Sholoson jungle. They lay hidden in gullies overgrown by the lush Sholoson vegetation. During the most successful years of jorftoss cultivation on Sholoso, the entire planet's crop might amount to little more than one-hundred and fifty kilos of dried leaves. However, given that a kilo of leaves could fetch a price equaling the total lifetime salary of a well-paid mining executive, even a tiny plot with a few plants could be worth a small fortune.

Hagatt led Fietlebaum out into the swamps. There was no visible trail where they walked, and Fietlebaum marveled at Hagatt's ability to navigate through the seemingly undifferentiated landscape of endless swamp, thick vegetation, hills, and gullies without any map, trail, or electronic guidance. After several miles of slogging through jungle, Hagatt stopped in a place indistinguishable from what they had been through for the last hour. He pulled aside the branches of an overhanging, palm-like shrub, and revealed to Fietlebaum his first glimpse of jorftoss.

Jorftoss was an unusual looking plant. It's leaves were large, bright red, with scalloped edges of iridescent blue. Spots of the same iridescent blue were aligned in rows along the central vein, large at the stem and decreasing to barely visible size near the tip. The leaves grew at the ends of blue stems, each about a foot long, that radiated from the ground in spoke-like fashion. The central hub was the tap root that extended several feet down into the fertile Sholoson mud. Each plant had seven to nine stems and leaves.

"This plant is still healthy," Hagatt told him. "Take it with you, and I will lead you to some plants that have become infected with the virus."

They hiked further into the jungle. After another hour or so, Hagatt again stopped, and pulled back the branches of a large plant with the appearance of a bright yellow philodendron. Underneath were several jorftoss plants that showed dramatic signs of viral infection. The bright red leaves were wilted and brown, and the striking iridescent blue had turned dull gray. Fine, fern-like tracings of black stretched across the leaves like patterns of frost on a winter window pane.

"This is what the virus does," Hagatt said gravely. "In another day, these plants will be nothing more than piles of black slime on the ground." He reached down and pulled the plant, root and all, out of the ground. "Take this, too," he said. Fietlebaum placed the infected specimen in a bag, stuffed it in his knapsack separate from the other samples, and they headed back toward the village.

After a few minutes of walking in silence, Hagatt spoke up. "I need to ask you something important, Dr. Fietlebaum, and I need an honest answer."

"Of course," Fietlebaum replied. He suspected that Hagatt wanted a dispassionate assessment about what their chances were of finding a cure for the virus and when results might be expected.

"My wife and I have been married for twenty-two years," Hagatt began.

What does that have to do with curing the jorftoss? Fietlebaum naively wondered. Then the reality of the situation hit him. He had neglected to consider that he was a psychiatrist and thus seen as a combination mind reader, lie detector, and expert in all things that motivate sentient beings. Oy, he thought. *Here it comes.*

"She has been angry and irritable lately," Hagatt continued. "She hardly talks to me anymore. I can't remember the last time we had sex. Maybe it's the change of life, maybe it's the kids growing up, maybe it's me. I don't know anymore." He shook his head, and with one of his left arms, he wiped away what was the Sholoson analogue of a tear.

Fietlebaum struggled to recover the professional, therapeutic persona that circumstances had of late stripped away. He reached deep inside himself for empathy. Thankfully, he found some. He was then legitimately able to sigh the sigh of wisdom born of pain, and give counsel on that most painful of all phenomenon, the troubled marriage. It didn't matter if a sentient being was Sholoson, Human, Silesian, Drusidi, or any other species. The same problems, losses of affection, fears, grudges, miscommunications, and doubts were there. All across the Galaxy, relationships were hard.

"I am sorry to hear that you and your wife are having problems," Fietlebaum told him with all the sincerity he could muster.

"I appreciate your sympathy," Hagatt replied.

"Have you asked her why she is behaving this way?" Fietlebaum inquired.

"Well, no," Hagatt sheepishly replied. "I've been afraid to say anything."

It occurred to Fietlebaum that if he had a *shekel* for every time he had heard that answer to that particular question, he could buy off Glesh and still retire a wealthy man. "Do yourself a favor," he told Hagatt. "Talk to her. Ask her what's wrong."

"She won't get mad?" Hagatt asked tentatively.

"She's already mad!" Fietlebaum bellowed.

Hagatt shrugged. "Hmmm, I guess you're right."

They arrived back at the village. Teysoot Motzo was being held there, "for safe keeping," as Hagatt put it. But, he was content. He had a fondness for Sholoson food, even the kind that wriggled on your plate, and he particularly enjoyed the local brew, *nasqua*. It was made from fermented leaves of a native tree, and it gave him some of the same relaxing, mood elevating effects of the best Janpooran *burzet*. He also enjoyed how the Sholoson children were attracted to him. A crowd of them followed wherever he went in the village.

Considering how their elders behaved, it was astonishing how playful and endearing the young Sholosons could be. It wasn't until they were about ten years old that some hormonal, neurodevelopmental process kicked in and turned them mean and sullen. An analogous process happened in human children in their teen years. The effects were less dramatic in humans, and the period of insufferable behavior eventually waned when they reached their twenties and their frontal lobes came fully on line. In the case of Sholosons, with rare exceptions such as Hagatt, the older they got, the meaner and more sullen they became.

Teysoot Motzo saw Fietlebaum and Hagatt enter the village. "Hey, Fietlebaum," he called out, "you fix jorftoss, we make big money!" Then he toasted Fietlebaum with a raised glass of *nasqua*.

"*Le'chayim*[93], you *shmuck*!" Fietlebaum yelled back.

"Come on," Hagatt said. He placed an arm around Fietlebaum's shoulder and led him to the lodge house. Fietlebaum followed him inside. He noticed that the décor had changed. The floor had been swept, woven mats had been placed on the floor, and in a corner of the hut, in a vase that more resembled an old galvanized bucket, was one of the huge, colorful flowers whose aroma had nearly made him vomit. All of it it was obviously for his benefit and, though he kept his distance from the nauseating flower, he appreciated the effort. "Stay awhile," Hagatt implored him. "Stay and have some food before you return to Dasholos.

93 The Jewish toast, "To life!"

I've had some Silesian pastries brought in for you. And I'll make some coffee."

"Coffee?" Fietlebaum asked with pleasant surprise.

"Yes, coffee," Hagatt said with a laugh. "It's a bad habit I picked up from some Humans I worked with while I was with the company."

Hagatt paused for a moment, struggling to phrase what he suspected might be a disconcerting revelation. "I must tell you, Fietlebaum, that I looked into your history. I am responsible for the village and Sholoson lives. It was the prudent thing to do."

Fietlebaum shrugged. "I can't blame you for being cautious, "he conceded.

"I found nothing of concern," Hagatt quickly added.

"No doubt," Fietlebaum replied.

"In any case," Hagatt more blithely continued, "I found that you were adopted and raised by a Human on Hijdor. They all drink coffee, so I figured you might enjoy some as well."

"I would love some coffee," Fietelbaum replied.

"I have to admit that I've never enjoyed working with Humans," Hagatt confessed as he filled the French press coffee maker with steaming hot water and fresh grounds. "They're so emotional, and they think they're so damned smart! You can't tell them anything."

Fietlebaum nodded in half-hearted agreement.

Hagatt finished brewing the coffee, and brought a fresh cup to Fietlebaum, along with a tray of pastries. After a moment of pause for the first sips and bites of refreshment, Hagatt inquired, "So, how do you intend to cure the jorftoss?"

Fietlebaum chewed a bite of pastry and considered his answer. He swallowed and took another sip of coffee. "Viruses are like clever little spies," he began. "They forge molecular passkeys and use them to enter the plant's cells under false pretenses. Once past the gates, they break into headquarters and take over operations. They take over by replacing the cell's operations manual, its DNA, with their own, destructive DNA manual."

"It sounds like war!" Hagatt remarked with enthusiasm.

"It *is* war!" Fietlebaum quickly retorted.

"But, what can you do to stop it?" Hagatt implored.

"One way," Fietlebaum answered, "is to identify the protein the virus uses as the counterfeit key, and then plug up the keyhole so it can't let itself in."

"Is that hard to do?" Hagatt naively inquired.

"It takes work," he was willing to admit. "But there are standard ways to approach the problem. The protein the virus uses as a key must be similar enough to one of the plant's own proteins that the plant mistakenly takes it for one of its own and allows the invasion to happen. Thus, the shortcut to identifying that molecular key is to look for proteins shared by the virus and the plant. Those proteins will be coded for in both the viral and plant DNAs."

"What do you do when you find the protein key?" Hagatt asked.

"Good question," Fietlebaum replied. You synthesize a molecule that mimics that protein, and spray the plant to plug up the keyholes. That molecule is medicine for the plant."

"I see," Hagatt said.

"Plugging up the keyhole would be the fastest way to stop the virus," Fietlebaum continued, "and it may be necessary to keep some plants alive. But it wouldn't be a permanent solution."

"What would be a more permanent solution?" Hagatt asked.

"A more permanent way," Fietlebaum said with discernibly more enthusiasm, "would be to change the lock. It may be possible to genetically engineer the plant cells to no longer accept the virus' counterfeit key. If such genetically altered plants could be propagated, the offspring jorftoss plants would forever be free from their vulnerability to the virus. That would be the best solution. But it would also be the most difficult and time consuming one."

The look of fascination on Hagatt's face quickly turned to one of solemnity, perhaps defeat. "Time isn't on our side," he noted with gravity.

"No," Fietlebaum admitted, "It isn't."

They sat in silence. Fietlebaum swallowed the last bite of pastry, and washed it down with what remained in his coffee cup. "I must go," he said. Hagatt sent for an aircab to transport him back to Dasholos. The cab arrived to pick him up, and Fietlebaum headed back to the hotel.

On the way, Fietlebaum reconsidered his conversation with Hagatt. He hoped he hadn't misled Hagatt into thinking that saving the jorftoss was a sure thing. Then, despite his best efforts, he entertained a series of misgivings. *For one thing*, he wanted to explain to Hagatt, *I'm working out of a* farshtunkeneh[94] *closet! And I'm out of my element. I'm a psychiatrist, not a botanist.* He took a deep breath to rein in his anxiety. He let it out slowly. Nu? he figured, *a virus is a virus.*

No matter whether the host was a plant or an animal, all viruses shared similar strategies and mechanisms. Once the tissue of the plant was broken down and centrifuged into its component parts, the jorftoss cells would be little different from cells he had previously studied. He had several times before used such strategies to treat aliens with viral infections of their brains. In some cases, it was not entirely clear if those aliens were plants or animals. "Those *meshugeneh* Fontids," he muttered in recollection. "They contracted the ciret virus. The Fontids had roots and leaves. They looked like begonias, for God's sake. Who knew they could grab you by the throat and try to run off with you?"

---

[94] stinking

The cab set down in front of the Dasholos Hotel. The Sholoson security guard sidled out the door to perform his perfunctory investigation. He looked Fietlebaum over and gave a reluctant nod of acceptance. Then he sauntered back to his position just inside the door. Not to give the impression that he was a mere doorman, he stood and scrutinized Fietlebaum as he struggled with his bags and key while trying to push the front door open.

"Would it kill you to give me some help?" Fietlebaum implored. The Sholoson turned his head in Fietlebaum's direction, then slowly turned away without responding. "A real *mensch* you are," Fietlebaum said. "*Platsin zuls du*[95]!"

He pushed his way through the door and walked across the lobby to the elevator. A sign on the elevator door read, "Out of order." "Of course," Fietlebaum thought. He reversed his steps and walked back across the lobby to the stairs, and climbed up to his floor. When he got to the Presidential Suite, he unpacked his knapsack and laid the jorftoss samples on a table in his new, makeshift laboratory. He sat to rest and reflect for a minute in a chair by the window.

He considered the gravity of his situation. He thought about Glesh. *When will he pick up our trail?* he wondered. *He must know as well as Teysoot Motzo that Sholoso is the last place where jorftoss plants are growing. He will surely be on his way. No drug dealer will sit idly by while the source of his ill-gotten gains dried up.* "Let's not forget, he's also mad as hell at me," he muttered.

He got up, padded across the room, and dug through his still unpacked bags for the half-full bottle of scotch he had brought with him from Polmod. "Hello *boychik*," he murmured as his fingers found the slender neck of the bottle.

As he sipped his *schnapps,* the psychotherapeutic conversation with Hagatt returned to him. He thought of

---

95 You should explode!

his own departed wife. "Sophie," he called out to her, "It's a good thing you're not here to see this. You would *plotz*[96]*!*"

He took another sip of *schnapps* and continued his talk with his long departed wife. "Who would have dreamed that at this time in my life I would be on this *farkakteh* planet with a fat Janpooran drug dealer, running away from a rogue Drajan intelligence agent, trying to save our grandson's life. I always thought by now we would have that little place on the beach by the Morplon sea. This is not what I had in mind."

He shook his head in slightly bemused bewilderment. "*Nu*?" he said as he lifted himself up out of the chair, "as Rabbi Goldman used to say, "*Der mensch trakht un Got lahkht*[97]." He sighed another big, "*Oy!*" "It's not too late in the day," he added in resignation. He sat up and stepped over to his makeshift laboratory. "I'll talk to you later, Sophie," he sighed. "It's time to get to work."

---

96 collapse

97 Man plans and God laughs.

CHAPTER 23

The choppers chopped and the grinders ground. Fietlebaum hummed an old, Yiddish folksong to the rhythm of the solenoids clicking up and down in the solid phase DNA synthesizer. In the centrifuge, he had spun out a fraction of infected jorftoss extract, rich in virus. He was completing another fraction rich in healthy plant cells. The first segments of DNA would soon be ready to probe for codons translating into the protein the virus was using as a forged pass key. He was a scientist, and the prospect of new data excited him. Still, he could only hope that the variants of DNA in these organisms from across the galaxy were not so foreign as to defy his efforts to unravel their secrets.

Thankfully, the alien DNA yielded. After several days, he had found hundreds of surface proteins in the jorftoss genome that could conceivably be the target of the virus' guile. Then he found a structural match in one of the viral proteins. His computer's proteomics program determined that the viral protein and one of the jorftoss proteins fit together like a hand in a glove. Such a protein was a perfect candidate for the virus' pass key protein. "Now we're getting some place," he said to himself.

He synthesized a batch of the suspect viral protein, radiolabeled it with tritium obtained from the starship's fusion reactor, and incubated it with live jorftoss cells. The radiolabeled protein bound to the jorftoss cells, and that binding could be displaced by adding extra unlabeled protein. These were the characteristics he had expected. *This could be it*, he thought.

Next was to see if blocking the keyholes in the cell's walls, by flooding the jorftoss with that protein, could prevent the virus from using the protein in its coat as a counterfeit key to gain entrance to the cell. If plant cells incubated with the virus alone died of infection, and those incubated with virus plus extra protein did not, then he would have his positive answer. He placed the various permutations of virus, protein, and jorftoss cells in petri dishes in the incubator and prepared to wait. It would take a few days to get the results. It was time to relax.

"*Vey iz mir*!" he exclaimed. "I haven't left this room for nearly a week. I need to stretch my legs." He had decided to stroll around town. He got dressed and went downstairs. He pushed through the front door. He said, "Good afternoon, *nudnik*[98]," to the Sholoson security guard, and stepped out onto the sidewalk. It was a beautiful day for Sholoso. The pink sky was clear and the red sun shone brightly. The breeze blew toward, not from over, the swamps, so the air smelled relatively clean and fresh. He felt optimistic, even buoyant. He walked around the corner and his heart froze.

A Drajan was sitting in a window seat of the diner next door to the Dasholos Hotel. At first he thought it was Glesh, then quickly realized it wasn't. *Who is he?* he desperately wanted to know. He turned and walked briskly back to the hotel. He pushed open the door and rushed in. He paced across the floor of the lobby several times before he stopped and simply stood still trying to regain his clarity of thought. He attracted the attention of the Sholoson guard who strolled over to investigate.

"You're acting strangely," the Sholoson said. "Is something wrong?"

"No—no," Fietlebaum stammered. "Everything is fine."

---

[98] nuisance

The guard gave him a wry look. "Then stop acting like an idiot in my lobby," he snarled, then returned to his post by the door.

Fietlebaum calmed himself, noting that there were billions of Drajans in the galaxy. It certainly wasn't Glesh, and in all likelihood this other Drajan had never even heard of that *groisser gornisht*. He was probably here on business. There was nothing to worry about. He steeled himself to go back and take another look through the window of the diner. But, when he got there the Drajan was gone. "*Oy gevalt*!" Fietlebaum exclaimed. He had to talk to Teysoot Motzo back in Hagatt's village.

He hailed an aircab, and directed the cabbie to the Sholoson village. The flight seemed to take forever. He couldn't stop the thoughts flying through his mind. *Was the Drajan working for Glesh? Was Glesh on his way? Was Glesh already here?* He had never felt such fear before. *Am I having a panic attack*? he wondered. Suddenly it struck him that Glesh may have already found Teysoot Motzo at the village. Maybe Teysoot Motzo was dead. "*Mein Got*[99]!" he cried out. The cabbie turned back to see what was going on. "You okay, pal?" he asked.

"Yes, yes, I'm fine," he cried. "Please hurry. Hurry!" The cabbie shrugged and pushed a little harder on the throttle.

In another few minutes, the cab was over the village and swooping in for touchdown. The approach of the aircab had coaxed the Sholosons out of their huts. They gathered in the center of the clearing and waited for it to land. As the cab dropped toward the ground, Fietlebaum peered frantically out the window for Teysoot Motzo, but did not see him. The cab landed.

"Wait here!" he screamed at the cabbie, as he jumped out to search for his Janpooran friend. He ran through the village, sticking his head into this and that hut, and calling

---

[99] My God!

out Teysoot Motzo's name. Teysoot Motzo casually strolled out of one of the larger mud hovels. He had a glass of *nasqua* in his hand. "*Got tsu danken*!" Fietlebaum cried out as he ran up to Teysoot Motzo and hugged him.

"What happen?" Teysoot Motzo asked him. "You look like you see ghost."

"*Vey iz mir,*" Fietlebaum said as he sat and tried to recover himself. "I'm too old for this *meshugas.*"

"Why you act so crazy?" Teysoot Motzo demanded to know.

"I saw a Drajan in the diner by the hotel," he explained. "At first I thought it was Glesh, but it wasn't. I got scared and ran back to the hotel. When I went back for another look, he was gone."

"Uh oh!" Teysoot Motzo said.

"I panicked. I got carried away," Fietlebaum confessed. "I even imagined that Glesh was on Sholoso and had found you. For a moment I even thought you might be dead."

"Oh, Fietlebaum!" Teysoot Motzo said with a laugh. "You crazy!"

"Maybe I am crazy," he replied. "But that Drajan scared the hell out of me. We have to find out who he is, and if he works for Glesh."

A moment later, Hagatt walked up to where Fietlebaum and Teysoot Motzo stood. "What's the matter with you?" he asked Fietlebaum. "You look like you saw a ghost."

"See," Teysoot Motzo said to Fietlebaum, "I tell you so."

Fietlebaum told Hagatt about the Drajan he saw in the diner. Hagatt nodded thoughtfully. "I don't ever remember seeing a Drajan on Sholoso, not even Glesh himself," he replied. "I wonder what he's doing here?" He was obviously concerned. "Take Teysoot Motzo with you back to Dasholos," he told Fietlebaum. "He's no good for me here. He drinks all the *nasqua* and corrupts the children. Maybe he can help you stay safe. Meanwhile, I'll look into this."

"Thank you," Fietlebaum told Hagatt.

"Come on," Fietlebaum said to Teysoot Motzo, "you're coming with me back to the hotel."

"Okay," Teysoot Motzo answered with shrug of ambivalence. He paused, then added, "just a minute." He turned and trotted back to the hut from which he had earlier emerged, and came out with his arms folded around some jugs full of *nasqua*. "I might get thirsty back in town," he said. Then they climbed into the waiting aircab to fly back to Dasholos. Before they took off, Hagatt trotted up to the cab. He knocked on the glass, and Fietlebaum opened the door. He had a blaster in his hand. "Here," he said, "take this." Fietlebaum took the blaster and closed the door. The cabbie took off.

For a few minutes Fietlebaum sat in much needed silence. Then he turned to Teysoot Motzo. "It's getting to me," he confided to him. "It seems crazy now, but for a moment I really had it in my head that Glesh had killed you. I feel like a perfect *schlemiel*."

"No, you not *schlemiel* like you say, Fietlebaum. Everybody get scared," Teysoot Motzo said to console him. "Hah!" he added, "even Teysoot Motzo get scared sometime. But you not tell nobody."

Fietlebaum smiled. "Thanks," he replied sincerely, "it helps to hear you say that."

"I not say nothing," Teysoot Motzo said with the Janpooran equivalent of a wink.

The aircab flew in over the town and dropped down in front of the hotel. The Sholoson guard immediately popped out of his lair and sauntered over. "Hmmm," he grunted as he stood by the side of the cab, "fatso is back."

As the guard bent down to look inside, Teysoot Motzo abruptly forced the door open and slammed it into his face. The guard was knocked to the ground. As he lay there groaning, Teysoot Motzo jumped out, bent over him and offered an apology. "My goodness!" he said. "Can you ever forgive me?" He gave the Sholoson his hand and helped him up to a sitting position. "There you go," he said, but as he pivoted away he caught the guard in the side of the head with his knee. "We just have *terrible* day," he said as he turned to walk on into the hotel. The guard slowly dropped back down on the sidewalk, where he lay moaning and rubbing his head. Fietlebaum got out of the cab, stepped over the guard, and followed Teysoot Motzo into the lobby.

They walked across the lobby to the elevator and rode up to the third floor. Fietlebaum didn't feel like being alone. He invited Teysoot Motzo to his room. He opened the door of the Presidential Suite and walked in with Teysoot Motzo close behind. "Wow!" Teysoot Motzo exclaimed when he saw the scientific equipment that Fietlebaum had set up in the room. "How you know what do for all this stuff?" he asked.

"Well, it's all pretty straightforward when you know what the instruments do," Fietlebaum replied. He gave a brief description of all of them, what they did, and what he was trying to accomplish. Aside from the fine technical details, Teysoot Motzo understood what Fietlebaum explained. Fietlebaum was impressed. "In another day or two I should know if the protein I have isolated is the one that the virus uses to infect the jorftoss. If it is, then I can make a drug to block the virus' effects. That will save the jorftoss long enough for me to genetically engineer it to resist infection in the future."

"Hah!" Teysoot Motzo almost shouted, "You real bighead, Fietlebaum. I glad we on same team."

Then Fietlebaum grew somber. "But we might be in big trouble, my friend. I don't know if that Drajan is part of Glesh's team or not. But sooner or later, Glesh *will* find out we are here and he will come for us. I don't want to be here when he does."

"Yah, maybe he come, and maybe not," Teysoot Motzo said dismissively. "Come on, let's go grab bite for eat. Forget about it little while."

"I suppose your right," Fietlebaum replied.

They rode back down to the lobby. When they stepped off, the Sholoson guard saw them and tried to limp away. But Fietlebaum spotted him. "*Gai, nudnik*," he called out. "*Gai strashe di vantsen*[100]."

They strolled out the door, around the corner, and into the diner. Teysoot Motzo looked around the room for the Drajan. "No worry," he told Fietlebaum. "He not here."

They found a table and sat down. Teysoot Motzo had snuck a flask of *nasqua* into the diner, and he poured himself a glass. Fietlebaum had few sips, too, but it did nothing for him and tasted terrible on top of it. They ordered dinner, and it was surprisingly good. The diner served food to please the palate of the Silesians patrons who used to frequent it when the mining industry was still booming. Fietlebaum had always enjoyed the exotic flavors of the Silesian cuisine. Teysoot Motzo, on the other hand, ate almost anything.

After the meal, they sat and talked. Fietlebaum was finally able to relax. He felt good. He paid their bill and walked back to the hotel. They pushed through the door, and as they walked into the lobby they saw the Drajan sitting in one of the folding chairs watching the Galactic news on the communicator screen.

"*Oy gevalt*!" Fietlebaum muttered under his breath.

"You can say that again," Teysoot Motzo whispered back.

---

[100] "Go on, you nuisance," he called out. "Go intimidate the bedbugs."

CHAPTER 24

Fietlebaum's night was restless. Every creak in the building was a foot step. Every breeze bore a whisper. The shadows that crept across the walls robbed him of sleep, and when he was able to snatch a moment of sleep, those shadows crept through his dreams. All night, the blaster stayed on his chest. When morning arrived, he felt more exhausted than when he had first climbed into bed.

First thing, he flew out to the Sholoson village and told Hagatt about the Drajan having a room in the Dasholos Hotel. Hagatt again promised he would look into it. He explained that Sholoso had no police department or even any government to speak of. But, he had connections with several of the interplanetary law enforcement agencies in that sector of the Galaxy. His friends there could use the data base to identify the Drajan and see if there was anything concerning in his files. Only mildly relieved, Fietlebaum returned to the hotel.

Several days went by. It came time to examine the cell samples. Fietlebaum pipetted out some of the cells that had been incubated with live virus. He placed a drop on a slide and placed a slide cover on top of it. He placed it on the microscope stage, clipped it in, and adjusted the focus. As he twisted the fine focus knob, cells sprang into view. Dead, infected, cells were all he saw. The virus had done its work.

He removed the slide, and retrieved a petri dish that held jorftoss cells and live virus, plus extra amounts of the protein he believed the virus used like a pass key to attach and gain entrance to the cells. If he was right, the extra protein would have competed with the virus for keyholes on the surface of the cells and thus deprived the virus of access and ability to infect them.

He placed a drop on a new slide, covered it, and placed it on the stage. He prayed that the cells would still be alive. He adjusted the focus. The microscope revealed plump, healthy plants cells that showed no signs of having suffered viral infection. "*Mazel tov*, Dr. Fietlebaum!" he sang out loud. "*Mazel tov* to you!"

Teysoot Motzo heard Fietlebaum's exultation from down the hallway, ran down, and knocked on his door. Fietlebaum pulled the door open. "Come in Teysoot Motzo," he sang, "I'm going to give you a big kiss!"

"What you do, Fietlebaum?" he asked." You act crazy again."

"It worked!" Fietlebaum cried out. "I know how to save the jorftoss!"

"Hah! You smart boy, Fietlebaum," Teysoot Motzo said. "You real bighead."

I need to tell Hagatt the news," he said, and while I'm there I want to find out if he has learned anything about that Drajan.

"You might pick up little more *nasqua* while you there, too," Teysoot Motzo suggested.

Fietlebaum caught an aircab. He landed in the village, and Hagatt came out to meet him. He told Hagatt about his success with the protein and what his next steps would be. Hagatt was pleased.

"Good work!" he told Fietlebaum. Then he paused for a moment and changed the subject. "I asked around about the Drajan. His name is Plestet, Jord Plestet. Word is that he's in Dasholos on business. He is looking to salvage old mining equipment left here on Sholoso, take it and sell it as scrap. They found nothing that should make you worry."

"Thank you," Fietlebaum told him, "That makes me feel a little better." He dutifully collected a few jugs of *nasqua* for Teysoot Motzo, then called the aircab back on his communicator. A few minutes later, it landed to return him to the hotel. As he climbed into the cab, Hagatt placed a hand on his shoulder to tell him one more thing. "They told me Plestet is clean," he said, "but if I were you, I would keep taking that blaster to bed with me."

Fietlebaum landed back at the hotel. An Astaran came out the door dressed in an ill-fitting security uniform. He looked in the window at Fietlebaum, turned his head a few times for appearance's sake, then gave the cabbie an affirmative nod.

"Where's the Sholoson?" Fietlebaum asked him as stepped out of the cab.

"He quit," the Astaran answered.

Fietlebaum pushed through the door and walked through the little lobby toward the elevator. There in the middle of the lobby, by the communicator screen, sat the Drajan, Jord Plestet. As Fietlebaum walked past him, Plestet lifted his head and said "Good afternoon." Then, without waiting for a return salutation, he turned his attention back to the galactic news broadcast. *Nothing so menacing about that*, Fietlebaum admitted.

He got to the elevator, and before he could push the up button, the doors opened and the Drusidi trio spilled out into the lobby. They were in the midst of a heated argument. The females were angry at the male for what they felt was unequal dispensation of affection. They gurgled, snarled and shrieked at one another. The new Astaran guard quickly mobilized from behind his desk and ran to the scene.

He stopped and stood before them, arms akimbo. "What's the trouble?" he demanded to know. The Drusidis paused in their argument. They glanced at the Astaran, turned back to each other for a pregnant moment, and then, with instant and fervent unanimity, jumped on the Astaran and started mercilessly pummeling him. Fietlebaum momentarily considered intervening, but talked himself out of it. He gingerly sidestepped the melee and slipped onto the elevator. "The little *nebbish*[101] will be fine," he told himself. "His skin is like leather."

He got to his floor and walked to the Presidential Suite. He pulled out his key to unlock the door, but at the mere touch of his key on the lock, the door swung open. A broch[102], he thought. *I know I locked this door. I am certain I did.* He paused, and struggled unsuccessfully to recreate in his mind all of his recent comings and goings. "*Oy*," he said as he shook his head in self-recrimination. "Maybe I didn't lock it." He pushed the door the rest of the way open with his foot. He slowly reached his arm around the door frame to turn the light on, then he cautiously peeked in. Nothing. No one was there. He stepped into the room, examined his equipment, scanned the bedside table, the closet, and the chest of drawers. Nothing was missing. Nothing was misplaced. "I'm going *meshugeh*," he said to himself.

He got undressed and laid down in his bed. The door was now securely locked. The blaster was on the bedside table. But, he couldn't sleep. "*Nu*?" he said out loud, "as long as I'm up, I might as well do something useful." He got out of bed and stepped a few feet over into his walk-in laboratory. "There's work to do."

The protein he had synthesized blocked the virus in the petri dish. But in the jungle, on living plants, the protein might be too large to be a useful medicine. He needed a smaller protective molecule that could be sprayed on and absorbed by the leaves of the plants. He sat at his table and worked through the night at producing a series of smaller molecules that he hoped would mimic the anti-viral effects of the protein he had synthesized. By morning he had several likely candidates. He added each of his new

---

101 little nerd

102 Damn it

compounds to a dish of cells, along with live virus, and set them in the incubator to do their work. Then he shuffled off to bed.

He awoke the following afternoon and sprang out of bed to examine his samples under the microscope. In three dishes, there was evidence of viral infection, while in the other two there was none. In one of those two, there were signs that the compound itself was mildly toxic to the cells. But in the other dish the jorftoss cells remained both healthy and free of viral infection. The last compound had worked. Fietelbaum was ecstatic. He got dressed, grabbed a flask full of the successful compound, and headed downstairs to hail an aircab to the village.

When he arrived at the village, Fietlebaum hopped out of the cab to look for Hagatt. He found him in a dark mood. Fietlebaum told him about the new compound that could be sprayed on the jorftoss to prevent infection. But, Hagatt was preoccupied. He sighed and shook his head. "It's too late," he lamented.

"What do you mean?" Fietlebaum demanded to know.

"All of yesterday I was out looking for jorftoss," Hagatt replied, "and after searching through forty or fifty plots, I found only two living plants. Even those two plants were sick, and for all I know, they're dead today. The virus has spread like wildfire."

"We can't give up now!" Fietlebaum asserted. "Get your crew together. We'll spread out through the jungle and hunt down and treat every plant within fifty miles of the village. Even if they plants are sick, this medicine should save them."

Sholosons were pessimistic by nature. It required every bit of skill Fietlebaum had to persuade Hagatt not to give up. He finally succeeded. Hagatt called an assembly, and every able-bodied member of the village was given a small jug of diluted treatment compound. After a brief explanation from Fietlebaum on how to apply it to the leaves and soil around the base of the plant, the Sholosons struck out into the jungle to find and rescue as many jorftoss plants as they could from the virus.

Fietlebaum walked into the jungle with Hagatt and several other high ranking Sholosons. After half an hour they came to the first plot of jorftoss. Hagatt pulled back the leaves of the larger plants that shielded them and revealed three twisted heaps of black slime that had once been full grown jorftoss plants. There was nothing to save. They pressed on through the hills and swamps. The next plot of jorftoss looked like the first. "These were the two living plants I saw only yesterday," Hagatt said dejectedly. One of the Sholosons wailed with grief, and Hagatt sent him reeling with a forceful backhand to his head. A second Sholoson kicked him to the ground. "Get up. Let's go!" Hagatt barked at him.

They trudged for hours through the dense Sholoson jungle, and every few miles they were greeted by the sight of dead and decaying jorftoss plants. The air around them carried wisps of the odor of rotting vegetation. Mein Got, Fietlebaum thought. *Maybe, Hagatt was right. Maybe it's too late to save the plants.* At the next plot they came to, Hagatt pulled back the covering vegetation and wailed. The plants were dead. "There are no more beyond this place," he cried. "Unless the others have found living plants on the far side of the village, the jorftoss is gone!"

They made their way back to the village. All were somber. No one spoke as they trudged back through the mud and swamp water. As they rounded a bend in the trail, Fietlebaum heard a commotion from the rear of the line. A Sholoson screamed. There was splashing, more screaming, then thrashing about in the water and mud. The sound of the struggle got further away, then disappeared altogether. "A gorbo snake got him," Hagatt told him in utterly dispassionate fashion. Oy, Fietlebaum thought, *Teysoot*

Motzo wasn't kidding about those snakes. I thought he made that up.

A moment later, Fietlebaum heard laughter. At first he assumed it was the paradoxical laughter that sentient beings sometimes exhibit when faced with enormous fear or inexplicable loss. It wasn't. The Sholosons thought the death-by-snake incident was hilarious. One acted out the scene of being dragged off through the swamp by his neck. He gasped and gurgled, much to the delight of his audience. Hagatt saw that Fietlebaum was disturbed and confused by it. "Welcome to Sholoso," he said.

They neared the village, and Fietlebaum was praying they would learn that one of the other groups had found still living plants and treated them with the protective compound. If not, his work would have been in vain, and his grandson's life would be forfeit. But the news was bad. The others had visited every plot of jorftoss they knew of and saw the same thing every time. The virus had reduced all of the magnificent red and iridescent blue plants to pitiful, stinking piles of black slime.

It was apparent to the Sholosons that the jorftoss, their only source of income, was dead. No more money from jorftoss. No more money for bribes, blasters, and instruments of death. The mood at the village darkened. Tempers flared. They blamed each other for having allowed jorftoss traders to visit the growing plots. Some blamed Hagatt. One ran toward him screaming threats and was quickly vaporized by Hagatt's blaster. Others blamed Fietlebaum and Teysoot Motzo, the last off-worlders to come to the village. Some cried that it was they who brought the fatal virus. Shouts went up to kill Fietlebaum and to hunt down Teysoot Motzo and kill him, too. Hagatt quickly put a stop to the cries for Fietlebaum's death. The one voice that continued to demand death was silenced by another shot from his blaster. "No one is touching him," Hagatt shouted. "He's our only hope."

"Come on," Hagatt said to Fietlebaum, "we have to talk." Hagatt strode off to his hut with Fietlebaum close behind. He held the curtain over the entrance open, and beckoned him in. "This is bad," Hagatt said. "If we lose the jorftoss we lose everything. Please, give me some good news. What hope do we have now?"

Fietlebaum heard the anguish in Hagatt's voice. The situation had grown desperate. He fell into thought. It occurred to him that if all of the plants in the jungle were dead, then the only living jorftoss cells in the entire universe were those back in the Presidential Suite of the Dasholos Hotel. They were merely cells, only ground-up slurry of plants, no longer whole plants that could grow and reproduce. He still needed to genetically engineer those plant cells to resist the virus. But, if he could do that, then, with the right nutrients and hormones, the cells could be cultured and coaxed to regenerate new roots, stems and leaves of complete jorftoss plants. *This could work,* he thought. But it would be difficult.

Fietlebaum explained what he might yet be able to do. "What are your chances," Hagatt implored. The scientist in him resisted a simple answer. There were too many unknowns. But, he couldn't remain silent. "Fifty-fifty," he replied.

"When will you know?" Hagatt asked.

"I should know if the genetic engineering works within a few days, but it will take longer to see if I can culture the cells and grow new plants from them," Fietlebaum replied.

Then Fietlebaum realized something disturbing. He might be able to overcome the obstacles of engineering the genome of the jorftoss. But regenerating new plants from tissue culture might take weeks. He wondered how long would it be before Glesh finally did show up on Sholoso looking for him and Teysoot Motzo. Glesh would demand jorftoss, not green specks floating in culture medium.

Without the jorftoss, or the piles of money jorftoss could bring, Fietlebaum would have no way to bargain for his grandson. *As angry as Glesh must be*, he thought, *I would be as good as dead myself*, he thought. *I'm running out of time.*

The two of them sat for several minutes lost in thought. Fietlebaum broke the silence. It may be possible to resurrect the jorftoss," he said. "But, I fear for my grandson. If I have no jorftoss or money to offer, I'm afraid that Glesh will kill him."

"I understand," Hagatt told him. "If you are unable to bring the jorftoss back to life, then we will have nothing, and I will not be able to help you. The Sholosons will want something for their losses, and I fear they will reconsider holding you and Teysoot Motzo for ransom. I will try my best to get you off the planet safely, but unless you save the jorftoss I can promise you nothing." He paused. "Come with me," he said.

Hagatt stood up and walked to the back of the hut where there was another curtain hanging over a door way. He stepped through and told the two guards stationed at the back entrance to allow no one past. He beckoned Fietlebaum to follow. He led Fietlebaum about fifty yards down a pathway to where another mud hut sat hidden by dense foliage. He pulled the grass curtain aside and the two of them went inside. Hagatt pulled aside a primitive woven mat and revealed a steel vault set into the floor. His voice disarmed the security system, and a second command started the vault rising up out of the ground. When the vault reached chest level, its thick steel doors slowly opened. Inside the vault were several shelves, and on the shelves were vials containing a dark brown liquid. Hagatt glanced behind, to make certain no one was spying on them. Then he reached into the vault and picked out one of the vials to show to Fietlebaum.

"This is pure extract of jorftoss," Hagatt told him. One vial is an entire year's harvest. Each is worth a fortune. If you succeed in engineering the jorftoss plants and growing new plants from the altered cells, I will give you three of them."

Fietlebaum was greatly moved by Hagatt's generosity, particularly in view of his keen suspicion that most of the Sholosons would just as soon roast and eat him. "Thank you, Hagatt," he replied.

Hagatt replaced the vials, closed the vault doors, and commanded the vault to return to its underground position. He pulled the mat back over it, and they walked back out through the curtain. As they walked back up the pathway, Hagatt stopped for a moment. "You were right, Fietlebaum," he said.

"About what?" Fietlebaum asked.

"About my wife. I asked her why she was so angry and distant, and she told me that she thought I was the one who was angry and distant. She thought I was going to leave her. Who knew?" Things are better now. Thank you."

"*Nu*?" he replied with a shrug. "It's what I do for a living."

They returned to the village where fights were in progress. One Sholoson lay dead, and two others lay wounded and bleeding. "Enough!" Hagatt bellowed. The fighting stopped, but murmurs of anger and discontent persisted. "You should go," Hagatt told Fietlebaum. "You're not safe here."

Hagatt called for an aircab to come to the village to pick Fietlebaum up and return him to Dasholos. It was a tense ten minutes waiting for the cab to arrive. Two more fights broke out. Hagatt's guard stopped the first with a shot from his blaster. The second ended when the unfortunate combatants simultaneously shot and killed each other.

When the aircab arrived, Fietlebaum jumped in and told the cabbie to take off quickly. As the cab lifted off the ground, a few of the villagers hurled stones and rotten fruit at it. Even from high above, Fietlebaum saw several more flashes of light from the blasters. He hoped that Hagatt would be able to manage the fear and anger that riled the village. He greatly appreciated Hagatt's offer to give him vials of extract, and prayed that he could fulfill his own side of the bargain.

CHAPTER 25

When Fietlebaum's aircab dropped in for a landing in front of the Dasholos Hotel, he was surprised to see yet another new security guard scuttle out to meet him. It was one of the Gorsids that had been serving behind the front desk. *The poor* shmuck *drew the short straw*, he suspected.

"Where is the Astaran?" Fietlebaum asked.

"He quit," the Gorsid replied with a tone of disdain.

The uniform looked even worse on him than it did on the Astaran. Four of his tentacles slipped through the arm holes of the coat that had been designed for the Sholoson, but the coat gave no allowance for the other six. Three of them slid out between the buttons in front, while the other three bunched up inside the front of the coat where they wriggled like cats in a burlap bag. For a moment, Fietlebaum considered asking him the name of his tailor, but thought better of it. *Gorsids never know how to take a joke*, he reflected.

He walked into the hotel, and immediately saw the Drajan at his usual place beside the communicator screen. "Good evening," the Drajan said. After a moment of hesitation, Fietlebaum relented and echoed back, "Good evening." When he reached the elevator, he sighed. "I don't know why I was so worried about him," he muttered. "He seems a harmless fellow. It goes to show you what fear can do to your perspective. It drives you *meshugeh*!"

It had been a long day tramping through the jungle with Hagatt. He was tired, but didn't feel like calling it a day. When he got to the third floor, he walked the few steps to Teysoot Motzo's room and knocked on the door. He intended to ask him if he wanted to join him for supper at the diner, but no one answered. He went to his room, splashed water on his face, put on a clean shirt, and headed back down the elevator. He had a second wind.

He walked back through the lobby, nodded to the Drajan, walked to the door and stepped out on the sidewalk. There he paused to look at Sholoso. It was dusk, and the usual pink sky glowed blood red. In the darkening northern half of the sky, a few stars were beginning to glimmer. The small cigar-shaped Sholoson moon, Bogdon, tumbled slowly through the sky. A huge flock of dragonfly-like creatures flew across the setting star. Their crystalline wings caught the fading starlight, and scattered the light into thousands of little explosions of color. In their graceful flight across the sky, the creatures passed over Fietlebaum. One shat on top of his head. "*Mazel tov*, my friend!" he called out as he wiped his head clean with a handkerchief. "A perfect shot!"

He walked on to the diner and ordered his food. He was halfway through his meal when he got a text message on his communicator, "Return to Dasholos Hotel immediately!" "*Vey iz mir*!" he exclaimed. "What's happened now?" His mind buzzed with countless emergencies that might have necessitated the call. Teysoot Motzo drank too much and started a fight. The Sholoson guard was back for revenge. The Drajan made his move and Teysoot Motzo had him cornered in the Presidential Suite. "*Got in himmel*!" he whispered out loud. "Maybe Glesh is here." His heart pounded. "*Oy*!" he quickly told himself. "Don't go there again!" Still, at this point, nothing would have surprised him.

He wrapped a napkin around two spicy stuffed Silesian pastries that remained on his plate and stuck them in his pocket. He laid more than enough money for the meal and tip on the table, and ran out the door. He rounded the corner and was surprised to see a crowd gathering on the sidewalk outside the hotel. The new Gorsidian security guard, the trio of Drusidi lovebirds, the now not so ominous Drajan, and a number of pedestrian passers-by stood out on the sidewalk with their heads tilted up. He reflexively looked up too, and immediately saw the reason he had been called. The old human tenant was standing on the ledge of his window on the third floor of the hotel about to jump off.

The flustered guard sidled up to Fietlebaum. "We sent for you," he said, "because we heard you were a psychiatrist. Please, can you help this Human? Suicides are bad for business."

"How can I refuse so compassionate a plea?" Fietlebaum asked rhetorically. "What's the Human's name?"

"Joe Henderson," the guard replied.

He ran to the hotel door, pushed it open, ran to the elevator and rode it up to the third floor. His chest heaved from the effort. He bent down and put his hands on his knees. "How did an *alter kocker* like me fall into this?" he panted. "I'm about to *plotz*." The elevator arrived, and he huffed out the door to the old man's room. Several other guests had already gathered around the room's open door. He collected himself, walked in, and stepped toward the window. He stuck his head out and saw old Joe Henderson standing on the ledge, shifting his weight from one foot to the other, muttering to himself.

"Joe?" Fietlebaum asked.

"What do you want?" the old man asked without turning his eyes away from the sidewalk below.

"I'm Dr. Fietlebaum."

"So what?"

"I 'd like to talk with you if you'll let me."

"Fuck off!" the old man barked.

"I know you want me to go, Joe," Fietlebaum told him, "but I'm going to stay here." He climbed out onto the window sill and sat down.

"Suit yourself," Henderson said in resignation.

He paused for a moment to allow Henderson to adjust to his presence. "You must feel awfully lonely out here," Fietlebaum said.

"Yah? How would you know that?"

"I *don't* know. But I would feel lonely and angry, standing on the ledge of a *farkakteh* little hotel, in a *farkakteh* little town, on a *farkakteh* little planet waiting to jump off and die in front of a bunch of gawking *Chaim Yankels*[103]."

Fietlebaum, and timely cybertranslation, so accurately described what Henderson was thinking at the moment that the old man was briefly taken aback. He looked at Fietlebaum and said, "Boy howdy!" then turned away again.

Fietlebaum was happy to get the eye contact. It was a good sign. "Did something happen to make you feel this way?" he asked.

"No," Henderson replied. "Nothing ever happens."

"I heard that you left Earth and came here years ago. Why did you leave, Joe?"

"There was nothing there for me."

"Did there used to be something there for you?"

The old man paused, sighed a deep sigh. "Yah—a long time ago."

"What was there?"

"Ah, you'll think I'm stupid," he replied. After a moment's hesitation he added, "It was a dog!"

"What was your dog's name?"

He turned his head toward Fietlebaum again and answered, "Lily."

---

103 A name, like Bubba, or Johnny Hayseed, suggesting dim-witted country bumpkins

"What did Lily look like?"

"Ahhh, for Christ's sake!" Henderson growled. "You don't want to hear about the damn dog!"

"Yah, I do want to hear about her. What did she looked like?"

"Like a dog, nothing special."

"But she was special to you."

"Yah—she was."

A tear rolled down Henderson's cheek. *Good*, Fietlebaum thought. *He is starting to let go*. "So, what did she look like?" he asked again.

"She was part Dachshund and part Cocker Spaniel—a funny looking dog." He gave a little chuckle that turned to sobbing. "I'm sorry," he said. "She was just a damn dog."

"It's alright," Fietlebaum said. "Tell me more."

Henderson went on talking about his dog. He seemed to come more alive as he talked about how the dog had followed him everywhere and slept at the foot of his bed. He told Fietlebaum that he brought her home one night as a surprise for his wife. "But she had a surprise for me, too," he bellowed. "She was gone when I got home! She took off with her boss—never heard from her again. After that, it was me and Lily." He hung his head and shook it slowly. "When Lily died," he said, "I felt more lonesome than I ever had in my life."

No doubt, Fietlebaum thought. *The dog was the last link. When he lost the dog, he finally lost his wife too.*

"I didn't want to stay on Earth anymore. I picked the farthest away place I could find and came here." The old man paused, hawked something up from his throat and spit. "I don't know why I did. I'm lonely as hell here too!" He wiped his eyes and sighed. "I sure miss that dog sometimes."

"Life is lonely," Fietlebaum said. He stayed silent for a moment before proposing to Henderson, "Do you want to climb back in and talk some more? Maybe we can go next door and get a cup of coffee."

"I haven't talked to anybody for years," he replied. The old man hesitated. "Yah," he finally said. "Why the hell not."

Fietlebaum helped him climb back through the window. "Come on," he said. "I want to hear more about that dog of yours."

They walked to the diner. The rubber-neckers on the sidewalk backed away from them as they walked by, as if the old man had something contagious. A Sholoson on the sidewalk yelled, "You should'a jumped!" Fietlebaum gave him a withering stare and a one word assessment, "*shmuck!*" They strolled into the diner and talked for an hour or so more. It was what the old man had needed.

After their chat, and some coffee and spicy Silesian pastries, they walked back to the hotel. The old man thanked Fietlebaum and rode the elevator back to his room. Fietlebaum was alone again. He looked around the lobby. The Drajan was not at the communicator screen. He had not seen Teysoot Motzo all day. He asked the Gorsid behind the desk, but he had not seen him either. "He's cozied-up somewhere with a jug of *nasqua*," Fietlebaum told himself. "He'll come crawling in tomorrow morning." He headed for the elevator, got in, and pushed the button for the third floor. "*Mein tuches*[104] is dragging," he said with a sigh. "I'm too old for this."

He stepped off the elevator and walked down the hallway. He pushed the door of his room open, stepped in, and locked it behind him. He pulled off his shirt, hung it up, and had sat down to take off his shoes when someone in the room called his name.

He spun around and saw Jord Plestet, the Drajan, standing in a darkened corner of the room. "Good evening," Plestet said.

"What are you doing here?" Fietlebaum demanded. He was shocked by the fear and trembling in his own voice.

---

104 My ass

Plestet took a step towards him. "I came to talk," he replied. Fietlebaum snatched the blaster from the table and pointed it at the Drajan. Plestet kept walking. "I'm not going to hurt you," he said. "and you're not the murdering kind. Put the blaster away."

"Not a goddamn step closer!" Fietlebaum cried.

"We have to talk about your grandson," the Drajan calmly said. "I have a message from Glesh." He kept coming.

Fietlebaum yelled at him to stop, one more time, and when he didn't, he pulled the trigger. Nothing happened. He pulled it again, and then again, with no effect. Plestet stepped within two feet of Fietlebaum. He pulled a large knife from his coat pocket, pointed it at him, and sneered.

As the Drajan drew back his arm to plunge the knife into Fietlebaum's heart, Teysoot Motzo burst through the door and threw all five-hundred and thirty seven pounds of himself on him. The force pushed Plestet's face forward onto the floor, and the impact of Teysoot Motzo's body falling on him knocked the wind out of his lung. The knife flew from his hand. As the Drajan recovered his wits a moment later, he tried to stretch out his arm to retrieve it, but it was beyond his grasp. With Teysoot Motzo's full weight on him, he was not about to inch himself any closer to it. But, with his eyes on the fallen knife, Teysoot Motzo did not notice the Drajan struggling with his partially free arm to retrieve a second knife hidden in his boot. He felt a sudden sting in his leg, and the intensity quickly swelled to an excruciating pain. The painful stab infuriated him. He loosed a deep and furious howl of rage, grabbed Plestet's neck, and, with a sudden twist of his powerful arms, broke his neck like a dry twig.

He got up off of the floor, brushed himself off, and walked over to Fietlebaum. "You okay?" he asked.

"Certainly," Fietlebaum gasped. "I'm terrific."

Teysoot Motzo took the blaster out of Fietlebaum's trembling hand and inspected it. "Oh, Fietlebaum!" he groaned in disillusionment. "You need shoot Drajan and you got safety on."

"Safety, *schmafety*, I'm Jewish psychiatrist," Fietlebaum pleaded. "What do I know from blasters?"

"Hah!" Teysoot Motzo exclaimed as he shook his head. "Dr. Bighead Fietlebaum."

Fietlebaum suddenly felt faint. He shuffled to a chair and slowly lowered himself down. He began to shake. "Thank you!" he said. "You saved my life."

"Well," Teysoot Motzo answered with a shrug, "somebody have to."

Fietlebaum sat. He shook his head slowly from side to side as the gravity of what had happened sunk in. He sighed as he began to work free of it. "*Vey iz mir,*" he said. "Dead bodies in your room are always so difficult to explain."

"Hah! You funny boy, Fietlebaum!" Teysoot Motzo replied. "We call Hagatt. He send his crew for tidy up place."

Fietlebaum sat silently. When he spoke again, he was deadly serious. "Teysoot Motzo," he said, "the jorftoss is dead. All across the jungle, the plots of jorftoss are infected with the virus. I was too late."

Then Teysoot Motzo himself felt faint and searched for a chair to lower himself down upon. "Oh no, Fietlebaum, not say that! That just not true."

"It's true, my friend. It's true. The jorftoss is dead. But there is still one hope for my grandson and the jorftoss. Hagatt has vials of extract in his vault. If I can revive and culture the cells here in the laboratory, and make the new plants resistant to the virus, Hagatt will give us three vials to use in the trade for Aaron. But we are in grave danger and running out of time. We will have to get out of here soon. If I am successful and we get the extract from Hagatt, we will need a plan to get it to a safe place where we can bargain with Glesh." Then he stopped and looked up at Teysoot Motzo. "It looks like Glesh wants me dead now, too," he admitted. "I need your advice. What do you think we should do?"

"Well," Teysoot Motzo said, while scratching the side of his head, "best place for be safe from Glesh is place where he scared do something crazy. He may be no good rotten crook, but he still agent with Galactic Intelligence. If we go Government Capital District on Silesia, he have lot other agent eye on him. He be careful there."

As Fietlebaum considered Teysoot Motzo's idea, he half-heartedly nodded his head in agreement. "That's clever," he said, "but if we get caught with extract of jorftoss on Silesia, Glesh won't have to kill us. The Government will."

"So, we put extract someplace for safe keeping, then meet Glesh on Silesia for bargain."

"We don't even know where he is," Fietlebaum protested. "How do we get the message to him to meet us on Silesia?"

"Hah!," Teysoot Motzo laughed, as if the explanation were obvious. "Glesh GIA agent. Agency know where he at. We tell Galactic Intelligence we have something very important for tell him, some big, Galactic Security news. Then they tell him come back Silesia."

"Yes, very good," Fietlebaum replied. "It just might work."

"Hah! Not you worry, Fietlebaum. I old crook myself! You get us extract, we talk Glesh, we have you grandson safe and sound."

CHAPTER 26

Fietlebaum awakened. He had been so exhausted he didn't remember climbing into bed. But as the fog of sleep lifted, all that had transpired the night before vividly returned to his mind. He hurriedly raised himself up on one elbow to see the spot on the floor where Teysoot Motzo had killed the Drajan the previous night. He was relieved that the body was gone. He got out of bed, stretched, and put his clothes on. He needed to talk to Teysoot Motzo.

He walked down the hall way to his room and knocked on the door. "Go away!" Teysoot Motzo bellowed.

"It's me, Fietlebaum," he insisted.

"Oh, just a minute," Teysoot Motzo replied. He fiddled with the lock, and after a moment the door swung open a few inches. Through the cracked door, Fietlebaum saw one of Teysoot Motzo's six eyes looking out at him. Just to the side, he made out the figure of a young Janpooran female in his bed. "Where did she come from?" Fietlebaum asked in amazement.

"After I tuck you in last night, I go on prowl. I meet her at singles bar. She work for starship line. She in town for big business deal with starport and Dasholos Chamber of Commerce. She very sweet!"

"I'm sure she is," Fietlebaum allowed. "When you're ready, come down to the diner. I will buy the two of you breakfast. Then we need to talk."

"Okay," Teysoot Motzo said, and closed the door.

"*Vey iz mir*," Fietlebaum said to himself. "The jorftoss is dying, Drajans are trying to kill us, my grandson is kidnapped by a sociopathic drug dealer, and he's chasing skirts!" He shook his head. "*Nu?*" he said, "as my father use to tell me, *ven der putz shteyt, der seychel geyt*[105]." As he turned from the door, he heard the footfalls of Teysoot Motzo bounding across the floor; a sudden, deep groan of severely stressed floor boards; a split second of silence; then a crash of bedsprings. As he stepped onto the elevator, he heard high pitched laughter explode from the room and echo up and down the hallway. "Well," he muttered, "if nothing else, he knows how to enjoy himself."

He rode down to the lobby, stepped off, and headed toward the door. "Fietlebaum," the Gorsidian guard called out as he walked by his desk, "the old man is dead."

"What?" Fietlebaum asked. "You mean Joe Henderson?"

"Yah, Henderson," the Gorsid replied.

Fietlebaum's heart sank. His first thought was that the old man had completed his suicide, and a sense of failure swept over him. "What happened?" he asked the guard.

"Nothing," the Gorsid told him. "He died in his sleep."

Fietlebaum was relieved to hear that. "Thanks for telling me," he said. He stepped out the door and toward the diner. He was glad he had spent the extra time with Henderson. *He shared his thoughts, some laughter, some tears,* Fietlebaum reflected. *He returned to the living before he died. That's about all anyone can expect.*

He walked into the diner and found a table. About twenty minutes later Teysoot Motzo came barreling through the door by himself. "Where's your girlfriend?" Fietlebaum asked.

"She back on starship," Teysoot Motzo quickly replied. "I not think she love me anymore. What for breakfast?"

"Don't worry," Fietlebaum told him. "You'll get over her in time."

---

105 When the penis stands up, common sense walks away.

"Hah!" Teysoot Motzo shot back. "You funny boy, Fietlebaum."

"Old man Henderson died in his sleep last night," Fietlebaum told him. He said it as much to inform Teysoot Motzo as to allow himself to more completely digest the fact.

Teysoot Motzo had heard about the events on the ledge. "So, he want kill himself because he miss dog?" he asked Fietlebaum.

"No!" Fietlebaum replied. "He wanted to kill himself because he didn't have anyone to tell that he missed his dog."

"Oh," Teysoot Motzo said. He paused and gave Fietlebaum a puzzled look. "What the difference?"

Fietlebaum sighed. "He was alone," he explained. "No one cared about him, and he believed his life wasn't worth living. He needed to talk. There's a lot of healing power in letting someone tell their story. It's the best gift you can give."

"I not know about that," Teysoot Motzo said. "Everybody listen Teysoot Motzo." He smiled and raised his fist in Fietlebaum's face. "They better listen!"

Fietlebaum nodded in agreement. "I hear you loud and clear," he said, "but let's change the subject. I think the plan you came up with last night to meet Glesh on Silesia is brilliant."

"I think so, too!" Teysoot Motzo replied.

"But we still have to decide on a place to hide the jorftoss extract Hagatt will give us," Fietlebaum noted. "We will need to arrange starship passage there, then on to Silesia, and we have to make sure that we'll be safe while we do it."

"You right, Fietlebaum," Teysoot Motzo replied as he scratched his head and fell deep into thought. "I know good place. We hide jorftoss on Jinkor, second moon of Janpoor. I know place like back of hand. Nobody go there. Glesh may still have agents on Janpoor. So, we take starship for Borgost, planet next by Janpoor, and take star taxi Jinkor. We go back Borgost, then Silesia for meet Glesh."

Fietelbaum considered the plan. "I trust your judgment," he said. "That's what we'll do." He paused for a moment to capture the details. "I will need four days to complete my work," he added. "Find out when the next starship leaves Sholoso for Borgost, and if the timing is right, book us on that flight."

"You got it, Fietlebaum, but first I got finish my breakfast."

Fietlebaum got up and told Teysoot Motzo that after breakfast would suffice. He laid money on the table. "*Ess gezunterhait*[106]," Fietlebaum wished him, and walked away.

Fietlebaum returned to the Presidential Suite. He had work to do. He had to genetically engineer jorftoss cells to be resistant to the virus. Then he would have to coax the altered cells into becoming full grown plants by culturing them. "It won't be easy," he advised himself.

The virus gained entry to the cells by attaching to a keyhole made of protein on the cell's surface. Thus, he needed to insert into the jorftoss cell a new segment of DNA that would generate a new keyhole protein. It would have to be similar enough to the native protein to allow the plant to thrive, but different enough so that the virus could not use it to attack the cell.

He designed a series of likely proteins, then made the corresponding DNA segments in the automated synthesizer. He inserted the DNA into the cells by zapping them with an electric charge. At the same time, he inserted enzymes to snip out and destroy the old DNA, and others to stitch the new segment into place. He spent the day and most of that night working, then set half a dozen petri dishes of

106 Eat in good health!

the altered cells floating in tissue culture medium into the incubator.

He expected that only a small percentage of the healthy jorftoss cells would take in the genetic material in the desired fashion. Then, many of the successfully treated cells would not survive the tissue culture process. He hoped to treat several thousand cells and create perhaps a hundred plants in culture. If he was lucky, five or six of those plants would be resistant to the virus. He didn't want to think about being unlucky. After keeping the treated cells in culture medium for two days, he added live virus and waited. If any plants survived and grew, they would be plants resistant to the virus.

Two days later, Fietlebaum placed the tissue culture dish under the microscope, and top-lit the stage. After adjusting the fine focus he saw five tiny, red islands drifting in the medium. As the tiny plantlets turned, the nascent leaves caught light and flashed iridescent blue. At this point, the cells had only partially differentiated, but leaves and rootlets stretching down into the medium were visible. These were five, virus resistant, jorftoss plants. "*Got tsu danken,*" Fietlebaum whispered. "Aaron is saved."

He stood up from the microscope, grabbed the tissue culture dish to return it to the incubation chamber, and sighed a tremendous sigh of relief. He walked down the hallway and knocked on Teysoot Motzo's door.

"Go away!" Teysoot Motzo boomed.

"It's me," Fietlebaum told him.

"Oh, just a minute," Teysoot Motzo replied. He padded across the floor, cracked open the door, and peered through at Fietlebaum. Fietlebaum looked around him, and saw someone on the bed. He craned his neck forward and made out that it was the female Gorsid that worked behind the desk.

Teysoot Motzo shrugged and confessed, "I say hello and she get frisky. What can I do?"

"I don't want to hear about it," Fietlebaum said. "But something has happened, and I need to tell you about it. Then we need to go tell Hagatt. Get dressed and come to my room as soon as you can."

"You got it," Teysoot Motzo replied.

Fietlebaum walked back toward his room to wait for Teysoot Motzo. He smiled and shook his head. *You can question his taste*, he thought, *but you have to admire his initiative.*

Fietlebaum got back to his room. He heard the Gorsid slither down the hallway, and a moment later Teysoot Motzo burst through the door. "So, what you got for me?" he asked.

"It worked," Fietlebaum replied.

"We got new jorftoss plants that not get sick?"

"Yes! The jorftoss has survived, and Hagatt will have more of it to grow on Sholoso."

"And I have more for sell!" Teysoot Motzo added.

"Well, yes," Fietlebaum admitted. "That too."

"Oh, you wonderful!" Teysoot Motzo cried, then he gave Fietlebaum a crushing hug.

"Okay, okay," Fietlebaum gasped, "a simple thank you would be sufficient."

"Hah!" Teysoot Motzo said. "You got it, Fietlebaum. Thank you! I glad you on my team! Now we go tell Hagatt. He be happy."

"Let's go!" Fietlebaum concurred.

They rode to the lobby. Teysoot Motzo was so cheered by the turn of events that he absently hummed a catchy Janpooran pop tune on the way down. The independence of his Janpooran mouth and respiratory slit allowed him to hum the melody while he separately ground his teeth and clicked his tongue to accompany his melody with a complex, syncopated rhythm section. Fietlebaum found it astonishingly annoying, but felt too happy to bother him about it.

They hit the ground floor, crossed the lobby, and went out the door to hail an aircab. As they waited on the sidewalk, Fietlebaum glanced behind them and pointed out to Teysoot Motzo that the guard uniform was now slung on the back of a chair by the guard's stand. Apparently the Gorsid, too, had abandoned the position.

The aircab landed and they climbed in. "Where to?" the cabbie inquired.

"Hagatt's village," Fietlebaum told him.

They strapped in and lifted off. The aircab glided up through the sky over Dasholos, then out over the jungle and swamp lands of Sholoso. On the way there was time to talk.

"Things are wrapping up," Fietlebaum said. "We need to get ready to fly to Borgost and on to Jinkor. Did you arrange tickets for the starship?"

"I do just what you ask," Teysoot Motzo replied. "Next starship fly for Borgost tomorrow afternoon. We on it. I already pack and ready for go."

"Good work!" Fietlebaum told him. "Now we have to give Hagatt the news and arrange to trade off the virus resistant jorftoss plants for the extract he promised to give us."

"I going miss Sholoso," Teysoot Motzo said nostalgically as he gazed out across the jungle. "It not such bad place."

"I suspect it is one of the better places you've been kidnapped and held for ransom," Fietlebaum interjected.

"Well, other than that," Teysoot Motzo replied, "it been very pleasant." He pulled a flask of *nasqua* out of his pocket and took a sip. "Very pleasant indeed."

The cab neared the village and swooped in for a landing. The sound of the approaching aircab had alerted Hagatt to their arrival, and he was standing in the clearing waiting for them. The moment they touched down, Teysoot Motzo hopped out and trotted off to find more *nasqua* to replenish his supply. Fietlebaum stepped out to speak with Hagatt. He didn't look good. He had stopped tending to his appearance. He was covered in mud, and he smelled bad. He had stopped trimming the quills on his face. Still, Fietlebaum took heart in seeing his friend. He shook Hagatt's hand, and walked off with him to give him the news about the jorftoss.

"I've got good news, Hagatt," Fietlebaum said. "Success! In my laboratory back at the Dasholos Hotel, there are five virus resistant jorftoss plants growing in a dish of culture medium."

"Wonderful news!" Hagatt replied. "You have no idea how happy and relieved I am to hear it. You have saved the only source of income we have on Sholoso. Without the jorftoss, we have nothing." He paused for a moment and added, "But, I also know that your success will save your grandson's life, so I am happy for you as well."

"Thank you," Fietlebaum told him. "Teysoot Motzo and I will be leaving tomorrow," he added, "and we will need to take the jorftoss extract with us. You and I need to agree on how to trade the plants and the extract. The jorftoss plants are still very small and fragile, so they will need to stay in the culture medium for another week or so. Perhaps you can bring the extract to the hotel tomorrow, and simply leave guards in the room to watch over the plants until they are big and strong enough to be planted into the ground."

"It's a deal," Hagatt replied. "I will meet you tomorrow morning at the hotel to give you three vials of jorftoss extract and take control of the plants in your room." They shook hands, and Fietlebaum called an aircab to return him and Teysoot Motzo to Dasholos.

In the silence of the waiting, they sensed the volatile mood of the Sholosons. The village was still in upheaval. The dying of the jorftoss had been profoundly unsettling, and most of the villagers continued to view Fietlebaum and Teysoot Motzo with suspicion and resentment. As they waited for the aircab, they bore insults and threats. Hagatt allowed the emotional venting, but only to the point when several villagers hurled rocks and mud at them. His blaster ended that.

The aircab arrived to fly them back to town, and as they lifted up into the air a sobering thought occurred to Fietlebaum. The next morning Hagatt could arrive at the hotel, take the genetically engineered plants, keep his extract, and leave him and Teysoot Motzo dead on the floor of his room. *It could happen*, Fietlebaum thought, *there is really nothing to stop him, and many of the villagers are crying out for just that.*

He looked out across the swamps and jungles of the alien planet. *I hope*, he thought to himself, *that all my years of dealing with hearts and minds has given me some insight into what makes sentient beings do what they do. I might be wrong. God knows I've been wrong before. But this time, I don't think so. For some reason, I trust Hagatt.* He sighed. "*Nu*?" he said out loud, as he raised his hands and let them fall. "At this point, what would not trusting get me?"

CHAPTER 27

It seemed odd for there to be no one standing guard when they arrived at the hotel. They had grown used to the insulting, perfunctory inspections at the door. *Just as well*, Fietlebaum thought as he climbed out of the cab and walked into the Dasholos Hotel with Teysoot Motzo.

The lobby was empty. The Silesians were gone. The Drusidi trio had broken up and gone their separate ways after a jealous, knockdown, drag-out fight in the diner. Joe Henderson had died. Fietlebaum and Teysoot Motzo were the only two guests left in the hotel. For Fietlebaum, it was a welcome chance to get some peace and quiet, as he knew that tomorrow would be a hectic day. Teysoot Motzo, however, was not thrilled with the prospect of an empty hotel. He asked Fietlebaum if he wanted to visit a few of the Dasholos "hotspots" before they called it a day, but Fietlebaum declined. He said goodnight and retired to his room.

Fietlebaum got undressed and poured himself two fingers of *schnapps* he had bought the day before at the convenience store beside the diner. He had drunk up the bottle of prized scotch he had brought with him from Polmod. The new bottle was distilled on Borgost, and came highly recommended by the Sholoson teenager behind the counter. *Any port in a storm*, he had thought.

He took a sip of the Borgostian *schnapps* and ran to the sink to spit it out. "*Vey iz mir*," he howled. "Pure *drek*[107]*!*

[107] crap

Why did I listen to that little *pisher?*" His mouth burned and a taste reminiscent of formaldehyde lingered on his tongue. He abandoned the idea of a relaxing nightcap and crawled into bed.

Sleep wouldn't come. He tossed and turned. Fietlebaum had often heard his patients complain, "I can't stop my thoughts." Now it was his thoughts that would not stop. His mind generated one catastrophic scenario after the next. Frightening visions kaleidoscoped in his mind's eye—his grandson's severed finger, the Drajan agent dead on the floor, gorbo snakes slithering out of the swamp. There was nothing to do but let the chaos in his mind play out. "Go ahead you frightened little brain," Fietlebaum said. "Do your best to terrify me. You can't think of anything worse than what has already happened."

Though he never felt himself drift off to sleep, he was awakened by a noise. The leg of a chair scraped across the floor. There was the sound of breathing. He raised himself up on his elbows to look around. A shadow appeared beside the bed. The shadow quickly took on form, materializing out of the very substance of the wall. A knife gleamed. It was Glesh! "I've got you!" Glesh screeched as he lunged upon him. Fietlebaum tried to scream, but he had no voice. He tried to push Glesh away but his arms would not move. The knife pierced his chest. Then, much to Fietlebaum's horror, Glesh's hand and arm followed the knife into his chest. Glesh burrowed his way in, insinuating his arms, head and shoulders into his body. Fietlebaum finally found his voice and sat up screaming. He struggled to free himself from the apparition that had penetrated his body. The door flew open and Teysoot Motzo burst through. Teysoot Motzo turned on the light to reveal Fietlebaum wrestling with bed clothes that had wrapped around his torso.

"Fietlebaum!" he cried. "Okay, okay. Everything okay. Teysoot Motzo here now."

"*Got in himmel*!" Fietlebaum cried as he came to his senses. "What a nightmare!" He sat on the edge of the bed to catch his breath and regain his composure. "Glesh had a knife. He was cutting me open and climbing inside."

"Wow!" Teysoot Motzo exclaimed, as he walked over and sat down on the bed beside him. "You psychiatrist, Fietlebaum," he went on to observe. "What you think you dream mean?"

Fietlebaum turned and looked at him in amazement. "It means that Glesh is trying to *kill* me, you *shmuck*! What do you think it means?"

"Umm hmm," Teysoot Motzo replied thoughtfully, "I suppose that most obvious interpretation."

Fietlebaum sighed. "Go to bed, Teysoot Motzo," he told him. "I'm okay now."

"You sure you okay?" Teysoot Motzo asked.

"Yes, I'm sure," he replied. "I need to stay away from Glesh and *schnapps* from *farshtunkeneh* convenience stores. I'll see you in the morning."

"Okay," Teysoot Motzo said. "But I hear anything funny, I run back."

After Teysoot Motzo left, Fietlebaum leapt off the bed, grabbed the bottle of cheap *schnapps* off the bureau, and poured what was left down the sink. He hopped back into bed and crawled in under the covers. "That dirty *momzer* Glesh," he said with a sigh. "When he's not trying to kill me with his goons, he's trying to kill me himself in my dreams. Perhaps my nightmare was to warn me to never drop my guard. He is ruthless and cruel. He's coming." He turned over and plumped his pillow. "Tomorrow," he told himself, "we'll get out of this place—and it won't be a minute too soon."

He awakened several hours later. He jumped out of bed, padded over to the walk-in closet laboratory, and pulled the culture dish out to look at the jorftoss again. He didn't have to check it. He wanted to—just to be on the safe side. The nascent plants were thriving, several millimeters across, and now readily visible to the naked eye. Hagatt would be pleased.

Hagatt would be arriving soon. Fietlebaum sent Teysoot Motzo to the diner to fetch some Silesian pastries for breakfast. He sat at his table, drummed his fingers, and waited. All was well. He had lived up to his end of the bargain. Yet he suffered a vague, uneasy feeling. He tried to be philosophical about it. "*Vos vet zein, vet zein*[108]," he told himself. Still, the uneasiness persisted.

Teysoot Motzo returned, but neither of them was hungry for a morning meal. The pastries sat on the table. Fietlebaum could see that Teysoot Motzo, too, was restless and uneasy. *We're both on* shpilkes[109], he judged. He saw no benefit in broaching the subject in conversation. Each would have to work it out for himself.

Fietlebaum caught the sound of a swarm of aircabs swooping down in front of the hotel. Doors opened and slammed shut. Voices called out. Orders were given. *This is Hagatt*, he thought, *but, something's wrong*. A minute later he heard the gears of the elevator grind into action. The door opened onto the third floor, and marching footsteps grew louder as Hagatt and his crew approached the door. There was a loud series of bangs on the door that came from the butt of a blaster being slammed against it. "Open up!" a loud voice demanded.

Fietlebaum opened the door, and seven armed Sholosons pushed their way through with blasters drawn. They pointed the blasters at him and Teysoot Motzo, and directed them into a far corner of the room. A moment later, Hagatt entered the room. Teysoot Motzo called out a tremulous but otherwise cheerful, "Good morning."

"Shut up!" Hagatt replied.

---

108 What will be, will be

109 Pins and needles

Hagatt stepped in front of Fietlebaum and demanded, "Where are the plants?" Fietlebaum started toward the walk-in laboratory to show him, but was stopped by Hagatt shoving the barrel of his blaster against his chest. "Tell me," he barked, "don't show me."

Fietlebaum's heart sank. "They're in the gray incubation cabinet on the counter," he replied.

Hagatt stepped to the cabinet. He slowly opened the incubation cabinet and carefully lifted the dish that held the plants off the tray and into the light of the room. Hagatt looked and saw the red and iridescent blue of the five small plants and smiled. He returned the plants to the incubator, then directed three of his crew to stand by the incubator and maintain guard around it.

"Get your things," he growled at Fietlebaum and Teysoot Motzo.

"You not tell us what for do!" Teysoot Motzo angrily protested.

Hagatt slammed the butt of his blaster against the side of Teysoot Motzo's head, and his crew simultaneously pointed their blasters at his chest. "Shut up and get your things, I said."

Hagatt gave them five minutes to gather their belongings, then he marched them to the elevator at the point of his blaster. They rode down, and when the door opened he pushed them out into the lobby. "You are getting into an aircab and going to the starport. Then you are leaving Sholoso and never coming back. You are lucky that I don't kill you."

One of Hagatt's crew flagged down an aircab. Hagatt opened the door. He shoved Teysoot Motzo in, then Fietlebaum. As the cabbie was purging his thrusters preparing for takeoff, Hagatt leaned into the cab and dropped three vials of jorftoss extract into Fietlebaum's lap. He winked at Fietlebaum and then, for good measure, gave

Teysoot Motzo one more smack in the face with his blaster. "Get off Sholoso! Don't come back!" he bellowed.

As Hagatt was withdrawing his head from the cab, the rattled but greatly relieved Fietlebaum regained enough presence of mind to whisper one last message to Hagatt. "Glesh must never know about the plants."

Hagatt responded with a barely perceptible nod, then ordered the cabbie to fly Fietlebaum and Teysoot Motzo to the starport. "Get them the hell out of here!"

The aircab sped off. They were on their way to the starport. Fietlebaum flashed the vials of jorftoss extract in Teysoot Motzo's direction, but he didn't react. He was pouting over the way Hagatt had treated him. He rubbed the sore and swollen side of his face.

"Why not he hit you?" he asked plaintively.

"Because you are bigger and easier to hit," Fietlebaum replied.

The answer was not immediately satisfactory, but the certainty and authority in Fietlebaum's voice lent the explanation credence. After a moment, Teysoot Motzo acquiesced. "I suppose so," he said.

Letting the issue go left Teysoot Motzo better able to be excited about the jorftoss vials. "Can I hold one?" he asked.

Fietlebaum sighed. *Like a little kid*, he thought, but he relented. Teysoot Motzo grabbed a vial, planted a kiss on it, then handed it back to Fietlebaum.

"She very pretty," Teysoot Motzo said.

The aircab arrived at the starport. Fietlebaum and Teysoot Motzo climbed out and walked to the terminal where they would catch a transporter to the starship to Borgost. As they rounded a corner in the terminal, Fietlebaum stopped and pulled Teysoot Motzo back around the corner from where they had come. "*Got in himmel!*" he exclaimed. "A Drajan stepped off the transporter down from the last starship." Fietlebaum peeked around the corner and quickly shrank back again.

"He's coming!" Fietlebaum gasped.

"Act nonchalant," Teysoot Motzo immediately suggested.

"Act nonchalant? Are you *meshugeh*?" Fietlebaum demanded to know. "How many old Hijdoris and fat Janpoorans do you think are touring Sholoso together this time of year? Do you think he'll look past us if we're nonchalant?"

"I suppose not," Teysoot Motzo admitted.

"We have to hide, you *schlemiel!*" Fietlebaum whispered insistently.

Fietlebaum saw the door to a utility closet and pulled Teysoot Motzo in with him. A few seconds later a group of travelers padded by the closet and seemed to walk on past to the aircab stands outside. Fietlebaum waited a few more minutes before peeking back out the door. No one was there, and no one was coming. They stepped out and walked briskly to the transporter and got onboard. "That Drajan belongs to Glesh," Fietlebaum said. "I know he does. We're leaving Sholoso just in the nick of time."

The transporter started its engines and took off towards the starship orbiting Sholoso. Fietlebaum now had the vials of jorftoss extract Hagatt had given him in a secret pocket in his jacket. He patted them in front of Teysoot Motzo to show him that the vials were safe and sound.

After a few minutes of silence, Fietlebaum revealed his thoughts to Teysoot Motzo. "I have to admit, that up until the moment Hagatt gave us the jorftoss extract, I had thought he had betrayed us. I am sure he had to be brutal to hide our working together. His crew would not have allowed cooperation with us. They would much rather have killed us. To have made and kept an agreement with us would have been far too soft and civilized for Sholoson tastes."

"I just wish he not hit me," Teysoot Motzo said, again rubbing his face.

"Ah, you don't look so bad," Fietlebaum told him. "The bruises give you a rakish look. The ladies will love it."

"Hah! You very funny, Fietlebaum," Teysoot Motzo replied. "But those ladies love me fine before Hagatt hit me."

The transporter arched up through the pink Sholoson sky. The sky turned from pink, to deep red, and then to black as they penetrated the last layers of atmosphere and touched space. The transporter docked with the starship bound for Borgost. Fietlebaum and Teysoot Motzo stepped off onto the starship, presented their tickets, then walked to the observation gallery to wait. As the starship continued to board, they sat and took their last looks at Sholoso. With the squalor of Dasholos, and the swamps and mud of the Sholoson jungles far below them, the planet was again a beautiful sight.

As he looked out upon the gleaming red and white planet, it occurred to Fietlebaum that in another few years, Sholoso would again have a rich harvest of jorftoss. He had mixed feelings. Genetically engineering the jorftoss was a remarkable accomplishment. But jorftoss was illegal, and for years the jorftoss trade had spawned violence and death across the galaxy. He wondered if his work would perpetuate it. On the other hand, as he had always told his pharmacology students, "There are no bad drugs, just drugs used badly." It was possible that some good could yet come of jorftoss if proper scientific attention were paid to its remarkable properties. He wanted to believe that he saved a plant with medicinal effects that someday might heal rather than harm sentient beings. But now it made little difference. He did what he had to do to save his grandson and himself. When he could, he would redeem himself, but for now redemption was a luxury he could not afford.

With the last of the stragglers finally on board, the public address system directed all passengers to the extended travel dorms. They stepped into their suspended animation chambers and said good bye to each other, as they would not re-awaken for another thirty-two months.

"Bon voyage!" Fietlebaum called out.

"Bon voyage for you, too!" Teysoot Motzo said in return.

They laid back in their chambers, the lids closed, and they drifted into nothingness. The starship accelerated into hyper-drive and sped off to Borgost.

CHAPTER 28

The starship decelerated and entered Borgost's atmosphere. From the observation gallery, they watched a panorama of the planet come into view. It was mostly ocean, with only a few land masses along the equator. Most of the life on Borgost remained in the sea. Millions of years of organic matter settling onto the sea floor provided the planet with a wealth of petroleum deposits to exploit. The economy of Borgost depended on the export of petrochemicals to other planets in its star system. The export of seafood to planets poor in protein resources was the second pillar of the Borgostian economy.

Like the Polmodi, Borgostian anatomy was radial in design. However, unlike the Polmodi, the Borgostians never achieved compartmentalization and elevation of body structures. They remained flat. They looked like star fish. They had six tentacle-like appendages radiating from a hub that contained vital organs; one large, black, compound eye; olfactory antennae; and a mouth lined with hundreds of very sharp, pointed teeth. On their underside were excretory and reproductive organs. They were dark gray in color, with smooth, moist, slippery skin. They exuded an odor of old, but not yet rotten, fish.

Although Borgostians were flat, by lifting the back three appendages up in the air and curling them up and over their central hub, they were, for short periods of time, able to balance on the tips of the three forward appendages and ambulate upright with astonishing speed and agility. Even their language reflected the considerable degree of pride that arose from being able to elevate to great heights on the front tentacles. The Borgostian phrase cybertranslated as "tip toe" meant something quite different from the English language phrase meaning to slowly and stealthily creep across a floor in an effort to remain discreet and undetected. In Borgost, to tiptoe was to be courageous, bold, and commanding. Whereas human children tiptoed into kitchens to steal cookies, Borgostian generals tiptoed into battlefields to wage bloody war.

It was unfortunate that in modern galactic life, the Borgostians' flat-to-the-ground anatomy often led them into awkward compromises of their integrity. Often, they were simply overlooked because of their lack of stature. They got stepped on a lot at inner galactic mixers, particularly when the functions were well attended by species with loftier anatomical architectures. At a recent diplomatic dinner party, an interplanetary incident was only narrowly averted when a near-sighted Klagdaggi official pulled up a chair and mistook the Borgostian ambassador for an ottoman.

Fietlebaum and Teysoot Motzo disembarked from the starship and walked into the terminal. The starport was bustling with Borgostians. Most were slithering across the floor, with the occasional tip toe-er running down the concourse while balancing upright, either in an effort to avoid missing his flight or to impress a girlfriend with his skill and prowess. The hordes of Borgostians turned the concourse into an obstacle course. On their way to the star taxi stand, Teysoot Motzo turned to ask Fietlebaum a question and promptly stepped dead center into the big eye of an elderly female Borgostian who at that moment was scuttling by him. Had he himself not been so startled and upset by the incident, he would likely have been taken into custody for battery and given a hefty fine. However, he screamed when he felt his foot sink into the squishy creature. He lost his balance, almost fell, and had to sit down for a moment to reconstitute. "Stepping in that old lady's eye almost give me heart attack!" he breathlessly complained. The starport security guards who witness the event told him to be more careful or face arrest the next time he was so reckless.

"My friend," Fietlebaum said after the incident, "you are a hopeless *schlemiel.*"

"Is that bad?" Teysoot Motzo asked.

"Not in your case," Fietlebaum said. "Somehow it suits you."

Fietlebaum spotted the star taxi counters at the far end of Concourse C and made a bee-line toward it with Teysoot Motzo in tow. A young Borgostian sat behind the counter. He was on a raised platform and propped up by pillows to sit at a more business-like eye level for the off-world customers. Fietlebaum asked him how they might arrange transportation to Jinkor.

"Jinkor? Sure, we can get you to Jinkor. You did say Jinkor didn't you?"

"Yes, Fietlebaum said. "We did and *do* say Jinkor. We want to go to Jinkor! Can't you take us?"

"Yes, we can take you to Jinkor, no use getting huffy about it," the Borgostian answered."

"Good," Fietlebaum replied. "How much will it cost to get there?"

"You mean to Jinkor?" the Borgostian asked.

"*Vey iz mir*!" Fietlebaum barked. "Of course to Jinkor! What the hell have we been talking about?"

"Yelling is not going to help, sir. So, you want to know how much it will cost to take a star taxi to Jinkor?"

"G*evalt*!" Fietlebaum bellowed. "Listen, you little *Chaim Yankel,* take your taxi to Jinkor and *shtup es in tuches*[110]!"

---

110 "Shove it up your ass!"

Teysoot Motzo pulled on Fietlebaum's jacket. "Fietlebaum," he said, "there another star taxi. Come on before you make you self crazy."

"Maybe it was me," Fietelbaum was willing to admit as they walked away. "Maybe it was being frozen in a starship for the last four years. But, that Borgostian was driving me *meshugeh*! I was ready to give him a *klop*."

"Borgostians make me crazy too," Teysoot Motzo agreed. "Come on, we see about other star taxi."

They walked further down the concourse and up to the service counter of the "Super Excellent Star Taxi Service." Teysoot Motzo rang the bell on the counter to call an attendant. No one came. After a few moments, he rang it again, but to no avail. Fietlebaum gave the bell a smack for one last try, and just as they had reluctantly turned around to head back to the Borgostian-run service, a deep voice boomed, "Super Excellent Star Taxi Service at you service. Where you want for go?"

The sound of the Janpooran voice from the behind the counter immediately spun Teysoot Motzo around. He turned and saw a huge fellow in a scarlet caftan with large, lime green chevrons emblazoned on the front and back. "Sessi Bosso?" Teysoot Motzo asked. "That you?"

"Teysoot Motzo?" the voice asked in reply.

The two old friends had recognized each other. They laughed and embraced. "This my old buddy, Sessi Bosso," Teysoot Motzo told Fietlebaum. Then, turning to his old friend, he added "and this my new buddy, Dr. Isaac Fietlebaum. He bighead psychiatrist."

"Oh, so you got you own psychiatrist now," Sessi Bosso said. "It about time. Has he help you, or you still crazy?"

"Hah! You funny boy, Sessi Bosso," Teysoot Motzo replied, then asked, "What you do here?"

"Well, after little problem I have with Janpooran Taxation and Revenue Board, I decide some change of scene might do me good. I be here five year now, flying star taxi at Borgost starport." Then Sessi Bosso stopped, cocked his head, and looked at Teysoot Motzo. "I think I might need little adjustment," he said with a wink. "Come with me." Sessi Bosso led them around the counter and into his office. He opened a drawer and pulled out a bag of *burzet* and a *moozore.*

"I need little adjustment myself," Teysoot Motzo noted with a laugh. Sessi Bosso filled the *moozore* with *burzet* and handed it to Teysoot Motzo, who proceeded to take a deep draught and hold it in his lungs. He handed the *moozore* back to Sessi Bosso who did the same. Sessi Bosso offered the *moozore* to Fietlebaum, but he declined. "No, thank you," he said.

In a few moments, the Janpoorans were giggling like school boys. They chattered away, catching up on friends and acquaintances. They reminisced about old girlfriends, petty larcenies, and unsubstantiated rumors. "It good see you, Teysoot Motzo," Sessi Bosso said with a laugh. "It good see you, too," he replied. They stared at each other in silence for a few seconds then exploded into laughter.

"So, where you go?" Sessi Bosso asked.

Teysoot Motzo looked puzzled for a moment, apparently having forgotten that he was tens of millions of miles away from home at a star taxi counter in the Borgost starport. Suddenly it came to him. "Oh yah!" he exclaimed with a laugh," We on way Jinkor for hide jorftoss."

"Jorftoss?" Sessi Bosso asked. There was an awkward silence.

"Uh oh," Teysoot Motzo said.

If looks could kill, Fietlebaum's glare would have been lethal. But murdering Teysoot Motzo would have been useless at that point, as the cat was already out of the bag. Fietlebaum could only sigh and shake his head. Then Sessi Bosso asked the obvious but devastating question, "Why you go hide jorftoss on Jinkor?"

It was no use trying to hide the truth. Fietlebaum explained that a jorftoss dealer, Erd Glesh, had kidnapped his grandson, and the jorftoss extract was the ransom to get him back. They were going to Jinkor to hide the jorftoss and later meet Glesh there to trade the extract for the boy.

Sessi Bosso fell silent. He was lost in thought. "Jorftoss illegal," he finally said with blatantly theatrical concern, "and it worth big money. Fietlebaum, this dangerous business you drag my friend into."

"Oh, he not drag me," Teysoot Motzo protested.

"Please, shut up," Fietlebaum said to Teysoot Motzo. Then he turned to Sessi Bosso and said, "Alright, say what you need to say. I'm listening."

"You sound suspicious," Sessi Bosso replied, feigning deep emotional injury, "but there no need for feel that way. I not greedy fellow. I not want jorftoss. It too nasty for me. But if I break law take jorftoss on my taxi, I want triple fare, both ways. In advance. Now."

"I understand," Fietlebaum grumbled in response. "It will cost us money to violate your high moral principles. Do you mind if Teysoot Motzo and I discuss it?"

"Please do," Sessi Bosso answered.

Fietlebaum took Teysoot Motzo by the arm and walked him into a corner to talk. "We have no choice," he said. "We have to agree. He knows too much. If he wanted to, he could turn us in right now for a big reward and we would be as good as dead. But, I don't like it. I don't like it at all. He may be an old friend of yours, but I don't trust him."

"Fietlebaum," Teysoot Motzo solemnly replied, "Sessi Bosso old, very dear friend of mine, and I not trust him either! We go along with what he say. We just got be careful."

They walked back to where Sessi Bosso sat. "Okay," Fietlebaum told him. "We'll pay you triple the regular fare in advance. But we need to leave this afternoon."

"Grab you things, Sessi Bosso said. "We almost there."

CHAPTER 29

It was a two week trip by star taxi from Borgost to Jinkor. It soon became evident to Fietlebaum and Teysoot Motzo that the Super Excellent Star Taxi Service had been misnamed. The quarters were cramped. The cabin smelled of reactor coolant and over-heated wiring. Every few hours, the startlingly loud hull breach alarm sounded. On each occasion, humidifiers automatically clicked on to pump water vapor into the cabin so that the site of the breach in the hull could be visualized as a spray of ice crystals out into the frigid void of space. Ostensibly, such a visual sighting might direct repairs. But it only served to make it unbearably wet and clammy inside. Drops of condensation rolled down the walls and shorted out equipment. No telltale fountains of crystalline spray into space ever emerged, and Fietlebaum finally convinced Sessi Bosso to "turn that *farkakteh* system off."

Along with having the disconcerting feeling of being back in the humid Sholoson swamps, they also suffered persistent hunger for something decent to eat. The food synthesizer on-board the star taxi was of the same brand as Fietlebaum's poorly functioning one back in his flat on Polmod. However, this one was two models older. No matter what was ordered, scrambled eggs, oatmeal, roasted *frelks*, or mashed potatoes, the meal it delivered tasted like crunchy, two day old tuna salad.

The only redeeming feature of the accommodations, at least from Teysoot Motzo's perspective, was that Sessi Bosso had a seemingly endless supply of potent, high quality *burzet*. It was his and Sessi Bosso's intention to become and remain very stoned for the entire trip. If they had failed, it would not have been for lack of trying. The two Janpooran friends spent most of their days alternating between inhaling *burzet* from the *moozore*, lying down, listening to loud music, and unsuccessfully trying to obtain something edible from the food synthesizer.

Fietlebaum read, meditated, and enjoyed simply staring out the portholes and watching the changing pattern of the stars and planets. After the first few days, the reservations Fietlebaum and Teysoot Motzo held about Sessi Bosso waned. Fietlebaum was willing to accept the possibility that Sessi Bosso was greedy and socially inept, but not evil. Teysoot Motzo had forgotten all about the suspicions he had voiced to Fietlebaum when they had first discussed making the trip with Sessi Bosso. His misgivings evaporated in a *burzet* haze.

A week into the trip, Fietlebaum was awakened by a subtle rush of air across his face and a pungent, camphorous aroma wafting past his nose. He eased an eyelid open enough to peek through and see Sessi Bosso bending over him blowing through the end of his *moozore*. As best he could, he shifted his gaze toward where Teysoot Motzo was bunking and could not see him. He shifted his gaze in the other direction, and in his peripheral vision he was able to make out what appeared to be Teysoot Motzo stuffed in the trash ejection tube.

Sessi Bosso continued to blow *burzet* vapors into Fietlebaum's face, apparently laboring under the false assumption that Fietlebaum, too, would become intoxicated and incapacitated by overexposure to the drug. Sessi Bosso was not aware that *burzet* had no effect on Hijdori. On the other hand, Fietlebaum correctly suspected that Sessi Bosso himself was, as the saying went, stoned to the gills.

Fietlebaum was in no position to sit up and simply demand that this six-hundred pound intoxicated Janpooran looming directly over his face stop what he was doing. Moreover, despite all indications, he wasn't entirely certain that the Janpooran was intending to harm him. *Who knows?* he allowed himself to consider. *Perhaps in his own awkward fashion, he is trying to be sociable.* For the time being, he decided to lie still and wait for Sessi Bosso to finish what he was trying to do. However, when he felt Sessi Bosso's fingers probing the pockets of his jacket, he knew he was searching for the jorftoss. He had to do something.

Fietlebaum built up his courage. With all the strength he could muster, he punched his fist into the center of Sessi Bosso's face. Then he pulled his knees to his chest and pushed out with his legs as forcefully as he could against Sessi Bosso's substantial belly, both forcing him back and knocking the wind out of him. The astonished and incredibly stoned Sessi Bosso stumbled back against the wall next to where Teysoot Motzo lay in the trash ejection tube. He quickly reached up with his hand to trip the button that would propel Teysoot Motzo out of the ship to certain death in space. However, in his haste and intoxication, he reached for the wrong switch and instead turned on the stereo music system, prompting a barely conscious Teysoot Motzo to reflexively sit up to better appreciate the tune. Sessi Bosso fought to push him back down in the tube to make it possible to eject him. At the same moment, Fietlebaum sprang up to retrieve the blaster Hagatt had given him out of his duffel bag. Sessi Bosso forced Teysoot Motzo back into the tube and was reaching for the proper switch to eject him into space when Fietlebaum found the blaster, turned it toward Sessi Bosso and fired. A flash of light, then a haze of acrid smoke filled the cabin of the Super Excellent Star Taxi.

Teysoot Motzo, having been startled into full consciousness by the blast, sat up and rubbed his eyes. "What for breakfast," he asked. "It smell terrible!"

Fietlebaum was shaking. "It's not breakfast you smell," he gasped, "it's your friend, Sessi Bosso."

"Hah!" Teysoot Motzo exclaimed. "You funny boy, Fietlebaum." He stood up and stretched. "Sessi Bosso," he called out, "Fietlebaum say you smell bad. You need bath!"

"Teysoot Motzo!" Fietlebaum screamed, "Shut up! You don't understand! The smell *is* Sessi Bosso. He's dead. I had to kill him with the blaster. He was about to eject you into space from the trash tube."

"What?" Teysoot Motzo asked with an increasingly serious look on his face. He stood up and realized that he was indeed standing in the ejection tube. He stepped out, then looked around for Sessi Bosso. He did not see him. "You not kidding, are you?"

"No," Fietlebaum said, "I wish I were, but I'm not."

Teysoot Motzo was shocked back into reality. "What happen?" he demanded. Fietlebaum told him everything. Teysoot Motzo sat and shook his head in astonishment.

"I've never killed anyone," Fietlebaum tearfully confessed. "I feel terrible. But I had no choice."

"Well," Teysoot Motzo said with a smile, "at least you take safety off. This time I got thank you for saving my life. Don't you worry about Sessi Bosso. That no good crook got what he deserve. I tell you I not trust him."

"Um hmm," Fietlebaum grumbled. "So now what do we do? Do you know how to fly this thing?"

"Well," Teysoot Motzo replied, "I fly a little ship like this when I work for mining company many year ago." He stepped up to the control panel. "Let see," he murmured to himself. He absently flipped a switch that activated the primary retrorocket. The star taxi immediately decelerated, and both he and Fietlebaum were violently thrown against the fore polycarbonate plate. "No, that not what I want," he said as he reached up and flipped the switch back off. Before Fietlebaum could stop him, he flipped the yaw control switch that sent them into a rapid spin. "No, that not what I want either."

"Stop!" Fietlebaum yelled. "Don't touch another goddamn switch!" He pushed Teysoot Motzo aside, and flipped the second switch back into its original position. Gradually, the spinning ceased.

"Don't worry," Teysoot Motzo told him, "I get hang of it before we land on Jinkor."

"Well I hope so," Fietlebaum shot back, "because it won't do us a damn bit of good for you to get it after we land on Jinkor."

"Better late than never," Teysoot Motzo said demurely.

Fietlebaum had to laugh. "Late *will* be never, you damn fool!"

"Hmm," Teysoot Motzo had to agree. "I suppose you right."

Fietlebaum slowly came to terms with what happened with Sessi Bosso. He was then able to focus his attention on the more pressing problems of how to fly the ship. He searched through the drawers and cabinets of the taxi, and found a few old, dog-eared, operation manuals. He demanded that Teysoot Motzo stop *burzet*, and the two of them spent several days reviewing the equipment and features of the star taxi. Teysoot Motzo recalled how the little space craft operated. Thankfully, while many of the systems on the ship were old and in disrepair, the computers, flight control systems and the automatic pilot modules were all fully operational. Fietlebaum reached the point where he no longer assumed their flight would end in a crash landing and certain death. *You sleep better that way*, he decided.

Jinkor grew larger in the view of space through the polycarbonate panels in the cockpit. Janpoor also shown in the distance, sparkling brightly from the sunlight reflecting off its blue oceans. They discovered that most of the instructions for the approach and orbital insertion had already been programmed into the flight computers by Sessi Bosso before they left Borgost. "He may have been crook," Teysoot Motzo noted, "but he was good pilot." However, there were too many variables for the final descent and landing to be programmed beforehand. The system expected the pilot to provide input at the necessary time. Hopefully, Teysoot Motzo would be up to the task.

That night, Teysoot Motzo stayed up and performed the remaining calculations. The next morning they inserted into orbit, and in the afternoon Teysoot Motzo decelerated in preparation for landing. The atmosphere of the large moon was thin, but the speed of the craft was high enough that it carved into the upper layers of atmospheric gas. Turbulence buffeted the craft, and the skin of the ship glowed red with heat. A steady hand was needed to steer the ship. Fietlebaum glanced at Teysoot Motzo for reassurance and noticed something funny about his eyes. Then he smelled a familiar, sweet camphorous odor.

"Teysoot Motzo," Fietlebaum barked, "you're stoned!" Indeed, he was absolutely ripped on *burzet*.

"I sorry, Fietlebaum," Teysoot Motzo said, "but I start thinking and remember how every time I ever land ship anywhere, I high on *burzet*. I not know how else to do it."

"Well, it's too late to do anything about that now," Fietlebaum reluctantly admitted. "Do your best."

The craft shuddered and groaned as it plummeted down through the atmosphere toward the surface of Jinkor. Fietlebaum swallowed hard. The pupils in his bright orange eyes opened wide. The rows of hairs on his arms and fingers stood up. "Do you think we're coming in a bit steep?" he asked.

"Maybe so," Teysoot Motzo said as he fought to level the craft. The G forces nearly flattened them to the floor as the craft carved a trajectory that abruptly changed from perpendicular to parallel to the moon's surface.

"Do you suspect we might be travelling a tad too fast," Fietlebaum inquired.

"We could be," Teysoot Motzo replied. He fired the retrorockets, the velocity noticeably decreased, and the shuddering craft calmed in its attitude. They were now swooping gracefully above the surface of Jinkor. Teysoot Motzo initiated the autopilot landing computation module.

Teysoot Motzo guided the craft to a level area of the moon while the computer worked velocity, direction, gravitation, and atmosphere characteristics into the landing calculations. He spotted a suitable area on the horizon, entered coordinates into the computer, and ordered the autopilot mechanism to set down on that point. There was then a series of whooshes, clicks, lifts and turns that were the system's fine adjustments of direction, speed, pitch, and yaw. "It sound like it working," Teysoot Motzo said with satisfaction.

The craft reached the selected area and hovered several hundred meters above the surface before slowly and gently easing itself down to the surface. "I think I do pretty good job," Teysoot Motzo remarked as he stood, chin out, arms folded, in the cockpit. Fietlebaum resisted the comments that came to mind. They touched down, light as a feather.

Fietlebaum sighed an enormous sigh of relief, then congratulated Teysoot Motzo on his remarkable success. "You did it, my friend," he said, "and I'm proud of you!"

Once on the surface, Teysoot Motzo determined from maps and celestial positioning system data where on Jinkor they were. He had made many excursions to the moon of Janpoor when he was younger, and he was familiar with its landmarks and terrain. "I know where we land," he said excitedly. "We in equatorial plane close by Jivitz Crater. There a place nearby—big cave. We used go there get high on *burzet* and have parties when I young," he told Fietlebaum. He winked and elbowed Fietlebaum in the shoulder, "I surprised I remember this place at all."

"Is the cave a place where we could hide the vials of extract?" Fietlebaum asked.

"Absolutely!" Teysoot Motzo replied. "It good place."

"Good," Fietlebaum concluded. "Then we can hide the jorftoss in the cave, and then arrange to meet Glesh back here to make the trade for my grandson."

The atmosphere of Jinkor was not compatible with life. It was thin and contained percentages of methane and nitrogen that were toxic for most life forms in the galaxy. The star taxi had various sizes and types of space suits, and plenty of tanks of air of various combinations to suit most species. Fietlebaum and Teysoot Motzo zipped into space suits, and stepped into the air lock to exit the star taxi. A four wheeled surface rover was strapped securely inside the airlock. They unfastened it and climbed in.

When the airlock doors flew open, Teysoot Motzo engaged the electric motor and pulled forward. The battery powered rover whined and kicked up clouds of dust when they rolled off the landing ramp and onto the soil of Jinkor. It was a bleak place. The atmosphere was just thick enough to capture light and give the landscape an eerie, orange glow. Looking straight up, the sky was too thin to provide color, and the black of space was stark. Still, the landscape was not without its own, austere beauty. The rocks and stones strewn across the surface were orange and green. They lay in fine, purplish gray sand. Silver stars glimmered in the blackness, and Janpoor, blue and brilliant, rose slowly on the horizon. "A remarkable place," Fietlebaum admitted.

Teysoot Motzo accelerated and rolled off toward the distant rim of Jivitz Crater. "The crater about seven kilometers away," he said. "Just before we get there, we drive down little canyon two kilometers before cave."

"So you remember how to get there?" Fietlebaum thought to inquire.

"Oh sure," Teysoot Motzo replied with a laugh and dismissing wave of his hand. "I been here million time!"

Fietlebaum found Teysoot Motzo's unbridled confidence disconcerting, but decided it best to say nothing for the time being.

They drove about twenty minutes. The rim of the crater loomed ahead. The arms of a large, convoluted canyon came into view. There were several possible routes through it. Teysoot Motzo slammed on the brakes. He thought deeply, talked to himself, drew maps with his finger in the palm of his hand. After several minutes of deep concentration, he turned to Fietlebaum and said with utmost assuredness, "I not think we get there from here."

"*Oy*," Fietlebaum replied. "A *kopveytik*[111] you're giving me."

Fietlebaum sat in silence and thought. State-dependent memory was well known in Fietlebaum's neuroscience circles. There were thousands of instances in the literature. A common example was a drunk who could not remember where he hid his bottles of whiskey until he got drunk again. *Maybe*, Fietlebaum thought, *the* burzet *did help Teysoot Motzo remember how to pilot the taxi. At least he didn't kill us! If he was always stoned on* burzet *when he came here, perhaps the* burzet *will help him remember how to get to the cave.*

"Teysoot Motzo," Fietlebaum said, "do you have your *moozore* and *burzet* with you?"

"I thought *burzet* not do nothing for you," Teysoot Motzo replied.

"Not for me, damn it, for you!" Fietlebaum barked.

Teysoot Motzo patted himself through the thickness of his life support suit. He felt the hard outline of his *moozore*, but nothing else in his jacket. "I got *moozore*," he said, "but no *burzet*."

"Well, the *moozore* is something," Fietlebaum mumbled. He hoped that the smell and feel of the *moozore*, and the

---

[111] headache

act of inhaling and holding his breath might be enough to jog his memory for all the times he made the turn in the canyon toward the cave while stoned on *burzet*. He had Teysoot Motzo fish out his *moozore* and slip it up through the neck of his suit.

"Okay," Fietlebaum told him, "smell your *moozore*. Smell the *burzet* that has been in it. Feel the *moozore* against your *ahzha*. Inhale it and hold it deep." Fietlebaum had him do it again and again. He hoped that the residue of *burzet* left in the *moozore* might give him a little buzz, and the smell, the feel, and the going through the motions would do the rest."

"Party at the cave!" Fietlebaum suddenly sang out. "Drive, drive, drive!" At first Teysoot Motzo resisted, but Fietlebaum insisted. "Don't think," he insisted. "Drive!"

"Here we go," Teysoot Motzo cried out. "It party time!" He hit the accelerator, threw dust, fishtailed, spun out and headed down one of the canyon roads.

"Drive, drive, drive!" Fietlebaum demanded. Teysoot Motzo took a sudden left, then a right. As they drove further down the canyon, the terrain began to look familiar. "This it!" he called out. "Bighead Fietlebaum, you right!"

They drove several more kilometers and stopped by the entrance of the cave that Teysoot Motzo had described. They got out and walked in, with the lights of the rover left on to illuminate their way. "Does anyone ever come here anymore?" Fietlebaum asked.

"No," Teysoot Motzo asserted. "After penalties for *burzet* decrease years ago, no one fly all the way Jinkor just for get high. Now, they stay home and get high without all of bother."

The two of them looked around the cave.The sandy floor was littered with candy wrappers and empty bags that had at one time contained *burzet*. Teysoot Motzo suddenly let out a whoop and ran to the far wall of the cave. There he pointed out to Fietlebaum some graffiti that he had scrawled on the rock forty years before. "See!" he exclaimed. "I tell you I here before."

"Yes, I suppose you must have been," Fietlebaum replied. "What does it say?"

"It say, "Girls! For good time, call Teysoot Motzo, ABA-GHW40."

Fietlebaum laughed. "You *shmuck*!" he exclaimed. "That's the kind of thing other people write to embarrass you. You don't write that about yourself!"

"Why not?" Teysoot Motzo asked in perfect innocence, "It work real good!"

"Come on," Fietlebaum said. "Let's find a good place to hide the vials."

"Follow me," Teysoot Motzo called out with a laugh. He spun a half-turn clockwise from where he stood next to the graffiti, and strode ten paces along the wall. His foot wound up next to a rock that he pushed to the side, revealing a small hole in the wall.

"Hah!" Teysoot Motzo cackled. "This my old hidey hole! It serve me well many year ago."

He held out his hand for Fietlebaum to give him the vials of jorftoss extract. Fietlebaum handed them over. Teysoot Motzo slid the vials into the hole and pushed the rock back in front of it.

"That's that," Fietlebaum said with satisfaction. "Let's head back to Borgost."

CHAPTER 30

The fortune in jorftoss extract was hidden on Jinkor, and they were on their way back to the Borgost Starport to catch a starship to Silesia. For Fietlebaum, it was an opportunity for a tranquil two weeks of reading, meditating, and gazing at the stars. Unfortunately for Teysoot Motzo, the only *burzet* that had left the Borgost starport with them had vaporized along with Sessi Bosso when Fietlebaum hit him with the blaster. He spent much of the first day grieving the loss of the *burzet* until Fietlebaum got tired of it and put his foot down. "Get over it," he demanded in no uncertain terms. Much to his credit, Teysoot Motzo did. But it left him with a good deal of time on his hands. Fietlebaum noticed the distress and boredom Teysoot Motzo was suffering and engaged him in conversation.

"So," Fietlebaum inquired," what were those days like when you and your friends got high and partied on Jinkor?"

Teysoot Motzo immediately warmed to the subject. "Hah!" he laughed. "Back then we terror of galaxy. When we around, daddies hide daughters and mommas turn boys' heads other way."

"I can't imagine why," Fietlebaum noted with tongue firmly in cheek.

"Ahhh, we young, have good time," Teysoot Motzo replied. "There nothing we not do on bet, and no bet too small. I remember my friend, Fotto Bozzi, dare me take police cruiser for ride. At first it going be little ride around block. But I never in first class machine like that. Just around block not do at all. Boys pile in. Off we go. That our first trip for Jinkor. We stay two day then fly back for Janpoor. We push cruiser off cliff into lava flow, then stow away on freight cruiser flying back for Pinshett. I glad I not get caught. I still be in jail. Now you tell me good story about boys on Hijdor."

Fietlebaum was at a serious loss. "I could tell you about my *bar mitzvah*," he said, "but I'm not certain it would hold your attention. There wasn't much adventure or intrigue involved. The only danger we faced was the remote, but grim possibility of the *gefilte*[112] fish going bad before the reception."

"What? Fietlebaum, I think you crazy," Teysoot Motzo exclaimed. "I not know what you talk about."

"Ironically, that's exactly what our caterer said," Fietlebaum replied. After a moment's pause, he asked, "So why didn't you ever settle down and raise a family on Janpoor?"

"Oh, I not family raising kind I suppose."

"Did you ever fall in love?"

"Oh, Fietlebaum, what kind question you ask me?"

"Apparently the kind you don't like to answer."

Teysoot Motzo sat silent for a long time, and Fietlebaum decided it would be unkind to pursue the question any further. But Teysoot Motzo himself continued the conversation. "Yes," he said, "I in love once."

"When were you in love?"

"Oh, maybe twenty year back, long time ago. Her name Uttu Esso. She very beautiful and sweet. We talk about marry. We talk about kids. I young and stupid. I make money. Work for mine company. Stay away from home. Fly around galaxy for overtime pay. There *burzet*, females, big times. Sometime I not want go home. She get sad. She get

---

112 "wrapped," referring to chopped fish being cooked wrapped in fish skin. Very tasty!

sick. I should have known. Maybe I did know. When I away she stop her life. She dead three week when I get back."

"I'm sorry," Fietlebaum said, "I shouldn't have asked those questions."

Teysoot Motzo sighed. "No," he replied philosophically, "it okay. You good boy, Fietlebaum. It not good that nobody ask. Sometime it start feel too heavy inside. It bad what I do. I do many bad things. Sometimes I think I no good at all. Then I think, maybe I not so bad after all. I keep going."

"There's a lot of heartache in this life," Fietlebaum said. "It's not easy."

"No, it not," Teysoot Motzo agreed. "But life only show in town."

They sat quiet for several minutes before Fietlebaum asked, "You hungry?"

"Yes," Teysoot Motzo replied, "but food on star taxi worse than terrible."

"You're right, it's wretched," Fietlebaum agreed. "Maybe we can find something else to eat in the storage bins." They rifled the storage compartments, and after half an hour of searching they came up with a can of smoked KorpianVorplebeast, a packet of freeze dried foopet berries, and a pouch of Astaran mesterberry juice. "God knows how old these are," Fietlebaum said, "but anything is better than what that *farkakteh* synthesizer puts out."

They gathered the booty they collected and sat at the fold-down table by the control panel. Fietlebaum poured each of them a glass of the mesterberry juice and offered Teysoot Motzo a toast. "*Le' chayim*, my friend," he said.

"*Le' chayim* for you too," Teysoot Motzo replied.

After years of flying the star system, the approach to Borgost starport from almost every direction had already been programmed into the computers and autopilot system of the Super Excellent Star Taxi. Over the following days, rockets would abruptly fire for a few seconds in complex patterns, then shut off. On a few occasions, the mid-course corrections gave them a jolt, but, for the most part the return trip was uneventful.

After another week, Borgost loomed large in the front polycarbonate panels. The fine course adjustments became more frequent as they reached the planet. The autopilot inserted them into orbit, then decelerated for descent to the surface. They descended over seemingly endless expanses of water before finally seeing islands peeking up above the waves. The land mass broadened, and the first indications of cities and civilization appeared. They swooped down over the city and over the Borgost starport. The control tower overrode the autopilot and had the star taxi circle for half an hour before being cleared for landing. Then the autopilot clicked back into operation, and the star taxi settled down on the tarmac.

Fietlebaum had avoided the subject on the flight, but had realized they would have some explaining to do. They would have to report the circumstances surrounding the death of Sessi Bosso to the Borgostian authorities.

Teysoot Motzo objected. "Can we let bygone be bygone?"

"A dead star taxi pilot isn't exactly a bygone," Fietlebaum was quick to point out.

"I suppose not," Teysoot Motzo reluctantly admitted.

"Don't worry," Fietlebaum told him. "We can skip the part about the jorftoss that would get us both executed."

"Good plan," Teysoot Motzo replied after a moment of consideration.

They climbed off the taxi and walked into the terminal. They looked around and spotted a sign directing them to the starport police station. They strolled through the door and up to the sergeant's desk. Fietlebaum told the Borgostian sergeant, "We need to report the death of a star taxi pilot."

"What was his name?" the sergeant asked, without diverting his eye from the paperwork he had been filling out.

"Sessi Bosso."

The sergeant quickly looked up and shifted his big eye toward Fietlebaum. "What happened?" he inquired.

Fietlebaum went on to relate that they had hired Sessi Bosso to take them to Jinkor, but all along the way he abused *burzet*. He became psychotic and attacked them both. At one point he even tried to eject Teysoot Motzo out into space through the trash ejection tube. Fietlebaum explained to the sergeant that he had to fire a blaster at him to prevent he and his traveling companion from being killed. "It was an act of self-defense," he asserted.

The sergeant listened to Fietlebaum's story, then sent several officers out to inspect the taxi. "Just between you and me," he said after the investigators left the room, "Sessi Bosso was a well-known *burzet* addict. We had had him under surveillance for months. It's a scourge, that *burzet*. It drives the Janpoorans wild. They can't help themselves. It leads them to exhibit disgraceful, despicable behavior."

"Oh, it not so bad as all that," Teysoot Motzo interjected.

Fietlebaum cast a disapproving glance and said, "I think the sergeant knows more about these matters than we do."

Teysoot Motzo leaned forward into an argumentative stance. But before he could launch into a defense of *burzet*, Fietlebaum leaned forward to meet him with a wide-eyed glare. He acquiesced.

The investigators returned from the Super Excellent Taxi about an hour later to file their report. After reviewing the information they brought him, it all seemed perfectly reasonable to the sergeant that the killing of Sessi Bosso was an act of self-defense made necessary by the homicidal effects of *burzet*. This was all the more evident given the taxi was returned, nothing was stolen, and the two of them went immediately to the police to report the incident. "We will investigate further and contact you if more information is required," he said, "but for now you are free to go."

Fietlebaum sighed with relief, and he and Teysoot Motzo had turned to leave when a Borgostian police captain who had overheard discussion about the case sidled up in front of them and blocked their exit. "What were you doing on Jinkor?" he asked.

"We can't tell you, Teysoot Motzo blurted out.

"*Vey iz mir*," Fietlebaum muttered to himself.

"Why can't you tell me?" the captain demanded.

"Why can't we tell him?" Teysoot Motzo frantically asked Fietlebaum.

"Uh, doctor-patient privilege," Fietlebaum quickly answered.

"Please explain," the increasingly suspicious captain ordered.

"I am Dr. Isaac Fietlebaum," he said as he flashed his medical license to the captain. Then he quickly set his mind to constructing a plausible explanation.

"I'm a psychiatrist and Mr. Teysoot Motzo is my patient," he tentatively began. "I did not want to reveal the nature of our therapeutic interaction, but let the record show that I am being forced to divulge it." He cast a lingering glance of disdain at the captain, which served not only to intimidate the Borgostian, but to provide himself a few extra seconds of creative breathing room. "The trip to Jinkor," he asserted, "was a necessary and fundamental part of Teysoot Motzo's psychiatric treatment." Then Fietlebaum hit his stride.

"When Teysoot Motzo was very young," he explained, "his grade school class left Janpoor and went on a weekend fieldtrip to Jinkor, which is, as you know, the moon of Janpoor. Excuse the indelicacy, but on the way he crapped his pants and became an object of ridicule among the other students. He never got over that traumatic event.

Thereafter, whenever he travelled by public conveyance, he has suffered a paralyzing fear of crapping his pants again. It has been a very difficult and disabling condition for the unfortunate fellow. For years, he sought help for the problem without success. When finally he came to me, I realized that it would be necessary for us to return to the scene of the psychological trauma. That is why we hired the Super Excellent Star Taxi Service and met Sessi Bosso. We travelled to Jinkor, and the therapeutic intervention I performed was quite successful. Unfortunately, this current embarrassment you've created will probably be a major setback in his therapy." He cast another rueful glance at the captain. "I hope you are satisfied," he added.

The sergeant giggled, and the captain reprimanded him. "I'm sorry, doctor," the captain stammered. "Be on your way."

"Come on," Fietlebaum told Teysoot Motzo, and they walked briskly out of the station.

"Why you have for tell him I crap my pants?" Teysoot Motzo asked plaintively.

"Well it wouldn't have made much sense to tell him that I, the doctor, had crapped *my* pants, now would it?" Fietlebaum asked in reply.

Teysoot Motzo stopped for a moment and scratched his head in puzzlement. "Well, you got me there," he admitted, "but I still not like it."

"Your embarrassment is all for a good cause," Fietlebaum told him as they continued walking through the terminal. Again, the concourse was full of flat, tentacled Borgostians slithering across the floor to and from ticket counters, starships, and baggage terminals. Teysoot Motzo was careful where he stepped, wanting to avoid another, old lady incident. At one point he narrowly avoided a collision with a tip-toer, but beyond that he negotiated his way to the ticker counter without difficulty. They bought tickets for the starship flight to Silesia, and made their way back across the bustling concourse to the gate from which the starship was departing. They found the gate and waited to board the starship to Silesia.

They were exhausted, pensive, and sat silently at the gate for nearly half an hour until Teysoot Motzo stirred. "I never crap my pants," he asserted in dejected tone.

"Let's drop it, shall we?" Fietlebaum responded. They sat silently for another few minutes. The departure of the starship was announced, and they boarded the starship for Silesia where they intended to meet Glesh.

CHAPTER 31

The crew of the starship led the passengers into the main observation gallery where they were assembled for identification, security clearance, and review of starship safety procedures prior to take-off for Silesia. Many of those boarding the starship were Silesian, but the passenger list also included Gorsids, Humans, Korpians, Drusidis, an Astaran, several Borgostians, and a Janpooran or two. There were also a few passengers of species that Fietlebaum recognized from pictures, but had never before encountered in his travels across the galaxy. After the procedures in the gallery were completed, the passengers filed into the suspended animation dormitories where they would be spending the next three years in transit to Silesia.

Before they were led to the dormitory, Fietlebaum had asked to use the starships communications center to send a message to Silesia. His message was directed to the Galactic Intelligence Agency. He informed them that it was of utmost importance that he speak directly with agent Erd Glesh about an extremely important matter of Galactic security, adding that Glesh would know what the matter concerned. He concluded by informing them that he and Teysoot Motzo would be arriving on Silesia in approximately three years, and hoped to speak directly with agent Glesh around that time.

After sending the message, Fietlebaum and Teysoot Motzo retired to the dormitory to be placed in suspended animation. "With any luck," Fietlebaum told him as he stepped into his chamber, "they will contact Glesh, and he will arrive on Silesia not long after we do."

"Not for worry," Teysoot Motzo said. "Our plan work. You see."

By chance, their starship journey to Silesia coincided with Transgalactic Lifespan Synchronization Time, a time in which every sentient being in the galaxy was placed into suspended animation. After hundreds of years of experience with transgalactic starship travel, the central galactic government saw the need for a method to adjust the pace of ordinary life to mesh with all of the years starship travelers had to spend in suspended animation to get from one place in the galaxy to another. It was deemed unacceptable for diplomats to travel to an area of conflict in the far end of the galaxy only to arrive twenty-five years after nuclear devices had destroyed the planets in question. It was also awkward for them to awaken after arrival on a planet only to find that those they were to have negotiated with had been dead for ten years. The solution was to have every sentient being in the galaxy go into suspended animation at the same time for three out of every nine years.

Transgalactic Lifespan Synchronization Time, or TLST as it was called, was first seen as heavy handed. Wags in the press referred to it as daylight savings time on steroids. Also falling under media scrutiny was the awkward fact that the brother-in-law of the galaxy's Vice-President was also the galaxy's largest manufacturer of suspended animation chambers. Nonetheless, after lengthy litigation in central galactic court, TLST was seen as the only reasonable way to coordinate life in a galaxy where a significant number of important individuals were at any one time lying frozen and unconscious on a starship.

It was the powerful beings in the galaxy who were the primary beneficiaries of the plan. The only selling point of TLST for the masses was the highly touted thirty percent increase in the length of one's life. The fact that this thirty percent of their increased life span would be spent in a state not half as stimulating as a full coma did not detract from the allure of longevity. It was like a poor man's jorftoss. Thus, the rank and file of the galaxy eventually lent their support, and TLST became a reality

Ordinarily, there was something comforting about going into suspended animation with every other sentient being in the galaxy. But Fietlebaum had a lot on his mind as the suspension gas enveloped him. Lives were at stake. In his last minutes of lucidity, Fietlebaum struggled with the sudden realization that Glesh might ignore the TLST mandate and use the time to gain advantage. He fought against the sedation to strategize, as a numbing cold swept over him. "But, what can I do about it now?" he asked plaintively, "*Gornisht*[113]*!" The word, "gornisht,"* reverberated in the last operating neural network in his brain, and he sighed a sigh of resignation before he fell into unconsciousness.

Fietlebaum felt himself rise slowly into awareness. He had experienced it many times, but this awakening was different. His visual field was illuminated by a burning bright light. From somewhere deep in the recesses of his mind, words from the ancient Bardo Thodol, the Tibetan Book of the Dead, floated up into his consciousness. *Remember the clear light,* the sacred words said, *the pure clear white light to which everything in the universe returns. Let go, trust it, merge with it.*

The light grew more intense. Mein Got*!* Fietlebaum thought. *I've passed to the other side!* There were murmurs and whispers around him. *Voices of eternal consciousness!* he suspected. There was rustling of fabric, shuffling of feet. *The gossamer gowns of angels,* he assumed, *but angels with*

---

113 Nothing!

shuffling feet? The sound of shuffling feet grew louder. Nu? *How do feet figure into this*?

Fietlebaum felt the painful tingling of energy surging back into his reanimated brain and body. He ached. The brilliant, white light again flashed into his eyes. "That's him," he heard a voice say. "Dr. Fietlebaum," the voice said. "Dr. Fietlebaum." He fought to slowly open his eyes, and was stung by the glare of a flashlight in the hand of a Silesian deck hand. "Dr. Fietlebaum," the voice asked, "are you awake?"

"Yes, yes," he murmured. "I think I'm awake. I'm not dead, am I?"

"No, you ain't dead," the deck hand replied.

"*Oy*," he groaned as he shook the sedation from his brain. "Are we on Silesia?"

"No," the deckhand said. "We're twenty-three days out from Borgost. Something has happened. There was a mistake in the programming of one of the suspended animation chambers. The chamber popped open and reanimated the passenger too early. It was a young Yorpigi girl. She was all alone when she woke up, and got scared half to death. She flew around and got stuck up in a ventilation shaft."

"Wait," Fietlebaum interjected. "Did you say she flew around?"

"Yah, that's what I said," the deckhand answered. "Those Yorpigi can fly pretty good! Anyways, her flying around where she shouldn't have set off an alarm, and the system reanimated us to wake up and take care of it."

"I see," Fietlebaum said, "but what does this have to do with me?"

"Well," the deckhand replied, "we looked at the manifest and saw that you're a psychiatrist." He furtively glanced at the other hand, who nodded his head in encouragement to continue. Then he turned back to Fietlebaum. "Doc," he insisted, "this little girl is nuts!"

The deckhands led Fietlebaum down a passageway, through a hatch, and into a utilities servicing area where the roof was high and the wiring, plumbing and ventilation systems of the ship were exposed. As soon as he ducked into the hatch, he heard a fluttering of wings and high pitch screeches. As he followed the Silesians further into the utility room, the fluttering and screeching grew louder. The air in the room was thick with a creosote-like odor. It was a pheromone, a signal of distress, exuded by the Yorpigi and wafted into the air by her frantic wing beats. After a few more steps, hc looked up and saw her.

The Yorpigi were insect-like creatures. They had exoskeletons and brilliantly colored, translucent wings. Their heads and faces resembled those of cicadas, with red, compound eyes on the top of their heads. They had long antennae on the sides of their heads that possessed olfactory as well as exquisitely sensitive vibrational transducers. Not unlike cicadas and crickets, the Yorpigi produced sounds by rubbing fine bristles on their arms against a ridged, hollow structure that extended out from the thoracic exoskeleton. The rubbing generated a continuous, high pitched drone almost indistinguishable from that of a violin. Through variation of pitch, rhythm, and tenor, they generated words and sentences in a sophisticated musical language.

Fietlebaum saw that the unfortunate young Yorpigi girl was extremely frightened. She screeched so many different notes, with such rapidity and intensity, that she sounded like the string section of a large orchestra tumbling down an endless flight of stairs. His cybertranslater could not keep up. He asked the device to analyze her speech in slow, time-delayed mode. Although he would not be hearing her words in real time, he would at least get a general sense of what she was trying to communicate. He was startled by what he heard. "Those boys were right," he said to himself. "The poor thing's gone *meshugeh*."

Reanimating could be a disturbing experience for anyone. However, awakening alone, with no one to talk to, and no one to ease her back into her normal state of consciousness, must have been truly terrifying for the young Yorpigi. Yet, Fietlebaum concluded that she was suffering from more than simple fear. A form of psychosis happened now and then in those awakening from suspended animation after transgalactic travel. There was confusion and disorientation in the disequilibrated brain. Sufferers often had the delusion that they were no longer the same or even unreal after having been frozen and reanimated. This seemed to be what she was experiencing.

She cried out to demons she believed had taken control of her body. She begged them to leave her alone. Not only had they taken her body, but she feared they were working on taking her soul as well. She screamed for help. She screamed for mercy. She screamed for her mother. She flapped her wings and lodged herself ever tighter into the air ducts and electrical conduits.

Fietlebaum called out to her, with aid of the cybertranslater, but she only became more frightened. He suspected it may have been due to the cybertranslater's poor rendition of the otherwise lovely and musically pure Yorpigi language. It must have sounded terrible to her, out of tune. He called to her again, without the aid of the cybertranslater, hoping that his natural voice might convey a sense of empathy to calm her. However, with his own voice so alien and abrasive, she took him for yet another demon and burrowed deeper into the ductwork.

"Maybe we can take her down with a blow dart," one of the deckhands suggested.

"*Bist meshugeh*[114]?" Fietlebaum hollered at him. Still, the Yorpigi girl continued to shake and scream, scraping

114 Are you crazy?

her arms across the exoskeleton in an endless cacophony of torment.

Fietlebaum trotted back to his compartment in the suspended animation dormitory and searched through his belongings. He returned and handed a memory cube to the deckhand. "Play selection three-hundred and twenty," he told him. The deckhand plugged the cube into the starship's sound system and the *Meditation* from Massenet's *Thais* flowed out of the speakers. The starship filled from stem to stern with the plaintive, ethereal cry of a lone violin.

Gorgeous! Fietlebaum thought. At that moment he longed to be a Yorpigi, for it occurred to him that for a being whose very language and soul was musical, the graceful, soaring voice of the violin must have seemed the most rapturous form of poetry. The tone, timbre, and inflection of the violin was so similar to the Yorpigian voice that the tormented girl immediately stopped her frantic cries to listen. The spasms of fear diminished, and she calmed down.

"Get me a ladder!" Fietlebaum ordered one deckhand, then he ordered the other to bring him the first aid cart from the starship's infirmary. The deckhand set up the ladder as Fietlebaum searched through the medications in the first aid kit. He knew next to nothing about Yorpigian psychopharmacology, but the kit did contain a substance that he knew was as close to a universal sedative as one could hope for under the circumstances. The drug, vicilidine, acted as a partial blocker of a variety of ion channels in the membranes of neurons. Almost every form of neural tissue, regardless of species, had such channels, and the dampening of activity through them tended to reduce overall neural activity and bring relaxation and sleep. He quickly read the packaging material and saw no contraindications in Yorpigi. He asked the deckhand for her name from the passenger list, then he headed up the ladder.

He climbed to where the Yorpigi had lodged herself. She was calmer than she had been, but still frightened. Fietlebaum realized that as different as he was in anatomy from Yorpigi, he must have been a hideous sight for the girl. "*Nu?*" he muttered. "A *ferkrimpter ponim*[115] I can't change." He had the cybertranslater sing her name, and she seemed to relax a bit more. He offered her the pill. "Please," the cybertranslater sang, "take this. It will help you feel better." She resisted. But, after a few more tries, she shot out her proboscis and snapped up the pill from his hand. "*Got tsu danken*," Fietlebaum murmured. He hoped that in another few minutes she would begin to calm further.

Fietlebaum stayed with her for the next few minutes. The shaking and rustling of her wings stopped. When he asked her how she was doing, she told him she felt better. She asked where the demons had gone, which let Fietlebaum know she wasn't out of the woods. But that was expected. Delusions never simply came and went. They always melted away slowly. He started to help her down the ladder, but she fluttered down to the floor on her own, and waited for him at the base. Then he and the deckhands led her back to the dormitory where they programmed another suspended animation chamber for her. She was drowsy by then, and no longer anxious or frightened. As she slipped into her chamber she looked up at Fietlebaum, yawned, and asked him what that was that she had heard on the starship's sound system. "I had never heard anything so beautiful," she said. "I thought an angel was singing to me."

"You know," Fietlebaum told her, "that's what I thought the first time I heard it." Before he turned off her light and closed the lid of her chamber, he kissed her on the forehead. "*A guteh nacht*[116]," he whispered, "*un ziseh droymer*[117]."

---

[115] A twisted face.

[116] good night

[117] sweet dreams

He walked back to his own dorm room to return to his suspended animation chamber. It felt odd and curiously lonely to know that he was one of only a few sentient beings out of hundreds of trillions in the galaxy that was awake and conscious. He walked by Teysoot Motzo's chamber and looked in on him through the glass lid. "*Schlofgezunt*[118], you charming *schlemiel*," he said. "We have work to do in the morning." He climbed into his own chamber, and the lid lowered and shut. He drifted back into unconsciousness with Massenet's melody swirling through his brain.

118 Sleep well

CHAPTER 32

Still cloudy in their thoughts, and with aches and pains throughout their bodies from reanimation syndrome, Fietlebaum and Teysoot Motzo sat and watched the surface of Silesia come into view through the portholes in the observation gallery. Of the five continents on the planet, Forgion, Torstina, Brioshi, Modlont, and Listaf, four were entirely urbanized. Each of those continents had grown to become a single, enormous city that stretched uninterrupted from sea to sea. The largest of these urbanized continents, Forgion, was more commonly referred to as the Galactic Capital Zone.

As they descended through the atmosphere toward the Galactic Capital Zone Starport, the surface features of Forgion slowly grew in size and definition. Teysoot Motzo stood up to better appreciate the view. "I never see place like this!" he gasped. The city below them seemed endless. It bristled with skyscrapers climbing ten miles or more into the sky. Twelve miles above the surface, skylanes bustled with local traffic. From their vantage point on the starship, no individual vehicles could be discerned. Rather, the skylanes appeared as organic Tattersall patterns, vibrating and shifting in color and shade, stretching from horizon to horizon. Ground traffic, also heavy throughout the day, could be discerned as yet another, deeper, set of shifting patterns of color and shade. At times in their descent, intersecting lines of skylane and ground traffic generated moiré patterns that dazzled their eyes.

"What all these creatures do here?" Teysoot Motzo asked in amazement.

"This is where the work of the galaxy gets done," Fietlebaum nonchalantly replied.

Dusk was falling as the starship approached the starport. Lights flashed on here and there across the Galactic Capital Zone fifteen miles below them. Soon the city was blanketed above by the darkness of night and spangled with lights below as far as they could see in every direction. The starport appeared as a wide depression in a vast expanse of towering buildings. Beacons identified boundaries and landing zones. Strobe lights warned of security areas. The tarmac far below them was dotted with thousands of starships from across the galaxy. Their red and green navigation lights flashed on and off like a field of fireflies on a warm Kansas night. A myriad feathered points of light, the headlights of ground transport vehicles, circled, danced, and dodged among the starships as passengers were sped to and from the terminals.

As the starship dropped below the level of the surrounding skyscrapers, they descended into a deep canyon of steel, glowing nanotube filament, and sparkling glass. The city around them pulsed with frenetic motion. Aircabs and commuter air transporters streaked to and from the air lanes high above, while thousands of floating optical display panels flashed traffic updates, directions and warnings. Elevators zipped up and down the sides of the skyscrapers. The streets stretching out between the buildings, beyond where the eyes could see, were lined with shops, restaurants, and theaters. They swarmed with pedestrians and ground cabs. Laser images of hotels and restaurants whirled across the sky. Video billboards blazed advertisements, customs requirements, and security information for travelers arriving on the starships.

The starship floated across the tarmac and nestled down. Offloading ramps were positioned, and passengers lined up to file off the ship. Farther ahead in the line, Fietlebaum was delighted to see the Yorpigi girl who had suffered the reanimation psychosis. He walked up to her and asked her how she was feeling. However, she appeared not to recognize him. She shied away and would not answer. *Just as well,* Fietlebaum thought. *She is better off not remembering.*

He walked back to rejoin Teysoot Motzo, who was busy staring out at the towering skyscrapers through the portholes in the deck of the starship. "I never see place like this!" he said repeatedly. He pressed his face against the polycarbonate for an ever so slightly closer look. One of the deckhands from the starship walked by, stopped, and tapped his shoulder from behind. "Please," he said, "kindly back away so as to not leave streaks on the window."

Teysoot Motzo turned and showed him his fist. "Please, kindly back away," he told him, "so as not get hit with this!" The deckhand scurried off, and Teysoot Motzo turned back to enjoy the view with his face plastered against the window.

Like a kid in a candy shop, Fietlebaum thought.

The starship crew gave the word to disembark. The passengers filed off the starship. Fietlebaum and Teysoot Motzo walked through the long concourse to reach ground transportation. They found the exit and passed through the doors out into the Silesian night. Even from the sidewalk of the starport, the energy and motion of Silesia was palpable. There was nothing you couldn't obtain in Silesia, and much you could find nowhere else. It was the center of everything new and exciting, whether intellectual, artistic, scientific, or culinary.

"I never see—" Teysoot Motzo began, before Fietlebaum cut him short.

"You've established that fact," he asserted. "I think it's time to go on."

The Silesians were a graceful and intelligent species. They were tall, hairless, and pale in skin tone. They had large cranial vaults, two large black eyes, tiny noses, and small mouths with thin lips. Like humans, they were bipedal, with two arms and hands with five long, graceful fingers. They were a highly evolved species with an extremely ancient and long-lived civilization. Their science was well developed, and their first sojourns into space took place while the ancestors of humans were still evolving from Australopithecines. They were among the first space travelers of the galaxy and for many planets, including Earth, they were the introduction to intelligent life beyond their own worlds. Thus, it was entirely fitting that Silesia became the seat of Galactic government. For Fietlebaum, being back on Silesia was being back in the center of the universe.

As they stood in line at the taxi stand, Fietlebaum realized that he was laboring under the lingering fog of reanimation syndrome. This was followed by the disturbing realization that he had absolutely no idea where they were going. When he conveyed this to Teysoot Motzo, the ever-hungry Janpooran resolved the uncertainty characteristically by suggesting they get something to eat. "I not eaten in three years," he said. "I starving!"

At that moment, the laser advertisement that serendipitously flashed across the sky was for Moishe's, "The Best Jewish Deli in the Galaxy!" "*Got tsu danken*!" Fietlebaum cried out loud. "We're back in civilization!"

Fietlebaum pointed out the ad to Teysoot Motzo. "Have you ever eaten a corned beef on rye?" he inquired.

"No," Teysoot Motzo answered, "but sound good for me."

"Then let's go," Fietlebaum said, his mouth already beginning to water. "We can figure out the rest later."

They slowly progressed to the front of the taxi line, a ground cab pulled up and they got in. "To Moishe's

Delicatessen, please," Fietlebaum said. "You got it," the Gorsid cabbie replied.

The Silesian ground cabs were sophisticated machines. Their guidance systems automatically provided them a quarter inch clearance on all sides of the cab at any speed up to two-hundred miles per hour. The cabbie peeled out into the street, accelerated further, and zipped into traffic at breakneck speed after coming murderously close to three other cabs, two pedestrians and a police cruiser. They arrived, twenty-seven blocks away, in three minutes flat. They stepped out of the cab and strolled a few more yards to the entrance of Moishe's Delicatessen.

The Best Jewish Deli in the Galaxy was smaller than Fietlebaum had expected. He and Teysoot Motzo squeezed through the door past several exiting customers and walked down a narrow corridor. The cash register counter was on their right, with a long, glass-covered counter of delicious looking food on their left. Deep dishes of rolled cabbages, bowls of chopped liver with caramelized onions heaped on top, *knishes*[119], *blintzes*, *lokshen kugel*[120], egg barley, roasted brisket, steaming pans of corned beef, pastrami, beef tongue, caldrons of chicken soup with *matzo* balls, *kreplach*[121], and egg noodles floating in the broth. Fietlebaum nearly swooned. At the end of the counter they stopped and waited to be seated.

As they waited for a table, a young Hasid with a black fedora, beard, and *lange peyes*[122] stepped up to the register. After paying his bill, he lingered at the counter a moment. He stuck his hand in his pocket, pulled out a small coin, and handed it to Moishe. He had inadvertently shorted Moishe a deci-*horki* the last time he ate. "I've owed you this

---

119 Stuffed roll

120 Sweet noodle pudding

121 A stuffed dumpling usually served in soup

122 Long sidelocks

for two weeks," he said sheepishly. "I wanted to clear my conscience."

"*Oy*!" Moishe shouted. "An entire deci-*horki*! That missing deci-*horki* explains why I couldn't sleep all those nights. A *groisser macher*[123] you are. *A gezunt der en pupik*[124]!"

"Hmm," Fietlebaum whispered to Teysoot Motzo. "A *farbissener*[125] we've got."

The waiter in a white shirt and black vest walked up and led them to a table. They walked past walls covered with signed holographic portraits of many of the celebrities and dignitaries that had eaten at Moishe's over the years. Many were long dead, forgotten, or both. When activated by the viewer's proximity, the holograms switched on. Again, if only for a few seconds, the old hoofers danced, the crooners crooned, and the comedians did their *shtik*[126] on their miniature stages.

Most of the customers seated at the tables in the back were Humans. Several were Hasids who had immigrated from Earth. There were many Hasids on Silesia. The planet was one of the commercial centers of the galaxy, and most were involved in the galactic diamond trade. There were always a few Hasids at Moishe's. It was the only restaurant that served kosher food on Silesia, and for them it was a lovely piece of home away from home.

For reasons that neither Moishe nor anyone else could fathom, Jewish food was also enormously popular among the Drusidis. There was a relatively large population of Drusidis living in the diplomatic quarter of the Galactic Capital Zone. They all flocked to Moishe's. At one point, Moishe had considered barring the Drusidis from the

---

123 A real big shot

124 Good health to your belly-button! A derisive form of thank you.

125 A grouch

126 bits

deli because of their predilection for ordering their corned beef sandwiches on whole wheat with mayonnaise and bread-n'-butter pickles. "What kind of *meshugeneh* does this?" Moishe was often heard to ask. But, after multiple entreaties from representatives from the Drusidi community, as well as a few from his accountant, he relented.

They were seated at a table squeezed in among several rows of tables, practically cheek to jowl with customers on either side. The deli bustled with activity, with five or six waiters continuously carrying trays piled high with food out from the kitchen. Three busboys just as persistently carted empty plates back. The food on the trays looked and smelled wonderful. One of the waiters burdened under an enormous tray loaded with food, reached into his back pocket with one hand, grabbed two menus, and slapped them down in front of Fietlebaum and Teysoot Motzo. Fietlebaum decided that he would have a bowl of *matzo* ball soup and a corned beef on rye. He urged Teysoot Motzo to try the corned beef, and to order a bowl of *kreplach* soup as an appetizer. When the waiter came by again, Fietlebaum called out what they wanted, and the waiter nodded in response.

The soup arrived. The waiter deftly slid the piping hot bowls in front of Fietlebaum and Teysoot Motzo, and in the same sweeping motion retrieved the menus and spun away to other duties. A plump *matzo* ball, floated in golden chicken broth, caressed by slivers of carrot, celery, and onion. But Fietlebaum was disconcerted. When the waiter passed by again, he called out, "Waiter, taste this soup." The waiter glanced down, and condescendingly remarked that the restaurant was known for serving the most delicious and well prepared *matzo* ball soup in the galaxy, and that his distaste for the soup could not possibly be anything more than a failure on his part to appreciate that obvious fact.

Fietlebaum was resolute. "Taste the soup," he insisted.

"Sir," the waiter curtly replied, "there is nothing wrong with the soup."

"Taste the soup," Fietlebaum again insisted.

With an air of having been unforgivably imposed upon, the waiter relented and agreed to taste the soup. But he hesitated. "There is no spoon," the waiter observed.

"Aha!" Fietlebaum retorted while waggling a reprimanding finger in the air. He then peered over the rims of his glasses with a silent, but withering stare. The humbled waiter turned, rolled his eyes, and retrieved a spoon so that the vindicated psychiatrist could finally savor his soup.

"*Oy, geschmakt*[127]," Fietlebaum said dreamily.

Teysoot Motzo was similarly enjoying his *kreplach*. "Umm, delicious," he said while simultaneously spooning broth and *kreplach* into his mouth. Fietlebaum resisted asking him to not speak with food in his mouth, as such a request of a Janpooran was both socially and anatomically irrelevant. Besides, Fietlebaum allowed that a sentient being perched before his first bowl of genuine *kreplach* soup could be forgiven his ill manners.

"*Vey iz mir*," Fietlebaum said with satisfaction as he patted his now bulging stomach. "A wonderful meal."

"Yes, very tasty," Teysoot Motzo agreed. "Too bad we not got *kreplach* back on Janpoor."

They got their check, left a tip, and stepped into line at the cash register counter to pay. Moishe Goldblat himself was at the register. In front of them, a Drusidi was paying his bill. He looked up from a search of his billfold with a pained expression. "Moishe," the Drusidi hesitantly said, "I'm a little short. Put it on my tab, and I'll pay you next time."

"You'll what?" Moishe asked.

---

[127] yummy

"I'm short," he said sheepishly. "I'll pay you next time."

"Hmmm," Moishe replied. "That's what I thought you said. Hmm, hmm, hmm" His face grew red, and his lip trembled. "This is a delicatessen!" he hollered. "Did I open a savings and loan? You want credit, yet?" He pointed in the direction of the door. "*Gai avec, gai*!" he bellowed, "*Zol dich chapen beim boych*[128]!"

Fietlebaum then stepped to the register, paid his bill, and mentioned to Moishe, "*Nu, afh yenems tuches is gut sepatchen*[129]."

Moishe did a double take at the orange-scaled, blue-lipped, Hijdori's perfect Yiddish. His astonishment robbed him of a clever rejoinder. All he could do is stare and mumble "*vey iz mir*" repeatedly as Fietlebaum and Teysoot Motzo walked out.

They caught a cab on the street and asked the driver to suggest a decent hotel within a mile or so. "The Silesian Guardian Hotel is a nice place," the Silesian replied.

"Please take us there," Fietlebaum requested.

"You got it," the cabbie said, and they zipped into traffic and zoomed off to the hotel.

Teysoot Motzo pressed his face against the window.

"So you've never been in a big city before?" Fietlebaum asked him.

"No," he said. "I thought I had, but not one like this. Biggest city I ever been in, Pinshett."

"There is nothing in the galaxy you can't find here in Silesia," Fietlebaum observed.

"Hmmm, I like this big city more all of time," he replied.

The cab pulled up in front of the Silesian Guardian Hotel. A young Silesian in a doorman's uniform immediately trotted out to the cab and opened the door.

---

128 "You should get a stomach cramp!"

129 "It's nice to smack someone else' ass."

Having recently become leery of doormen, Teysoot Motzo jumped out, grabbed his bag with one hand, and made a fist with the other, which he promptly shoved in the doorman's faced. "Back off!" he demanded.

"As you please, sir," the Silesian said. "Welcome to the Silesian Guardian Hotel." Fietlebaum was more civil, and allowed the Silesian to take his bag and escort them into the hotel.

They walked through the revolving door of the hotel and entered a new world. This was no Dasholos Hotel. The floors were of fine marble with multicolored inlays forming intricate geometric patterns. The high ceilings were hung with enormous, brilliantly lit chandeliers. They had finely detailed molding with gilded accents. Trees covered with blossoms rose to the ceilings from stonework planters scattered about the spacious lobby. Blossom covered vines twined around supporting columns that were themselves finely detailed with gilded molding, marble inlays and crystal light fixtures. Statuary and marble fountains graced the center of the lobby, where an Earth-style string quartet entertained, and tables were placed for the sipping of cocktails and fine wines. The hotel bustled with well-stationed guests from around the galaxy. Bell captains snapped their fingers to command cadres of bellboys carting luggage to and from the arriving limousines, the front desk, and the banks of elevators.

"I could get used to place like this," Teysoot Motzo remarked.

They checked in, sent bellboys up to their rooms with their bags, and followed them up in the high velocity elevators. Fietlebaum said goodnight to Teysoot Motzo at his door, then trudged down to his own room to sleep off the remains of his reanimation syndrome.

CHAPTER 33

Fietlebaum woke up that first morning on Silesia with a hankering for cheese blintzes. He thought he would ask Teysoot Motzo to join him for breakfast at Moishe's Deli. He got dressed, walked down the hallway to Teysoot Motzo's room, and knocked on the door. There was no answer. He knocked again, suspecting that his friend was either sound asleep or preoccupied with a young Janpooran female he might have met the night before—perhaps, that morning. Still, there was no reply. *Maybe he's in someone else's room*, Fietlebaum thought. *He'll show up. He always does.*

Fietlebaum took the elevator to the lobby and enjoyed the stroll through the sumptuous décor of the hotel. He stepped through the revolving door to the sidewalk, and the Silesian doorman whistled down a cab for him.

"Moishe's Deli!" Fietlebaum sang.

"Moishe's it is," the Drusidi driver replied, adding with a laugh, "Maybe I'll join you. I love Moishe's." The cab accelerated into traffic, and in only a few minutes they were in front of the deli.

Fietlebaum hopped out of the cab, his mouth watering in anticipation of the breakfast he had planned. He walked through the door and was immediately beset by Moishe and a customer having a friendly discussion.

"You don't like the *bialys*[130]? You don't like the cream cheese? You don't like Moishe's? Maybe you'd like the

[130] A bagel-like roll, but flat and chewy like an English muffin

cemetery better!" Moishe hollered. *"Gerharget zolstu veren*[131]*!"* The Human customer extended the middle finger of his hand, a gesture Fietlebaum recalled as being vaguely offensive on Earth, and stormed out. Moishe immediately turned in Fietlebaum's direction, smiled a broad, cherubic smile, and sang out "Good morning, *mein Yiddisher* friend! I'll have the waiter take you to your table."

Fietlebaum was promptly led to a table. The deli was buzzing with customers. Waiters stepped by with plates of scrambled eggs with pastrami, bagels, lox, *matzo brie*, omelets, blintzes. "A *mechaiyeh*[132]!" Fietlebaum said out-loud. He had ordered, gotten his food, and eaten half-way through his plate of eggs and blintzes when he received a call on his communicator. "Hello," Fietlebaum said. "What?" he practically shouted, "Again?"

It was Teysoot Motzo. He was calling from a tenement building in a tough, Janpooran section of town. He had gone there to buy *burzet*, but made the mistake of leaving his money bag behind. He was being held by a Janpooran drug dealer by the name of Posso Gotzi. He figured Teysoot Motzo was either a narcotics agent to hold for ransom, or a sucker to fleece. Either way, he was going nowhere soon.

"Come quick! Bring you money bag!" Teysoot Motzo cried plaintively." I tied up. They got blasters."

You stupid shmuck, Fietlebaum thought. "I'll be right there," he said.

First, however, Fietlebaum finished eating. "I've waited too long for a breakfast like this to let Teysoot Motzo ruin it," he muttered. He paid his bill and caught a cab for the address Teysoot Motzo had given him. As they sped down the streets, Fietlebaum had to wonder, *How many times in his life has this hapless* putz *been kidnapped?* He sighed.

---

131 You should drop dead!

132 A magnificent pleasure

"*Nu?*" he said, "as the saying goes, *tsum shlimazel muz men oich mazel hoben*[133]."

Halfway to Posso Gotzi's hangout, something occurred to Fietlebaum. He told the cabbie to change course and take him back to the hotel. The cabbie did a stomach wrenching u-turn, and sped off to the Silesian Guardian Hotel. When they arrived, Fietlebaum hopped out and asked the cab to wait while he retrieved something from his room. Fietlebaum zipped up to his room. He opened the door and trotted over to his bag. He was hoping his memory served him correctly. He could have sworn there was a small vial still hidden in the lining from when he placed it there on Janpoor. He felt around, patting here and there, and finally felt its outline. He reached his hand in through a loose flap in the lining and snatched the vial with his fingers. *This might help lubricate the negotiations,* he thought. He trotted back to the elevator, rode to the lobby, and walked briskly through the lobby to the front door where the cabbie had waited for him. "Let's go," Fietlebaum told him. The cab shot into traffic and zoomed off toward the tenement where Teysoot Motzo was being held.

The glitz and glamour of the hotel district faded. The cab entered what appeared to be a rundown part of town. The sidewalk traffic was sparser and less well-heeled. Many of the storefronts were empty. At the speed they were travelling, it was difficult to pick out details. But, if he moved his head just right, he could briefly fixate on objects outside. He thought he saw an inordinately large number of Janpoorans on the sidewalks. The cab came to a screeching halt at the address he had given the cabbie, and his suspicions were confirmed.

A burly gang of Janpoorans started his way when he climbed out of the cab onto the sidewalk. He was going to have to bluster his way through. He strode off to meet them

---

133 Even for *bad* luck, you need luck.

half-way. "I'm Isaac Fietlebaum, and I'm here to see Posso Gotzi," he declared. As an afterthought he added, "and don't fuck with me." They looked at one another and shrugged their shoulders. They let him pass, less out of being intimidated than simply taken aback. He sauntered over to the stairs of the building when he encountered a second group of Janpoorans, whom he also warned not to fuck with him. They let him pass, but not before they searched him for weapons. A third gang of Janpoorans stopped him inside the building by the elevator, but they figured that if he gotten this far there must be nothing of value left to take. They let him on the elevator, and he rode up to the floor where Teysoot Motzo told him he was being held.

He rode to the 527th floor and got out to look for the room number that Teysoot Motzo had given him, but it wasn't necessary. Down at the end of the hall, a gang of Janpoorans were out in the hallway, inhaling *burzet*. They saw Fietlebaum, and called out to him, "You dumb ass friend over here!" Fietlebaum strolled over, being as nonchalant as was possible under the circumstances, and told them that he was Isaac Fietlebaum. "Don't fuck with me," he was careful to include. No one replied, they just opened the door of the apartment where Teysoot Motzo was tied up and waved him in.

Fietlebaum peered in and cautiously stepped through the door. Raucous Janpooran music was playing on a cheap stereo, and the spicy odor of *burzet* hung heavy in the air. He heard Janpooran voices chatting and laughing. He saw silhouettes against the drawn drapes, but the light was too dim for him to make out who was in the room. From somewhere in the back of the room he heard Teysoot Motzo calling his name, and another Janpooran quickly telling him to, "Shut up!"

Someone switched a light on. The illumination revealed half a dozen Janpoorans, some standing, some sitting, all very big, with one even bigger fellow, whom Fietlebaum correctly assumed was the leader, sitting in a ragged, over-stuffed chair in the corner. He slowly stood up, as if very tired or very bored, and started lumbering over. It looked to Fietlebaum like a small mountain was coming his way.

"I, Posso Gotzi," the big Janpooran said in a deep booming voice. He stopped six inches away from Fietlebaum, towering several feet over his head. "You friend owe me money," he said looking down. "He owe fifty Silesian *horki* for *burzet*, five-hundred *horki* for being big pain in my ass. You bring you money bag?"

"No, I didn't," Fietlebaum said.

"Oh no!" Teysoot Motzo groaned, "you not mean that."

"Shut up!" Fietlebaum, told him.

Posso Gotzi cocked his head, bent closer, and scrutinized Fietlebaum. "You say you *not* bring you money bag?" he asked in decidedly menacing fashion.

"I've got something better than money," Fietlebaum declared.

"Oh no!" Teysoot Motzo cried, "not again!"

"Shut up!" Posso Gotzi told him. Then he turned back to Fietlebaum and asked him, "What you got?"

"Designer shodom," Fietlebaum replied.

"Oh no!" Teysoot Motzo cried, "not again!"

"Shut up!" Fietlebaum and Posso Gotzi demanded in unison.

"What in hell designer shodom?" Posso Gotzi inquired.

"I can't explain," Fietlebaum told him. "It's better to have some of your boys try it." He reached into his pocket and pulled out the vial of the molecularly engineered shodom that Beshted had returned to him after he used it to temporarily obliterate Teysoot Motzo's mind before the union meeting in Pinshett. He sprinkled a few flakes on the outstretched hands of two of the Janpoorans, and told them to lick it off.

The first Janpooran licked off the flakes of shodom with relish and a moment later felt his way backward to fall helplessly down into a chair. He stared into space for several minutes before giving out a loud, long exclamation of, "W-o-o-o-o-o-ow!" or at least that was what the cybertranslater made of it. The second one then quickly followed suit. He gasped and fell on the floor. "Wick-ked ba-a-a-a-a-a-ad," is what he appeared to say before his voice trailed off into nothingness.

It was an impressive display. Posso Gotzi and his crew stood and gawped at the stoned Janpoorans, both of whom were now staring into space and mumbling incoherently. They were quite taken by the quality of the drugs that Fietlebaum had access to. "It's yours," Fietlebaum said as he handed the vial to Posso Gotzi. "There are twenty more hits of the designer shodom left in here. It's my gift to you."

"Hah!" Posso Gotzi laughed. "You wicked bad boy!" Fietlebaum was now one of the crew.

"Here," Posso Gotzi excitedly said to Fietlebaum, "now I got something for you can try." He pulled out a bag of what looked like *burzet*, but it was deep red, and its aroma was far stronger than the *burzet* he recalled smelling before. The Janpooran loaded his *moozore* with the special *burzet* and inhaled deeply. He held his breath until he exhaled with a loud groan, then fell back into an empty arm chair. He was so incapacitated by the big hit of *burzet* that he was unable to lift his hand to offer the *moozore* to Fietlebaum. One of his crew had to trot it over to him. Fietlebaum put the *moozore* to his mouth and, knowing full well that *burzet* didn't do a thing for him, inhaled deeply and held the *burzet* infused air in his lungs. All eyes were upon him as he held it in and finally let it out with a rush of air. They waited for the lightning bolt of intoxication to strike him down, but he simply stood there, smiling and winking at them. Finally, he shrugged his shoulders and politely said, "That was very good shit, thank you." The Janpoorans were blown away. This Fietlebaum fellow was no one to trifle with.

"It's been lovely," Fietlebaum said, "but I would like to leave with my friend now." Posso Gotzi emerged from his *burzet* stupor long enough to tell him, "That okay, Fietlebaum, you good boy." He had his crew untie Teysoot Motzo's hands and give him an extra bag of the good stuff to take with him. He told one of the boys to go along with them out of the building and uptown a few blocks, where they could safely catch a cab back to the hotel. "Don't be a stranger!" he called out to Fietlebaum as he was leaving, then collapsed back into his chair.

They rode the elevator down, stepped out into the rundown lobby of the building and out to the street. The Janpooran gang on the street saw him and Teysoot Motzo, and gravitated toward them like moths to a flame. But, Posso Gotzi's fellow turned them away with a simple, "Don't fuck with Fietlebaum." He walked them up a few more blocks, and said, "You safe here." He walked away, but after a few steps turned around and added with a laugh and a shake of his head, "Fietlebaum, you wicked bad!"

Fietlebaum hailed a cab. "Thank you, Fietlebaum," Teysoot Motzo said as they climbed in. "I owe you one."

"Actually, you owe me two," Fietlebaum replied, "but who's counting?"

"Hah!" Teysoot Motzo said. "You funny boy."

"You hungry?" he asked Teysoot Motzo.

"I always hungry," Teysoot Motzo replied.

"Well, come on," Fietlebaum said. "We'll go to Moishe's. The *kreplach* is on me."

"Moishe's Deli," Fietlebaum called out to the cabbie. This cabbie was an Astaran with no interest whatsoever in what Moishe's Deli had to offer. "Moishe's," the cabbie echoed back matter-of-factly as he jetted out into traffic.

"I wish we have *kreplach* back on Janpoor," Teysoot Motzo said.

"Yes," Fietlebaum replied. "I know. You conveyed that desire yesterday."

"Well," Teysoot Motzo said with a shrug, "it still true."

They rode for a minute without speaking. Then Fietlebaum broke the silence. "We'll have a nice lunch," he said, "but then we need to deal with a less pleasant subject. After you load up on *kreplach*, we'll catch a cab over to the Galactic Intelligence headquarters and find out if Glesh is on his way back to Silesia."

CHAPTER 34

The scanning and identification devices at the entrance of the Galactic Intelligence Agency were unparalleled in sophistication. Upon entering the building, one walked through a sensory gate. Nuclear Magnetic Resonance spectroscopy activated vibrations in the molecular bonds between nucleotides in the DNA helices in predictable patterns, and the identification of characteristic spectra allowed the almost instantaneous sequencing of an individual's genome. The resulting genome was simultaneously compared with a hundred trillion existing genomes in the data bank, and the individual was identified within microseconds. The computational power required for the rapid accumulation, assimilation, and resolution of the enormous amount data generated in this process was impressive. It was roughly the same as would be needed to predict temperatures, wind velocities, and precipitation patterns for every square foot of a small planet for a year. No facilities outside of Silesia had such equipment.

Fietlebaum strode through the gate in three steps. "Good afternoon, Dr. Isaac Fietlebaum," the system said almost instantly in perfect Hijdori. "Please progress to the intake desk and state your business."

"Remarkable!" Fietlebaum cried.

A moment later, Teysoot Motzo bounded through the gate, and the system spoke in flawless Janpooran, "Good afternoon, Mr. Teysoot Motzo. Please address outstanding parking violation fee, precinct 27, Janpooran City, delinquent 9.72 Nirsten star system years."

"Wow!" Teysoot Motzo exclaimed wide-eyed. "This really some place!"

They strode over to the intake desk and informed the Silesian clerk that they needed to find out if a particular Galactic Intelligence agent to whom they were to give important security information was on his way back to Silesia and when he might be expected to arrive. The clerk took their names, entered them into the daily log, then directed them to the Information Retrieval Office on the 4378th floor. "The elevators are behind you," he said. "They will be expecting you there."

The bank of elevators ran for several hundred yards. The elevators that served floors 4300th to 4400th were down about fifty yards. They walked there and pressed the up button. The elevator door opened and a small crowd of nearly thirty beings of different species pushed their way off. The elevator cleared, and they stepped on, accompanied by a dozen other riders.

After a few minutes of travel, including several stops at lower floors, Fietlebaum and Teysoot Motzo reached the 4378th floor. The floor directory showed the Information Retrieval Office to be down the hallway. They reached the office and stepped up to the receptionist's desk. Fietlebaum informed the clerk who they were and why they had come, but the clerk cut him short. "We know why you are here, Dr. Fietlebaum," the Astaran clerk said, and he handed each of them a dossier. It described everything that had been recorded about them in the galaxy's information net or had been obtained through other, more ill-defined methods of surveillance.

Fietlebaum glanced through the most recent additions to his cyber history and noted the request he placed in the Borgost starport for the GIA to page Glesh and retrieve him for a transfer of important information. It was disconcerting to see that his travel to Jinkor had also been recorded. Mein Got[134]," he thought. *Glesh could have gotten hold of this information. He could have followed us there.* After a moment of rising anxiety, he sighed. Nu? *If Glesh had known these things I would probably be dead already.* "Please have a seat," the Astaran said. "Someone will come for you."

They waited two or three minutes, when a Drajan came out of a room down the hallway and turned toward them. Fietlebaum first thought it was Glesh, and his heart leapt in his chest. It was not. "Please follow me," the Drajan said.

They got up and followed the agent into an adjoining room. He gestured for them to have a seat, then he himself circled behind the desk and sat down. He leaned back and interlaced his fingers across his chest. "So," he said, "what can we do for you?"

Fietlebaum was struck with the disconcerting feeling that since the Galactic Intelligence Agency already knew everything, the conversation was a mere formality before dragging them away and executing them for jorftoss trafficking. He briefly fought a peculiar urge to simply confess and get it all over with. *Don't be meshugeh*, he had to tell himself. "We are here on Silesia to see agent Erd Glesh," he told the Drajan. "We have important information that is not for your ears."

The Drajan remained impassive for a moment. "We know exactly why you are here," he finally said.

Vey iz mir, Fietlebaum thought. *The jig is up*.

"Agent Glesh was contacted, and he has informed us that you have information about labor unrest on Janpoor that could jeopardize production of critical military equipment. He also informed us of how Teysoot Motzo was working with him to uncover a conspiracy to take control of the mining unions and disrupt productivity."

---

134 My God

He knows how to cover his tuches, Fietlebaum realized. "Yes," he replied to the Drajan, "The three of us were working together very closely."

"We are also aware of how you smuggled Teysoot Motzo off Janpoor to bring us the information," the Drajan noted. "Very clever," he added. "Everyone on Janpoor still believes that Teysoot Motzo went crazy, and then escaped the asylum." He paused in thought. "Kesset was on that case," he noted as if in reminiscence. "I had worked with him on Lorsid on the Plusirten affair, which doesn't concern you, of course. I never much cared for him." The agent became more animated. "That idiot, Kesset, was beaten senseless by the Gorsid before hospital security came in and rescued him." He laughed out loud. "Hah! That rotten sonuva bitch never knew what hit him. Couldn't have happened to a nicer guy!"

He laughed a big belly laugh, caught himself, then fought to regain his composure. He cleared his throat and took on a stony facial expression as he mechanically rattled off parting words. "Agent Glesh will be here, day after tomorrow, at fourteen-hundred hours. You are expected to be here. That will be all." He got up quickly, stepped around the desk, and strode out of the room. As he went out the door, he was gasping, snorting, and practically choking himself trying to stifle the laughter that continued to bubble up from his picturing Kesset being beaten, bitten, and strangled by the mad Gorsid.

"Charming sense of humor," Fietlebaum wryly noted. "He's probably a million laughs at autopsies." Then he turned his thoughts to the more serious concern. "Your plan worked, my friend," he told Teysoot Motzo. "Glesh will be here the day after tomorrow."

"We be here, too," Teysoot Motzo said firmly.

They said nothing more until they were down the elevator and outside the GIA building. "Glesh is no fool," Fietlebaum finally said. "He knows that he is potentially in as much trouble as we might be. The good part is that he thinks us so important that he is willing to let them see us as his collaborators. He obviously needs us to stay healthy, at least for the time being."

"He just in it for money," Teysoot Motzo said. "If you help make money, he keep you alive. If you cost money, he kill you. Here, he mind his p's and q's. So, here we got figure way stay safe when we go trade extract for you grandson. Out there, it be too late."

"Yes, of course," Fietlebaum replied. "You're right." Fietlebaum reflected for a moment. *Teysoot Motzo may act the buffoon half the time,* he thought, *but underneath it all, he's a very shrewd fellow.* "So what do you suggest we do?" Fietlebaum asked him.

"I not got slightest idea." Teysoot Motzo answered.

Well, Fietlebaum thought, *he tries.* He sighed. Again, there was silence. They flagged down a cab, and headed back to the hotel.

On the way, Fietlebaum considered their situation. Although Teysoot Motzo had no solution for it, he was right in noting that the most dangerous part of the misadventure would be back on Jinkor with the actual transference of the jorftoss to Glesh. On Jinkor, there would be nothing to prevent Glesh from killing them all after he had the extract placed in his hands. The more Fietlebaum thought about it, the more it seemed the most likely thing for Glesh to do. He and Teysoot Motzo, alone, would not be capable of fighting off Glesh. But, if he contacted authorities for help, he and Teysoot Motzo would be sentenced to death for trafficking. He considered having Teysoot Motzo enlist his Janpooran cronies to help. But, when he reflected on his own Janpooran acquaintances, Bostoff Metzee, Sessi Bosso, and Posso Gotzi, he realized he would be better off fighting Glesh alone. Then, it came to him. "Why didn't I think of this before?" he whispered.

They arrived at the hotel. "I believe I have a way to protect ourselves from Glesh on Jinkor," he told Teysoot Motzo as they climbed out of the cab, "but I will need the help of an old friend at the Medical School. I'll drop by tomorrow and speak with him. It has been a long time."

"I knew you figure it out, Fietlebaum," Teysoot Motzo said with pride. "You biggest bighead I ever know." Considering the source, the statement did not entail an estimation of great brilliance. But Fietlebaum accepted the compliment in the spirit it was offered.

"So, now what we do?" Teysoot Motzo asked as he pushed open the door to the hotel.

"It time for supper yet?"

"For you, it's always time for supper," Fietlebaum replied. "Why don't you pick a place to eat?"

"You know," Teysoot Motzo said wistfully, "I miss home cooking. How about we go Janpooran restaurant?"

Feh! Fietlebaum thought, but not wanting to disappoint Teysoot Motzo, he said, "I would be delighted." They walked toward the bank of elevators. "You ask the concierge the name of a good Janpooran restaurant," he said to Teysoot Motzo, "and I'll meet you in the lobby by the door in an hour."

Fietlebaum headed back to his room. He laughed when he pictured Teysoot Motzo asking the concierge the whereabouts of a good Janpooran restaurant. "It's like asking for a left-handed monkey wrench," he said to himself. He suspected the poor concierge would have to resort to flipping a coin. His levity ended when it occurred to him that he would be obliged to eat the food. "*Me ken brechen*[135]!" he said out loud.

He got to the 4907th floor. He was looking forward to a shower and even a few free minutes to think and decompress. Tomorrow, he would have to look up an old

---

[135] You can vomit from this!

friend at the medical school. He hoped he was still there. It was his old friend, Birshond Lishorn, a Silesian neurologist, and perhaps the best neurophysiologist in the galaxy. He needed his help to design an intention switch. Hopefully, Dr. Lishorn could enlist his technicians to build it, sans the explosives, of course.

He showered and changed. Then he sat for a few moments, gazing out the windows of his room, and enjoying a finger of *schnapps*. It was the good stuff, a rare, single malt Scotch, that he picked up in the gift shop in the lobby of the hotel. *Worth every penny*, he thought.

With the last drop drained, and no more excuses to exploit, he got up, steeled himself for the gastronomic ordeal he was about to face, and headed out the door. When he got to the lobby, he spotted Teysoot Motzo, surrounded by staff and security. "*Oy*," Fietlebaum mumbled. "What has he done now?"

Apparently, Teysoot Motzo had caused a minor scene when the Silesian concierge laughed at his request to find a good Janpooran restaurant. Teysoot Motzo had threatened to climb across the desk and "rip you cute little nose off." After some quick negotiations with the hotel manager, the incident was settled. The concierge conjured up the requested information and offered his apology. "There were simply too many to choose from," he deftly explained. "Perhaps I might suggest the Janpooran Delight."

"We going Janpooran Delight!" Teysoot Motzo declared with unbridled excitement.

"Yes, I'm sure," Fietlebaum replied.

Teysoot Motzo cocked his head and added, "It come highly recommended."

"*Oy*," Fietlebaum quite involuntarily retorted.

They walked out to the sidewalk, and the doorman flagged them down a cab.

They hopped in the cab. "To the Janpooran Delight!" Teysoot Motzo sang. The Silesian driver turned completely around and looked incredulously at Teysoot Motzo. Then he turned to look at Fietlebaum, craning his neck momentarily for closer scrutiny. Fietlebaum looked back at him and shrugged his shoulders. The cabbie shrugged in kind, turned back around and unceremoniously announced, "Janpooran Delight." They sped off.

CHAPTER 35

Fietlebaum heard it and smelled it before he saw it. A pungent, cheesy smell with a hint of pepper was in the air, along with loud Janpooran music. They neared an alleyway from where it all seemed to be emanating and, much to his chagrin, the cabbie turned into it. The cab rolled up and stopped by a storefront. There was a hand painted sign above its door that Fietlebaum could not read, but he correctly assumed that they had arrived at the Janpooran Delight restaurant.

"We here!" Teysoot Motzo sang out. "Now you get some real food, Fietlebaum."

Fietlebaum could not answer.

Teysoot Motzo bounded out of the cab, and Fietlebaum followed. The aroma and clamor in the air quadrupled in intensity when they opened the door and walked into the restaurant. Between the music, laughing, and talking, Fietlebaum could hardly hear himself think. The ability of Janpoorans to eat and talk at the same time made Janpooran restaurants particularly lively places. Janpoorans were always chatty, but in restaurants the usual non-stop talking was further augmented by blow by blow reports about their culinary experience. The usual complaints about the boss, detailed descriptions of their grandson's graduation, and the lurid details about the previous night's date, were punctuated by "Oh, this delicious bite," "Umm, they spice it just right this time," or "Uh, oh, I think they little bone in this bite."

The *maître d'* led Teysoot Motzo and Fietlebaum to a table, and immediately placed glasses of *squath* in front of them. *Squath* was a popular, mildly intoxicating drink often served in Janpooran restaurants and at social functions. Fietlebaum took a sip and nearly gagged. It had a flavor suggestive of ginger and feta cheese. However, even after that first sip, he felt something begin to happen. The neurochemistry of Hijdori was different enough from Janpoorans that Fietlebaum was usually unaffected, even by substances that sent Janpoorans into heights of delirium. However, the *squath* seemed to give him a pleasant buzz. After the second or third sip, it didn't taste so bad any more.

"It grows on you," Fietlebaum observed.

"Yes, it do," Teysoot Motzo said in agreement.

Fietlebaum looked around and, through his new found appreciation of *squath,* he felt less out of place among the room full of Janpoorans. It was obvious that Janpoorans loved their food. They threw themselves into it. They dug in. Elbows flew. At times, the bang and scrape of silverware on plates rattled the windows. Their infectious enthusiasm, or perhaps the *squath*, made Fietlebaum more eager to have a look at the menu the waiter had laid in front of him.

There was a problem. It was statutory that all retail stores on the planet, including restaurants, have a Silesian translation as part of every transaction form and document. But, the simple fact was that no Silesian would be caught dead in a Janpooran restaurant. The extra labor and printer's ink were utterly unnecessary expenses. Though Fietlebaum spoke and read Silesian fluently, the Janpooran script was completely unintelligible. Thus, he considered the unimaginable, which was asking Teysoot Motzo's suggestion on what to have for dinner.

"Oh, so many good things to eat!" Teysoot Motzo chortled. "Spicy noodle de-*licious*!" But for Fietlebaum, the vivid recollection of Bostoff Metzee juggling females on his knees with spicy noodles and sickly green sauce dripping from his poto was an insurmountable barrier to appetite. He asked for other recommendations.

Teysoot Motzo gave him a disappointed and slightly incredulous look. "Spicy noodle not sound good? Well, how about nice flamed leg of *gorzet* with spicy noodle, or spicy noodle with brazed minced *blebitt*?"

"Listen," Fietlebaum said, slowly and succinctly as leverage to avoid complete exasperation, "you need to forget the spicy noodle, either alone or with anything else."

"Hmm—it sound like you not interested in spicy noodle," Teysoot Motzo replied.

"No," Fietlebaum replied, with restraint he didn't know he possessed.

"Well," Teysoot Motzo offered, "why don't we order another glass *squath* and start over?"

Teysoot Motzo raised both arms above his head, snapped his fingers, and called for the waiter. "More *squath*," he said when the waiter reached the table. "This may help you decide," he told Fietlebaum. "Menu always look better after *squath*."

As the waiter was on his way with two more glasses, Fietlebaum glanced behind him and saw a Janpooran spooning simpler, blander looking fare into his *poto*. "What is that fellow behind me eating?" he asked.

Teysoot Motzo sat up slightly for a better view, then sat down. "Oh, you not want to eat that," he said with a pained expression. "That food for fellow who old and sick. The sauce got no *umph*."

"I'm prepared to sacrifice the *umph* on this occasion," Fietlebaum replied. "Perhaps you could order that for me."

"OK," Teysoot Motzo said with palpable disappointment. When the waiter returned with the *squath*, Teysoot Motzo ordered for himself, and then conveyed Fietlebaum's request for a plate of *horgus* root in *shorple* sauce.

The waiter leaned down to inspect Fietlebaum more closely. "You okay?" the waiter asked.

"Yes," Fietlebaum replied, "I'm fine, and that's what I would like." As the waiter rose back to full height, Fietlebaum added one more request. "Please, hold the *umph*." The waiter responded with a puzzled look on his face, but decided not to inquire any further.

"You gonna embarrass me," Teysoot Motzo said with feigned concern. Then he laughed and toasted Fietlebaum with the fresh glass of *squath*.

"You know," Fietlebaum said as he looked down at the glass in his hand, "this stuff isn't half bad."

The waiter returned with their food and slid the plates down in front of them. The *horgus* root was barely edible. However, Fietlebaum knew that he would be able to suffer through it and thus avoid offending Teysoot Motzo. At this point, that was the only important thing. Teysoot Motzo dove into his plate of spicy noodles and thoroughly enjoyed them. "Delicious! Oh, very good! The noodle just right" tumbled out without pause as he shoveled forkful after forkful of noodles into his *poto*.

Halfway through his own meal, Fietlebaum saw something moving underneath the *shorple* sauce. He wasn't certain if the creature was a stowaway or part of the recipe. In any case, eating it was not an option. Keeping the denizen of the sauce in his peripheral vision, he deftly maneuvered it to a corner of his plate. The action did not escape Teysoot Motzo's attention.

"You no want you *pord*?" he asked plaintively. But already knowing the answer, he reached across the table, grabbed the wriggling creature with his fingers, and popped it into his *poto*. "That best part!" he said with satisfaction. After finishing off the *pord*, Teysoot Motzo stood up and said, "Excuse me. I got go for little boy room."

For most of the night, a big Janpooran, several tables down, had been eyeing Fietlebaum. At first, Fietlebaum suspected that it was only his imagination or, perhaps, the *squath*. But when he let his gaze linger longer, he unmistakably noticed the Janpooran staring and sneering at him. He had decided to ignore him, but when Teysoot Motzo got up to relieve himself, the big Janpooran sauntered over to Fietlebaum's table and pressed the issue.

"What you anyway?" the Janpooran asked, "I not never see nobody look like you." He laughed. His belly shook, and his breath laden with *burzet* and spicy noodle billowed over Fietlebaum's face. Then he picked Fietlebaum up with one hand and lifted him up in the air. "Hah!" he laughed. "You itty bitty boy."

When Teysoot Motzo stepped back into the dining room, he saw the Janpooran lifting Fietlebaum in the air and exploded in anger. The blood rushed to his head and turned his face as green as a jungle python. He stormed across the room, pushed over tables, chairs, and customers, and flew at the big Janpooran in a rage. He hit the Janpooran and knocked him down. "That Dr. Fietlebaum!" he yelled. "Fietlebaum my friend! He save my life!" He jumped on top of the Janpooran and pummeled him further. Customers were screaming in fear, that is, the ones who weren't egging him on. Two big fellows who worked in the kitchen finally ran out and pulled him off. Teysoot Motzo was still seething with anger as they dragged him back across the room. "You ever touch Fietlebaum again," he screamed, "I kill you! You understand?" The big Janpooran struggled to his feet. Blood dripped down his face onto his chartreuse caftan. He knew it would be a mistake to say anything to Teysoot Motzo. The fun was over. He shut up, paid his bill, and walked out.

They let Teysoot Motzo up, and he ran over to Fietlebaum. He was laying on the floor rubbing the shoulder that was strained when the big Janpooran hauled him up into the air. "You okay?" Teysoot Motzo asked with fatherly concern.

"Yes, yes," Fietlebaum replied, "I'm fine, *Got tsu danken*."

Teysoot Motzo looked him in the eye and said in uncharacteristically serious tone, "As long as I alive, Fietlebaum, nobody hurt you." He looked intently at Fietlebaum for another moment then asked in the same solemn tone, "Do you want dessert?"

"God no," Fietlebaum replied, "Let's go back to the hotel."

Fietlebaum paid the bill, and they stepped out into the alleyway. The cool night air was refreshing. The moons of Silesia shone brightly. The red and white lights of traffic in the latticework of air lanes miles above appeared as sparkling strings of jewels moving across the sky from horizon to horizon. The ground cabs sped by in blurs of speed, casting reflections of the streets bright visual display boards and endless streams of laser advertisements. The boundless hum and rush of activity conveyed a strangely comforting sense of momentum. It was an enveloping sense that the massive, yet intricate, society had its own energy and purpose that would effortlessly carry you through moments when your own strength might falter. Being in Silesia was being in something very big and powerful.

They walked through the alley to the street, and flagged down a cab to take them back to the hotel. The traffic was speeding down the street bumper to bumper, but the cab almost magically slipped out of the line of traffic to pick them up and slipped right back into the two-hundred mile per hour lane without a bump, dent, or scrape. "How they do this?" Teysoot Motzo wondered aloud. Then after a moment he added, "Why they do this? Half fun of cab ride crash and bang. This not do on Janpoor."

When the cab stopped in front of the hotel, the Silesian doorman bounded out and opened the cab's doors for them. "Welcome back, Dr. Fietlebaum," the doorman said, "Welcome back Mr. Teysoot Motzo." It was a nice touch. Even Teysoot Motzo thought so. He closed the doors, and trotted around ahead of them to open the door to the hotel. They strolled into the lobby. It was alive with activity. Drinks were being served. Cocktail glasses tinkled. The murmurs of hundreds of simultaneous conversations echoed around the room.

The string quartet was playing by the fountain, and Fietlebaum stopped for a moment to listen. It was ancient Earth music. He smiled and mouthed the name, *Borodin.* The piece had always been one of his favorites. It may have been the resonance of a particular major chord, or the raspy timbre of a cello note that carried him across time and space. He was with Sophie, years ago on Hijdor, at Ethan and Sarah Rosenberg's wedding. They were playing the Quartet Number Two. He breathed in Sophie's fragrance and felt her hand grasping his.

"It's lovely isn't it?" he heard her say.

"Yes, it is lovely," Fietlebaum said aloud.

"What you say, Fietelbaum?" Teysoot Motzo asked.

A wave of melancholy swept over Fietelbaum. He missed her. She would have loved this place, he thought.

"You okay?" Teysoot Motzo asked, this time breaking his reverie.

"Uh, yes, yes. I'm fine," he replied. "This was one of my wife Sophie's favorites. I was reminiscing, and feeling a *bissel*[136] lonely, I suppose."

"I know," Teysoot Motzo said. "That happen for me sometime, too." They stood and listened a few more minutes. "I like that music," Teysoot Motzo declared. "It very sweet."

Fietlebaum looked at Teysoot Motzo and smiled. "Yes, it is. It is very sweet."

They rode up to their floor and stepped off the elevator into the hallway. "Good night," Fietlebaum told Teysoot Motzo.

---

136 A little

"Goodnight," Teysoot Motzo replied.

After a few steps toward his room, Fietlebaum stopped. "Teysoot Motzo," he called out. The Janpooran turned back to him, and Fietlebaum added, "Thank you."

Teysoot Motzo looked puzzled, and asked, "What I do?"

"Just thank you," Fietlebaum answered. "Thank you very much."

Fietlebaum walked into his room, got undressed, and slipped on his pajamas. He searched through the music library in his communicator for the piece by Borodin they were playing in the lobby. He found it, and plugged his communicator into the room's sound system. The music flowed into the room, and he sat in a chair by the window and listened. Again he thought of Sophie, but he told himself that there was no need for loneliness and despair. It was just as easy to find a sense of joy and gratitude that he had shared life with her, and that the two of them had lived together in a world where such music existed. When the music was over, he turned off the light and got into bed. "*A guteh nacht* to you, my dear," he said. "All my love and thanks to you, and to the universe that gave you to me."

CHAPTER 36

Birshond Lishorn was a Silesian physician and old friend of Fietlebaum's. After attending medical school and residency together, they both stayed at Forgion Transgalactic School of Medicine. There they often collaborated in research and in the resolution of difficult cases. Fietlebaum later left academia for a position in the pharmaceutical industry, while Lishorn stayed and became a Professor of Neurology and Molecular Neuroscience.

Lishorn was one of the galaxy's foremost experts in Comparative Noetics, that is, the study of similarities and differences among the various intelligent species of the galaxy in the ways their brains worked to produce the phenomenon of self-awareness. He formed the impression that all conscious beings, regardless of species, believed themselves not just fully, but perfectly conscious. However, he noted in one of his early theoretical papers, *In any sentient being, the brain's level of complexity and the complexity of the mind it generates are always at least one order of complexity above that being's ability to understand them.* This statement came to be known as Lishorn's Axiom on Consciousness. He further noted that his axiom had an unfortunate corollary, which was that, *Owners of very simple brains always have very simple notions about their brains, their world, and themselves, but can never be convinced of that fact.*

Lishorn concluded that the minds of all sentient beings in the galaxy were synthetic, utterly dependent on brain tissue, and virtual, rather than actual. Like well-animated cartoons, these minds created the perfect illusion of continuity and wholeness, while actually being full of gaps and holes. In some species, the neural animation was gorgeous, multi-dimensional, and full of color and detail. In other species, it was the simplest of black and white stick figures. Still, each individual was oblivious to any other form of awareness, and assumed their consciousness was all it could possibly be.

Even more famous than Lishorn's Axiom, was what came to be known among the cognoscenti as Lishorn's Retort. His eminently quotable response arose during a lecture at the university when a visiting scholar protested his stark conceptualization of the mind. He demanded to know how a sentient being could bear the existential dilemma of not having an actual, persisting, well defined consciousness, but instead having a virtual consciousness that was no more than an elaborate illusion. Lishorn famously answered, "What difference does it make?" That reply had always struck Fietlebaum as supremely wise and succinct.

A quick call from his room to the Department of Neurology informed Fietlebaum that Lishorn was still employed at the College of Medicine, and was expected to arrive at his office shortly. Fietlebaum was buoyed by the news. He immediately headed down to the lobby and out to the street to catch a cab. A cab zipped over to pick him up, then zipped back into traffic and off to the Forgion Transgalactic College of Medicine.

Fietlebaum had not been at the College for over twelve years, but it looked much the same. It was an old and venerated school. It had been at the same site for at least seventeen-thousand years. A few buildings still in regular use had stood for thousands of years. But the old ones were dwarfed in the shadows of the college's masterpieces of modern architecture that stretched five or more miles higher into the sky above them.

Sun glinted off the reflective glass of the towering buildings and illuminated the canyons between them. All around, and as far up as Fietlebaum's eyes could see, there was ceaseless activity. Cabs raced, pedestrians bustled through the street, herds of doctors and medical students crowded across the skybridges that connected higher stories of adjacent buildings, messenger bots zipped everywhere, and aircabs zoomed to and from the airlanes miles above.

The small courtyard in front of the old medical library was one of the few places of natural peace and solitude in the entire Galactic Capital Zone. A much prized tree, the only one within an area of ten square miles, had grown there for several hundred years. Fietlebaum would often meet Lishorn by the tree for lunch. They would eat and discuss their research and topics of interest in neuroscience. Seeing the place brought back fond memories.

He strode over to the Neurology and Neurosciences building behind the library, and rode five miles up to the floor where Lishorn had his office. He walked into the main office of the Department of Neurology, and asked if Dr. Lishorn had arrived yet. Hearing a strangely familiar voice, Lishorn himself peeked out of his office door, then slowly crept over.

"Isaac?" he asked quizzically, "Isaac Fietlebaum? My God, is that you?"

"Hello, Birshy," Fietlebaum replied. "It is good to see you, my friend."

"Isaac Fietlebaum!" Lishorn cried out as the reality sunk in. "It must be ten years since I saw you last. What a wonderful surprise!" They embraced, and Lishorn kissed each of Fietlebaum's cheeks in the Silesian manner.

"Shursit," Lishorn called out to his Silesian receptionist, "cancel all my morning appointments!"

"No, please," Fietlebaum protested. "I don't want you to alter your day for me."

Lishorn leaned close to Fietlebaum's ear. "Listen," he said, quickly glancing behind to ensure that no one of consequence could overhear him, "these aren't patients. These are graduate students. My nine o'clock is always full of excuses, my ten o'clock is a pain in my ass, and my eleven o'clock hasn't written a page worth reading in two years. To tell you the truth, you are doing me a big favor." He beckoned Fietlebaum to follow. "Come on!" he sang.

Lishorn led Fietlebaum into his office and closed the door. He pointed Fietlebaum to a leather lounge chair. Then he stepped to a large cabinet behind his desk, opened it, and grabbed a carafe of Scotch for Fietlebaum, a carafe of spiced methanol distillate for himself, and two cut crystal glasses. He poured the drinks and raised his glass in a toast.

"*Le'chayim*, old friend," Lishorn said.

"*Le'chayim*," Fietlebaum joyfully replied.

Lishorn took the spiced methanol down in one gulp, then planted the glass back down on his desk with perfect aplomb. "It's wonderful to see you, Fietlebaum," he said. "But what in the hell are you doing here after all these years?"

"*Vey iz mir*," Fietlebaum replied as he sipped his glass of Scotch. "I hardly know where to begin." He paused for a moment, sipped once more, then he tilted his head back and threw the entire glass of Scotch down his throat. "I've gotten myself into a great deal of trouble," he said.

"What else is new?" Lishorn replied, as he leaned in to hear all that Fietlebaum had to say. "Let's hear about it." Lishorn carried an uncommon genetic mutation that caused his eyes to be gray, rather than the jet black color that was typical of Silesians. Along with his placid facial expression, his huge, pale eyes, the size and shape of goose eggs, lent him an enormously empathic appearance. Fietlebaum had always found it easy to reveal himself to Lishorn. On many occasions he had thought he would have made an excellent psychiatrist.

Fietlebaum told how Glesh had kidnapped and tortured his grandson. He went on to speak about Teysoot Motzo, noting that he was a Janpooran labor union leader and part-time, small-time crook. "But a very nice crook," he felt compelled to add.

"I'm sure you keep company with only the nicest crooks," Lishorn conceded.

"He was in way over his head," Fietlebaum added, almost apologetically.

Fietlebaum described how he had manipulated Teysoot Motzo into the psychiatric ward, only to learn that Glesh had intended to kill both of them. Then he told the story of their harrowing escape.

"I suspect you've had some interesting scrapes," Lishorn surmised.

"We have," Fietlebaum admitted. "Teysoot Motzo has already saved my life once, if not twice." He paused. "*Nu*," he added parenthetically, "on the other hand, he has almost gotten me killed three or four times!"

Fietlebaum grew somber. He leaned toward Lishorn for emphasis. "There are things I won't tell you," he explained, "because the truth could be very dangerous for you. A forensic neuroprobe can't find things that aren't in your brain, so some things are best left unsaid. I myself could be sentenced to death for things I have done since this nightmare began, and I won't place you in that kind of danger." He leaned back in his chair and paused again to let Lishorn digest what he had said.

"What you need to know," Fietlebaum continued, "is that I and Teysoot Motzo are here on Silesia to meet Glesh in a safe place. We will meet Glesh tomorrow at the Galactic Intelligence Agency offices. I will give him instructions to meet us on Jinkor, a moon of Janpoor, where I will pay him a ransom for my grandson. We hid the ransom there. It is a deadly piece of contraband that you shouldn't know about." Lishorn said nothing, but nodded his head in acknowledgement.

Fietlebaum shifted in his chair, then reached over and poured himself another finger of Scotch. "Now, this is why I need your help," he said. "It occurred to me that Glesh has no reason not to kill us after we give him the ransom on Jinkor. There will be no one there to protect us, and no one of consequence to witness the crime. He will have nothing to lose." He paused, then added thoughtfully, "And, of course, there is the fact that he hates me!"

"An unfortunate combination," Lishorn interjected.

"What I need you to help me with," Fietlebaum said, "is an intention switch."

Lishorn had a puzzled look. "A what?" he asked.

"An intention switch," Fietlebaum replied. "Let me explain. The switch I envision would activate or deactivate an explosive depending upon whether or not my brain waves reflected my intention to do so. The explosive would be attached to the ransom package. The switch would have wires with electrodes on the ends to pick up my brain waves. It would also have computational capacity to interpret the meaning of those brain waves."

He paused for a moment and looked Lishorn in the eyes. "Are you with me?" he asked.

"Yes, I'm with you," Lishorn said. "Please, go on."

"If I decided to deactivate the explosive," Fietlebaum said, "the electroencephalographic signature of my decision would be recognized, and the switch would disarm the explosive. If this wasn't completely voluntary, my experience of coercion would also be reflected in my brain waves. The switch would recognize coercion and not deactivate the explosive. If my brain wave activity stopped, such as would occur if I am killed or if the switch is ripped from my head, the switch would detonate the explosive. Any attempt to bypass the switch by removing the explosive from the contraband ransom would also cause the explosive to detonate. The explosive would destroy the package and, with any luck, the dirty *momzer* who was trying to take it without my consent."

"Yes," Lishorn said, "an intention switch. I like it."

Fietlebaum was relieved that Lishorn understood what he was hoping to do and didn't dismiss the possibility of building the device. He went on to explain, "I'm hoping you can help me determine what areas of my brain and what types of brain waves would provide the strongest reflections of my willingness to disarm the explosive, or my need to detonate it. Then we could use that information to program the switch."

"That shouldn't be difficult," Lishorn said without hesitation. "Let's take you down to the lab and find out."

"Let's go," Fietlebaum said.

Lishorn and Fietlebaum rode a mile down to Lishorn's neurophysiology lab. As they descended, Lishorn told Fietlebaum how he was going to attack the problem. "What we need to do," he said, "is to run you through microvibrational imaging and see what areas of your brain become active when you, Isaac Fietlebaum, are intent on doing something. This should be straightforward. First I ask you to think about things that have nothing to do with you, like the weather on Silesia, the price of gruba beans on Janpoor, or the depth of the Hider Sea. Then I ask you to think about things that have everything to do with you, such as your name, what you want to eat for dinner, whether you are right handed or left handed. Then we look for differences. This helps us zero in on where the primary 'I am Fietlebaum' signal originates. Between you and me, in your Hijdori brain, I'm betting on the medial postgenistic body."

"I'm with you," Fietlebaum said.

"Once we know where the strongest *I am Isaac Fietlebaum* signals come from," Lishorn went on to say, "we'll snap an electroencephalographic electrode cap on your head and see what kind of electrical waves those areas of your brain generate when you strongly want or don't want something. Do you want me to stomp on your foot? Do you want me to punch you in the nose? Would you like a nice shot glass of your favorite s*chnapps*? Do you want your grandson back?"

When Fietlebaum heard the last question, he felt a surge of anxiety ripple through his body. Lishorn lowered his head and peered knowingly over the rims of his glasses at Fietlebaum. "I suspect that last question roused something we could measure." Fietlebaum sighed and gently nodded affirmation. It was a boundless relief to be transparent before a being who was not only a caring friend, but a towering intellect as well.

"In an hour or so," Lishorn stated firmly, "we should find out what you need to know."

"You have no idea how grateful I am for your help," Fietlebaum told him.

"But this is just the start," Lishorn was quick to note. "We need to take the neurophysiological information and build you a working device." He paused for a moment to consider, then added with an air of authority, "But that should be simple. Once we know what to look for, it shouldn't be difficult to build a device whose sensory system and logic board are able to decipher the presence of your intention to detonate or disarm the explosive. Then it can resolve a simple disarm, do nothing, or blow the son-of-a-bitch up decision matrix."

They reached the laboratory floor and stepped out into a suite of rooms bristling with scanning equipment, computers, and electronics. It was cutting edge, the best in the galaxy. "Let's get started," Lishorn said.

Lishorn led Fietlebaum through a series of questions and mental exercises while he was in the brain imaging machine and wired up to the electroencephalograph. After a few hours, Lishorn announced, "We have what we need.

I'll give the data to Hirzhod, then you and I can go get some lunch. There's nothing like quantum microvibrational tomography to work up a fellow's appetite."

Fietlebaum and Lishorn zipped down to the ground floor of the building to a little, hole-in-the-wall diner to grab a quick bite. The old place had long been popular with medical students and staff of the college. The two of them used to eat there when they were students together. They found a table and ordered a large plate of stuffed Silesian pastries to share, as was the custom among friends. The waiter brought a plate heaped high with steaming hot pastries. They smelled wonderful. Fietlebaum had eaten Silesian pastries on Sholoso in the diner next to the hotel, but those didn't compare. "Mmm, *geschmakt*!" Fietlebaum exclaimed. "I almost forgot how good these were."

The two old friends relaxed and reminisced. Lishorn had not known about Sophie's death. "I'm so sorry to hear that, Isaac," he said. "Sophie was a good soul."

"Yes, she was," Fietlebaum replied solemnly.

Lishorn knew how much he had loved her. He gazed briefly but unwaveringly into Fietlebaum's eyes, then offered a simple smile and a nod of recognition. There was no need for further elaboration. They sat silently for a moment, then continued the conversation.

Lishorn had heard about the trouble with Flodrisht and Plork Pharmaceuticals that led Fietlebaum to lose his position as chairman of the board. The company was based in Silesia, and Lishorn might have made a difference had he tried to intervene. But he was on sabbatical at the time, out in a distant star system for two years to study the embryological development of the nervous system of Mojir Desert worms. "I'm sorry I wasn't there for you, Isaac. It was a terrible shame," he said.

"Yes," Fietlebaum admitted. "It was a very tough time, especially when it came so soon after Sophie's death. But it led me to a simpler life. I gave it all up." He paused, then shrugged his shoulders. "Now I'm working at a clinic on Polmod. I'm employed by the Transgalactic Merchant Marine Academy."

Lishorn cringed. "My God, Isaac! Polmod? How can you stand that backward, wasteland of a planet?"

Fietlebaum laughed. "Oh, it's not so bad," he said. "Now I'm free to practice psychiatry full time without all the distractions of being responsible for a business. I have my music. There's a snifter of *schnapps* now and then. I can't complain."

"Well, I'm glad to see you content," Lishorn told him. "It is very good to see you."

"And you, my friend," Fietlebaum replied.

When Fietlebaum and Lishorn returned from lunch, a good two hours later, they popped into Hirzhod's office. They were delighted to find that Hirzhod and his team had already pieced the device together from the information Lishorn had given him. It was a standard, close fitting encephalography cap, designed to be belted snuggly against Fietlebaum's head, with a set of electrodes held firmly against the area of his skull overlying the left and right medial postgenistic bodies of his brain. The electrodes fed information directly to the sensory and logic systems of a microcomputer in the cap that, in turn, directed a wireless switch to send a signal.

"Consider it a cyber-*yarlmulke*[137]," Lishorn suggested, "with a chin strap yet." He gave Fietlebaum a wink.

"And stylish," Fietlebaum volunteered. "Everyone admires a psychiatrist who can accessorize."

Hirzhod included a pliable, but virtually indestructible, tamper proof, plastic satchel with a receiver inside. When acted upon, the receiver could either pop open the envelope safely, keep it shut, or generate a current to detonate an explosive that could be placed inside. Trying to bypass the

---

137 Prayer cap

switch stimulated current as well, which would set off the charge.

"Remarkable!" Fietlebaum exclaimed.

"Hirzhod does excellent work," Lishorn noted proudly. "The intention switch is built to your specifications. Now all you need is explosive, but I'm afraid I can't help you with that. For some reason, the Dean feels that dispensing explosives in the clinics reflects badly on the medical school."

"Go figure," Fietlebaum remarked.

The two old friends stood silent for a moment. It was time to go. "I can't thank you enough, Birshy," Fietlebaum said. "You may have saved my life and my grandson's life. I couldn't have done this without your help."

"Just be careful, my friend," Lishorn replied, "and when you get the chance, let me know how it all turned out." They embraced again, and Fietlebaum walked out.

The major pieces were in place. With the intention switch in hand and the meeting with Glesh scheduled at the GIA building, it was time to purchase starship passage back to Borgost. He took a cab to the ticket office of Intergalactic Starlines and purchased passage for himself and Teysoot Motzo from Silesia to the Borgost Starport. The question remained as to how they would get from Borgost to Jinkor. One thing was for sure—they would not be taking the Super Excellent Star Taxi.

CHAPTER 37

With tickets in his pocket, Fietlebaum walked out of the starship line's office and flagged a cab back to the hotel. On the ride back, his mind was abuzz with loose ends, unforeseeable contingencies, and catastrophic possibilities. He had the intention switch in his lap, and it raised his confidence that he and Teysoot Motzo would be able to pull off their plan. But, so much was at stake, and so many things could happen to jeopardize even the best of plans. Finally, he threw up his hands. "So, what do I get from all this worrying?" he asked himself. "*Gornisht*!"

The cab pulled up in front of the Silesian Guardian Hotel. The doorman trotted out to open his door. "Welcome back, Dr. Fietlebaum," he called out. He thought of how pleasant it was to receive such attention. He looked around and saw all of the energy and vibrancy of Silesia. He contrasted it with the dullness of the Polmodi, and their almost total lack of social graces. He wondered if Lishorn wasn't right in thinking he was a fool for living there. *Ach*, he thought, *why torment myself? Doubt, envy, indecision, remorse—a* farshlepteh krenk[138]!"

The lobby was more lively than usual. There was a convention in town. The Silesian-based company enticed housewives, college students, and dreamers temporarily down on their luck to sell vitamins and cosmetics from planet to planet in what was little more than a pyramid scheme. Many of the participants from around the

138 A sickness that never ends.

galaxy were staying at the Silesian Guardian. They were an enthusiastic bunch. Astarans, Humans, Janpoorans, and Korpians scurried about the lobby with flashing identification badges around their necks, funny hats on their heads, and powerful drinks in their hands. Fietlebaum nearly tripped over a Borgostian conventioneer who was scuttling across the lobby floor toward the exit to catch an airbus. He, too, had a badge, and if there had been a way to fasten it to his squat little body, he would likely have had on a hat as well.

On his way up to his floor, Fietlebaum shared the elevator with a Gorsidian couple also wearing hats and badges. He said hello, but they didn't respond. Each had their tentacles wrapped tightly around the other, and one was making a peculiar, rhythmic, grunting sound. Fietlebaum wasn't certain if they were engaging in sexual foreplay or if one was administering the Gorsidian analogue of the Heimlich maneuver to the other. He was about to ask them if they needed assistance, but his intuition told him to butt out.

Fietlebaum left the Gorsids to their endeavors, stepped out on the 4907th floor where he and Teysoot Motzo had rooms, and walked down to his friend's door. He was anxious to talk with Teysoot Motzo and see what he thought about all that had been worrying him. *He's very clever for a* schlemiel, Fietlebaum allowed. *Besides, God help me, I've grown rather fond of him.* But he knocked and there was no answer. He resisted placing his ear against the door. Not only did it seem an invasion of privacy, he was slightly apprehensive that he might hear something he wasn't prepared for. "I'll come back later," he mumbled.

He returned to his own room, and stashed the intention switch and satchel in a drawer beneath his underwear. He locked the door securely, and headed downstairs for some music and a glass of wine. He strode into the lobby. The music and ambiance lifted him. He sat at a table by the fountain and ordered a glass of rare Earth wine. It was costly, but he felt he deserved a treat. "*Nu*?" he asked himself, "what's money for?" The waiter brought his wine. He sipped it and listened to the music. His cares drifted away.

Then, out of the corner of his eye, he saw three Drajans approaching. He felt his stomach twist. He forced himself to turn and look at them, to appreciate the nature of the threat. "You *shmuck*!" he blurted out. The Drajans were a frail, elderly male and what were likely his two young granddaughters. They were probably on holiday. "You can't keep doing this, Fietlebaum," he told himself. "You're letting that son-of-a-bitch, Glesh, drive you *meshugeh*." But he couldn't regain the mood. He left the half-drunken glass of wine on the table and went back to his room.

He laid down for a nap, but sleep wouldn't come. When he finally did drift off, his sleep was disturbed by dark dreams. There were shadows, and murmurings he couldn't understand. Something was chasing him, but it made no sound and he could not turn around to see it. Whichever way he turned, it positioned itself just beyond his field of vision. He awoke several hours later, but didn't feel refreshed. "*Oy*," he exclaimed, "I'll be glad when this is over." He decided to check Teysoot Motzo's room again. It was early evening, and Teysoot Motzo would probably be thinking about dinner. Perhaps they could grab something at Moishe's Deli.

He strode down the hall and knocked on Teysoot Motzo's door. There was still no answer. *Well,* he thought, *maybe I'll go to Moishe's myself. A pastrami on rye is calling to me.* He went downstairs, caught a cab, and rode to Moishe's. By then it was dinner time, and a line of customers was forming outside of Moishe's door waiting to get in. When the line had led him a few feet inside the deli, he heard a commotion. Moishe was upset. His voice came from around the corner in the dining area. He was berating someone. He heard a miserable groan. That groan was familiar. *No*, he thought, *It can't be*. But his Hijdori auditory system rarely betrayed him.

"*Bist meshugeh*?" he heard Moishe holler. "You can't sit here all night. I need the table!"

"*Vey iz mir*," Fietlebaum murmured. "I hope he isn't involved." He pushed his way to the front of the line, turned the corner into the dining room, and his fears were substantiated. Teysoot Motzo was slumped over the table. There were empty soup bowls stacked all around him.

"*Gai avek*[139]*!*" Moishe hollered. Teysoot Motzo only groaned. His face was pale. Moishe's was bright red. He was so angry he was prancing around the table on his tiptoes and shaking both his fists in the air. "*Oy! Oy! Oy*!" he yelled, "*Ich vel dir geben a klop*[140]!"

Fietlebaum walked up to the table, where Moishe noticed him. "You know this *putz*, don't you?" Moishe demanded.

"Yes," Fietlebaum admitted. "This *putz* is my friend. I'll talk to him."

"Don't talk!" Moishe demanded. "Just get him out of here!"

"Alright already," Fietlebaum replied. "Stop *haken a chainik*[141]." Fietlebaum placed his hand on Teysoot Motzo's shoulder.

Teysoot Motzo slowly turned his head and looked up at Fietlebaum. His face was turning yellow. "Fietlebaum," he moaned, "I think I eat too much *kreplach*."

"Come on, my friend," Fietlebaum said. "Let me help you up." He grabbed his arm, and gave him the extra upward momentum he needed to stand. "Let's get back to

---

139 Get lost!

140 I'm going to give you such a smack!

141 "Beating a tea kettle," making a racket

the hotel where you can sleep off the *kreplach*." Fietlebaum tossed a few bills on the table to cover the meal.

"And don't come back!" Moishe hollered.

"Moishe," Fietlebaum calmly replied as he turned to look him in the eye, "We're leaving. So, *gai mit dein kop in drerd*[142]."

Moishe was taken aback. "Does that mean *you're* not staying for supper?" he was quick to ask.

Fietlebaum rolled his eyes and helped Teysoot Motzo out of Moishe's and on to the curb to flag down a cab. A cab zipped up to get them, and they zoomed off to the Silesian Guardian. "So, what possessed you to eat seventeen bowls of *kreplach* soup?" Fietlebaum inquired.

Teysoot Motzo shrugged. "I like *kreplach*," he whimpered.

"Well," Fietlebaum replied, "we'll go back to the hotel, you can lay down, and when this *kreplach*-drunk of yours wears off, we have some important things to discuss."

By the time they got to the hotel, Teysoot Motzo was already feeling better. At least, he no longer needed help walking. He got out of the cab and waddled to the door, groaning and holding his bulging stomach. They slowly made their way through the lobby, then rode up to their floor.

"I better now," Teysoot Motzo announced as they stepped out into the hallway. Fietlebaum invited him into his room, where Teysoot Motzo could lay down while they talked.

"I spent the day with my old friend, Birshond Lishorn, at the medical school," Fietlebaum told him, "and we put together the intention switch I told you about."

"That good, Fietlebaum," Teysoot Motzo replied. "I knew you do it, you bighead boy!"

---

142 Go stick your head in the mud.

"What I don't have is the explosive to make it work," Fietlebaum said. Then he added, somewhat sheepishly, "Do you have any thoughts on where we might obtain explosives on Silesia?"

Much to Fietlebaum's surprise, Teysoot Motzo quickly answered, "Sure! Borgind Island got mining operation. There be explosive there."

Fietlebaum was astonished. "I didn't know there was mining on Silesia," he said incredulously.

"Course not," Teysoot Motzo answered. "Nobody know." It occurred to Fietlebaum that Teysoot Motzo's being a mining union president might have made him privy to such information. "They not want nobody know because they mine iridium for starship propulsion computers," Teysoot Motzo added. "It classified military information."

"But how can we get anything from classified mines on Borgind Island?" Fietlebaum wondered aloud.

"Maybe we pay some crook get it for us," Teysoot Motzo suggested.

They both fell silent for a moment. Then, at exactly the same time, they blurted out the same name, "Posso Gotzi!"

"After we see Glesh tomorrow," Fietlebaum suggested, "we'll drop by and speak with Posso Gotzi. Perhaps he can do the job for us."

Suddenly, Teysoot Motzo sat bolt upright. Fietlebaum expected a razor-sharp new insight into the explosives problem.

"Fietlebaum!" Teysoot Motzo said excitedly.

"What?" Fietlebaum asked with great anticipation.

"I think I ready for dessert!" Teysoot Motzo declared.

"*Oy*!" Fietlebaum replied. "You must be joking."

"No, no," Teysoot Motzo said earnestly. "I never joke about something like that. *Kreplach* all digested now." He hopped to his feet. "Come on, Fietlebaum, we go down for lobby and grab something."

"Astonishing," Fietlebaum said, shaking his head in disbelief. But he felt hungry, too, having abandoned his pastrami on rye to save Teysoot Motzo from the enraged Moishe Goldblatt. "Let's go," Fietlebaum said.

"So," Fietlebaum idly inquired as they rode down to the lobby, "after all this, would you still like to bring *kreplach* to Janpoor?"

"Sure," Teysoot Motzo replied. "It not *kreplach* fault I get bellyache."

"I think it admirable that you're not blaming the *kreplach*," Fietlebaum asserted, with his tongue firmly planted in his cheek.

"That just way I am," Teysoot Motzo replied without hesitation.

When they got down to the lobby, it was still crowded with conventioneers. They pushed their way through to the tables by the fountain and found a spot to sit. They ordered dessert for Teysoot Motzo and a sandwich for Fietlebaum. They sat quietly and waited for their food. Fietlebaum broke the silence. "We meet Glesh tomorrow at the GIA building," he said, "and it's going to be a difficult day. I won't be able to say all the things I really want to say. Any discussions other than about labor unions will raise suspicion." He heaved a sigh. "I dread sitting right in front of him and not being able to ask him about my grandson," he went on to say. Somehow, we will have to slip him instructions to meet us somewhere else where we can talk about everything more freely."

"Maybe we tell him meet us right here, in lobby of hotel," Teysoot Motzo suggested. "It safe place, and big crowd be good cover."

"That's a good idea," Fietlebaum replied.

The waiter brought the food. Teysoot Motzo attacked his slice of *gorbetz* pie with relish. He finished it off in three big bites, looked down, and rubbed his stomach with satisfaction. Fietlebaum's sandwich, on the other hand, was a disappointment. The corned beef was made from round rather than brisket. It was dry, and it was served on a Kaiser roll. He took one bite and pushed the plate aside. *Feh*! he muttered. For a moment, he struggled with an urge to return to Moishe's and beg him for forgiveness. But, his appetite was gone. There was too much on his mind to eat anyway. He absently stared up into the distance. A moment later, he lowered his gaze to find Teysoot Motzo staring intently at him.

"What is it?" Fietlebaum asked.

"You going eat you pickle?" Teysoot Motzo asked plaintively.

"No," Fietlebaum replied as he lifted the plate and offered the pickle over. "Help yourself."

CHAPTER 38

The day began early. Fietlebaum woke up, and after a noble but unsuccessful try to return to sleep, he got up and stayed up. "Who can sleep?" he asked himself. He walked to the bathroom and splashed water on his face. He saw himself in the mirror and noticed he had lost more hair from the top of his head. It was once deep blue, like lapis lazuli, but the little that was left had gone completely white. The stripes of hair on his hands and fingers had faded to turquoise. This had been happening for the previous few years, but the process was accelerating. *This is what age and* tsuris *do*, he thought.

He got dressed and went down to the lobby to find some coffee. His Hijdori brain did not utilize the neurotransmitter, adenosine, that operated in the human brain to dampen arousal. Thus caffeine, which blocked the effects of adenosine, had no specific stimulating effect on him. However, his father, Morris, used to drink it every morning and would always make some for him as well. For Fietlebaum, waking up with coffee was a habit. The stimulation it gave him was a Pavlovian, not a pharmacological response.

Some early birds were already populating the lobby. A few were convention revelers from the night before who had never gone to bed. Here and there, less ambitious conventioneers were splayed out, asleep on the overstuffed chairs and couches. He walked to the fountain where a Silesian girl behind the counter served the many and various morning drinks that served to spark the galaxy's beings into wakefulness. He ordered a coffee, and sat next to the fountain to sip it and consider the day that lay before him. "I'll be face to face with that *momzer* today," he said to himself. As he sipped the coffee, he realized what he really wanted from the drink that morning was a moment to be immersed in the memory of his father. It strengthened and comforted him. "A *gitte neshomah*[143] you were," he said softly as he raised his cup ever so slightly in a toast to him. "*Vey iz mir*," he added. "You wouldn't believe what your boy has gotten himself into."

As he sat sipping the rest of his coffee, he considered ways to surreptitiously arrange the meeting with Glesh in the lobby of the hotel. There, out of earshot of the GIA, he could ask Glesh about his grandson, and propose to him the trade of a small fortune in jorftoss extract for the boy. Then, or later, they could discuss the fine details of how and when they might meet on Jinkor to make the trade.

Fietlebaum ran half a dozen elaborate schemes through his head before he decided he would just pass Glesh a note in his palm when they shook hands. "Why did I drive myself *meshugeh* over this?" he sighed. The note would simply say to meet him and Teysoot Motzo in the lobby of the Silesian Guardian Hotel by the fountain at seven o'clock that evening.

Well, Fietlebaum thought, *I'll mosey back upstairs, wake up Teysoot Motzo, and see if he wants to grab some breakfast somewhere. Then we can go to the GIA building and meet that paskudnyak, Glesh.* As he walked back toward the bank of elevators, he was struck by a sobering question. *What if Glesh doesn't agree to the trade*? The possibility stopped him in his tracks. *Mein Got*, he thought. *It was Teysoot Motzo who was so certain Glesh would go for it. I've only assumed he was right.* He stepped on the elevator to ride back to his floor. He let his head drop, and he shook it from side to

---

143 A good soul

side. *Oy vey*, he thought, *that possibility never even occurred to me.* The elevator opened, and he gathered himself. "Well," he said out loud, "I'll have to cross that bridge when I come to it."

He walked down the hallway to Teysoot Motzo's door and knocked. He heard nothing, and knocked again. "Who is it?" Teysoot Motzo sang out from behind the door.

"It's Fietlebaum," he replied.

"Oh," Teysoot Motzo said. "Just a minute."

Fietlebaum heard giggles and rustling of bedclothes. The door opened a crack.

"Good morning, Fietlebaum," Teysoot Motzo said.

Fietlebaum peeked in and saw two funny convention hats lying on his floor. It took him a moment to put the pieces together. "Two?" he asked with astonishment.

"No-o-o-o! Not two," Teysoot Motzo answered with a dismissive laugh. "They three," he declared. "Other girl keep hat on."

Fietlebaum could not help but laugh. "Teysoot Motzo," he asserted, "you are a most remarkable fellow. Meet me downstairs in an hour, and we'll catch a cab to the GIA where we'll meet Glesh."

"You got it," Teysoot Motzo said, and closed the door.

As he turned to walk back to his own room, Fietlebaum heard a chorus of laughter go up in Teysoot Motzo's room. *I hope an hour is long enough*, he thought.

He went back to his room, showered, and changed his clothes. Then he went down to the lobby to get a quick bite to eat and wait for Teysoot Motzo. He was finishing a Silesian pastry when Teysoot Motzo bounded up to his table. Fietlebaum offered him the plate. "Here," he told him, "there's one left. Why don't you take it."

"Not mind if I do," Teysoot Motzo replied. "Thank you, very much."

They sat another few minutes. Fietlebaum scribbled out the note to Glesh on a small piece of paper, folded it into a small square, and stuck it in his pocket. Then he said, "Let's go." They caught a cab, and told the Astaran cabbie to take them to the Galactic Intelligence Agency building. They zoomed off.

They arrived at the building, walked through the entryway, and rode up to the 4378th floor. They sat in the reception area of the office and waited. At a little after eleven o'clock, the Silesian clerk walked over to them, and asked them to follow him to the conference room. Fietlebaum instructed himself not to overreact. He walked down the hallway behind the clerk. They entered the room, and there sat Glesh.

Seeing him was strangely anticlimactic. Somehow he had recalled him as being much bigger. Perhaps it had been a trick of his mind to better explain all the misery he had brought upon him and his family. But there he sat, a small, almost shriveled looking fellow. The reality made Fietlebaum even more angry. "How can this puny little *shtik drek*[144] be the cause of so much agony?" he asked himself.

Glesh was still in the dark as to exactly why Fietlebaum and Teysoot Motzo had asked GIA to call him back to Silesia for a meeting. However, he correctly suspected it was a way for them to offer him a deal of some kind. He admired the cleverness of their ruse. Since he was up to his neck in illegal activity, he had little choice but to play along without making a fuss and raising suspicion.

In the galaxy, the phrase, *a Drajan's smile* carried the same meaning as *a crocodile's tears*. Glesh smiled broadly. "It's nice to see you, Dr. Fietlebaum," he said. Fietlebaum's anger and disgust almost made him forget about the folded message in his pocket, but he remembered at the last moment. He stuck his hand in his pocket as he stepped toward Glesh, fumbled for the paper, and reached out to

---

[144] piece of shit

shake his hand. "Hello, Agent Glesh," Fietlebaum replied. "It's nice to see you again, as well."

Glesh's eyes became ever so slightly larger when he felt the paper hit his palm. He quickly reached out with his free hand, and wrapped it around Fietlebaum's, as if it were a gesture of extra special affection, then slid both hands away with the slip of paper hidden between them.

"I believe you know Teysoot Motzo," Fietlebaum asserted.

"Yes, of course," Glesh replied with his Drajan's smile. "We have spoken many times by communicator, but I've never had the pleasure of meeting him.

"I *still* not have pleasure for meet you," Teysoot Motzo said with a growl.

"Perhaps we should sit," Fietlebaum quickly interjected.

The three of them were alone in the room, but Fietlebaum noticed the micro-cameras set around the room. They were being closely watched and recorded. They would have to fabricate information that would explain their request to meet with Glesh. It was his assumption that a few minutes of such conversation, laced with occasional references to Galactic policies and interests, would be sufficient to minimize any suspicion on the part of the GIA. He dropped names and voiced concerns peppered with patriotic platitudes, all the while staring at Glesh with intense hatred and distrust.

Having momentarily exhausted his own supply of imaginary plots and insurrections, Fietlebaum informed Glesh that Teysoot Motzo also had some important things to say. "As you know," Fietlebaum began, "Teysoot Motzo is a union leader on Janpoor, and has been in the position to observe some distressing events. He informed me of some activity that could possibly jeopardize important military production. Teysoot Motzo, perhaps you could relay some of these concerns to Agent Glesh."

Teysoot Motzo grimaced and stared at the table in silent consideration. Then he cleared his throat and proclaimed, "Everything I think happen, not really happen. Everything, okay. Let's go." Then he stood up and started toward the door.

For a moment, there was a real possibility of Fietlebaum and Glesh throwing in together and strangling Teysoot Motzo. Fietlebaum grasped for a way to restore credibility to the conversation and not stimulate an investigation of their relationship with Glesh. "You will have to excuse Teysoot Motzo," Fietlebaum said with an uneasy laugh. "He is still suffering a bit of reanimation syndrome. Besides, to be perfectly honest with you, he is not terribly articulate even under the best of circumstances. I believe what he was trying to say is that some of his worst suspicions were unfounded, but he is keeping an eye on things." He looked at Teysoot Motzo, with an expression half plaintive and half murderous, and asked him if that accurately reflected his thoughts.

"Yes, I suppose so," Teysoot Motzo answered sullenly.

With all of Glesh's faults, a lack of shrewdness and perspicacity was not among them. He, too, sprang to Teysoot Motzo's defense to their mutual benefit. "Yes, of course, perfectly understandable," he said. "Teysoot Motzo has been a valuable contributor to the safety and security of the Galaxy, and a reliable source of important information. I look forward to his continued participation in our intelligence efforts. Perhaps he should return to his hotel for a rest, and if he recalls anymore critical information, he can contact me."

"Well, there you have it!" Fietlebaum blurted out. He stood up from his chair, then he and Teysoot Motzo hurriedly left the conference room. As they walked down the hallway, Fietlebaum was beside himself with worry. He was desperately hoping the interaction the GIA recorded would not trigger an immediate investigation, but rather fall into the Galaxy's computer stores to be data mined more leisurely over the next year. If any suspicion was aroused, by then everything would likely have blown over. But when they got on the elevator, the still frightened and angry Fietlebaum could restrain himself no longer. "What's the matter with you?" he demanded, "*bist meshugeh*? Were you trying to get us arrested?"

"I hate that Glesh," Teysoot Motzo replied. "He try for kill me."

"Well, if you don't watch what you say," Fietlebaum asserted, "I might spare him the effort. You could get us both investigated and thrown into jail by making it look like this is all a trick to get to Glesh. You and I have transported jorftoss. That's a capital offense. And don't forget that the *groisser gornisht* has my grandson. This is no game we're playing here!"

Teysoot Motzo hung his head and said, "I sorry." He said it with such pathos and sincerity that it disarmed Fietlebaum of his fury.

"Well, damn it!" the more conciliatory Fietlebaum replied. "Think! Be more careful!"

"I will, Fietlebaum,' the contrite Teysoot Motzo replied. "I promise."

They rode in silence a few more minutes, until Teysoot Motzo casually inquired, "You hungry?"

"*Vey iz mir*!" Fietlebaum exclaimed with a cleansing laugh. "Do you have a hollow leg?"

Teysoot Motzo tapped several times on his legs, shrugged, and replied, "No, not leg. I pretty sure it my stomach that hollow."

"I suppose I could use something to eat myself, "Fietlebaum admitted as they stepped out into the lobby. "Where would you like to go?"

"You think Moishe forgive me yet?" Teysoot Motzo wondered.

"Probably so," Fietlebaum replied, "particularly if you walked in with cold, hard cash to buy some more *kreplach*. But the salient fact is that *I* haven't forgiven him. I don't like the way he treated you."

"O-o-oh," Teysoot Motzo said, "I not care so much."

"Forget Moishe's!" Fietlebaum stated emphatically as they stepped out onto the sidewalk.

Teysoot Motzo sulked for a moment. "Okay," he finally said with resignation.

Fietlebaum flagged down a cab, and they climbed in. "Janpooran Delight," Fietlebaum told the cabbie, trying to sound more enthusiastic about it than he actually was.

Teysoot Motzo broke into a big smile. "Oh, you good boy, Fietlebaum!" he exclaimed. "Lunch on me!"

CHAPTER 39

The Janpooran Delight was exactly as bad as Fietlebaum had recalled. That remained the case even after his third glass of *squath*. But, Teysoot Motzo was happy, and that's what Fietlebaum had intended. When they finished their lunch, he checked his communicator. It was two o'clock in the afternoon. "It's time to go find Posso Gotzi," he said.

They flagged a cab and gave the Silesian cabbie the address of Posso Gotzi's building. The cabbie hesitated a moment, caught Fietlebaum's eye in his rearview mirror, and asked, "You sure?"

"Yes, I'm sure," Fietlebaum replied. "Let's go."

"You're the boss," the cabbie said with resignation and zipped out into traffic.

A minute later, the cab rolled up in front of Pozzo Gotzi's building. As soon as Fietlebaum and Teysoot Motzo hit the sidewalk, the Janpoorans gravitated toward them and shook them down for cash.

"I'm here to see Posso Gotzi," Fietlebaum protested. "He's my friend."

"Yah," the largest Janpooran of the bunch said derisively. He pointed to Teysoot Motzo and added, "I suppose this you grandmother." He had Fietlebaum's hands up in the air and was patting down his pockets when another Janpooran stepped out of the building and saw what was going on. This one had been upstairs in Posso Gotzi's hangout the day that Fietlebaum and Teysoot Motzo had first been there. He recognized the two of them and trotted over.

"This Fietlebaum," he said. "You make Posso Gotzi wicked mad you hurt him. He say Fietlebaum good boy."

"Oh," the shakedown artist replied. He was annoyed to have his enterprise interfered with, but was unwilling to risk Posso Gotzi's wrath. "I just fool around," he added without the slightest hint of sincerity. "You go on up for see Posso Gotzi."

The Janpooran who had recognized them took them in arm. "Come on," he told them. "I myself take you boys up for see Posso Gotzi."

He led them into the building and took them up to Posso Gotzi's floor. Fietlebaum had apparently maintained his status as wicked bad boy and minor celebrity. When he stepped off the elevator and down the hallway, Posso Gotzi's gang made way for him. Posso Gotzi himself strolled out of his lair and gave him a bear hug. "Fietlebaum!" he exclaimed. "You back, you wicked bad boy. Come in, we talk."

Posso Gotzi led them into the suite of rooms that was his hangout. The room was dark and, as always, the air was heavy with the aroma of *burzet*. Fietlebaum was only slightly surprised to see that the two Janpoorans who had received the molecularly engineered shodom were still exactly where he had last seen them several days before. The one in the chair still stared straight ahead without moving. A twisted smile was plastered onto his face. The one on the floor also lay motionless, but every few minutes he lifted his head and said, "Wo-o-o-ow!"

"Hah!" Posso Gotzi laughed as he pointed to the two semi-conscious Janpoorans. "We say they be Fietlebaum-ed."

Posso Gotzi grabbed Fietlebaum by the arm and led him into his backroom office. "Before we talk, we get adjusted," the big Janpooran boss said. He pulled out his *moozore* and stuffed it with some of the best of his own special stash. "This extra special deluxe *burzet* from

Pogon Mountain," he proclaimed in almost reverent tones. "It strongest in galaxy." Unbeknownst to Fietlebaum, a demonstration was about to take place.

Before Posso Gotzi himself partook or offered any of the ultra-potent *burzet* to Fietlebaum, he beckoned his fellows forward with a subtle throw of his head and handed the loaded *moozore* off to one of the more elite members of his crew. This Janpooran, renown for his high tolerance to intoxicants, took the *moozore,* then waved the others back for some elbow room. He readied himself, inhaled deeply through the *moozore,* and held it in. All watched as his initially smug expression quickly morphed into one of fearful astonishment. He glanced at the *moozore* in a quick double-take a split second before falling backwards to the floor in a deep *burzet* stupor. Amidst a chorus of groans and derisive catcalls, Posso Gotzi removed the *moozore* from the tightly curled fingers of the Janpooran now lying crumpled on the floor and handed it to Fietlebaum. He waved the others in the room over. All leaned in, staring intently as Fietlebaum sucked in the super *burzet.* He inhaled deeply and held it in. "Now watch," Posso Gotzi said.

Fietlebaum held the breath of *burzet* as long as he could, then let it all go. He waited a moment, calmly meeting the gazes of all those who stared at him, then shrugged his shoulders. "Very nice," he said unfazed. "Now let's get started."

Janpooran mouths fell open. They stared at Fietlebaum, then turned and stared at each other. After the moment of silent awe, laughter rippled through the room. It was laughter born of the astonishment and disinhibited joy of being in the presence of true, benevolent greatness. "Hah! What I tell you?" Posso Gotzi exclaimed. "I tell you he wickedest bad boy ever!"

Posso Gotzi took the *moozore* from Fietlebaum, inhaled deeply from it, then sunk back into his overstuffed chair. With the demonstration over, he was ready to converse.

"Talk to me," Posso Gotzi said, with words not spoken outward, but sucked inward with the wisps of *burzet* vapor that remained in his *ahzha*.

Fietlebaum told him about his need of a small packet of high explosive. Posso Gotzi abruptly exhaled. "You strange boy, Fietlebaum," he said. "Why you need explosive?"

"For your own good, I can't tell you," Fietlebaum replied.

Posso Gotzi frowned.

"But I will pay you well, five-thousand Silesian *horki*," Fietlebaum quickly added."

Posso Gotzi's frown disappeared. "Now we talking!" Posso Gotzi cheerfully replied. "Why you want explosive you business, not mine."

"Wonderful," Fietlebaum replied. Then he called for Teysoot Motzo to come in and explain to Posso Gotzi where they might be able to find explosives on Silesia. Teysoot Motzo stumbled in, already exhibiting the effects of the high octane *burzet* he had partaken in. By the time he had walked the ten feet to the back room, he had entirely forgotten why he had come. He stood in silence for several minutes, until Fietlebaum jarred his memory.

"Oh, yah," Teysoot Motzo said. "There big iridium mine on Borgind Island. They use explosive every day."

"Iridium mine, on Borgind Island?" Posso Gotzi asked incredulously. "I not know that."

"Nobody know that," Teysoot Motzo answered. "Galactic Defense run it. Big military secret. They use tragonite explosive for blast out iridium. Tragonite all over place by mine."

"So, Mr. Bighead," Posso Gotzi ruefully inquired, "how we get tragonite from mine when it run by Galactic Defense? There be armed guards there."

"Yah," Teysoot Motzo said in agreement. "Mine guarded by Defense Department soldiers. But they guard mine and iridium, not tragonite. You make trouble on one side island,

and go in other side take tragonite before they know what happen."

"Hmm, you maybe right," Posso Gotzi said. "Maybe you not so dumb as I think."

"Of course not," Teysoot Motzo replied with considerable satisfaction. "I not so dumb as *every*body think."

"We have only a few days before we leave Silesia on a starship," Fietlebaum interjected. "When you get the tragonite—we only need an ounce or two—bring it to me at the Silesian Guardian Hotel. I'll pay you in advance." He counted out five-thousand *horki* into Posso Gotzi's hand.

"You got deal," Posso Gotzi cheerfully replied.

"One more thing," Fietlebaum told Posso Gotzi. He reached into his coat pocket and pulled out an envelope. "I also need you to deliver this letter to someone."

"Who that be," asked Posso Gotzi.

"You'll know the details when we leave. I will send you a message by communicator telling you when and where to deliver it." Fietlebaum placed another thousand *horki* in Posso Gotzi's hand. "Here's payment in advance for that, too."

"Hah!" Posso Gotzi exclaimed, "Fietlebaum, you good boy!" Then he cocked his head and leaned in close to Fietlebaum's face. "You wicked *bad*, good boy," he whispered admiringly.

"High praise indeed," Fietlebaum told him, though with less enthusiasm than he had intended to exhibit. "If there's trouble in the next few days, contact me at the hotel."

He and Teysoot Motzo walked out and were headed down the hallway when Teysoot Motzo stopped.

"You go on," he said. "There something I forget." Then he turned around and went back into Posso Gotzi's hangout.

"He forgot to stock up on *burzet*," Fietlebaum told himself. "Okay," he called out to Teysoot Motzo, "I'll meet you down at the front door."

Fietlebaum waited by the front door of Posso Gotzi's building, and Teysoot Motzo arrived ten minutes later. "Let's head back to the hotel," Fietlebaum said. "We meet Glesh in a few hours. I want some time to relax and think about what we need to say."

They waved down a cab, and it zigzagged it's way from the center lanes to the curb to pick them up. Fietlebaum opened the door to get in, but stopped short when he saw a Drajan behind the wheel. He quickly slammed the door shut and waved him on. "No thanks!" he called out." The driver made an upside down fist, extended his thumb down, and wiggled it vigorously at Fietlebaum before he darted back into traffic.

"He just flip you off!" Teysoot Motzo exclaimed. "Nasty cabbie."

"*Iz nisht geferlech*," Fietlebaum said with a shrug of his shoulders. "If that's the worst thing that happens to me today I'll be happy. Anyway, getting flipped off is certainly better than being driven to an alley, beaten senseless, and dropped into a sewer."

Fietlebaum shook his head and sighed. "I suppose it's silly," he confessed, "but I can't help it. I see a Drajan, and I see Glesh behind every one of them." He started to raise his arm again to flag down another cab, but said, "You know, to hell with it. The hotel is only a mile or so away. We've got time. Let's walk."

Fietlebaum realized he had not had any exercise for God only knows how long. He hoped the walk would do him good. Perhaps it might clear his head. But circumstances weighed upon him, and as they walked he waxed philosophical. His thoughts darkened.

Ordinarily, the anonymity of the big city was liberating, but at that moment he felt as if his very self was being diluted by the vastness of it all. He and Teysoot Motzo walked down block after block of busy city sidewalks. Hundreds of thousands of faceless, nameless individuals sped by in their vehicles in the streets and up in the air. Beyond the green Silesian sky, in the countless stars and planets, hundreds of trillions of other sentient beings were going about their lives. These were beings he had never met and never would meet. Some were on their way to weddings, some to sit by the side of a dying parent, some were fleeing painful marriages, others were off to their first day of an exciting new job. It even occurred to him, given the size of the galaxy and the number of sentient beings in it, that statistics demanded that one or two of those beings were flying across the galaxy arranging ransoms for their kidnapped grandsons. The realization provided him a second of comic relief, before it also grew oppressive in his mind. Though all of the beings that sped by had their own families, hopes, and cares, the nature of life was such that they were utterly indifferent to his. How many beings could one care about?

He had no idea if Teysoot Motzo had perceived the melancholy that had inexplicably come over him. But when Fietlebaum turned toward him, their eyes met and Teysoot Motzo smiled. He was astonished at how small an amount of affectionate interaction it took to bring him back from the brink of despair. The mind and its relationships with other minds remained a mystery. *He's a good friend,* Fietlebaum thought. No further explanation was possible or required.

They finally reached the Silesian Guardian Hotel, and the doorman welcomed them back. Fietlebaum checked the time. They had an hour before they met with Glesh. He decided to go upstairs, have a little *schnapps*, and relax before dealing with the *momzer*. He told Teysoot Motzo he would meet him in the lobby at seven o'clock.

He poured a finger of *schnapps* in a glass and sipped it. He had waited a long time for this moment to sit in front of Glesh and ask about his grandson. Then it occurred to him that Glesh would lie if it furthered his purposes. *He'll tell me what he wants me to know, and no more.* He felt utterly at Glesh's mercy, of which he had none. "Erd Glesh," he said out loud, "*a brokh tsu dayn lebn*[145]*!*"

He stared out the window and nursed his glass of *schnapps.* He remembered his grandson, Aaron, when he was a baby—his smile, his laugh. He recalled the way he called him "*zaidy*[146]" with his high, lilting voice. Though he had not been a believer for many years, he found himself praying. "Please, God," he said, "keep the little *pisher* safe." He noticed the clock on the wall. It was time to go.

He rode the elevator down and stepped out into the lobby. It was crowded, as he had hoped. He strolled over to the fountain and noticed Teysoot Motzo already seated at a table. He had a *nosh*[147] in his hand. Teysoot Motzo waved to make sure Fietlebaum saw him. "Over here," he called out. Fietlebaum went over and sat down. He checked the time. It was three minutes after seven. "He'll be late," Fietlebaum predicted. "A pusher always keeps you waiting."

At a quarter after seven, Glesh walked through the front door of the hotel and slowly made his way to the fountain area. He spotted Fietlebaum and Teysoot Motzo at their table, but that did not prompt him to move the least bit faster. He took his sweet time making his way over and sat down. He looked Fietlebaum directly in the eye and asked in slow monotone, "What do you want?"

"First," Fietlebaum said, with all the restraint he could muster, "you need to tell me how my grandson is."

---

145 A curse on your life!

146 Affectionate term for grandfather

147 snack

"His finger grew back," Glesh calmly replied. "But the scales on the new finger grew in slightly brown among the remaining orange ones. It embarrasses him. I asked him if I should cut the new one off and try again. You should have heard him squeal!"

Fietlebaum leaned close into Glesh's face. "You cruel, sadistic *shtik drek*. If it wasn't for my grandson, I would kill you here and now with my bare hands."

"Well," Glesh replied, unfazed either by Fietlebaum's torment or his wrath, "then it's fortunate for me that I have your grandson's life in my hands, isn't it?"

Teysoot Motzo shook his head in disgust. It did not escape Glesh's attention. He turned his eyes toward the Janpooran while continuing to address Fietlebaum. "It's nice you've brought your has-been, labor leader, lunatic with you," he said with a sneer. "The diagnosis was *leshte po noc*, was it not?

Teysoot Motzo jumped up and angrily stepped around the table toward Glesh. Glesh snapped his fingers, and the elderly Drajan whom Fietlebaum had seen and dismissed the previous day stood up at a nearby table. The two young females who accompanied him, the ones he assumed were his granddaughters, also stood up, pulled their silk jackets aside, and exposed holstered blasters. Fietlebaum then heard the sound of more chairs being pushed back from tables around the lobby, and five more Drajans stood and faced them with blasters exposed. Glesh smiled. He began to speak again, but was cut short when all around the lobby, Janpoorans arose, one after another. Ten Janpoorans, also carrying blasters, stood. Then, at a table across the lobby, Posso Gotzi slowly rose. The enormous Janpooran calmly sauntered over to the table and stopped in front of Glesh. He slowly bent down until his bright green face was an inch from Glesh's nose. "You want trouble?" he asked.

"Uh—no, no trouble," Glesh stammered as he waved his Drajans back down into their chairs. "Everything is—fine. I don't want any trouble."

Posso Gotzi slowly rose back up. "Ahhh, that too bad," he said. "If you change you mind, we be right here." Then he turned and calmly made his way back to his table.

Glesh was shaken. His face was pale and his tail limp. But he took a deep breath, collected himself, and turned his eyes to Fietlebaum.

Fietlebaum met his gaze. "It's *tuches ahfen tish*[148]," he told him. "I have three large vials of pure jorftoss extract. As I'm sure you know, all of the jorftoss in the Galaxy has been killed by a virus. These vials are worth a fortune. They might be the last jorftoss left in the Universe. I want my grandson back, safe and sound, in trade for the extract."

Fietlebaum had expected Glesh to start salivating upon hearing the proposition, and he was mildly disconcerted when he didn't. *Cool as a cucumber*, Fietlebaum thought.

After a long silence, Glesh asked, "How do I know I can trust you?"

"Because I have my grandson to lose, and you have nothing to lose," Fietlebaum replied.

"Maybe," Glesh said, "maybe not." Then he fell into thought. "I want to see this extract," he said.

"We were not so foolish as to bring jorftoss extract to Silesia to be caught and sentenced to death," Fietlebaum answered. "We have the extract hidden on a distant, desert moon."

"Hah!" Glesh laughed contemptuously. "A desert moon where you can have me ambushed and killed by your Janpooran goon squad! What kind of fool do you take me for?"

"That won't happen," Fietlebaum asserted. "I have devised a way to protect myself that I will explain to you.

---

148 Time to "put our asses on the table." Time to get down to business.

We will have no armed guards because we won't need them. If you're afraid, you are welcome to bring all the armed guards you want."

"Oh, I not think that such good idea," Teysoot Motzo volunteered.

Fietlebaum threw a piercing glance at him, then turned back to Glesh and re-emphasized his statement. "You can bring all the armed guards you want."

Finally, Glesh seemed intrigued. "Three vials of jorftoss extract for your grandson," he said out loud, partly to confirm the terms and partly to help himself think it through. "Perhaps it might be to my advantage to trust you. Where is this moon where you have hidden the jorftoss?"

"I won't tell you that now," Fietlebaum replied, "but if you agree, then in three days you will receive all the information you need to meet us there to make the trade."

"I will also need to know about this method you have to protect yourself. It sounds like the kind of protection that could get me killed," Glesh said.

"I want you to know everything about it," Fietlebaum told him, "because the more you know about it, the better it will work and the less chance you or I have of getting killed. The details of the device will be provided to you. All I will tell you now is that it is an explosive device sensitive to the presence and characteristics of my brain waves. It will allow you to have the extract if and only if I agree to your having it. If you tried to take it against my will, or if you killed me, both you and the jorftoss would be destroyed."

Glesh grew silent for a moment, then slowly nodded his head in appreciation of Fietlebaum's ingenuity. "Yes," he said, "It sounds like a very clever device. My compliments." He abruptly stood up and said, "I will trade your grandson for the jorftoss extract on this moon you've chosen." Then he extended his hand for Fietlebaum to shake, but Fietlebaum kept his hand at his side.

"I will make the trade with you, Glesh," he said, "but beyond that, you can *kish mir in tuches*[149]!" He and Teysoot Motzo stood up and started away. After a few steps, Fietlebaum turned back to Glesh. "Wait three days, and you will receive all the information you need. Don't try to follow or monitor us. Depart from the plan, and we all lose."

As they walked away, Fietlebaum was curious to know how Posso Gotzi ended up in the lobby. "Did you have something to do with Posso Gotzi being here tonight?" he asked Teysoot Motzo.

"Yes," Teysoot Motzo told Fietlebaum. "I hope you not mind, but when I turn around and go back for Posso Gotzi hangout, I take liberty of invite him and gang come join us tonight."

"Very shrewd," Fietlebaum told him. "Thank you." He paused for a moment and added, "Along with thanks, I probably owe you an apology. When you left me to go back to Posso Gotzi's I assumed you had just gone back for *burzet*."

"I *did* just go back for *burzet*," Teysoot Motzo admitted. "But when I there I think it be good idea we have help."

Absolutely without guile, Fietlebaum thought. *Vos iz ahfen kop, iz ahfen tsung*[150]. Then he turned to Teysoot Motzo and said, "Our work on Silesia is almost done. We have starship passage to Borgost, and we leave in three days from the Forgion Midcontinental Starport. By then, we will have the tragonite explosive and Posso Gotzi will have the information to get to Glesh." After brief consideration of necessity for complete secrecy, he turned back to Teysoot Motzo and added, "Keep this under your hat."

"I not wear a hat," Teysoot Motzo calmly replied.

"Oh, for God's sake!" Fietlebaum exclaimed. "Just keep it to yourself!"

---

149 Kiss my ass!

150 What's on his mind is on his tongue

CHAPTER 40

They had made certain one of them was always at the hotel waiting. But one day, two days, and the morning of the third day passed, and Posso Gotzi had not sent anyone by with the tragonite. The starship would be leaving for Borgost later that day. It was the makings of a catastrophe.

"I knew it not good idea pay advance," Teysoot Motzo lamented. "They probably at casino right now."

"I hope not," Fietlebaum said with a sigh. "Perhaps something went wrong." But as the morning wore on, he wondered if Teysoot Motzo wasn't right.

Then the news report came over the communicator. Four Janpooran fishermen had been taken into custody off Borgind Island. According to the report, the island was the site of a government experimental marine farming laboratory. The area was considered to be extremely important to the Silesian economy and strictly off limits to commercial fishing.

"*Oy gevalt*!" Fietlebaum cried out. "Those are our boys!"

"But they not fisherman," Teysoot Motzo protested.

"Of course not," Fietlebaum replied. "But they can't report the real facts. That would betray Galactic government secrets."

"I suppose you right," Teysoot Motzo admitted.

Fietlebaum stood and stared blankly out the window.

"So what we do now?" Teysoot Motzo asked.

"There's nothing we can do," Fietlebaum replied. "For all we know, Posso Gotzi may have been interrogated by now and implicated us in a plot to steal tragonite from the government. I wouldn't be surprised if the police were on their way right now."

Teysoot Motzo stepped over to the window and peered through the curtains to see if he could spot any police cruisers hovering outside. "Not yet," he said.

Fietlebaum paced. "Damn it!" he shouted. "We can't stay here. We will have to leave on the starship as we planned and hope we can arrange something when we get to Borgost. Maybe we'll have to make a side trip to Janpoor to obtain explosive from one of your friends before we get to Jinkor."

Then Fietlebaum was struck with the other terrible possibility. What if Posso Gotzi isn't able to get the instructions to Glesh? If Posso Gotzi and his crew were in jail, then there was little chance the task could be accomplished.

Fietlebaum checked the time. "Arrangements have been made that can't be unmade. We need to get ready. An ambulance is going to pick us up in half an hour," he told Teysoot Motzo.

"Ambulance?" Teysoot Motzo asked. "You get sick?"

"Of course not," Fietlebaum answered. "We can't let Glesh follow us, because we have to get to Jinkor early enough to prepare the intention switch and attach it to the jorftoss. If he got there at the same time we did, the jorftoss would be unprotected and we would be lost. I asked my friend, Dr. Lishorn, to send an ambulance to pick us up and take us to the hospital. He will tell them I am needed for a special psychiatric consultation, and that it is a matter of life or death. None of Glesh's agents will be able to keep up with us, because the ambulance has electronic clearance for high speed travel through the city. When we get to the hospital, there will be an aircab waiting for us to transport us to the Midcontinental Starport in the center of Frigion.

We will be able to get there and board the starship without Glesh having any idea where we've gone."

"Hah!" Teysoot Motzo cackled. "Very good. You clever boy!"

Fietlebaum completed his packing while Teysoot Motzo returned to his room to gather his own things. They then had another fifteen minutes to wait, and Fietlebaum insisted the two of them remain in the room by the phone until the last second.

Time passed. The phone didn't ring. Neither said a word until Fietlebaum took a last glance at his communicator and said, "No one's coming. Let's go."

They went downstairs, and less than a minute after they stepped out onto the sidewalk, the ambulance roared up with lights flashing and sirens blaring. The driver leapt out and opened the door for Fietlebaum. He was puzzled to see Teysoot Motzo also standing there, as he had not been told about a second passenger. "He is my assistant," Fietlebaum explained, and the driver immediately opened the door for Teysoot Motzo as well.

They jetted off, weaving in and out of the traffic that was automatically re-routed here and there to allow the ambulance to maximize its speed through the city. Fietlebaum looked through the rear window as they sped off, and he saw a vehicle collide with another while trying to edge its way into traffic. He thought he saw a Drajan behind the wheel, but they were too far away for him to be certain. If someone had been following them, they weren't any longer. Still, Fietlebaum's brain was ablaze with anxieties. The plan was on the brink of disaster.

They sped through the city at impossibly high speed and arrived at the hospital only a minute or two later. They jumped out and, much to the driver's consternation, they immediately climbed into the waiting aircab and flew off to the Midcontinental Starport. After a fifteen minute flight, the aircab landed and they hopped out. The walked through the doors of the terminal, checked their bags at the ticket counter, and headed to the departure gate.

There were only a few more minutes until boarding time, and the gate was crowded. The passengers were mostly Silesians bound for diplomatic and business offices on Borgost. Along with them were Borgostians on their way home. An entire family was at the counter on tiptoe, hoping to appear more intimidating as they demanded seating re-assignments. The youngest one was not up to the physical demands of the exercise, lost his balance and fell, taking the rest of the family down like a line of toppling dominoes. The father on the end struggled valiantly to remain on his toes. He reeled, twisted and turned, but finally fell backwards and landed on Teysoot Motzo's feet. Wanting to endear himself, and hopefully avoid another embarrassing incident with a Borgostian, Teysoot Motzo quickly grabbed the fellow's uppermost tentacles and hoisted him back up on his toes. Unbeknownst to Teysoot Motzo, for a Borgostian the only indignity worse than a painful, lingering death was being assisted onto tiptoes.

The Borgostian twisted out of Teysoot Motzo's grasp, scuttled a few feet away, turned, rose up on his tiptoes, and let loose a blood curdling shriek.

Oy vey, Fietlebaum thought—*when you think things can't get worse.*

"What in hell going on?" Teysoot Motzo pleaded. "What he get so hot about?"

A Silesian diplomat standing nearby quickly explained the situation to him, and warned him to expect the worst. According to Borgostian tradition, the only appropriate response to this gross insult was either challenging the offender to a fight to the death or hurling oneself into a pit of flame. With no pit of flame readily accessible at the starport, the death challenge remained the only viable option.

"Would it help say I sorry?" Teysoot Motzo asked the Borgostian, but the unspoken answer was, "No!"

After another shriek, the Borgostian ran tiptoe up to Teysoot Motzo and scurried up his big Janpooran body to his head. He skittered around his neck, over one arm, around his chest, and back under and around the other arm. While his intention was to display unbridled ferocity, he appeared more like a treed squirrel trying to escape the eyes of the hounds. He skittered back around Teysoot Motzo's back, then scrambled up on top of his head where he gnawed on one of his olfactory tentacles. Teysoot Motzo grew tired of it. He sincerely apologized one more time, but after the Borgostian failed to relent, he peeled the fellow off and hurled him across the room. "I sorry, I sorry, I sorry," he exclaimed, "but I not going kiss you ass all day!" It was then they heard the sirens.

Well, Fietlebaum thought, *that's it. I'm done . . . arumgeflecht*[151]! He heaved a sigh of surrender. *The police interrogated Posso Gotzi and he gave us up,* he concluded. *Galactic Intelligence used all their assets to ferret us out, and now we're about to get arrested.*

The sirens got louder. The walls at the departure gate grew dappled with dancing spots of blue and red light as three police cruisers dropped down onto the tarmac. Posso Gotzi hopped out of one cruiser accompanied by police. They poured through the door and bounded up to Fietlebaum.

"That him!" Posso Gotzi shouted.

"We're doomed," Fietlebaum sighed.

Posso Gotzi trotted up to Fietlebaum and held out a package. "Here is medicine, Dr. Fietlebaum," he said with a wink. "I tell police medicine was matter of life and death and had be in you hands before you take off for Borgost. They nice enough for give me escort."

---

151 milked, sucked dry, exhausted

He gave Fietlebaum a firm hug, and during the short embrace he added, "No worry. Tomorrow I drop off prescription you write for Dr. Glesh."

"*Got tsu danken!*" Fietlebaum exclaimed. He was tremendously relieved. "Thank you," he told Posso Gotzi. Then, considering the possibility that one of Posso Gotzi's crew might yet betray the plan, he felt the necessity of asking, "but what about your crew? I heard about them on the news."

"Hah!" Posso Gotzi answered as he broke the clench. "They get caught like I want. They crash boat on one side island while I sneak on other and grab tragonite. I hide out in bush two day until heat die down. Then I sail back. They be okay. They just have for play dumb." Then he leaned in closer one last time and added, "Between you and me, they not need play hard." Posso Gotzi and the police filed out of the doors and piled back into their cruisers. The sirens blared again, and they flew off in a blur of dopplered sound and flashing light.

The Borgostians were famous for short tempers, not long attention spans. By the time Posso Gotzi and the police had left the starport, the Borgostian had forgotten Teysoot Motzo's grave insult. The family had even forgotten their complaints over the seating arrangements that had initiated the ill-fated group tiptoe display in the first place. In the blink of an eye, the universe had suddenly come right again.

The starship crew announced that the starship would begin boarding, and Fietlebaum and Teysoot Motzo joined the line of passengers streaming onto the ship. An enormous burden had been lifted from his shoulders. They had the tragonite in hand, and Glesh would soon have all the information he needed to meet them on Jinkor as well as a run-down on the workings of the intention switch. They were boarding the starship and all was in order. But Fietlebaum was disturbed by something.

Had he and Teysoot Motzo been implicated in a conspiracy to breach Galactic security on Borgin Island, then Galactic Intelligence would have spared no effort in searching the entire Galactic data base to discover their travel plans and intercept them. However, they would not have gone to the trouble of hunting him down simply to help Posso Gotzi deliver a package, even if it were the matter of life or death. Posso Gotzi had to have already known where they were. But how? The obvious answer sprang to his mind.

"Teysoot Motzo?" Fietlebaum inquired. "Do you have any idea how Posso Gotzi knew where we were?"

"Maybe I do," Teysoot Motzo answered sheepishly.

"*May*be you do?" Fietlebaum asked in pursuit of a more substantive answer.

"Yesterday," Teysoot Motzo began, "I go Posso Gotzi's hangout for buy *burzet*. He not there, so I leave message where he find us over next few days."

"You left him all the plans for where we would be?" Fietlebaum inquired with growing agitation, "even after I asked you not to?" Teysoot Motzo nodded affirmatively.

"Did you suspect," Fietlebaum continued, "that Glesh might have had him tailed after the scene in the hotel lobby? Did it occur to you that Glesh could have had him tortured to spill the information?"

"Yes," Teysoot Motzo replied, "but at time it seem like chance worth taking."

"*Oy vey*!" Fietlebaum shouted out loud. The line of passengers turned toward him. Even the Borgostian that Teysoot Motzo had insulted turned to see what the commotion was. Fearing a new commotion might rekindle the flat fellow's memory of the aborted death challenge, he struggled to control himself. Yet, as he took himself in hand, Fietlebaum realized that had Teysoot Motzo not given Posso Gotzi the information, they might have left without the tragonite and their plans would have been ruined. Again, he sighed.

"My friend," Fietlebaum finally said, "I don't know if I should kiss you or strangle you."

"Well," Teysoot Motzo replied philosophically, "one can only hope for best."

Fietlebaum and Teysoot Motzo followed the line of passengers into the observation gallery of the starship from where they would be led to their suspended animation chambers. One of the crew called their names, and they were led into the dormitory. The chamber lids popped open, and they climbed inside their respective chambers.

"Sweet dreams," Teysoot Motzo called out as he slid down into his chamber.

"*Gai schlofen*[152]*!*" Fietlebaum ordered.

Fietlebaum nestled down as the lid of the suspension chamber lowered, then fastened itself shut. "God, I hate this!" he exclaimed. The sweet, peppery odor of the suspension gas washed over him. It was a complex mixture of gases chosen for his particular species. One component protected the body's cellular integrity during the freezing process. Another acted as an anxiolytic to calm the mind, and yet another as an anesthetic that smothered the brain's neural activity in preparation for what would otherwise be a painful drop into the rapid-onset freezing process. He closed his eyes. He felt a reflexive urge to refrain from breathing the gas, but coaxed himself into relaxing. He allowed his chest to expand and contract. His lungs took in the gas and his blood absorbed it.

As the gas-laden blood completed the cardiopulmonary circuit and pulsed into his thoracocerebral artery, he felt the familiar sensation of falling into darkness. The temperature of the suspension gas fell. As he felt his neural function slow down, he fastened his thoughts on how pleasant it would be

---

152 Go to sleep

to see his grandson again. The thoughts faded. They were no longer anchored in synaptic protein. They existed only in the evanescent waves of electrical charge that for those moments swept through the neural networks of his cerebral cortex. His thoughts slowed and fragmented, and as the electrical potentials across his neuronal membranes fell to zero, his consciousness vanished like the morning fog.

CHAPTER 41

The better starship lines employed physicians to prescribe hormones specific for each life form to help them re-establish their natural circadian rhythms and ease back into their normal activities before disembarking. But, Fietlebaum and Teysoot Motzo were not flying one of the better starship lines. Indeed, none of those lines flew from Silesia to Borgost. Few who travelled to Borgost could afford such amenities anyway, and hardly anyone travelled there by choice. Thus, none of the starship lines saw the need to offer the medical service on flights to Borgost. "Why bother?" they asked.

Borgost was a day away. The onboard computers had brought the starship back to life. Fietlebaum and Teysoot Motzo awakened. They climbed wearily out of their suspended animation chambers and shuffled to the observation gallery to sit and shake their reanimation syndrome. Fietlebaum was dizzy. He felt like his brain was full of oatmeal. *Oy*! he thought. I've got it bad this time.

As he struggled to collect himself, he heard a sudden cry of anguish and horror. The cry echoed through the corridors of the starship. The crew of the starship ran toward the apparent source of the cry. The fear in the cry was so intense and pure that, as a psychiatrist, he felt duty-bound to pursue it as well. He forced himself to rise, then stumbled after the crew down the corridor to a utility closet. There he saw a Gorsidian janitor slumped against a wall. The smell of decay hung in the air. On the other side of the small room lay the flat, desiccated body of a Borgostian stowaway who, without the benefits of the suspended animation chamber, had likely died of starvation and thirst. The janitor had awakened from suspended animation and restarted his usual cleaning routines on the starship when he inadvertently encountered the gruesome scene.

The janitor had a look on his face that Fietlebaum had seen many times before. It was the vacant look he had seen in the faces of many veterans of the wars that were constantly erupting here and there across the galaxy. It was the thousand yard stare. His own father had had nightmares when memories of the final Arab Israeli war returned to haunt his sleep. He remembered the times his father bowed out of celebrations and social events because it was, "just too much." Sometimes, in the quiet of the night, young Fietlebaum would wake up and see his father by the window with the stare on his face. The vision had always haunted him.

Fear was the natural response to mortal danger. The fear of combat arose with the risk of being wounded or killed. It came from seeing friends injured and maimed, or from viewing the bodies of comrades killed in battle. Fear kept soldiers sharp and alert. It kept them alive. Like physical pain, fear could be suppressed and endured long enough to get the job done. But choosing to endure overwhelming fear, day after day, extracted a price. In many veterans of combat, even years after the war had ended, the memories and demands of great fear not only persisted, but had ballooned until fear became a way of life.

While the crew carried away the dead Borgostian body, Fietlebaum tended to the janitor. As he looked down upon the unfortunate fellow, he felt the room spin. *I'm* farblondzhet[153], he thought. *It's reanimation syndrome.* He braced himself against the wall and eased himself down it to the floor. He drew from his years of residency at Forgion

---

153 Confused, lost, bewildered

Transgalactic. Then he would often go for days without sleep, finally fall into bed for desperately needed rest, only to be awakened after fifteen minutes to see a patient in the emergency department. From those experiences he had developed the ability to reach deeply into himself, past physical exhaustion and the fog of sleep deprivation, to focus his energy and skill on the patient. It became second nature. "Pull it together, Fietlebaum," he whispered to himself. "You have work to do."

"I'm Isaac Fietlebaum," he told him. "I'm a psychiatrist, and I would like to help you if I can." The janitor did not respond. But the intensity of his fear, and the depth of his nihilism and despair were palpable. "What's your name?" Fietlebaum asked him. After a long silence, the Gorsid answered, "Nesh Jorsiss."

Fietlebaum suspected Nesh suffered post-traumatic stress disorder. He carried a festering terror that had spilled out at the sight of the decaying corpse. The terror and despair needed lancing, like a boil, and Fietlebaum decided to pursue the source of the Gorsid's anguish. He scooted a little closer to him, but the move may have been too abrupt. One of Nesh's tentacles jerked and flapped wildly. The tentacle twisted so energetically that it tore free from Nesh's body and launched itself up into the air with a loud snapping noise. It fell to the floor, writhed, wriggled, then slithered in a bee line underneath a nearby cabinet with the apparent intention to hide itself.

"*Gevalt*," Fietlebaum muttered.

The most parsimonious explanation for the psychiatric symptoms suffered by war veterans was that they remained stuck in combat mode. They needlessly, yet persistently, engaged in reflexive, self-perseveration behaviors. In humans, and many other species in the galaxy, these were often described as components of the "fight or flight" response. Such behaviors arose from nervous systems primed either to engage in battle or to flee to live and fight another day. However, in cataloging the various forms of self-preservation behaviors across the galaxy, exo-psychiatrists expanded their view to allow the phenomenon to become known as the "fight, flight, freeze, flail, or fall apart" response. Gorsids were among those species who fell apart.

The "falling apart" of Gorsids fearful of injury or death was identical to the behaviors displayed by certain species of reptiles on Earth. When such species were cornered by a predator, their tails might snap off, then writhe and twist with such extravagant motion that the predator's attention was drawn from the tail owner to the tail alone, thus allowing the tailless creature to slip away. At the dawn of their evolution as a species, the response likely saved Gorsidian lives from larger, stronger predators. Yet, the loss of tentacles in "falling apart" was distressing for the Gorsidian sufferers of PTSD. Though deeply rooted in biology, for intelligent beings, such as the Gorsids, the response seemed primitive and unnecessary. It was embarrassing.

There were also significant medical sequelae from frequent falling apart. Tentacles were muscular pieces of tissue, and repeated loss and regrowth of tentacles caused depletion of the body's protein and amino acid stores. Such depletion could, in turn, exacerbate the aberrations of brain chemistry that themselves arose from depletion of amino acid-derived neurotransmitters. Thus, falling apart tended to worsen the comorbid depression of PTSD in Gorsids. Fietlebaum noted that several of Nesh's remaining tentacles were small, immature, and likely in the process of regrowth. *This boychik is sick*, he thought to himself.

"I'm sorry," Nesh said dejectedly about his falling apart. "I can't help it."

Fietlebaum dismissed his concern with a wave of his hand. "*Nu*?" he replied. "Whaddaya gonna do?" As he spoke, he heard his own voice reverberate in his head, as if the interior of his skull had become enormously spacious. Flashes of blue light sparkled in his peripheral vision. *It's never been this bad before*, he realized. He paused to collect his thoughts, then pressed on. "Nesh," he said, "I can see in your face that you have seen death many times before." The janitor nodded slowly, then sighed. By gauging the Gorsid's age, he quickly came to suspect the form of horror Nesh Jorsiss had been subjected to. "Did you serve in the Vorstian War?" This time he turned to face Fietlebaum and again nodded his head.

The Vorstian War between the planets Gors and Korpia was a brief, but brutal affair. There had long been conflict over mineral and mining rights in the Vorsti Asteroid belt that lay between the two planets. Thirty years before, the conflict had exploded into violence. A Korpian mining company hired mercenaries to clear one of the larger asteroids of the competing Gorsidian presence. Several dozen Gorsids were killed in the process. It was an election year on Gors, and the standing government felt political pressure to marshal troops and ship them off to defend Gorsidian interests.

Seven thousand soldiers were sent off to defend Gorsidian life and property. They were eager, young volunteers. Unfortunately, the popularity of the war plummeted when it was learned that the Gorsidian commercial interests at the center of the conflict were owned by the brother of the president of Gors. It was seen as a disgraceful conflict of interest. The effort foundered. The goals became unclear. Political adversaries initiated endless rounds of accusations and congressional investigations. But, as always, it was the soldiers in the field who bore the brunt of the political subterfuge and lack of military resolve.

"So many dead," Nesh Jorsiss whispered. From the stories Fietlebaum had heard, hundreds of Gorsids were slaughtered by Korpian troops when reinforcements failed to arrive to bolster defense perimeters. There was incompetence and equipment failures. Thousands more died of starvation waiting for supply ships that never came. The few thousand that remained alive lived amongst the corpses for months, waiting for rescue. With every passing day, the number of corpses increased on the floor of the mining company warehouse that served as their bunker.

"Many starved like this poor fellow, didn't they?" Fietlebaum asked.

The Gorsid nodded. "I should have died with them," he said. He wrapped four of his tentacles around his cephalic structure in a gesture often seen among Gorsidian children who were embarrassed or afraid.

Gorsidian soldiers who returned from the Vorstian War often drifted to the margins of society. They were wary and constantly on edge. It was difficult for them to be in crowds. Many, like Nesh, took on menial jobs that required little interaction with others. Even those jobs tended to be short-lived. Many of the veterans abused the drug, *ragatt*. It lulled them into sleep, and helped them avoid the nightmares that persisted even thirty years later. Many veterans went to jail for one reason or another. Some committed suicide. Few thrived.

"For many, it's smells that bring it all back," Fietlebaum explained. He hoped not only to help the Gorsid understand what he was experiencing, but also to give him a form of permission to follow wherever his memories and feelings might lead him. "Explosives, burning flesh, and the smell of death. This must be a horror for you." Nesh Jorsiss wept. For Gorsids, this was rapidly breathing in and out against a contracted membrane in the throat. It produced a deep, resonant, melancholy sound, like a tremulous bassoon. It was an overdue catharsis, and Fietlebaum granted him a long and cleansing cry.

"Those politicians that sent you off to that *farkakteh* war owe you," Fietlebaum finally asserted. "Have you gone to the Gorsidian Veteran's Bureau?"

"I don't want anything to do with them," he angrily replied. "Why should I ask for help from the ones that fucked me over in the first place?"

"I don't blame you for being angry," Fietlebaum told him. "But they aren't the same ones that sent you to Vorsti. A lot of years have passed and things have changed."

Nesh said nothing. The weeping had deflated the immediate horror and desperation, but the wound sealed back over more rapidly than Fietlebaum had anticipated. Nesh Jorsiss needed years of ongoing treatment, not a morning's heart-to-heart chat. Still, Fietlebaum hoped the door to his pathway back to life had been opened, if only a crack.

"Listen," Fietlebaum finally said, while writing him a note on a scrap of paper. "Here's my number. If you ever want my help, get a hold of me, and I will do whatever I can to arrange something for you." He held out his card for the janitor to take. Nesh made no move to take it, but Fietlebaum continued to hold it in front of him until he did.

After a long pause, the Gorsid said, "Maybe I'll give you a call someday."

That's the best I can do, Fietlebaum thought. *I can't save everybody.*

He stood up. The flashes of light intensified. The dizziness got worse. He left the Gorsid and headed back toward the gallery, holding on to the hallway railing as he walked. Midway, he stopped and reconsidered. He turned and headed toward the suspended animation dormitory where his things were stored. When he got there he pulled out his bag, unzipped it, and reached in for his *schnapps*. *A little couldn't hurt*, he thought.

He felt under underwear, shirts, and pants. "Hello, old friend!" he sang out loud when his fingers found the bottle. "If anyone deserves a little of your company right now, it's me," he told the *schnapps*. He looked around to see if anyone was watching, then tipped back his head and drank a gulp of scotch right out of the bottle. He wiped a few escaped drops off his chin with his sleeve.

Lacking a chair, he plopped on the floor, pushed his bag against the wall, and leaned back on it. His initial impression was that the *schnapps* was helping the reanimation syndrome, and took another swig. He thought of Nesh Jorsiss and shook his head in disgust. "Those fucking wars," he muttered out loud, "and those fucking politicians. They're all the same. It doesn't matter what planet they're from." He took another swig of *schnapps*. "They pump young soldiers full of patriotic nonsense, throw them into the slaughter, then forget about them."

He thought again of how his father suffered from the emotional scars of combat. Unlike many sufferers of post-traumatic stress disorder, he had managed to get on with his life. He was able to marry and share a long and rewarding relationship. But the horrors were always a memory away. Fortunately, his struggle to make sense of his suffering led him to medical school, and not to the maintenance crew of a third-rate starship.

His father had a ritual he followed whenever one of his patients died. He bought a fine cigar, poured himself a snifter of rare brandy, sat back and enjoyed them. He was not celebrating death. It was his way of celebrating the life his patient had lost but he, Morris Fietlebaum, still possessed. It took Fietlebaum a long time to understand why his father did that. It was his way of dealing with his post-traumatic stress disorder and his memories of the horrors of war.

He raised the bottle of *schnapps* to his father, said, "*Le'chayim*, Dr. Fietlebaum," and took one last swig. He tucked the *schnapps* back in the bag under some clothes. "I'll see you later," he whispered affectionately.

He struggled back to his feet and managed to find his way back to the gallery. Teysoot Motzo was waiting for him.

"You look like hell" Teysoot Motzo said. "You okay?"

"No, I'm not okay," Fietlebaum replied. "I'm sick as a dog. But we have things to discuss."

"You mean now?" Teysoot Motzo asked.

"Yes, now," Fietlebaum answered. "You flew the star taxi quite well the last time we went to Jinkor."

"Yes, I did," Teysoot Motzo whole-heartedly agreed.

"I was thinking we could rent a little ship like that taxi and you can pilot it to Jinkor this time, too," Fietlebaum told him. "Do you think you can do it?"

"Of course, I can do it!" Teysoot Motzo replied.

"Good," Fietlebaum replied. "Tomorrow, we land on Borgost. We'll rent a ship at the starport and you'll fly it to Jinkor.

"No problem," Teysoot Motzo replied.

"Any concerns?" Fietlebaum asked.

Teysoot Motzo fell lost into thought for a long moment. "Yes," he finally answered. "If food processor in ship as bad as last one, can we buy food for take with us?"

"I'll take that under advisement," Fietlebaum told him. He again felt dizzy and nauseated, and fell silent for a moment. "*Oy*," he finally groaned, "if I keep talking to you I'm going to vomit."

"That not nice thing for say," Teysoot Motzo protested.

"Oh, for God's sake," he replied. "I'm sick from the flight."

"I a little sick, too," Teysoot Motzo admitted.

Fietlebaum closed his eyes. *It will all be over soon*, he thought. *I'll have Aaron back from that momzer Glesh.*

Then a painful thought struck him. *Would Aaron have post-traumatic stress disorder?* Only an hour before, he had watched Nesh Jorsiss live out a horror that had taken place thirty years before. It was as real and intense as if it had happened only yesterday. But, Nesh had been a trained soldier when he suffered his trauma. Aaron was just a boy. What trauma would he have to work through after his torture and torment at Glesh's hands? His only certainty was that he wasn't going to survive it unscathed.

CHAPTER 42

Fietlebaum was suffering unusually severe reanimation syndrome. He turned to ask Teysoot Motzo to watch out for him, but drifted off to sleep instead. He fell into a dream. He was being chased by Drajan GIA agents. They were eating spicy noodles and accused him of adding too much *pokra* to the sauce. They pointed blasters and chased him down a long, dark hallway in the basement of the Silesian GIA office. He jerked awake to find he had left his seat and wandered down the starship's main corridor to an employee locker room.

He trudged back to the gallery, sat down next to Teysoot Motzo, and promptly fell back to sleep. He awakened when crew members came around to announce they would be landing at the Borgost Starport in thirty minutes. *Borgost*? he wondered, *What the hell am I doing here*? He turned to Teysoot Motzo for answers, but he was sound asleep. Fietlebaum shook him and Teysoot Motzo resurfaced into a state of relatively full consciousness. But, he, too, was suffering reanimation syndrome and could offer no useful information. Teysoot Motzo fall back to sleep. Then, for no obvious reason, Fietlebaum suddenly recalled where he was and what he was doing. *Got tsu danken*, he sighed, "This is no time to go *meshugeh*."

He shook Teysoot Motzo awake again. "We'll be landing soon at the Borgost Starport," Fietlebaum told him. "Get your things together." After a moment to reflect, he added, "and for God's sake, when we get there don't touch anybody!"

"Not for worry," Teysoot Motzo replied, "I not even look at Borgostian!"

"Good!" Fietlebaum replied, then promptly fell back to sleep.

The starship shook as it penetrated the turbulent Borgostian atmosphere. The shaking awakened Fietlebaum. He sat and vacantly gazed through the portholes. The again sleeping Teysoot Motzo bobbed back and forth in his seat until Fietlebaum gave him a swift elbow to the ribs. "Look!" Fietlebaum told him, as he pointed to the landscape of Borgost growing visible through the atmospheric haze. The starport came into view. Stabilizing rockets roared and landing gear clicked into position in a series of deep, resonant *thunks* from underneath the starship. The landing gear touched ground, and the whine of the engines slowly decreased, then disappeared.

"We're here," Fietlebaum announced.

"Where?" Teysoot Motzo inquired.

"Borgost, for God's sake!" Fietlebaum barked.

"Oh," Teysoot Motzo responded.

They grabbed their bags and walked off the starship into the arrival concourse of the starport. The now fully awakened Teysoot Motzo spotted a starship rentals sign a hundred yards down the concourse and pointed it out to Fietlebaum. "Let's go," Fietlebaum said.

They strolled over to the starship rental counter and rang the bell. A moment later, a Borgostian clerk peeked out from an adjoining office and scuttled over to help them. Teysoot Motzo saw the Borgostian and, tossing his head toward a row of seats by a window, told Fietlebaum, "I think I wait over there."

"Splendid idea," Fietlebaum replied.

Fietlebaum explained to the clerk that they were interested in renting a starship for a trip to Jinkor. He described the small star taxi they had last flown there—leaving out the uncomfortable fact that it was the late, Sessi Bosso's Super Excellent Star Taxi—and asked if it were possible to rent a craft similar to it. "We have a craft of the same make," the clerk explained, "but it's a slightly smaller model." Fietlebaum turned to ask Teysoot Motzo his opinion.

Meanwhile, Teysoot Motzo had fallen back asleep in his chair, and an errant Borgostian infant had crawled up onto his lap. The little fellow's parents had just noticed the whereabouts of their baby boy and where steaming toward Teysoot Motzo to set things straight. Fietlebaum turned in time to watch hell break loose. "*Vey iz mir*!" he exclaimed.

The Borgostian mother grasped the handle of her overstuffed travel bag firmly with two tentacles, scooted around the chair behind Teysoot Motzo, and proceeded to wallop him over the head with it. The startled Teysoot Motzo sprang up in shock. When he arose, the infant slid off his lap and scurried away with his mother in hot pursuit. Teysoot Motzo frantically searched for the cause and source of the pummeling without success. "What in hell going on?" he cried in bewilderment. "Where am I?"

Fietlebaum ran over. "Why do you insist on tormenting these creatures?" he demanded to know.

"I victim of circumstance!" Teysoot Motzo pleaded.

"*Got in himmel*!" Fietlebaum howled, "leave them alone!" He shook his head in consternation as he strode back to the starship rental counter. "The sooner we get off this *meshugeneh* planet the better," he muttered.

Fietlebaum signed the papers, and the Borgostian clerk handed over the keys to the economy-sized starship. The clerk also gave him a memory cube with auto-pilot commands to lift them off Borgost and start them on a trajectory to Janpoor's moon. "Excellent," Fietlebaum told the clerk. After receiving directions, he fetched Teysoot Motzo and they walked out to the rental lot where the starship stood.

Fietlebaum took in a deep draught of Borgostian air and let it out slowly. He was beginning to feel himself again as they approached the ship. "So, what do you think of her?" he asked Teysoot Motzo. But before he got an answer, he was struck by a powerful new wave of dizziness and confusion.

Teysoot Motzo saw him struggle to maintain his balance and took him by the arm. "I think you need something for eat," he told Fietlebaum with fatherly concern, "Maybe some of you *schnapps* and a nap."

"You're probably right," Fietlebaum replied. "This reanimation syndrome is kicking my *tuches*."

"Come in ship with me and sit down," Teysoot Motzo told him as he walked him through the starship's hatch. He led Fietlebaum to the captain's chair and sat him down. "I got something for you," he said with a smile. He dug through his bag and pulled out a helium-packed corned beef on rye from Moishe's. "I buy it couple day before we leave Silesia."

"You mean, after he threw you out?" Fietlebaum asked incredulously.

"Yes," Teysoot Motzo replied. "He not want sell for me. He say he not sell for *schlemiels*. But I convince him." He raised his fist to demonstrate his method of persuasion.

"Hah!" Fietlebaum laughed with delight. "You are a *mensch*, my friend." He unwrapped the sandwich. It was surprisingly well-preserved and tasty. "I'm amazed," he said, "It's still fresh and delicious!"

"It probably help bring sandwich into suspended animation chamber with me," Teysoot Motzo volunteered. "We *both* stay fresh."

"Very clever!" Fietlebaum exclaimed. *He even had the decency to include a packet of yellow mustard*, he noted. He felt it would be a nice gesture to offer Teysoot Motzo one of the kosher dill pickle spears that accompanied the sandwich.

Teysoot Motzo graciously accepted the pickle, raised it high, and toasted Fietlebaum with it. "*Le'chayim*," he said with gusto.

"*Le'chayim*," Fietlebaum answered in kind as he lifted his own pickle high in the air.

After Fietlebaum finished his sandwich, Teysoot Motzo announced, "I got important business." He pointed out the front porthole to a snack shop a short way down the concourse. "You have sip *schnapps* and close you eyes awhile," he told Fietlebaum. "I be right back."

"Go grab your *chazerei*[154]," Fietlebaum told him, "and get right back to the ship. I don't want to be alone. I don't know how I'm going to be from one minute to the next." He retrieved his remaining *schnapps*, sat, and looked around the ship. It was musty inside. There was a layer of dust on the control panel. *When was the last time this thing flew*? he wondered. He took a sip of *schnapps*, sat back down to wait for Teysoot Motzo to return, and promptly fell asleep.

He heard a familiar cackle, looked up, and saw Senator Lornst from the Senatorial gestiron investigation committee. Oy! he thought. The senator was riding a horse down the corridor of the starport and driving a herd of Borgostians ahead of him. He cracked his whip across their backs and commanded them to run faster.

"Leave them alone!" Fietlebaum demanded.

Lornst swiveled his head completely around and stared into Fietlebaum's eyes. "This is your fault, Fieggenblot," he growled. He cracked his whip again, causing the largest Borgostian to break from the herd. He reared up and galloped toward Fietlebaum on tiptoe. Fietlebaum tried to move, but his legs would not respond. "*Gevalt*!" he cried as the Borgostian trampled over him.

---

[154] Pig swill, junk food

He awoke with a shout. He glanced around—no Borgostian, no Lornst. "What a nightmare," he croaked. "Like *a loch in kop* I need this."

Teysoot Motzo strolled back to the ship with a large bag of food and snacks in his arms. He glanced at Fietlebaum, then craned his neck in for closer inspection. "You look terrible," he said.

"Another nightmare," Fietlebaum admitted, "but I feel fine, now. Go figure"

Teysoot Motzo shrugged. "I okay, if you okay," he said. He stored his goodies, switched the control panel on, and began a perfunctory examination of the instruments. When everything seemed in order, Fietlebaum handed him the memory cube, and Teysoot Motzo inserted it into the auto-pilot interface. The on-board computer whirred and hummed, lights flashed, and the control panel confirmed that Jinkor had been chosen as the destination. A holographic display projected the planned trajectory in the air for the approval of the flight crew.

"Were set," Fietlebaum chirped as he punched the flight plan confirmation into the system. "Let's fly to Jinkor."

"That sound good for me," Teysoot Motzo proclaimed.

They buckled into their seats and taxied out onto the tarmac. After the control tower reviewed their flight plan and trajectory, they were given permission for take-off. Teysoot Motzo lifted the safety hatch from off the ignition button and pushed it. They were off.

As they accelerated up through the Borgostian atmosphere, Teysoot Motzo leaned back, folded his hands behind his head, and lifted his feet up onto the edge of the control panel. "I think I do terrific job!" he said with satisfaction.

"Absolutely," Fietlebaum replied. "Your button-pushing skill is unparalleled in the galaxy."

"I just have knack," Teysoot Motzo proudly replied.

Let him bask in his glory, for now, Fietlebaum thought. *The real work will begin when we get to Jinkor.*

After an orbit around Borgost, Teysoot Motzo blasted the main engine. The gravitational pull of Borgost and the thrust of the starship's sturdy engine combined to slingshot them toward Jinkor. After a final confirmation of their flight path, they unbuckled and took their ease.

Teysoot Motzo gazed through the starboard porthole at his planet. It was still a mere point of light in the dark of space. "I feel good we fly back toward Janpoor, even if we not go there right away," he said. "I miss my home," he added wistfully.

"It has been a long time, hasn't it?" Fietlebaum asked.

"Yes, too long," Teysoot Motzo replied with a sigh. "You miss you home, Fietlebaum?" he asked.

Fietlebaum was taken aback. "I'm not certain where my home is anymore," he finally confessed, "not since Sophie died. I live on Polmod, but that planet isn't my home. It's a place to stay."

"You gotta have home, Fietlebaum," Teysoot Motzo replied with concern. After a thoughtful pause, he added, "Maybe you work like you home. It keep you steady. It place where you can be best Fietlebaum."

"Yes, perhaps you're right," Fietlebaum replied.

"My work just something keep me busy," Teysoot Motzo admitted. "Janpoor my home."

"When we're done on Jinkor, you'll go back home," Fietlebaum told him, "and I'll go back to my work."

"Then we both be happy," Teysoot Motzo said with a nod.

CHAPTER 43

A week into the trip, they made their midcourse corrections. Fietlebaum's cybertranslater was fluent in machine code, and it interfaced perfectly with the on-board computer. Through the device, Fietlebaum was able to have a chat with the navigation system and convey to it exactly where on Jinkor they wanted to go. He had the cybertranslater give the computer the positioning coordinates of the cave where they had hidden the jorftoss, and the flight path was planned to the finest detail. Teysoot Motzo had the navigation system project the holographic display of the new trajectory. The landing it showed them was perfect. "*Got tsu danken*!" Fietlebaum exclaimed.

The images of Janpoor and Jinkor loomed larger in their view from the cockpit. No longer a mere point of light, the oceans and continents of Janpoor took on definition. It made Teysoot Motzo's longing for home more poignant. As for Fietlebaum, the increasing clarity of the surface features of Jinkor made the task before them less abstract in his mind. "This is serious business," he said to himself. "Someone could get killed. Who knows what might happen? *Der toyt klapt nit in tir*[155]." Grim possibilities paraded through his mind. What if Glesh was waiting in ambush? What if he wasn't coming at all? What if Aaron wasn't with him? "*Ich hob es in drerd*!" he cried. "I'm going *meshugeh*!"

---

[155] Death doesn't knock at the door.

They were three days out from Jinkor. With the final flight adjustments having been made, there was little to do but enjoy the ride. But it wasn't easy. Fietlebaum was now entirely free to worry. More troubling was that Teysoot Motzo had eaten his way through his yummier snacks. He was more obsessive about food than Fietlebaum was about imminent catastrophe.

"It almost supper time," Teysoot Motzo called out.

"No, it's not," Fietlebaum replied. "We ate lunch only an hour ago."

"I thought it been longer than that," Teysoot Motzo said sullenly.

He sat and brooded until Fietlebaum could stand it no longer. "Teysoot Motzo," he said in exasperation, "*ess gezunterhait*!"

"You good boy, Fietlebaum," he replied enthusiastically.

He opened some canned foods for an early supper, two cans of Special Spicy Noodle for himself and a can of Chicken Noodle soup for Fietlebaum. After Teysoot Motzo had gulped down his supper, he sat silently, staring at Fietlebaum. "Now I got nothing for do," he said petulantly.

Oy, Fietlebaum thought, *if it's not one thing, it's another*. "Here's a suggestion," he snapped, "*gai shlog dein kup en vant*[156]!"

The cybertranslation made Teysoot Motzo laugh. "Hah!" he said, "My papa use say, '*Saab boga mas po hasha*'. That mean in Janpooran, "Go shove you head in mud!" He paused in fond remembrance. "He count for ten, then do it for us." He sighed. "Dear old papa."

"Your father was a prince," Fietlebaum allowed.

"Umm," Teysoot Motzo grunted with a nod of agreement.

---

156 Go knock your head against the wall! (A suggestion sometimes made to bored children who become annoying.)

Fietlebaum rolled his eyes. "Go entertain yourself," he told Teysoot Motzo. "I have some serious worrying to do."

Teysoot Motzo trundled off to occupy himself. For the hundredth time, Fietlebaum prepared for their rendezvous with Glesh. He pictured the landscape on Jinkor around the cave where they hid the jorftoss. Again, in his mind's eye, he hooked up the intention switch to the packet of jorftoss extract. He practiced the speech he planned to give to Glesh, and wondered how best to comfort Aaron when he finally had him safe in the starship and heading back home. Lost in his thoughts, he didn't notice the time go by until he heard the sound of Teysoot Motzo snoring in his bunk. "Time for bed," he told himself, and he joined Teysoot Motzo in slumber.

"I hungry," Teysoot Motzo said in the middle of the night.

"*Got in himmel!*" Fietlebaum growled as he awakened from sleep. "Why couldn't you have kept that startling realization to yourself?"

"Sorry," Teysoot Motzo said sincerely. "I not realize I say it so loud. I guess I more hungry than I thought."

"Go look for something to eat and shut up!" Fietlebaum insisted.

"Good idea," Teysoot Motzo replied. "But finding something good for eat in starship getting harder all of time. Nothing I got quite hit spot." He got up and padded across the floor and down the short corridor to a small, but hitherto unexplored, back storage closet to rummage around for a forgotten can of stew or a long lost bag of desiccated fruit.

Fietlebaum had drifted off to sleep again, when he was awakened by a scream and the sounds of struggle. He leapt from his bunk, grabbed his blaster, and ran to the source of the commotion. He raced through the control room and jumped through the hatch into the corridor. Beside the open storage closet he saw Teysoot Motzo struggling to wrestle a large Borgostian off his neck.

"*Gevalt*!" Fietlebaum screamed. He pointed his blaster, but could not get a clean shot at the intruder. The risk of hitting Teysoot Motzo was too high. He watched helplessly, until he saw a glint of steel in the cabin lights. "He's got a knife!" Fietlebaum cried out.

Teysoot Motzo struggled more vigorously to maneuver his arms around the body of the Borgostian and pull him away, but he was too slippery. Fietlebaum watched in horror as the Borgostian found his mark with the knife and slashed across Teysoot Motzo's face. Dark green Janpooran blood dripped onto the floor.

Teysoot Motzo screeched in pain. With strength enhanced by rage, he ripped the knife from the Borgostian's tentacle and thrust it deeply into the intruder's body. The blade must have penetrated one of the creature's hearts, as he instantly loosened his grip and fell to the floor in a heap. Without a moment's hesitation, Fietlebaum fired the blaster and the Borgostian evaporated.

After a moment of shock, Fietlebaum grew livid. "*A broch*!" he screamed. "I told you to leave those creatures alone. They're all *meshugeh*! I knew they couldn't let all those insults of yours go. It was a vendetta, for God's sake!"

Teysoot Motzo was contrite as he wiped the blood off his face. "I never see him before," he meekly protested. "He in closet waiting for me. Nothing I can do." He stood, turning the knife over and over in his hand. Then he glanced down at the knife in a double take. "This not Borgostian knife, "he exclaimed after closer inspection. "This government issue." He held the knife out for Fietlebaum to see. "Look," he insisted. "Look at insignia on blade. This GIA knife!"

It took Fietlebaum a moment to digest the significance of Teysoot Motzo's observation. "*Mein Got*!" he cried. "This had nothing to do with your insults. The Borgostian worked for Glesh!" At the same moment, he recalled his dream in the starport. "*Vey iz mir*," he gasped. A wave of guilt swept over him. "Teysoot Motzo," he confessed, "I think I saw him come aboard the ship."

"What?" Teysoot Motzo asked incredulously."

"I—I thought I was dreaming," Fietlebaum struggled to say. "At least, I know *part* of it was a dream. I must have been delirious from reanimation syndrome." He shook his head and heaved a sigh of regret. "I'm so sorry," he added. "The Borgostian could have killed you. I should have *done* something."

"Not for worry, Fietlebaum," Teysoot Motzo said with a dismissing wave of his hand. "You sick boy then. Besides, on Janpoor, we have old saying—"Shit happen!"

"Several species lay claim to that old saying," Fietlebaum duly noted.

Teysoot Motzo nodded his head and solemnly asserted. "It saying you can always depend on."

They made their way back to the cockpit to sit and collect themselves. Although Fietlebaum was relieved by Teysoot Motzo's survival, he soon realized how narrow his own escape had been. "Why do you think he didn't kill me when he had the chance at the starport?" he asked Teysoot Motzo.

"No smart crook cause ruckus like that in starport," Teysoot Motzo replied, as if the explanation were obvious. "And Glesh want us both dead, not just you." He paused, seeming to appreciate the plan Glesh had hatched. "It smart for wait be in space," he admitted. "That way I would do it."

"It's nice that you and Glesh both agree on that matter," Fietlebaum grumbled, with no attempt to hide his disgust.

"What right is right," Teysoot Motzo replied without pretense.

It was unsettling. *Oy*, Fietelbaum groaned as he fought to comprehend the new turn of events. "Why would Glesh do this?" he demanded to know. "He can have a fortune in jorftoss extract. Why would he make this so difficult? It doesn't make any sense?"

"You psychiatrist, Fietlebaum," Teysoot Motzo noted. "You think maybe he crazy?"

"Maybe he is," Fietlebaum admitted. "But maybe he knows something we don't, or maybe he still doesn't trust us."

"Hah!" Teysoot Motzo laughed, "Glesh not trust his own mamma!"

"One thing is for certain," Fietlebaum lamented, "We can't trust him." He rubbed his chin as he fell into thought. "I don't mind not being able to trust him," he explained. "It's not understanding him that bothers me."

"One way or another," Teysoot Motzo replied with a shrug, "it all be over soon, and maybe you not be so grumpy all of time."

CHAPTER 44

After several swings around Jinkor, Teysoot Motzo initiated the landing sequence. The auto-pilot had been programed to place them in close proximity to the cave where they had stashed the jorftoss extract. The ship slowed itself and fell out of orbit. Unlike in their previous landing, the ship swooped gracefully down through the thin atmosphere of Jinkor in a smooth, well calculated trajectory. It glided, banked, and turned above the moon.

The view through the portholes gradually revealed a familiar landscape. Fietlebaum peered through the polycarbonate panel, and strained to make out what lay on the surface below. He spied the canyons that lay near the cave, the dusty roads, and then the mouth of the cave itself. He scanned the ground carefully and was relieved to see what he had so desperately hoped to see—nothing. No other spacecraft were there. There were no new tracks of ground vehicles in the dust, nor any other evidence suggesting anyone was there or had recently visited. They had arrived first. They would be able to retrieve the jorftoss from the cave and activate the intention switch without interference.

"We have the jump on Glesh!" Fietlebaum declared. It was an enormous relief.

The starship floated down, buoyed by rocket blast, and gently touched ground. They spent several minutes in the mandatory safety check of the integrity of the ship after landing. All was well. After eating a frugal canned lunch, at Teysoot Motzo's insistence, they opened the utility closet to find space suits. Fietlebaum grabbed one his size off the rack of suits for tailess, bipedal passengers and slipped into it. The suit stank of its last occupant. It was the smell of stale sweat—either Human or Nochian. He could not determine which, but quickly decided the distinction was inconsequential. "*Feh*!" he gasped. "Don't they ever launder these things?"

After Teysoot Motzo slipped into his suit, they entered the airlock and closed the lock behind them. Teysoot Motzo loosened the straps that fastened the rover to the wall. He lowered it and prepared it for travel. After the pressure equalized, the airlock opened to the atmosphere of Jinkor, and they sped off onto the moon's surface. The rover's tires kicked up purple dust that billowed high into the thin air. As the dust floated down in the moon's low gravity, crystals caught the starlight and sparkled like a slow motion fireworks display.

They had landed the starship about five-hundred yards from the edge of Jivitz Crater. The cave lay another thousand yards beyond. They drove to the road that dipped into the canyons and headed for the cave. Janpoor's red sun was low on the moon's horizon, and Janpoor itself was rising above the orange cliffs. Its blue oceans shined like sapphires against the black, starry sky. Teysoot Motzo stopped for a moment to gaze at it. He sighed. "Everything I have up there, Fietlebaum," he said. "She my beautiful home."

Fietlebaum admitted that Janpoor was a beautiful sight, but he was anxious to get the job done. "Let's go," he said. "When this is over, you'll have time to look as long as you like. Now, we have work to do."

"Okay, Fietlebaum," Teysoot Motzo replied. He shot his arms up over his head and gleefully shouted, "It party time—drive, drive, drive!"

Teysoot Motzo suffered no confusion this time. He drove straight to the cave. They hopped off the vehicle and bounded in. Teysoot Motzo strolled over to his hiding place in the wall of the cave, pushed aside the covering rock, reached in, and snatched the vials of jorftoss extract. He lifted the vials of jorftoss extract and looked at them. "This seven thousand year supply of *squath*, *burzet*, and female," he lamented. "Too bad it go for big jerk, Glesh."

"Yes," Fietlebaum agreed, "it is too bad. But when we get back to Borgost to return the starship, I will personally buy you a tall glass of *squath*."

"Hah!" Teysoot Motzo replied with a laugh. "Then I guess it not so bad after all." He handed the jorftoss over to Fietlebaum, then pushed the rock back in front of the hole. They walked out to the rover, hopped in, and started back to the ship.

Janpoor's star had set, but the planet had risen full in the Jinkor sky and reflected the star's light. It was nearly as bright as day. Several times, Teysoot Motzo glanced longingly over his shoulder at Janpoor. But he did not stop. They returned to the starship, stowed the rover, and re-entered through the airlock.

"It almost supper time," Teysoot Motzo was quick to point out after climbing back into the ship. They dined on the half-stale, Silesian stuffed pastries he had picked up in the Borgost starport.

After they ate, Fietlebaum put the finishing touches on the intention switch. He opened the package of tragonite, and inserted the lump of explosive into the detonation packet that was wirelessly connected to the intention switch. He placed the vials of jorftoss into the armed explosive packet and sealed it. It was ready. All he would have to do is slip the electroencephalographic sensor cap onto his head before they met Glesh. If Posso Gotzi had passed on the information to Glesh as they had expected, then he should be arriving in another two or three days. There was nothing to do but wait.

Fietlebaum read, meditated, and tried his best not to dwell on all that could go wrong. Teysoot Motzo spent most of his time rummaging through the nooks and crannies of the starship for something to *nosh*. When he didn't search, he paced. He paced until Fietlebaum could stand it no longer. "Sit still for five minutes!" he bellowed. "You're driving me *meshugeh*!"

"Sorry, Fietlebaum," Teysoot Motzo sincerely replied. "I nervous. I want finish and go home."

"Yes," Fietlebaum agreed. "I'm nervous too, and a little irritable. I'm sorry for snapping at you. Maybe I'll have a little *schnapps* to take the edge off." He reached in his bag for the nearly empty bottle of Scotch. As he poured what remained of it into a glass, he mentioned to Teysoot Motzo, "I thought you had given Posso Gotzi our whereabouts at the Starport so that he could deliver some *burzet* for you. Didn't he bring you any?"

"No," Teysoot Motzo replied dejectedly. "He bring only tragonite."

Fietlebaum cocked his head and thought. He trotted over to the trash tube, reached in, and fished out the package that had held the tragonite Posso Gotzi had given him at the Silesian starport. He felt in the hidden folds and pockets inside, and after a few moments his fingertips hit pay dirt. He pulled out a little handmade envelope of folded paper and handed it to Teysoot Motzo.

Teysoot Motzo grabbed it and quickly held it to his *ahzha* to sniff. He smiled. "Hah!" he said. "You good boy, Fietlebaum. This make wait for Glesh much better." They each took their favorite chemical escape, and enjoyed them together. They talked a few hours until they became drowsy, then headed for bed.

"What you want for breakfast tomorrow?" Teysoot Motzo asked as he climbed into his bunk.

"Forget about breakfast!" Fietelbaum demanded in reply. "*Gai schlofen*. Maybe you'll dream of *kreplach*." Before the last word had left his lips, Teysoot Motzo was already asleep and snoring like a Polmodi sandstorm.

They awakened the following morning to more of the same. Glesh was expected any day, but days came and went. They had been on Jinkor four days with no sign of him. Wanting to remain positive, Fietlebaum had worked hard to abandon any suspicions of Glesh not coming. Now, he felt he had to construct a contingency plan. But the more he considered it, the more helpless he felt. "*Nit gut*[157]," he thought out loud. "I have absolutely no idea what to do if he doesn't show up." At that moment, a beeping sound came from the cockpit and grew louder. *Now what's going on?* he wondered. "What the hell is that sound?" he yelled out to Teysoot Motzo.

"I look see," Teysoot Motzo answered. A moment later he came back. "It radar beep," he said excitedly. "It show something come this way."

They both ran to the cockpit to look more carefully at the radar screen. Fietlebaum saw a small blip on the screen and requested computer calculations. "The system says the object is heading to Jinkor, and should reach orbit in six hours," he said. "This is Glesh."

The beeping of the navigational radar continued until Fietlebaum told Teysoot Motzo it was driving him *meshugeh* and had to be turned off. But by that time, a tiny point of light could be seen by the naked eye moving slowly, yet steadily, in the sky toward Jinkor. Fietlebaum watched for several more hours until all remaining hints of doubt about who was coming were erased. Glesh would be in orbit in another hour. Another hour or two after that, he would land.

By late in the day, the faint point of light had become a bright spot shooting across the black sky above. Teysoot Motzo had fallen asleep, but Fietlebaum could not. He

157 Not good

watched Glesh's ship enter orbit, race across the sky, and disappear beyond the horizon. He waited impatiently the hour it took for the ship to reappear at the opposite horizon. A few degrees above that edge of the moon, Fietlebaum saw a feathering of flame appear at the front of the point of light. Glesh was beginning his descent.

It won't be long now, Fietlebaum thought. *Soon, I'll have Aaron back, and Glesh will be out of my life.*

The trajectory of the incoming object changed. It arched downward. It grew larger in the sky, and with proximity came the ability to discern the finer features of the craft. With its antennae, extended landing gears, ladders, and stabilizing wings, it looked to Fietlebaum like an enormous insect dropping in from space for a landing. *Hmm*, he thought. *He's flying around in a cockroach. It suits him.*

Glesh's starship fired its stabilizing rockets to control its descent. It was close enough to predict where it would land. By Fietlebaum's eye, that would be several hundred yards away in the direction of the crater. He raced to awaken Teysoot Motzo. "They're landing!" he cried. "The ship is landing!"

After waking Teysoot Motzo, he scrambled to grab the intention switch, place the electroencephalographic cap on his head, and slip into his space suit. Then he grabbed the explosive packet of tragonite and jorftoss. "Get up!" he yelled at Teysoot Motzo, "*Gib zich a shukl*[158]! We are going for a ride!" After Teysoot Motzo slipped into his suit, they hopped in the rover and zipped out of the airlock.

Glesh's starship eased down on the surface of Jinkor as they drove out to meet it. Fietlebaum's heart was pounding as they covered the last few yards and stopped at the base of the starship. They got out and waited for Glesh and Aaron to walk out of the airlock of the ship. They waited

---

158 Give yourself a shake! (hurry up).

an hour—then two. Fietlebaum seethed. *The pusher is still making me wait*, he thought. *A chazer bleibt a chazer*[159]. He waited yet another hour, until his frustration and rage burst through. He picked up a rock and hurled it at the ship. "*Momzer*!" he yelled. "*Geharget zoltstu veren*[160]!"

Teysoot Motzo grabbed him. "Fietlebaum," he said, "not make you self crazy. Let's go back ship. We make him come for us."

"You're right," Fietlebaum replied, still churning with anger. He turned back to Glesh's ship and yelled, "He's right, you *shtik drek*!"

They climbed back into the rover, and had begun to turn around, when the airlock of Glesh's ship opened. They stopped and watched. A small creature in a space suit popped out and ambled down the ramp to the surface of the moon. Fietlebaum's heart leapt at the sight. It was Aaron. His grandson saw him as well. The boy waved his arms wildly and ran toward him. But suddenly, he stopped and turned his head back toward the ship. Unbeknownst to Fietlebaum, Glesh had commanded Aaron to stop. Glesh himself then came out and slowly stepped down the ramp. He came up behind the boy and yanked him back. After what appeared to be a tongue lashing, Glesh pushed the boy forward again. As the gap opened up between Glesh and the boy, Fietlebaum saw that Glesh had a blaster.

"A blaster?" Fietlebaum wondered out loud. "Why does that *shmuck* need a blaster? What is he thinking?" Fietlebaum could not restrain himself. He ran across the remaining twenty feet that lay between himself and Aaron. Glesh responded by shoving Aaron towards Fietlebaum, causing them to collide and fall to the ground. When Fietlebaum arose, he found Glesh holding the blaster on

---

[159] A pig stays a pig

[160] Someone should strangle you!

the both of them. Glesh waved Teysoot Motzo over to join them with the tip of his blaster.

Glesh dialed his communicator to the frequency in their suits. "It's nice to see you and your grandson together again," he told them. Then he looked past Fietlebaum to the ship, craning his neck to scan around it. "I thought you might have had a guest on board," he said. "But perhaps I was mistaken."

"You Borgostian dead," Teysoot Motzo quickly replied. "I stab him in heart with his own knife."

"I see," Glesh responded without emotion. "It's hard to find good help these days."

"Stop this *meshugas*!" Fietlebaum screamed at him. "Put the blaster away, and let's finish this so I can have my grandson. I have the jorftoss extract, right here. It's worth more money than you could make in ten years. But you can only have it if I agree to it." He held out the packet containing the jorftoss to Glesh.

"I'm wearing the intention switch I told you about," Fietlebaum continued to explain. "You received a note describing exactly how it works. This package is wired with an explosive that's controlled by my brain waves." He pointed with both hands to the encephalographic cap. "If you kill me," he told him, "the jorftoss explodes and you get nothing. If you open it without my permission, it explodes and you get nothing. If you try to force me to open it, it explodes and you get nothing. But if you take it, and give me my grandson as we agreed you would, then you walk away with a fortune."

Glesh was impassive.

"For God's sake!" Fietlebaum cried frantically. "Don't be a fool. Make the trade!"

Glesh looked at Fietlebaum, then he looked at the packet of jorftoss. He hesitated for a long moment, seeming to weigh his options, then, in apparent acquiescence, he held out his hand for the packet.

Fietlebaum felt an enormous relief as Glesh took it from him. "*Got zu danken*!" he cried. Glesh cautiously looked at the packet, turned it over and around, bounced it up and down in his hand to gauge its heft. He raised his head toward Fietlebaum and smiled. He stared into Fietlebaum's eyes, and his smile slowly turned into a sneer. As he held fast his gaze, he extended his arm out across his chest, and with a powerful backhand he flung the package as far as he could toward the canyon. In the low gravity of Jinkor, the package sailed an unimaginably long distance before it disappeared over thc rim of the canyon. A moment later there was an explosion so large that even the rarified air of Jinkor was able to carry the concussion back to them. Now satisfied that Fietlebaum had been reduced to utter insignificance, Glesh's Drajan smile returned. His tail curled with satisfaction.

Fietlebaum's mouth fell open. He was in shock. "*Bist meshugeh*?" he finally cried. "What have you done? Why did you do that?" he demanded to know.

Glesh laughed. "I did it because I don't need your jorftoss or your pathetic bargains. I went to Sholoso after you left, and Hagatt told me how you saved the jorftoss from the virus. He didn't want to tell me. But, after I cut off three of his arms and started on the fourth, he changed his mind. Now, I know there will be plenty of jorftoss. I have nothing to worry about." He paused for effect and added, "But you do."

Glesh calmly turned his blaster toward Fietlebaum. "Now you, the brilliant Dr. Isaac Fietlebaum, will pay for making a fool of me." He extended his arm out to blast Fietlebaum and told him, "You will be the first to go. Your grandson and idiot friend will watch."

"*Dos iz alts*[161]," Fietlebaum groaned as he reached for Aaron's hand to hold.

As Glesh was pulling the trigger, Teysoot Motzo leapt between him and Fietlebaum. "You not kill Fietlebaum!"

---

161 This is it

he screamed. Glesh fired the blaster and Teysoot Motzo disintegrated in a blinding flash of light and smoke.

"No! No! No!" Fietlebaum cried. His knees buckled as the gravity of the loss pulled him to the ground. He shook his head in anguish and bewilderment. "*Gotteniu*!" he cried. "Teysoot Motzo, my friend, how could this have happened?" Then there was motion in his peripheral vision, and he reflexively turned toward it. Two more cruisers descended to the surface.

Glesh saw Fietlebaum's head turn and looked around himself to see the cruisers land. He glanced at his communicator. "They're late," he said with mild annoyance. "I hate it when they're late."

Two more Drajans jumped out of the cruisers and bounded over with blasters drawn. "Hmm," Glesh murmured as he turned back to Fietlebaum. "I would enjoy killing both of you. But why have your murders in my neural circuits for the forensic neuroprobes to discover? I had the satisfaction of killing your fat friend—a criminal, lunatic, and known drug dealer. No one could blame me for that. But, it would be smarter to let my fellows take the blame for killing you and your grandson." He twisted around to the other two Drajans. "Kill them," he calmly ordered.

Fietlebaum pulled himself up to stand next to his grandson and offer him comfort the best he could. *At least we will die together*, he thought.

The Drajans stepped forward. One of them fired. The blast hit Glesh and he vanished in a haze. The shooter then turned toward the other Drajan and fired again, causing him to vanish as well. Fietlebaum watched in astonishment as the Drajan stepped toward him out of the smoke that arose from what only seconds ago had been living, breathing Drajan flesh. He looked through the polycarbonate visor in the Drajan's helmet, and recognized the face. It was Beshted.

CHAPTER 45

Fietlebaum's head was spinning as Beshted helped him and his grandson onto the rover. The airspace above Jinkor was suddenly ablaze with flashing lights and rocket engine flames. Dozens of police and Galactic Intelligence Agency cruisers converged on the area. Sirens, which would have blared on Janpoor, sounded like a distant swarm of lazy mosquitoes in the rarified air of Jinkor. Detectives strode about writing in notepads. Cameras flashed, and yellow tape was strung to prevent the trampling of evidence. Beshted climbed into the driver's seat, and sped Fietelbaum and Aaron back to the starship.

Aaron held tightly to Fietlebaum as they rode back. The boy maintained a firm grip on Fietlebaum's hand as he helped him off the rover and into the airlock of the ship. The airlock closed, they stripped off their space suits, and embraced in a long, strong bear hug.

"How are you my boy?" Fietlebaum asked his grandson.

"I'm fine, *Zaidy*," Aaron answered.

Fietlebaum knew these were only the words of a boy who wished that none of the horrors had ever happened. There would be many struggles for him to go through—fear, nightmares, bewilderment. But there would be plenty of time to deal with that later. Now, it was enough to be together.

It was a joy for Fietlebaum to have Aaron back safe and sound. But he felt a boundless anguish from Teysoot Motzo's death. It seemed unreal. "I can't believe it," he said repeatedly, shaking his head. "I can't believe he's gone."

Seeing Beshted on Jinkor was also a shock, "like seeing someone who had risen from the dead," Fietlebaum told him. "What are you doing here?"

"I discovered Glesh wasn't in it for the money," Beshted replied. "When I realized that, I had to find you and help you, because I knew he wasn't just going to kill Teysoot Motzo. He was going to kill you and your grandson, too."

Fietlebaum was utterly confused. "Not in it for the money?" he asked. "I don't understand. What are you talking about?"

"I know, it's confusing," Beshted admitted. "Let me explain."

Fietlebaum pulled his grandson closer to him, and sat back to listen to Beshted.

"After Glesh dismissed me on Janpoor," Beshted began, "he had me transferred to an intelligence outpost on a godforsaken planet called Wistat in the Clorpot-12 star system. While I was there, I got to know an old Silesian agent named Dorsh Geshond. He had been stationed on Korpia, but was transferred to Wistat for what was alleged to be insubordination. That transfer had taken place a good twenty-five years before I arrived."

Beshted stopped when he saw Fietlebaum shivering. "Are you okay?" he asked.

"Yes, I'm okay," Fietlebaum replied. "It's just all been a terrible shock. Please, go on."

"One day," Beshted continued, "Geshond and I were talking about how we had ended up in such terrible assignments. He talked about his supervisor on Korpia that had accused him of insubordination. His description of how that supervisor acted, the things he said and did, reminded me of Glesh. His supervisor had also been a Drajan whose name was Arls Bosh. But, I thought nothing more about it."

Aaron squirmed. "Are you doing okay?" Fietlebaum asked him. The boy shook his head to say, "yes." Fietlebaum curled his arm more tightly around the boy. "I'm sorry, Beshted," he said. "Please, continue."

"Months later," Beshted went on to say, "Geshond was reminiscing and showing me photographs of his old crew on Korpia from before the time he was transferred. One of the faces in the picture was that of his old supervisor, Arls Bosh, of whom he had spoken. The scales rose up on my back when I saw him. He was a dead ringer for Glesh. I thought perhaps the lighting or camera angle in the photo was playing a trick on my eyes, but when I asked him to show me more pictures of Bosh, I was positive. Arls Bosh and Erd Glesh were the same person."

Fietlebaum shook his head in puzzlement. "How could that be?" he asked. "What does that mean?"

"Keep listening," Beshted told him.

"I checked the dates on the pictures Geshond was showing me, and they were almost fifty years old. This Arls Bosh, the one you and I knew as Erd Glesh, hadn't changed a bit in those fifty years from then until now. After I saw those pictures, I was so puzzled I searched through some of the older picture archives of the department. I saw pictures going back fifteen or twenty years before the ones that Geshond had shown me, and he looked the same way then."

"*Gevalt*!" Fietlebaum exclaimed.

"One night, after I was convinced something strange was going on, I snuck into the agency's central computing system to use its facial recognition program. I entered one of the pictures of Glesh and searched the Galactic data base for matches of his face." Beshted paused, as if he were still surprised. "I found pictures of Glesh that were over four-hundred years old."

"*Mein Got*!" Fietlebaum shouted. "That's more than three times the life span of a Drajan. That would be possible only if he had had the Chang Tze procedure!"

"That's exactly what I concluded," Beshted replied. "So, after I found the evidence of how old he must have been,

I went the extra step of restricting the facial recognition search to pictures taken around known locations of illegal Chang Tze Immortality clinics." He reached into his pocket and pulled out his communicator.

"Load the Glesh file," Beshted ordered the device, "and screen picture number four." He showed Fietlebaum the communicator screen. "Look," he said, "this was Glesh walking into the entrance of what was known to have been a Chang Tze Clinic on Gors. This picture was taken by the security camera outside the restaurant next door. It was taken four-hundred and thirty-seven years ago."

"*Oy vey*!" Fietlebaum said. "So that's what you meant. He didn't need the jorftoss for the money. He had to have his own, secure supply of jorftoss to stay alive. There was nothing he wouldn't have done to keep a safe and steady supply of jorftoss, even killing me and—" He stopped as he realized he was about to say Teysoot Motzo's name. He was furious. "That no good, *momzer*!" he cried. "He killed Teysoot Motzo to keep his own selfish *tuches* alive! He deserved exactly what he got."

"Of course," Beshted noted, "the need for jorftoss also explained why Glesh was so intent on getting Teysoot Motzo out of the picture. I realized quite early that the story about Teysoot Motzo fomenting labor unrest was a lie. On the other hand, your Janpooran friend had been under surveillance for suspicion of jorftoss trafficking. He had made connections on Sholoso through a few of the shadier mining officials and politicians who had some power when mining was still important on the planet."

Beshted paused again, appearing to weigh his next statement. "As much as you liked him," he added, "the sad fact was that Teysoot Motzo was a petty crook and a fool."

"*Nu*?" Fietlebaum admitted. "As much as I liked him, I can't argue with you."

"Teysoot Motzo's great misfortune was that his jorftoss connections were on the planet that was the last to fall to the virus that was killing jorftoss around the galaxy. Glesh probably thought the only way he could maintain a certain supply of jorftoss was to control the jorftoss trade on Sholoso. That meant taking out Teysoot Motzo."

"But how did you know to come rescue us on Jinkor at the last second?" Fietlebaum asked Beshted.

"It wasn't difficult," Beshted replied. "I knew Glesh would use all of his resources to track you, and that wherever you went, he would follow. He got to Sholoso only a few days after you and Teysoot Motzo had left. I ran searches with your names in all of the starports in that sector of the Galaxy. I found that you flew from Sholoso to Borgost, and then hired a star taxi to Jinkor. I had no idea why anyone would visit that Godforsaken place except to hide something."

Beshted added with a clearly discernible look of disdain, "I learned that Teysoot Motzo used to play hooky on Jinkor when he was a young, juvenile delinquent. He knew the place pretty well. I put two and two together."

"That's where he flew his first stolen cruiser," Fietlebaum noted in passing.

"No doubt," Beshted remarked in wry tone. "Later," he continued, "I learned that you and Teysoot Motzo had met with Glesh on Silesia. Neither you nor Glesh would have dared to do anything illegal on Silesia, so I figured the next place you went would be the site of the final meeting, and where your lives would truly be in danger."

Fietlebaum nodded in appreciation of Beshted's analysis. Then he tapped the side of his forehead. "You've got *seychel*[162]," he added.

"By the way," Beshted added parenthetically, "meeting Glesh on Silesia was very shrewd."

"That was Teysoot Motzo's idea," Fietlebaum felt compelled to acknowledge.

---

162 Good sense, a solid mind.

"Oh," Beshted remarked with surprise and palpable disappointment, "I wouldn't have suspected that." He had a mildly pained expression on his face for a moment, but surrendered to the distressing fact.

"After you met on Silesia," he went on, "you booked a starship to Borgost, and Glesh booked a flight to Janpoor. The most obvious common denominator of those destinations was proximity to Jinkor, where you had already been."

"Damn clever!" Fietlebaum remarked.

"Maybe it was," Beshted replied, "and maybe it was a good guess. But I headed to Janpoor anyway. A few days ago, I learned that Glesh had requested back-up for a security detail on Jinkor, so I knew I was right. He asked the GIA office on Janpoor for two cruisers. One of his goons flew one, and I slipped into the other. Just to let you know, that fellow of Glesh's I blasted would not have hesitated for a second to kill you had I not killed him first. You've no need to feel guilty about his death."

After a long and pregnant pause, Beshted noted in grave tone that the events would have to be reported. "I need to go out, take some notes, collect some evidence, and contact the regional office on Janpoor," he said. "There will be an in-depth investigation."

"Of course," Fietlebaum acknowledged.

"But don't worry," Beshted said. "The story I will tell will completely exonerate you. You were a victim of extortion. You had your grandson to consider, and the two of you were lucky to even get out alive. I'll make sure Glesh is revealed as the criminal bastard he really was. This was his doing, not yours."

Beshted walked out, and Fietlebaum was alone with his grandson and his thoughts. He sat, trying to collect himself and make sense of it all. He was at a loss.

"Why did this happen?" he asked himself.

"Why not," was his reply.

"Why did Aaron have to suffer?"

"*Nu*? Who doesn't suffer?" was his answer.

He wanted to help Aaron understand, but there was no making sense of it. "Like my father used to say," he concluded, "*emes is der beste ligen*[163]."

"Aaron," Fietlebaum said, "I want you to understand that none of this was your fault. Terrible things can happen in this life. But never forget that the world is also full of goodness." He held Aaron close and kissed his head, then added emphatically, "and love." *Not altogether satisfying*, he thought, *but true enough. It will do for now.*

He sat for another moment with his arm around Aaron until he spied Teysoot Motzo's *moozore* on the control panel of the starship. He felt compelled to touch it. He stood up and walked the few feet to the panel. Aaron got up with him and stayed right next to him, as if he was glued to his side. *Poor frightened boy*, Fietlebaum thought.

He reached out and touched the *moozore.* He gently ran his fingers over its contours. He picked it up and held it. As he held it, his fist clenched tightly around it. He felt a terrible rage at Glesh and the unfairness of it all. He thought of all he had been through with Teysoot Motzo. He had been infuriating at times, but he had also made him laugh. *If it wasn't for him*, he reminded himself, *I wouldn't be alive, nor would Aaron*. Then he wept. "Good bye, you sweet *schlemiel*," he murmured. "I will miss you."

As Fietlebaum wiped his eyes, it occurred to him that perhaps those tears were the truth he had been seeking. Then he noticed that Aaron, too, had begun to weep as he clung to him. "*Got tsu danken*," Fietlebaum thought. "Glesh didn't turn the boy to stone." He pulled him close and said, "You go ahead and cry, my boy. You have suffered a lot, but you are back with someone who loves you. Everything will be okay."

---

163 The truth is the best lie.

Beshted returned to the ship, and discussed with Fietlebaum what would be happening over the next few days. Fietlebaum and his grandson would be flown to Janpoor to file depositions at the regional GIA office in Pinshett. They might be asked to stay a few more days to tie up any loose ends in the investigation, but after that they would surely be free to go. The starship they rented to fly to Jinkor from Borgost would be held as evidence for the investigation. Thus, they would have to arrange other transportation for him and his grandson at the Pinshett starport.

Just as well, Fietlebaum thought.

Fietlebaum had Beshted send a message to Aaron's parents on Hijdor through the GIA's transgalactic quantum entanglement communication system. That was the fastest way to inform them Aaron was safe and would be on his way back home as soon as possible. "My son and his wife will be thrilled to hear the good news," Fietlebaum said. "If the Galactic government won't have a conniption fit, perhaps you could expend a few extra qubits to add that I love them and miss them."

"Will do," Beshted replied.

He hugged Aaron, and kissed his head. "We are going to get you home," he told him.

CHAPTER 46

The flight from Jinkor to the Pinshett starport on Janpoor was short, but sweet. Beshted arranged everything for the flight. A Gorsidian GIA agent piloted the ship, thus sparing Fietlebaum any further concerns about orbits or trajectories. For the first time in months, he relaxed. "It's a *mechaiyeh*," he told Beshted.

The seven hour trip gave Fietlebaum time to get re-acquainted with his grandson. It also gave Aaron more opportunity for emotional ventilation. After he divulged some of what he had experienced, it became clear that his time with Glesh had been even worse than Fietlebaum had suspected. Much of the time he was completely alone. Glesh gave him a few computer games to play with, but only to make him less of a nuisance and not out of any concern for his wellbeing.

Glesh had been a master sadist. He wore a knife on his belt, and there were frequent threats of further finger amputations. He often told Aaron his family had stopped looking for him and no longer cared. Fietlebaum felt terribly guilty in learning that Aaron had borne the brunt of Glesh's anger over his escape with Teysoot Motzo from the psychiatric ward. Glesh beat him, and withheld food and water for several days. Aaron suffered similar punishment when Glesh was upset over his agent's failure to kill Fietlebaum on Sholoso.

Aaron clung to Fietlebaum for much of the trip. Several times he pushed his face into Fietlebaum's shoulder and cried. Much of the time he sat holding his hand without saying a word. Only now and then did Aaron leave his side to look out the portholes or to see what the cockpit instruments read. Fietlebaum allowed him to do whatever he pleased. He was confident that with time, love, and skill, Aaron's emotional wounds would heal. Still, he knew there would always be scars.

When they landed at the Pinshett Starport, the concourses were crowded with passengers. The Janpooran holiday, *Pozonto*, was approaching, and many travelers were on their way home to spend time with their families. The holiday atmosphere and the families travelling together made Fietlebaum's reunion with his own grandson all the more poignant. It also made him wonder who, if anyone, would be grieving Teysoot Motzo's death at the *Pozonto* banquet table. A painful thought occurred to him. *Will anyone even know he's gone?* He made a mental note to contact the miner's union officials on Janpoor to inform them of his death. He also intended to tell them that what had been suspected of being *leshte po noc* had been the effects of being drugged by the Galactic Intelligence Agency. "No use dragging that shame with you to the next world, my friend," he whispered in the direction of Jinkor.

Beshted had called in arrangements for Fietlebaum and his grandson to stay at the Pinshett Grand Hotel. Since they would be giving important evidence in the governmental investigation that Beshted was initiating, the Galactic government would pick up the tab. Janpooran redcaps carried their luggage to the taxi stand, and Beshted hailed a cab to the hotel. A Janpooran cab swooped down out of the sky and landed in front of them. They hopped in and directed the cabbie to the Pinshett Grand.

The cabbie shot out into the air lanes. He banged into three other cabs and a freight hauler on the way. Fietlebaum feared Aaron might be too unstable to tolerate that kind of stimulation, but he saw him giggle and smile. He seemed to be enjoying it, like a carnival ride. After several peculiarly uneventful minutes of flying, the cabbie swerved sharply into the neighboring lane, clipped the fender of another cab, yelled several oaths Fietlebaum was reluctant to translate for Aaron, and nosedived toward the front drive of the hotel. He pulled out of the dive at the last moment and leveled out into a picture perfect landing at the hotel's door. Fietlebaum marveled at how the Janpooran cabbies maneuvered around town every bit as quickly as the Silesian cabbies, but without any of their sophisticated guidance systems. "All they need," he whispered to Beshted, "is a foot of lead, *beytzim*[164] of steel, and none of the encumbrances of good sense."

The accommodations at the Pinshett Grand were impeccable. They were given a lovely suite with two bedrooms, each with its own large bed. But Aaron did not want to be alone, and Fietlebaum was glad to allow him to sleep next to him. The boy thrashed throughout the night, cried out, and struggled against phantoms. These were symptoms of PTSD Fietlebaum had feared. In one bout of nightmares, Aaron swung his fist and caught Fietlebaum in the eye. *The boy may have PTSD,* he thought, *but he's still got a good left hook.*

During a period of relative calm in the night, Fietlebaum got up, fished his *schnapps* out of his bag, and poured himself two fingers. He stood at the window, sipped his *schnapps*, and gazed out at Pinshett. "*Got in himmel*," he thought, "it's been like a dream—a nightmare." Teysoot Motzo was dead. He still agonized over how such a big, vibrant being, so full of life and rich with plans and memories could have so suddenly vanished into nothingness. Not only was it painful emotionally, but difficult to grasp intellectually. "I thought I had come to understand death and the evanescence of life," he told himself, "but it's beyond me."

---

[164] balls

It was almost *Pozonto*, the Janpooran holiday of ancestor worship and remembrance of the dead. Thus, it was particularly fitting that as he thought of Teysoot Motzo, the words of *Kaddish*[165] came to his lips. "*Yitgaddal veyitqaddash shmeh rabba . . .*" he recited over the city of Pinshett that lay below. He finished the prayer with, "amen," then he lifted his glass to the memory of Teysoot Motzo. "*Le'chayim*," he added. He slipped back into bed next to Aaron, who awakened briefly. "*Zaidy*?" he asked drowsily, then quickly dropped back to sleep. "Yes, Aaron," Fietlebaum murmured, "*Zaidy* is here. *Gai schlofen*."

Beshted arrived the next morning to take Fietlebaum and Aaron to the GIA office to be deposed. He was wearing a splendid new service uniform—deep green with iridescent purple buttons, and the silver epaulettes of a sub-regional assistant manager. It was a significant position for an agent his age. *He's even grown an inch or two*, Fietlebaum suspected.

They strolled through the lobby and out to the street where an agency cruiser was waiting. Beshted took the driver's seat. He started the engine with a roar, and switched on the siren and flashing lights, which Aaron enjoyed. Then they sat. They were on Janpoor in Janpooran traffic, and there the accoutrements of authority were worthless. The cabs and freight haulers sped by as usual, utterly ignoring his urgent and official status. After waiting for several minutes Beshted said, "to hell with it," and bullied his way into traffic like any other Janpooran pilot would. *He's learning*, Fietlebaum mused. They arrived a few minutes later at the GIA office.

The regional GIA office on Janpoor wasn't as impressive as the central office in Silesia. But, with its huge steel doors, armed guards, and surveillance cameras, it was clearly a no-nonsense kind of place. They rode to the twenty-sixth

165 The Jewish prayer for the dead

floor, and Beshted spoke to the receptionist. “Down the hall, the second door,” Beshted relayed to Fietlebaum. “They’re expecting us.” They walked down the hallway, and as they stepped through the doorway, Beshted added, “Just tell your stories. I have arranged immunity for you, so you have nothing to fear.”

The room was full of cameras and other recording equipment. There were lawyers, agents, and low level government officials. “Have a seat Dr. Fietlebaum,” one of them said.

It was a relief for Fietlebaum to tell his story. He got some things off his chest. He explained how Glesh had first contacted him and coerced him into helping him by kidnapping and torturing his grandson. He went on to explain how Teysoot Motzo was an obstacle to Glesh’s ability to control the jorftoss trade on Sholoso, and that this was why he had wanted him dead. He noted that Beshted would provide further details, but explained that Glesh needed the jorftoss to maintain his Chang Tze immortality procedure. Thus, there was every reason to believe he would have stopped at nothing to achieve his goals.

Fietlebaum was thanked and excused, but before he arose from the table, he told the panel there was one more thing he wanted to say. “I know,” he began, “that Teysoot Motzo was involved in the jorftoss trade. He was a petty criminal and, because of his trafficking in jorftoss, he might well have received the death penalty had he not been killed by Glesh on Jinkor.” He paused to collect himself. “Still,” he went on, “aside from all that was unsavory about Teysoot Motzo, I want you to know that he saved my life on several occasions, and were it not for his intervention on Jinkor, it is likely that neither I nor my grandson would be alive at this moment.” He stood up from the table with the final words, “I wanted that in the record.”

Then it was Aaron’s turn to testify about what Glesh had done to him. He began by telling them how Glesh had kidnapped him and cut off his finger. He held up his right hand to show them the discolored finger that had grown in as a replacement for the one that was amputated. He told them about being isolated and beaten at Glesh's hand. But soon the telling became too much for him. He began to cry. Fietlebaum rushed back to the table and told the panel that Aaron's testimony was over. Two members of the panel demanded that Aaron continue, but Fietlebaum was adamant. "No," he said. "He's done." He helped Aaron up from the table, and they walked away. As they passed through the door, Fietlebaum informed them over his shoulder, "If you want to arrest us, we'll be at the Pinshett Grand."

They rode the elevator to the ground floor, then stepped out on the sidewalk where Fietlebaum flagged a cab. On the way back to the hotel, they stopped at a travel agency and Fietlebaum arranged passage for Aaron on a starship back to Hijdor. Beshted arranged another series of communications through the agency's quantum entanglement system so that Aaron's parents would know what plans had been made. Fietlebaum informed them that Aaron would be returning on the next starship to Hijdor, and that he should arrive in eighteen months.

Fietlebaum's son, Dovid, signaled back, "Wonderful news!" He added, "Please come, too, Dad. Polmod is no place for you. We have room. Now that mom is gone, Rebecca, Deborah, the kids, and I are the only family you have."

"Thank you," Fietlebaum signaled back, "I will return to Polmod. I can take or leave the place. But my home is my clinic, my patients, and my practice. That is where I want to be."

Fietlebaum woke up early to help ready Aaron for the morning starship flight. He was concerned that because of all the trauma Aaron had experienced, he might be too anxious to deal with the stress and excitement of the starship. Two of the cardinal symptoms of PTSD were wariness and hyper-vigilance. These were particularly intense around strangers and crowds, both of which would be the case on the starship. He considered the possibility of a sedative for Aaron, but since the two of them were the only Hijdori within light-years of Janpoor, it was unlikely any pharmacy in Pinshett would carry medications useful for their unique neurophysiology. The next best solution was to give him a little *schnapps*, which had a mild anxiolytic effect in Hijdori. He gave him a spoonful of scotch before they left. "Not enough to get him *shikker*[166]," Fietlebaum told himself, "just to calm him down." He poured some *schnapps* into the spoon and gave it to Aaron.

After Aaron's loving spoonful, Fietlebaum hesitated for a moment, then shrugged and said, "I think I'll join you." He poured a spoonful, and lifted the spoon in the air in a salute to Aaron. He gave a hearty, "*Le'chayim,*" and slurped the *schnapps* like it was a spoonful of his Sophie's chicken soup. Then he poured himself another two more.

They rode the elevator to the ground floor and strolled through the lobby to the door. The doorman flagged them down a cab, and it whisked them off to the starport. Aaron remained suitably subdued by the *schnapps*. They arrived at the departures concourse, and walked to the starship gate where Fietlebaum made special arrangements with one of the starship attendants to look after him. She was a human female from Hijdor. Her name was Esther Rabinowitz, and her grandfather, Efron Rabinowitz, had been one of the crew of the starship *Mogen Dovid*, as well as one of the first settlers of Hijdor. He had been a friend of Fietlebaum's father.

"He's been through a lot," Fietlebaum told Esther. "He was kidnapped and tortured. Now he's on his way back home to his parents on Hijdor."

---

166 drunk

"Ach!" Esther exclaimed. "How could anybody do such a thing?" She shook her head in disgust. "Don't worry, Dr. Fietlebaum," she added. "I'll be a second mama for this boy."

"Thank you, so much, Esther," Fietlebaum replied. "He's a good boy."

He returned to a seat next to Aaron and waited for the starship to board. When the call came to board, Esther walked over and told Aaron it was time to go.

"Goodbye, *Zaidy*," Aaron told him. "I love you."

"Goodbye, Aaron," Fietlebaum replied. He gave him a long bear hug and kissed his head. "I'm sorry all of this happened to you. I hope you understand there was nothing you did to deserve it." He kissed his forehead a second time. "Goodbye, sweetheart. Have a good trip, and remember that I love you."

Esther led Aaron away. When they got to the gangplank, they turned for one last look. Esther gave Fietlebaum a confident nod, and prompted Aaron to wave a final goodbye. Then Fietlebaum watched Aaron and Esther walk onto the starship. He waited another twenty minutes to see the ship lift off and disappear into the Janpooran sky. Then, he caught a cab back to the hotel and prepared for his own flight back home the following morning.

That afternoon at the hotel, Fietlebaum called Beshted to thank him and say goodbye. "The goodbyes will have to wait," Beshted told him. "I'll be by tomorrow morning to take you to the starport myself."

He picked Fietlebaum up bright and early the next morning. After exhaustion of the hellos and small talk, they fell into an awkward silence. For a while, Fietlebaum thought they might not say anything until they reached the starport.

It was not his habit to push conversation, but there was something Fietlebaum wanted to know. He cocked his head and looked at Beshted with a quizzical expression on his face. "I want to ask you something," he said.

"What is that?" Beshted asked in response.

"Why did you go to so much trouble to save me?"

Beshted was silent for a long while. "My father was cruel," he finally began. "He chased my mother away, then he made life miserable for me and my brothers. Nothing we did was ever good enough for him. Nothing was fun." He sighed. "I tried to escape him. I left home. I even left the planet, and all I did was replace my father with Glesh." He wiped his eyes. "Drajans aren't supposed to be able to cry," he said with a awkward laugh, "but I think that's what I am doing now."

"*Deigeh nisht*[167]," Fietlebaum told him with a dismissing wave of his hand. "As the saying goes, *nor a nar filt nit*[168]."

Beshted nodded his head, then paused for a moment, trying to formulate what he wanted to say. But words failed him. "I was thirty-two years old when I met you," he was at last able to say, "and you were the first person in all of those years who ever asked me how I felt and really wanted to know the answer." He shook his head and sighed again. "I wasn't going to let Glesh kill you."

"You're a good boy," Fietlebaum replied. He quickly thought better of what he said, and qualified it. "I suppose I shouldn't call you a boy," he admitted, "but when I have affection for someone and I'm old enough to be their father, I say things like that. I hope you don't mind."

Beshted shook his head. "No," he answered, "I don't mind."

"What I most want you to know," Fietlebaum continued, "is how much I appreciate you, and how much I admire you for what you did. You didn't have to risk your life for me and Aaron. You weren't just kind and clever, you were incredibly brave. You know as well as I that Glesh would have gladly killed you along with us."

---

167 Don't worry

168 Only a fool feels nothing.

"He wasn't going to kill me," Beshted replied. "I wouldn't have allowed it. I wouldn't have given him the satisfaction."

"Hah!" Fietlebaum laughed. "Now I know I shouldn't have called you a boy, because you're a *mensch*!"

They arrived at the starport. Fietlebaum asked Beshted if he wanted to come in, "maybe for a coffee, a little *nosh*." Beshted declined. He said he had business to attend to, but Fietlebaum suspected a long, drawn out good bye would have been too painful for him. There was no use pressing the point.

"*Nu*?" Fietlebaum said, allowing Beshted his dignity, "then it's time to say goodbye." He gave him a hug. "It's not everyday somebody saves your life. *Zeit nit a fremder* [169]. Let me hear from you now and then." He watched Beshted speed off. "Goodbye, my hero," he whispered, "and good luck to you."

He walked to the concourse and found the departure gate shown on his ticket. There were several Polmodis waiting to board the flight, and he was surprised how comforting it was to see them. There were also Janpoorans and Silesians. "Probably on their way to Polmod to wring a few more *horki* out of the old mines," he figured.

The starship crew announced that passengers could begin boarding. He stood up and walked to the line that was forming. As he approached the line, he caught himself absently turning to see what was keeping Teysoot Motzo. He sighed. "He's going to miss this flight," he told himself.

The starship attendants led the passengers into the gallery for the safety briefing before leading them into the suspended animation dormitories. His name was called, and he followed the attendant and a dozen fellow passengers into his dormitory. He found his name beside one of the suspension chambers, and he stowed his bags in the cabinet beside it.

---

169 Don't be a stranger.

He climbed into the suspended animation chamber and prepared himself for the fall into unconsciousness. "*Oy*," he said as he laid down, "this again. I'm getting too old for this business." He gave a *kvetch* as he nestled down into the chamber in a futile effort to make himself comfortable. The chamber made a whirring sound, and the lid slowly descended upon him. "Like a *loch in kop* I need this," he grumbled as his lungs filled with suspension gas. "No more travelling. From here on out, *mein tuches* is staying put." He gave one more *kvetch* and drifted into darkness.

CHAPTER 47

It was late when Fietlebaum's starship landed at the Industrial City Starport on Polmod. A lone aircab waited at the taxi stand, and he grabbed it. The cab lifted off and drifted lazily out in the direction of his flat on the edge of town. Fietlebaum was anxious to get back home. His impatience rose. He missed the efficient cabs of Silesia. Oddly enough, he even missed the slam bang excitement of the Janpooran cabbies. At least, they were fast. "Come on, come on," he muttered under his breath. "*Gib zich a shukl.*" But he was too spent to be assertive.

Far above the sleeping planet, Fietlebaum gazed out upon the lights of Industrial City twinkling in the urban haze. Feh! he thought. Yet as the slowly moving aircab approached his home, he felt his pulse begin quicken. He was surprised to have such a reaction. Nu? *Home is home,* he allowed as the aicab dropped out of the sky for landing, *I suppose it's not such a bad place.* The cab slid to a stop in the dust in front of his bungalow. He paid the cabbie, grabbed his bag, and walked to the door as the aircab took off behind him.

"Good evening, Dr. Fietlebaum," the front door said. "You have been gone longer than we expected. We were growing concerned. We trust you are well?"

"I'm fine," Fietlebaum replied. "Thank you." The door opened and he stepped across the threshold. The door closed itself behind him.

He walked into his living room, put his bag down, undid his collar, and loosened his belt. He put on some music, a fantasia by William Byrd, and poured himself two fingers of *schnapps*. He took a sip, lowered himself into his chair, and released a loud, long, heartfelt "*Oy!*" He was asleep before the fourth bar of music ended.

He awakened early the next morning. He saw the untouched *schnapps* in the glass by his chair. W*hat the hell*, he thought. He looked toward Sophie's picture on the wall and lifted the glass in her direction. "*Le' chayim*, my dear," he sang, and gulped down what remained. "*Oy*!" he chirped. "I almost forgot. I have something for you!" He trotted over to where he had left his bag, snatched it up, and carried it over to where Sophie's picture hung. "I've brought you some company!"

He unzipped the bag, and inside were three new pictures for the wall—one of his grandson, one of Beshted, and the other of Teysoot Motzo. He reached into his desk drawer where he kept a device that was a combination screw driver, knife, bottle opener, pliers, wire cutter, file, and hammer. It was for emergencies. He had never used it before, "thank God." He rifled through the detritus that had collected over the years at the bottom of the drawer and uncovered a few tacks. He tapped in tacks, and mounted the pictures of Aaron and Beshted. Then he placed Teysoot Motzo's picture on the wall, and paused a moment to look at him. "*Olov ha sholem*[170]," he whispered fondly. He stepped back to admire his handiwork and gave a nod of satisfaction. "You must have been lonely up there all these years, my dear," he said. "I'm sorry."

He padded into the kitchen and made himself some breakfast, a plate of *matzo brie*[171]. His food synthesizer delivered a product with a perfect appearance and texture but an aftertaste of cilantro. He glanced at the *matzo brie*

---

170 May peace be upon him

171 Fried matzo, a Jewish breakfast dish halfway between an omelette and French toast.

on his fork in a quick double take, and philosophically shrugged his shoulders. "*Nu,*" he said out loud, "*iz nisht geferlech.*" He gobbled down the last bites.

He showered, changed clothes, and walked to the front door that opened for him. He climbed into his transport capsule and told it to fly him to the clinic. The capsule lifted into the air and flew off. The familiar landscape of Industrial City, the vacant industrial parks, the grubby suburbs, and the dingy downtown, moved beneath his capsule. He tried to think if Polmod had changed in the years he was gone. He decided it hadn't.

He reached the campus of the Transgalactic Merchant Marine Academy. The capsule hovered above the clinic, then lowered itself down into his personal parking place and shut itself off. Fietlebaum pressed the door release button. The retaining ring gave way, and the spring-loaded button shot up through the air and down under the passenger seat. "I'm back," Fietlebaum sighed. The door opened anyway. Fietlebaum got out and walked the remaining distance to his office door.

When he strolled through the door, he was met with joyous shouts and cries. The receptionist burst into the loud, yodeling cry of the Polmodi. "Dr. Fietlebaum!" she cried, "I'm so glad to see you! I was so worried!"

"My God!" the Silesian nurse shrieked when she saw Fietlebaum. "Where were you?" she demanded as she ran up to him. "What happened to you? Not even a phone call! Why did you make us worry?"

"Secret government business," he replied, "and a *Yiddishe mama*[172] I don't need." He struggled to get away from her, but she grabbed him and hugged him, all the while berating him for "making us worry 'til our hair fell out!" More hugs came from the security guard, the pharmacist, and the social worker. He relented and let them hug.

---

172 Jewish mother

"Thank you, thank you," Fietlebaum found the strength to say, "but *shoyn genug*." He walked into his office and shut the door for some peace and quiet. He circled the desk a few times, slowly, to get the feel of it, and sat down in his chair. He took a deep breath, let it all out, and again he was Dr. Isaac Fietlebaum.

"Time to get back to business," he told himself. He had been greatly troubled by leaving his patients so precipitously, and he felt compelled to see how they had fared while he was gone. He activated the computer system and opened the patient files. He read what had been written by others who had seen his patients in his absence. He was glad to see Burb Plorbus, the Drusidi cadet with pseudotrigortism, was doing well. He had undergone radiation therapy to destroy the small tumor. The procedure went splendidly, and he recovered without complications. He had returned to his classes and graduated with an advanced degree at the end of the term. It was a successful case. *That's nice*, Fietlebaum thought. *He was a bright and promising young fellow.*

Minforp Graj, the Polmodi with severe Major Depression, had also done well. He had started her on medication, and by the next time he saw her, she was feeling better. Apparently, she had made a remarkable recovery over the subsequent months. She started psychotherapy, at his suggestion, and there she discovered strengths she never knew she had. Her husband had lost his job, and the family went into a tail spin. But she took some risks. She decided she could pursue a career. She took some classes and started work as an interior designer and consultant for several of the large businesses that remained alive around Industrial City. "Wonderful!" Fietlebaum noted with satisfaction. "*Mazel tov*, Ms. Graj."

On the other hand, James Dennison had not done well. He was the human who believed he had been cloned from tissue harvested from the real James Dennison's foot. Fietlebaum started him on an antipsychotic medication, but did not have high hopes at the time. He knew the delusional disorder would be difficult to treat, and apparently it was. James had since dropped the notion that he was his own clone and had inexplicably come to believe he had been cloned from the mummified foot of Pharaoh Amenhotep III of Egypt. "Go figure," Fietlebaum muttered. He suspected he would be seeing James again in the near future, perhaps on the inpatient ward.

The little Horgentian pisher, Hisht Jorvond, eventually got better, though not without having scared the hell out of everyone first. Though the first visit seemed to settle him down, he later blew up, stole a personal transport capsule, and took it for a joy ride to the other side of the planet. Two weeks later the police brought him back. After a few days in the Polmodi jail, something clicked. *That jail must have scared the crap out of him,* Fietlebaum suspected. *Sometimes a jail cell can be therapeutic. We should think of building one here at the clinic.*

He called up the records of Fejdut Lops, the Korpian female with Borderline Personality Disorder, but was puzzled to see that the file was open. "That's odd," he said out loud. Not a second later, a call came from the receptionist. "Mr. Lops is in the waiting room and hoping to see you," she said. He heard screaming from the other room. "It's *Miss* Lops! Miss! Miss!"

"*Vey iz mir*," Fietlebaum sighed. He steeled himself, and said, "send her in."

"Where were you?" Fejdut Lops cried the second she saw him. "I needed you and you weren't here!"

"No, I wasn't, Fejdut," Fietlebaum calmly replied. "You needed me and I wasn't here."

"I trusted you, and you let me down!"

"Yes. You trusted me, and I let you down."

"All you care about is yourself, you selfish son of a bitch!"

"You feel that all I care about is myself, and that I'm a no-good, selfish son of a bitch!"

"That's right!" she screamed. "You're a no-good, selfish son of a bitch, and you make me want to cry!"

"Yes," he unabashedly admitted, "I'm a no-good, selfish son of a bitch, a real *groisser gornisht*, and I make you want to cry."

Immediately, the loud, gargling sound of Korpian weeping began. It became so loud that at one point a concerned nurse opened the door to peek in to see if everything was alright. Fietlebaum waved her away. Fejdut gargled and shook her head in the Korpian fashion. Her olfactory tentacles flew back and forth across the top of her head. Along with the gargling, the high velocity flapping of her tentacles created a loud whooshing, whirring sound reminiscent of an old, hand-cranked egg beater. *Nu*, Fietlebaum thought, *this is what she wanted.*

She gargled and shook for ten minutes or so, then stopped as suddenly as she had begun. "I feel better now," she said, with what Fietlebaum suspected was a Korpian smile.

"Yes," Fietlebaum said in validation. "You feel better now."

"I'll make an appointment to see you next week," she said as she arose from her chair.

"I'll be here," Fietlebaum replied. As she walked out the door, he muttered, "She's *meshugeh* . . . but, *iz nisht geferlech.*"

GLOSSARY

The Yiddish words and phrases in *Fietlebaum's Escape*

A

A broch! Damn it!

A brokh tsu dayn lebn! May there be a curse on your life!

A chazer bleibt a chazer. A pig stays a pig.

Afh yenems tuches is gut sepatchen. It's nice to smack someone else's ass.

A freint bleibt a freint biz di kesheneh. A friend stays a friend up to his pocket.

A gezunt der en pupik! Good health to your belly-button! A derisive form of thank you.

A leben ahf dir. Live and be well.

alta kocker. an old fart

Alt genug iz alt genug. Old enough is old enough.

Alts, dos hartz hot mir gezogt! I always knew in my heart it would happen!

arumgeflecht. milked, sucked dry, exhausted

Az der oks falt, sharfen alleh di messer. When the ox falls, everyone sharpens his knife.

Az di bubbe volt gehat beytsim, volt zi gevain mayn zaideh If my grandmother had balls, she would be my grandfather.

Azes vert nit besser, vert memaileh erger. If it doesn't get better, it will probably get worse.

B

beytzim. balls
bialys. bagel-like rolls, but flat and chewy like English muffins
bissel. a little
Bist meshugeh? Are you crazy?
b'nai mitzvah. the ceremony celebrating religious maturity of boys and girls
boychik. affectionate term for boy
bupkis. goat turds, nothing

C

Chaim Yankel. A name, like Johnny Hayseed, suggesting a dim-witted country bumpkin.
chazer. a pig
chazerei. pig swill, junk food
chuppa. a wedding canopy

D

Deigeh nisht. Don't worry.
Der mensch trakht un Got lahkht. Man plans and God laughs.
Der shuster gaien borves. The cobbler is barefoot.
Der toyt klapt nit in tir. Death doesn't knock on the door.
Dos iz alts. This is it.
drek. crap

E

Emes is der beste ligen. The truth is the best lie.
Ess gezunterhait. Eat in good health.

F

farbissener. a grouch on steroids
farblondzhet. confused, lost, bewildered
farkakteh. shitty
farshlepteh krenk, a sickness, often an imaginary one, that never ends
farshtunkeneh. stinking
Feh! an expression of disgust
ferkrimpter ponim. a twisted, ugly face

G

Gai avec! Go away!
Gai mit dein kop in drerd! Go stick your head in the mud!
Gai, nudnik. Gai strashe di vantsen. Go, you nuisance. Go intimidate the bed bugs.
Gai schlofen. Go to sleep.
Gai shlog dein kup en vant! Go knock your head against the wall! This is a suggestion sometimes made to bored children who become annoying.
Gai tren zich! Go fuck yourself!
Gefilte. As in *gefilte* fish. This means "wrapped," referring to chopped fish being cooked wrapped in fish skin. Very tasty!
Geharget zoltstu veren! Someone should strangle you!
Genug es genug. Enough is enough.
Gerharget zolstu veren! You should drop dead!

geschmakt. delicious, yummy
Gib zich a shukl! Give yourself a shake! Come on, hurry up!
gitte neshomah. a good soul
gonif. a theif
gornisht. nothing
Got in himmel! God in heaven!
Got tsu danken! Thank God!
groisser gornisht. a big good-for-nothing.
groisser macher. a real big shot
gruber yung. a rude boy
guteh nacht. good night

H

haken a chainik. beating a tea kettle, making a racket

I

Ich hob dir lieb. I love you.
Ich hob es in drerd! To hell with it!
Ich vel dir geben a klop! I'm going to give you such a smack!
ipish. a stink
Iz nisht geferlech. It's not so terrible.

K

Kaddish. the Jewish prayer for the dead
Kish mir in tuches! Kiss my ass!
klug yingl. a smart boy
kopveytik. a headache
kosher. acceptable as food according to Jewish law
knishe. a meat—or cheese-stuffed roll

kreplach. a meat-stuffed dumpling usually served in soup
kvetch. a groan of complaint

L

lange peyes. the long sidelocks worn by religious Hasidic Jews
le'chayim. the Jewish toast, "To life!"
loch in kop. a hole in the head
lokshen kugel. a sweet noodle pudding

M

macher. a big shot
Magen Dovid. Star of David
matzo brie. fried matzo—a Jewish breakfast dish.
mazel tov! Congratulations!
mechaiyeh. a great pleasure
Mein Got! My God!
mein tuches. my ass
Me ken brechen. You can vomit from this.
mensch. a good man, a real person
meshugas. craziness
meshugeh. crazy
meshugeneh. a crazy woman
Moishe Pupik. Moishe Bellybutton—a Yiddish version of Mr. Nobody.
momzer. bastard

N

nebbish. a little nerd
nit gut. not good

Nor a nar filt nit. Only a fool feels nothing
nosh. a snack
nu? well? so?
nudnik. a nuisance

O

Olov ha sholem. May peace be upon him
ongeshtopt mit gelt. stuffed with money, rich
Oy! Oh! with a hint of dismay or annoyance
Oy gevalt! God forbid! An expression of surprised dismay

P

Paskudnyak. a scoundrel
pisher. (usually a "little pisher"). a pisser, a little, snot-nosed kid.
Platsin zuls du! You should explode!
plotz. collapse
putz. prick

S

schleger. a bully
schlemiel. a silly fool
schlofgezunt. sleep well
schnapps. whiskey
schvitz. sweat
seychel. good sense, a solid mind
shekel. an ancient Hebrew coin
shikker. drunk
shikseh. A non-Jewish girl, most often blond and blue-eyed.
shlump. a nerdy slob

shmuck. A derisive term. A prick, a fool, a jerk
shpilkes. pins and needles
shtik. a piece, a bit, as in a performance
shtik drek. a piece of shit
shtik naches. a great pleasure, sometimes used in a tone of voice to mean exactly the opposite.
Shtup es in tuches! Shove it up your ass!

T

tchotchkes. decorative doodads and trinkets
Trog gezunterhait. Wear it in good health.
Tsum shlimazel muz men oich mazel hoben. Even for bad luck, you need luck.
tsuris. troubles
tuches. ass
tuches ahfen tish. "asses on the table" It's time to get down to business.

V

Ven der putz shteyt, der seychel geyt. When the penis stands up, common sense walks away.
Vey iz mir. Woe is me.
Vos iz ahfen kop, iz ahfen tsung. What's on his mind is on his tongue.
Vos vet zein, vet zein. What will be will be.

W

wunderkind. a wonder child

Y

yarlmulke. a prayer cap worn throughout the day by religious Jews

Yiddishe kop. a Jewish head or mind

Yiddishe mama. a Jewish mother, with a flavor of being stifling and overprotective

Z

zaideh. grandfather

Zeit nit a fremder. Don't be a stranger.

ziseh droymer. sweet dreams

Zol dich chapen beim boych! You should get a stomach cramp!